T0037515

"Mesu Andrews yet again proves her mastery of weaving a rich and powerful biblical story! With unexpected color that brings the world of Egypt, Canaan, and Crete to vivid life, *Potiphar's Wife* offers depth and compassion to the tale of a woman so easily called a villain while also upholding the integrity of the story of Joseph we all know and love. Andrews has an amazing knack for helping us see the heart and life that may lurk behind the few words about a person we read in the Bible."
—ROSEANNA M. WHITE,
Christy Award–winning author of *A Portrait of Loyalty*

"*Potiphar's Wife* has all the elements I've come to expect from a Mesu Andrews book: settings so vivid I can smell the sea air and taste the salt on my lips, characters who draw me in from the first moment, and a story that compels me to turn page after page. Mesu's research is flawless and brings the biblical account to life with captivating clarity. A book not to miss!"
—VIRGINIA SMITH,
bestselling author of *The Last Drop of Oil: Adaliah's Story*

PRAISE FOR
MESU ANDREWS

"Mesu's stories are immersive in the best sense of the word."
—JAMES L. RUBART,
bestselling author of *The Man He Never Was*

"Andrews gives readers a fascinating inside look at familiar biblical accounts, all while developing beautiful and timeless love stories."
—JODY HEDLUND,
Christy Award–winning author of *Luther and Katharina*

"Once again, skilled storyteller Mesu Andrews has accomplished what so many of us wish to do—peek into the lives of cherished and sometimes mysterious Bible characters."

—CYNTHIA RUCHTI,
award-winning author of more than a dozen books,
including *Miles from Where We Started*

POTIPHAR'S WIFE

POTIPHAR'S WIFE

A Novel

MESU ANDREWS

WATERBROOK

POTIPHAR'S WIFE

All Scripture quotations are taken from the Holy Bible, New International Version®, NIV®. Copyright © 1973, 1978, 1984, 2011 by Biblica Inc.™ Used by permission of Zondervan. All rights reserved worldwide. (www.zondervan.com). The "NIV" and "New International Version" are trademarks registered in the United States Patent and Trademark Office by Biblica Inc.™

This book is a work of historical fiction based closely on real people and real events. Details that cannot be historically verified are purely products of the author's imagination.

Published in the United States by WaterBrook, an imprint of Random House, a division of Penguin Random House LLC.

WaterBrook® and its deer colophon are registered trademarks of Penguin Random House LLC.

Interior map created by Stanford Campbell

Library of Congress Cataloging-in-Publication Data
Names: Andrews, Mesu, author.
Title: Potiphar's wife : a novel / Mesu Andrews.
Description: First edition. | [Colorado Springs] : WaterBrook, 2022.
Identifiers: LCCN 2021052469 | ISBN 9780593193761 (paperback ; acid-free paper) | ISBN 9780593193778 (ebook)
Subjects: LCSH: Joseph (Son of Jacob)—Fiction. | LCGFT: Bible fiction. | Novels.
Classification: LCC PS3601.N55274 P68 2022 | DDC 813/.6—dc23
LC record available at https://lccn.loc.gov/2021052469

Printed in the United States of America on acid-free paper

waterbrookmultnomah.com

2nd Printing

First Edition

Book design by Diane Hobbing

To Gene and Daphne Woodall: Your generous hospitality provided the bank of Jabbok where the Lord and I wrestled over this book—He won. Thank you, precious friends.

NOTE TO READER

Have you read the Bible story of Joseph and Potiphar's wife? Let curiosity compel you—as it did me—to discover her name. *Zuleika.*

In both the Koran and *The Legends of the Jews,* Joseph's notorious seductress is named. The research has been both fascinating and overwhelming. Placing Joseph's life on ancient Egypt's time line is no small feat; in fact, many scholars deem it impossible.

Why would Egyptologists confess such uncertainty? Think about it. If they can't ever be certain, their work becomes faith-based. Or perhaps their search is like mine—a combination of facts, faith, and informed fiction.

Though I researched intensely and made every effort to be biblically accurate, I am neither an Egyptologist nor a scholar. The story you're about to read is faith-based and informed fiction. As with all my books, you'll find more information about the research and creative decisions in the author's note at the end of the book. But beware! It contains spoilers. For now, I hope you'll simply turn the page and meet Zuleika, Potiphar's wife, as you've never known her before.

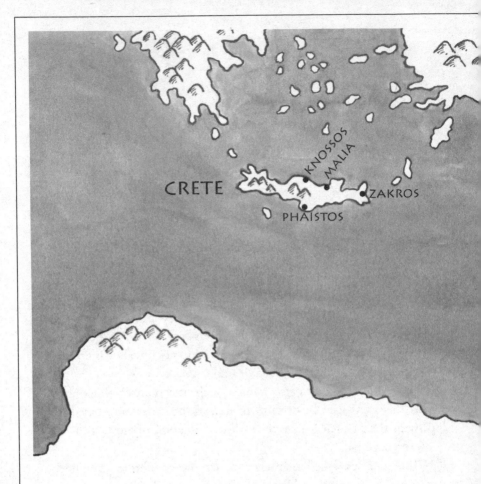

CRETE

KNOSSOS
MALIA
ZAKROS
PHAISTOS

TEMEHU
(TEHENU)

CHARACTERS

Abasi	Potiphar's old steward
Ahira	Hebrew slave; daughter of Jacob's chief shepherd
Apophis	Tani's brother; general of Pharaoh's army (separate from bodyguard)
Gaios	King Rehor's street rat; Zully's childhood friend
Hami	Medjay commander; Potiphar's keeper of halls
Joseph	Potiphar's Hebrew slave
Khyan	third Hyksos ruler of Lower Egypt
Kostas	Minas's younger brother
Medjays	hired warriors from Cush
Minas	crown prince of Knossos District
Minos	king of Knossos District
Mitera (Queen Daria)	Zuleika's mother
Pateras (King Rehor)	Zuleika's father

Potiphar	captain of Pharaoh Khyan's elite bodyguard
Pushpa	Potiphar's surrogate mother; his villa cook
Sanura	Wereni's wife
Tani	Khyan's first wife (Egyptian)
Ubaid	prison warden
Wereni	second-in-command to Pharaoh
Ziwat	Khyan's second wife; daughter of a Medjay chieftain
Zuleika	Zakros's princess; Potiphar's wife

GLOSSARY

ABBA (Hebrew)	father
ABI (Egyptian)	father
AMU	an Egyptian term for Canaanites or those from Canaanite ancestry
BARQUE	a large, flat-bottomed ship made for navigating the Nile
EYE OF HORUS	a symbol derived from a mythical conflict between the gods Horus and Seth and used in art and cosmetics to signify well-being, healing, and protection
FAIENCE	earthenware embellished with opaque colored glazes
GREAT-SABA (Hebrew)	great-grandfather
HATHOR	Egypt's goddess of love, beauty, dancing, music, and fertility
HYKSOS	a Semite dynasty that ruled Egypt during the Second Intermediate Period, circa 1800–1550 BC

INUNDATION	the Nile floods, marking Egypt's first of three seasons; the other two: Sowing and Harvest
KA	a principal aspect of the soul, in a human being or a god, with the ba and the akh
MA'AT	Egypt's goddess of truth, justice, harmony, and balance and/or those qualities imbued through Pharaoh
MINOAN	a native or inhabitant of ancient Crete
MISTRESS	a married noblewoman
MITERA (Greek)	mother
NEHESU	the inhabitants of the region on Egypt's southern border
OMMI (Egyptian)	mother
PATERAS (Greek)	father
SABA (Hebrew)	grandfather
SCARAB	a piece of art fashioned after a dung beetle, Egypt's sacred sign of renewal
SCHENTI	a single strip of linen wrapped round the hips
SETH	the Hyksos's patron god of chaos
SHOREEK	Egyptian sweet bread
TEHENU	a tribe that belongs to the nation of Temehu and shares the delta's western border
VIZIER	Egypt's second-highest-ranking official

A slave doesn't always wear chains, nor does a master possess all power.

PART I

Joseph had been taken down to Egypt.

GENESIS 39:1

He shakes the earth from its place
and makes its pillars tremble.
JOB 9:6

The sea was choppy, angry, spitting its salty mist on my lips. My stomach grumbled, anxious to sample whatever delicacies our Minoan sailors brought home from their eight-month trading season.

A group of ships passed at a safe distance from Zakros's sturdy quay. I could barely make out their flags, but the wind eased, revealing the leaping bull. Knossos flags—the largest of Crete's districts. My husband's fleet. The oarsmen's progress was painfully slow, the wind too strong to hoist a sail. The steersman leaned into the wind, guiding the vessel with one arm on the large oar while holding the raised stern with the other.

Hundreds gathered on the sandy shore beside the quay, but crashing waves drowned conversation. Children clung to their miteras' skirts as their sand creations succumbed to the frothy sea.

I reached for the ivory figurine tucked inside my belt and rolled the

Mother Goddess over and over in my hand, remembering how the earth had trembled the day before. Had we somehow angered our island creator, the giver of all life? Had the sailors given insufficient offerings during their journey? *Sacred Mother, my husband is so close to home now. Protect him from the wrath of other gods. Keep him safe until my duties in Zakros are complete and I can go to him.*

Mitera pulled me into a sideways hug. "Don't worry, my girl. Always remember that Minoan sailors are the best in the world. You'll see Minas as soon as you finish the ledger work for this year's cargo. Duty before pleasure, my girl."

I'd heard the same mantra since I was a child. *Your sums before painting, Zully. Mopping before pottery. Reading before sculpting.* I loved Minas more than my art, but I no longer needed coaxing to protect Zakros District. "Duty *is* my pleasure, Mitera."

"Longing for a husband is different than a princess missing her pateras." She squeezed me tighter. "I know it will be hard to complete your record keeping before leaving for Knossos to see Minas, but your crown prince will have duties to attend to as well. Your pateras will sail with you to Knossos when you finish your tasks. You need not travel overland through the villages."

I nodded absently, calculating the cargo on each passing ship to estimate the time my record keeping might require. If our Zakros ships returned with the same bounty, it could be a week before I saw Minas. I'd been responsible for our district's ledgers since I was thirteen. Numbers for necessary supplies and census figures ran through my mind like the blood in my veins, but I'd never before tried to concentrate on them while yearning for a husband. "I don't know how you've endured so many years of Pateras's seafaring."

She released me. "There's no other choice, Zully. How would Zakros survive if Queen Daria or King Rehor decided to skip a year of trading?" She spoke of herself as Queen Daria and Pateras as King Rehor only when teaching me the hard lessons of royalty. "When Rehor steps aside and Minas becomes king, you'll become the first queen to rule over *two* Minoan districts. If Minas never went trading, our people would be deprived of their queen's gracious and efficient rule. And think of what a mess our well-meaning husbands would make of our island."

We shared a wry grin. My mentor and confidante was right, of course. Though I missed my husband, Crete was as unique as the octopuses in our waters largely because of the vibrant women who ruled most of the year. We lived differently from other lands. Men and women sacrificed and celebrated together in four separate kingdoms on a single island, living in relative peace.

Another boat passed with the Knossos flag. Searching frantically, wind and ocean mist blinding me, I didn't recognize the oarsmen. "When I finally see my husband," I shouted over the waves, "he'll not leave my sight for a week."

"Why do you think your pateras and I spend so little time at welcome feasts?" Mitera winked.

We giggled like young girls as the last Knossos ship sailed past. It was close enough to make out the steersman.

"Kostas!" I waved at my brother-in-law, the second of King Minos's sons. "Minas is usually steersman. I wonder why—" Dawning fear stole my breath.

Mitera braced my shoulders. "You can't imagine the worst first. Rehor would have sent a messenger if anything happened to Minas."

Unless it happened in these rough seas.

"King Rehor's standard!" someone shouted.

Everyone turned as the next fleet approached from the east. Pateras flew a flag bearing an octopus—our district's eight-legged symbol, a fascination that initiated trade conversations in every port.

Anticipation of our reunion, heightened by angst for my husband's welfare, sent me into the angry sea to wait. I fought to stay upright as the salty force of it battered me toward shore.

Pateras stood like a god at the stern, pushing and pulling the heavy steersman's oar while riding the bucking ship like a galloping horse. No statue sculpted from the rock-crystal cliffs of Crete could fairly represent King Rehor.

"Pateras!" I shouted over the rough water and wind. "Pateras!" Letting the water buoy me, I leapt and waved both arms.

He raised his hand in reply and steered the ship toward the quay. Six others followed. Thirty oarsmen—fifteen on each side—moved in perfect rhythm to pull the sleek and sturdy cargo ships through the fiercest waves. I was proud to be Princess Zuleika of Zakros, but I'd also married the Knossos crown prince. When I glanced toward the horizon beyond our ships, no more sails approached.

Where is Minas?

I swam toward shore, my strokes cutting through the waves, my legs churning, and arrived before the lead ship docked. I hurried to the quay and noticed a scuffle near Mitera. A palace servant had slapped my childhood friend. "Leave me alone, Gaios!"

"Pffft." He dismissed her with a flip of his hand. "Don't be so sensitive, Aronia," he called as she ran from him.

"Lovers' spat?" I teased when I reached him.

"Something like that." Though he was slender and barely taller than me, women seemed to flock to him. His impish grin was likely part of the reason. "Other women on this island are much friendlier." My street urchin friend had an arrogance born of resolve.

When we reached Mitera, a sea breeze made me shiver. Gaios removed his cloak and placed it around my shoulders. "The dove I sent yesterday returned, Princess. The message read, *Zakros hooked giant fish. Knossos eats tuna.*"

"It said 'giant fish,'" I clarified, "not 'whale'?"

"Yes, Princess."

I applauded the triumphant report.

Mitera was always frustrated by our code. "Speak plainly, Gaios."

"Forgive me, my queen." He bowed. "King Rehor must have signed a trade agreement with Egypt's *giant* king!"

"That is good news!" she shouted.

Commotion at the quay stole our attention. Families rushed toward our sailors, and Mitera suddenly lifted her hem and darted in the same direction.

My blood ran cold. I'd never seen Queen Daria run. "Come, Gaios."

I followed Mitera, pulling him with me, too afraid to face my fear about Minas alone.

Gaios steadied me as I stumbled across the sand toward the quay. Stealth and quickness had made him the best street rat in Crete. I hated the term, but my friend bore it with pride. Pateras had given him the moniker when Gaios was only seven yet clever enough to recognize the danger of unrest in Malia District. He'd eluded Zakros Palace guards and gained entrance to Pateras's private chamber, then informed him of the planned coup and asked only for a sweet cake as payment. That day, Pateras made him my playmate and, later, part of my guard detail.

Thirty oars retracted as the ship nestled against Zakros's sturdy quay. Sailors leapt from Pateras's vessel and tied its thick hemp ropes to trees by the shore. A trumpeter blew the announcement: *King Rehor has returned to Zakros.*

I should have been shouting with joy at the return of our ships and at Gaios's skilled sleuthing. Instead, I could barely breathe for fear Minas was lost.

Pateras stowed the steersman's oar and descended from his perch into Mitera's waiting arms. I plowed into them both without slowing and wrapped them in all the fear, joy, relief, and trepidation a soggy hug could express.

"What were you doing in the middle of the sea, girl?" Pateras laughed. "I thought you were a dolphin and almost speared you."

"Is he safe?" I stepped back, ignoring the jest. "Minas. I didn't see him steering a Knossos ship."

"Because I couldn't wait to see my dark-eyed little goddess."

"Minas?" I shaded my eyes from the sun's glare and looked more closely at a sailor who had followed Pateras. "You're here!" It wasn't the eloquent welcome I'd practiced, but my husband swept me into his arms, and his kiss was exactly as I'd dreamed.

A cheer rose as he twirled me around. Bare-chested, dressed in a rough-spun kilt, and smelling of sea air and sweat, he looked like every other sailor. Yet the leaping bull tattooed over his heart made him mine—and the next king of Knossos.

"You must put me down at once!"

He obeyed, but I felt as if my world spun, though it was he who should have complained of sea legs.

He pulled me into his arms again and stared at me. How I had longed for this moment. "Quickly finish your record keeping, Wife. We'll not attend tonight's feast until we've made every effort to produce an heir."

"While you still smell like a sailor, Son-in-law, you can help with heavy lifting in the banquet hall." Mitera tugged at his arm and then winked at me. "Leave Princess Zuleika to her duty."

He groaned as he released me. "Why must a crown prince do the heavy lifting?"

He kissed my cheek and offered his arm to escort Mitera to the palace, sneering as he passed Gaios. "Are all the servants at Zakros Palace as scrawny as you, street rat?"

"Minas!" But my husband had already walked away with Mitera, her servants, and the villagers to finish preparations for tonight's feast. Should I apologize for my husband's rudeness? Minas would one day be king and—if like his pateras—might never apologize. When I turned to face Gaios, he'd already followed Pateras back to his ship, his stylus poised over a wax pad to record the cargo as the sailors unloaded.

I ran to catch up, determined to at least explain. "Minas is simply angry. The information you gather makes Zakros a viable competitor with Knossos for trade agreements with larger nations. Knossos kings aren't used to that. They secured every treaty along Canaan's coast until you came to Zakros."

He gave a dismissive snort. "You and King Rehor are the reason Zakros succeeds, Zully. I provide information, but you use it to improve the lives of our villagers. King Minos never needed to compete to secure trade agreements until—"

"Until Pateras made you and me his secret trade counselors." I linked my arm with Gaios's. "And my husband will realize that growing Zakros is the same as growing Knossos. Our children will benefit from two equally strong—"

A strange rumble shook the ground beneath my feet. The sailors stopped unloading the ships, and everyone stood as still as one of my sculptures. Pateras glanced at me and then searched the path between the shore and Zakros Palace. Mitera and Minas must have already gone inside. A few villagers had stopped on the path and looked out across the sea, but most of those already ashore were inside Zakros's sturdy walls.

The waves' steady sound promised that the rhythm of our lives would return. I exchanged a relieved look with Pateras. "Let's get the cargo logged so we can both enjoy a reunion before tonight's feast."

He pulled me into a ferocious hug. "I expect a grandchild by the time I return next year."

"Uhh!" I playfully shoved him away. "Am I only capable of making babies now that I'm a wife?"

His smile faded as the earth beneath us rumbled and an otherworldly roar turned violent. Shrieks and screams filled the air, and I glanced, terrified, at my king. Staring at the sea, our lifeline and guide, I watched the tide recede and the shore extend into the waters as far as a stone's throw.

Pateras turned and grabbed my arm. "Get everyone out of the palace!"

"No! We must take shelter!" We stumbled in shifting sand, frustrated in our race toward the most stable structure in Zakros. Gaios kept pace. He'd grabbed my other arm, both men pulling me toward home. Thighs burning, feet churning uphill, we made it to the crest. Thrown against a waist-high palace wall, I caught myself, but Pateras and Gaios slid down the sandy mound.

A woman screamed. I held on to the shaking rock wall as she raced from the southeast palace gate. The earth before her opened in a terrifying yawn. The deafening roar drowned out all other sound.

"Zully!" Pateras shouted.

I reached for him and Gaios as the ground beneath us heaved, casting us on our faces like beggars before an angry god.

"Are you all right?" Gaios scrambled toward me.

When I rolled onto my side, I saw them. Mitera and Minas stood on the palace balcony overlooking the courtyard. She extended her hand, beckoning me, as a deep, ugly crack crawled up the wall.

"Nooo!" I lunged toward the massive stone building as it began to crumble. Fighting to keep my footing as the ground shook, I tried to run, but an olive tree fell across my path. I crumpled and covered my head.

Once the shaking ceased, I lifted my head. Dust billowed upward from a large pile of stones where Zakros Palace once stood. The earth was silent for one lonely heartbeat. Then the wailing began. I leaned forward, unable to speak, and pressed my fists against my eyes. Groaning. Growling. Gasping. I retched.

"Zully!"

Shuddering violently, I peered toward the voice calling my name. *Gaios.* I couldn't answer. Unwilling to think. My mind throbbed with disbelief. Voices rose around me. Shrill and piercing. Bass and rumbling.

"Zully girl." This voice strong and commanding.

"Pateras?" I flung myself into his arms. Sobs racked me.

He trembled and cried out, rocking as he held me. I was lost in the nightmare.

As my tears ebbed, Pateras released me. When I opened my eyes, I saw Gaios standing alone, his head bowed. I remembered the day his mitera left Crete, and Gaios watched silently on the quay, weeping. "How did you ever live without your mitera, Gaios?" I pulled him into a hug, but he stiffened and nudged me away.

"You and King Rehor are my only concern." He swiped at his cheeks, smearing the dust into mud. "I'll never leave your sides."

TWO

Do people make their own gods?
    Yes, but they are not gods!
JEREMIAH 16:20

Zuleika

Though the midwives had used the freshest herbs to wrap Minas's and Mitera's remains, three days' decay and incessant wailing made these final moments more nightmare than reality. I leaned over my husband's floating pyre and kissed his cloth-covered lips.

Pateras stood beside me in the waist-high sea and placed a purple cloth over Mitera's body. He'd brought the gift from Tyre but never had the chance to give it. Covering a sob, I regained the control demanded of me. Pateras furtively brushed my hand before commanding his sailors to shove the funerary pyres out to sea.

I reached for the Mother Goddess tucked in my belt—but remembered I'd tossed her into the palace flames after retrieving the mangled bodies of the people I loved most.

A single sailor rowed alongside the funerary rafts, shoving them farther from shore with his oar. When they were a sufficient distance away, Pateras inhaled a shuddering breath. "Nock!" he shouted to his archers. "Aim." The men raised their flaming arrows. "Loose!"

At their king's command, fire rained down on the two boats. At first, only smoke rose, billowing like specters around the wrapped figures. When the flames caught on the kindling arranged beneath the bodies, all of Zakros District watched as my beloved husband and mitera returned to the elements from which they were created—earth, water, air, and fire.

As the rafts continued on the tide, a small vessel passed them on its way to our harbor, flying the familiar leaping bull standard. A lump the size of a boulder rose in my throat. It was inevitable that King Minos must learn of his crown prince's death, but I'd dreaded greeting him. A sigh escaped as I turned toward the private inlet used by royalty.

"No." Pateras stopped me. "I'll tell him."

"Thank you," I said. "I wasn't sure how to survive King Minos's temper."

We'd all taken an emotional beating while digging through rubble to find our loved ones during smaller yet still terrifying tremors.

"My king, look." Gaios pointed at the boat. "It's Prince Kostas, not King Minos."

I relaxed. "I'll go with you to tell him. He loved Minas, but he won't be unkind—as his pateras would be." My greatest fear had been that King Minos would somehow blame Pateras for my husband's death and use it to instigate conflict between our districts.

Gaios and I followed Pateras to the inlet, where Kostas skillfully moored the prow of his small vessel. He dragged himself from the boat and approached us. "My pateras is dead." His eyes were as empty as those of the corpses we'd pulled from the palace ruins. "Tell me my brother isn't on one of those funerary boats."

"Kostas, he . . ."

"Nooo!" He doubled over and laced his fingers together, squeezing until his knuckles turned white.

I started toward him, but Pateras stopped me, shaking his head in unspoken warning. Though I didn't know Minas's brother well, we shared a love of sculpting. He'd always been kind to me, and my heart broke to watch him suffer alone. Had his mitera survived? What about their cargo? Would they have enough to trade for supplies and rebuild? So many questions of concern for this man and the people of Knossos. Suddenly, the same thoughts crossed my mind about the people of Zakros. Some of our cargo had been saved, but it wasn't nearly enough to rebuild a palace. Much of our salable art had been destroyed, leaving nothing to trade. Harvests were over, and our food stores were ruined.

Prince Kostas exhaled and slowly stood. "King Rehor, as the only remaining heir to the Knossos throne, I extend an offer of cooperation to you. It seems prudent that Zakros and Knossos—as the two largest districts on the island—join in a plan to rebuild lest we all perish."

Gaios, considerably shorter than most Minoan men, nudged Pateras and motioned him to lean down for a private conversation.

Kostas's jaw clenched. "This must be the street rat my brother mentioned."

My defenses soared. "His name is Gaios, and—"

"Yes, he's the street rat," Pateras interrupted. "During the past three days, he's gained information that the Phaistos and Malia Districts have sustained similar damage to ours. However, their palaces are considerably smaller, and the villagers live in mud huts. The cost to rebuild those districts will be less."

Kostas examined Gaios, his right eye slightly closed as if he were sighting his bow, then returned his attention to Pateras. "There's no way he could know that with certainty. It's a two-day overland trip to Malia—one way—and another four days overland to Phaistos. By sea it would be quicker, but—"

"He uses doves." In response to my answer, Kostas crossed his arms, but his doubt only made me more determined to defend Gaios. "Armies have used them for decades to communicate military strategies. Why not use them on Crete when our districts are so far apart?"

His features relaxed. "It's the first good news I've heard in three days. Forgive my skepticism." He appeared too weary for a man who'd barely reached his twentieth year—only a year older than me. "I sent my mitera and pateras to sea on a funerary pyre yesterday and sailed here today, hoping to drag my brother back to Knossos as reigning king. Our immediate issues are finding clean drinking water and unspoiled food stores. The earth's shift ruined some of our springs and wells, and we're salvaging what grain we can from broken and over-turned pottery."

"The long-term effects are the most daunting," Pateras said.

Kostas pressed his lips in a tight line. "I'm relying on your wisdom, King Rehor. I've got a strong back, a willing spirit, and the largest district on Crete relying on me."

Minas had been wrong when he described his little brother as irre-sponsible and flighty—or perhaps Kostas *had* been those things before the earth's quaking. But the man who now sat on Knossos's throne seemed to be everything good I'd seen in my pateras. Humble enough to ask for help yet confident enough to forge his own path.

Pateras massaged the back of his neck.

Gaios looked at me, his brow lifted in a silent query, but I knew the king of Zakros needed no prodding or suggestions while so deep in thought. I shook my head, discouraging any further input from my sometimes-overzealous friend.

Finally Pateras turned to Gaios. "How long until Egypt hears of our disaster?"

"We turned away a merchant ship yesterday." Gaios shrugged. "If they catch a good wind, they could reach Egypt in five days."

"Assuming the merchant ship doesn't use doves." Kostas's sarcasm, even the quirk of his lips, reminded me of Minas.

Overwhelmed with a wave of grief, I turned away.

"Zully, I'm sorry." He laid his hand on my shoulder.

I backed away. "How can we go on as if they were never here? How can I rebuild a world without Minas in it?"

"Shh." Pateras pulled me close. "We rebuild to honor them, my girl. It's the only way we bear the unbearable." He released me. "Kos-tas, I negotiated a trade agreement with Egypt's Hyksos king."

The Knossos prince lifted both brows, but I couldn't interpret the emotion behind his expression as I could with Minas. "Congratulations, King Rehor," he said. "My pateras would be drowning his sorrows in our new cargo of wine if he'd heard the news."

Pateras didn't acknowledge the humor. "If Pharaoh Khyan hears of the destruction, he'll assume we're unable to trade."

"We *are* unable to trade." Kostas's tone was caustic.

"Then I must travel back to Egypt now."

"In that?" I pointed to the rough seas.

"It's a risk, I know," he said, "but we must prove to Pharaoh we can weather the storms on both sea and land."

He was right. We had little choice. Two of our ships had floated away during the quake and capsized, sending hard-earned cargo into the deep. The remaining goods were divided into two categories: supplies for the island and wealth to be traded. But even if Pateras traded all the luxury items for double their worth, we would be barely able to feed Zakros for the winter. "Surely we have something on this island to trade for our people's lives."

The profound sadness in his eyes slowly hardened into the cool, detached countenance of King Rehor. I'd seen it before when he pronounced the death sentence on a man who'd murdered his wife. I prepared myself for whatever judgment he was about to pronounce on me.

"There is something on this island that we could trade for enough supplies to rebuild both Zakros and Knossos—but I refuse to ask it of you."

Confused, I started to question, but the awful realization dawned with the finality of death.

He wished to trade *me,* Princess Zuleika of Crete, to Pharaoh. I straightened my shoulders, acknowledging the sense of the idea, but my heart wailed louder than the mourners had.

"The choice is yours, Zully." Pateras's declaration merely confused Kostas.

"What choice?" He glanced between us. "I don't underst—"

"It's too dangerous," Gaios said. "Until seven years ago, Egypt was one land ruled by an Egyptian. Now it's two lands where confusion reigns. Zully should stay in Crete."

"You can't mean . . ." Kostas turned to me, eyes wide as he knelt and reached for my hand, then placed it against his forehead. "Marry me, Zully."

But I saw Minas and pulled my hand away. "Wha—"

"I'm not as handsome or charming as my older brother," he said, still on his knee, "but we can rebuild Crete together. We'll find a way to feed our people."

We'll find a way. What sort of plan was that? I turned to Pateras for help.

His eyes glistened, the cool, detached mask slipping. "You must choose, my girl, and I'm afraid you must make your choice quickly."

I looked to the smoldering funerary rafts, barely visible on the horizon. The future I'd imagined, the dreams I'd embraced were dissolving into ashes. Pateras now placed a new future in my hands, like a fresh lump of clay or an uncut stone, but how could I craft another masterpiece so soon after my first was destroyed?

"If I'm to reach Pharaoh Khyan before news of our disaster," Pateras said, "I must set sail for Egypt tomorrow."

"Tomorrow?" The word came out in a squeak.

I glanced at Kostas and found him staring. He looked away—not in a coy lovers' game but with bowed head and slumped shoulders. Would he always bear the weight of what Minas might have been? Was I another of his brother's trophies just out of reach?

I gathered my courage. "Kostas, I'm honored that you would think me worthy to be your wife and join our districts as Minas and I had dreamed of doing. But I can't marry you—"

"Because I'm not Minas." His words were sharp as a blade.

"Because I don't want you to try to be Minas." I paused, letting my words soften the deep lines between his brows. "You're gifted, intelligent, and capable just as you are, Kostas. If you married me, Minas would always stand between us—overshadowing you and hiding the real Kostas."

"But you'll stay in Zakros," Gaios blurted.

I turned to Pateras. "Do you really believe if I sail to Avaris and win Pharaoh's favor, he'll offer enough as my bride-price to provide the food and building supplies for the whole isle of Crete?" I could hardly believe one trading stop could provide so great a sum.

"He will. Pharaoh Khyan will see my daughter's beauty and sharp mind as a sound investment for his household." Pateras's eyes locked on mine. "I would never suggest a man I didn't think worthy of you, Zul."

I looked away and brushed a finger over my lips, remembering Minas's last kiss. His passion had made me dizzy. The thought of another man's touch made my skin crawl. Could I give myself to another? My body tingled at the thought of passion. Yes, my body would respond, but my heart would never sing as it had for Minas. But if my sacrifice meant Minoans would have a chance to rebuild . . .

A wave soaked the hem of my tiered skirt, and I wiggled my toes deeper into wet sand, searing the sensation into my memory. I would miss the sea, my long swims, and the island flowers. Perhaps if . . . No. Wishing couldn't feed our people. I nodded at Pateras. "I'll go."

Gaios bowed on one knee, grasped Pateras's hand, and pressed it to his forehead. "My king, let my service to you continue with Princess Zuleika on the dangerous path she's chosen. She'll need—"

"Get up, Gaios." Pateras pulled his hand from my friend's grasp. "You will remain on Crete and help King Kostas with rebuilding and communication between the districts."

"But, my king, to deliver Zully to the Egyptians and leave her unprotect—"

"I will protect my daughter." Pateras glowered at his servant.

Gaios bowed. "Of course, my lord and king." Standing, my best friend lifted his eyes to meet mine and then respectfully inclined his head toward Pateras. "Binding Crete to Egypt in a marriage alliance is brilliant."

Pateras ignored Gaios's surrender and pulled me close for a quick kiss on my forehead. "We sail at dawn."

THREE

Woe to those who go down to Egypt for help.

ISAIAH 31:1

"There it is." Pateras pointed to a bustling seaport in the distance. "Sena is the eastern gateway to Egypt by sea and land."

I pressed a hand against my belly, still fighting nausea after more than a week of roiling seas. "I've never been more anxious to walk on dry land."

We'd sailed along Egypt's northern coast for two days, seeking the Nile's Pelusiac branch to carry us into the heart of the delta.

The gentler waves pushed us toward shore, the lapping against our ship feeling as though the gods applauded our arrival. The calmer water called to me, and I ached to dive in, but we were too close to shore for diving. "I need to swim!" I declared, twirling on the ship's deck. Making the threat appear real, I climbed atop a cargo crate on the starboard side.

"Princess Zuleika!" Pateras's eyes bulged. "Get down from—"

Pateras lunged at the same moment I realized I was falling. Flying really. The boat had jerked with an unexpected wave, thrusting me toward Egypt. I plunged into the warm, frothy sea and was more startled by the familiar joy of the sensation than the fall. Egypt's sea had greeted me: *Happy to meet you, Zully.*

And I, you. I pushed against the muddy seafloor and shot upward. Our sailors, having dug their oars into the seafloor to anchor the ship where I'd fallen, whooped and shouted when I emerged.

Pateras was the only one not celebrating.

Two of our men helped me climb one of the oars to get back into the boat. Pateras met me there, pointing at my dripping hair and clothes. "Is this how you wish Egypt to see Minoan royalty? Change into something dry and do something with your hair." He turned to his men. "Lift oars and dock!"

I strode to my small cabin as elegantly as a one-shoed, soggy, humiliated princess could manage. I changed quickly from my wet clothes into the only other tiered skirt and short jacket I'd salvaged from my wardrobe, then worked my long brown hair into four braids and joined them with a leather tie. When I returned to the deck, Pateras and his chief oarsman were checking my cargo ledger on the wax tablet while the others lay snoring in the sun. It had been a long, hard voyage.

Pateras looked up from the record, and his lips relaxed into an approving smile. "You look lovely, Zul."

Tears threatened, his tenderness harder to move past than a reprimand. "To the market?" We'd planned our arrival in Egypt during the short respites between storms. After docking, Pateras would requisition both a barque and an escort to Avaris from Sena's dockmaster. While we waited, Pateras would introduce me to the famed Sena market, the largest trading post on Egypt's northern shore.

"To the market," he said. "But first we endure the dockmaster." He offered his hand to steady me as I debarked.

With a deep breath, I took my first step onto Egyptian soil, and my foot sank into mud. I looked up at him, horrified.

"That's another thing Sena is famous for." He grinned. "Minoans call this Port Pelusium—Port Mud." His arm circled my waist, and he guided me through the mud, which sucked at my leather boots. Finally we reached some wooden stairs that led to a platform where a man surveyed Sena's docks like a god from above. As we approached, he mumbled something in a language I presumed was Egyptian.

"What did he say?" I whispered to Pateras.

"He called us 'lazy Cretans.'" Pateras spoke to me in Akkadian, the trade language he'd taught me, and spoke loudly enough that the Egyptian scoffed.

"Your men sleep before they unload?" I understood the rude Egyptian's insult this time since he spoke in perfect Akkadian. "They do nothing when I've provided donkeys on the banks for any trader to haul their goods to the mark—"

"My men will transfer my cargo to a barque *you* provide, Thabit."

Thabit arched a kohl-lined eyebrow. "Your destination?" His knee-length, fine-linen schenti and braided gold belt distinguished him as a man of some means. Clearly he was paid handsomely for his services, likely by both those requesting the barques and those providing them.

"Avaris. With a Medjay escort." Pateras was unflinching.

"The king's royal guards at the Sena fortress have likely already spotted the flag on your ship," he said. "I'll provide Egypt's regular army escort until the Medjays arrive from there. I'm sure they'll be anxious to discover why King Rehor returned unannounced so soon after he concluded trade for the season."

Dread stirred within. Would gossip on the docks reach Pharaoh before we did? "Trade season never concludes for hardworking Minoans, Thabit. As soon as you secure our barque, our men will transfer the cargo."

The man spit at my feet and shouted something at Pateras in Egyptian, then turned and walked away.

Enraged, I stared after him. "How dare he—"

Pateras grabbed my wrist and turned me to face him. "You have no authority here, Zully." He'd warned me of the differences between Egypt's culture and Crete's, and I'd even agreed to abide by their unsettling practices. But to experience the bigotry was another matter.

He pulled me closer. "We're only Sea People to them," he whispered, "one of four classes in an Egyptian's eyes, no matter our rank elsewhere. The Tehenu People share Lower Egypt's western boundary and are feared because they threaten to seize for themselves the delta's fertile farmland. The Nehesu People's skilled warriors are Medjays, who for generations have protected Egypt's kings. The Amu People are sometimes called Hyksos, a word as offensive to those who emigrated from Canaan as *Cretan* is to you and me. The Amu now outnumber native Egyptians in Lower Egypt's government—one of whom is Pharaoh Khyan."

He stepped back and searched my face as I pondered the dangerous consequences of Egypt's prejudices. "If you can't accept the harsh realities of this culture, Zul, there's still time to return with me to Crete. We haven't yet presented you to Pharaoh, and you haven't signed the marriage contract."

I could leave. Maybe I *should* leave. But how would Crete survive?

Shouting on the docks below drew our attention. Pateras pointed. "I'm sure that's the barque we'll take to Avaris." Egyptian sailors in rowboats tugged a larger, flat-bottomed ship toward our Minoan sailboat. "Thabit is rude and obnoxious but good at his job. That barque will see us safely to Pharaoh's quay."

Our sailors stood on the deck, waiting to unload the small amount of cargo we'd salvaged from Crete's ruins as gifts for my groom. Our people's hope of survival—including me—was about to be transferred to that ship. "Thank you for leaving the decision in my hands, Pateras, but you know I can't sail home. Our sailors have brought me this far. I'll trust them to deliver me safely to Avaris."

He turned to me, his face fallen. "Zully, our men aren't sailing us to Avaris."

The realization was another jolt. "Who else?"

"Only experienced Egyptians can navigate a barque down the Nile after Inundation has started to recede."

I watched the men who had so courageously brought me here. The unexpectedly swift goodbyes would feel like more death. "Why didn't you tell me?" I looked away, trying to hide the rising panic.

"I've told you many times about the barques that sail up and down the Nile. They're different from Minoan boats designed for open seas."

Silence fell between us. I surveyed the men we'd soon trust with our lives. The lithe Egyptian sailors maneuvered the barque alongside our sailing boat, then worked furiously with our stout Minoan friends to secure the vessel for the cargo transfer. My dread increased as the two distinct groups formed a labor chain and performed the task with solemnity uncharacteristic of our boisterous Minoan crew.

I squeezed my eyes shut, the sight of Gaios's frenetic waving on Zakros's shore emblazoned in my memory. We were Minoan. Full of life and color, flowing in whatever direction the gods called us. Egyptians seemed gloomy and dark, bound with indelible cords of tradition and bias. I opened my eyes and watched the final crate transferred to the waiting barque. Our chief oarsman offered the ledger to an Egyptian sailor who took the wax tablet and stylus to acknowledge receipt of the goods. The transfer was complete.

I sighed. The battle between mind and heart was done—at least for now. "You must return to Crete before the winter seas become impassable, which means you must teach me all you can about Egypt before you leave." I forced a smile and lightness into my tone. "A trip to the market should help."

"I've sent a messenger for your Medjay escort, Sea King."

I turned to find Thabit standing with two burly Egyptian soldiers dressed in white schentis, their chests covered only with the leather straps of a bow and quiver. "When the Medjays arrive, they'll wait for you on the barque. The Hyksos king's soldiers will escort you to Sena's market."

The Hyksos king? Amazed at the Egyptian's blatant disregard for Pharaoh Khyan, I stared at him brazenly but held my tongue. Thabit sneered and strode away, shouting at the slaves below.

Pateras offered his arm, and I fell naturally into step beside him. The two soldiers from Pharaoh Khyan's army followed, silent and looming. A sea of mud separated the world of sailors from the world of sellers, and I wholeheartedly agreed that this place should be renamed Pelusium. My mood improved when we approached Sena's market. Its merchants hawked everything from oil and grain to exotic animals and shackled slaves. Minas would have dragged me to the wine booth and sampled the best vintages from Canaan. *Minas.* The memories of our year together—meeting traders on the docks of both Zakros and Knossos Districts—were some of the sweetest of my life. I reached into my belt and rubbed my husband's ring between two fingers. *If only I could wake in your arms and realize this has all been a terrible dream.*

"Praying to the Mother Goddess?"

I pretended not to hear him. I'd dreaded telling him the truth about the goddess since we left Zakros.

I wandered toward a market stall of small figurines, hoping he'd follow. There were strange images of all shapes and sizes, made of various materials suitable for both peasant and prince. Pateras lagged behind me, his question hanging in the market's fetid air.

I picked up a figurine to avoid his gaze. "I tossed the Mother Goddess into the fire at Zakros Palace when she destroyed nearly everything I loved."

He didn't respond. I still couldn't face him, so I motioned toward the swampy flatlands and greener pastures beyond the market. "Perhaps I'll adopt whatever god takes such good care of the delta."

"You must choose Seth, Zully."

His definitive tone surprised me. Pateras seldom said I *must* do anything. "Why Seth?" I took the figurine, examining the awful-looking clay image with a human body, square-tipped ears, and long, slender snout.

"Of Egypt's hundreds of gods, Seth is the only one Amu nobility and kings have adopted as their own." He shrugged. "Besides, Seth is the god of chaos. He's the logical choice for us now." He tried to smile, but I returned to my perusal of the icon. Why waste our efforts on feigned pleasantry now? We'd both need all our wits and wisdom when we faced Pharaoh Khyan.

"You need god?" The merchant spoke in broken Akkadian. He likely hadn't understood anything we'd said in our Minoan-Greek dialect.

Thankfully, Gaios had taught me several languages he'd learned on the Zakros docks. "How much for this one?" I showed him the image Pateras had chosen.

He lifted one eyebrow. "I no haggle with woman."

I tossed Seth back onto the man's table, knocking over several other gods. A string of Egyptian curses ushered us away. I giggled at Pateras. "Gaios taught me what those words mean."

We moved freely through the market, and I feasted on the variety, my senses coming alive with every sight, smell, and sound. I watched women weave intricately patterned cloth and touched every fabric. Drooled over Persian pottery and encountered Egypt's famed faience baubles. Unlike porous earthenware, faience was smooth and glazed, and it glimmered in the sun. While I chatted with one artist about how she created faience beads, Pateras leaned over me and lowered something in front of my eyes. "This will look beautiful for your wedding."

I turned to face him and gasped at the sight of Mitera's most prized possession. "Pateras, we shouldn't. It's worth far more in trade."

"I'll give you twenty pieces of silver for it," the artist offered. "Or your woman can choose any necklace in my booth." The faience beads in Mitera's necklace were the color of the sea, more lovely than anything the woman offered on her tables.

Pateras ignored her offer, his eyes holding mine. "I purchased this necklace for your mitera here in Sena when she told me she was pregnant. Now the baby girl she gave me is giving up her life for the people of Crete. Daria would be proud of you for living out the sacrifices of royalty, Zul." He secured the jewelry behind my neck. "I'm proud of you."

Had we been in the familiar environs of the Zakros market, I would have thrown my arms around him, and we could have wept together. But in this strange land, where I'd already made too many mistakes, I touched the cool beads hugging my neck and pressed down my conflicting emotions. Grief. Fear. Adoration for a man who was sacrificing as much as me. "I'll treasure it, Pateras. Thank you." We inclined our heads in respect, the regal thing to do.

At midday we stopped at a bread cart and shared a meal with our escort. Relaxing under a sycamore tree, I asked the soldiers what distinguished them from the Medjays of Pharaoh's elite guard. They looked at me as if I were an octopus.

"We're not mercenaries from Cush." The shorter soldier cast his last bite of bread to the waiting birds. "We defend Egypt because it's our home, not because—"

His comrade elbowed him. "We're part of Lower Egypt's army. We serve on a regular rotation of alternating months. General Apophis calls us to full-time service only when our nation is threatened."

"I'm grateful for your service today."

They exchanged confused glances.

"I wish you well."

"Our Medjay escort should be at the docks anytime now," Pateras said, saving them from the awkward silence that followed. The men were on their feet and ready to escape before I'd swallowed my last bite of bread.

As we strolled back through the market, we passed a booth I hadn't noticed before. Three tables, arranged like a horseshoe, were covered with hundreds of thumb-sized faience ovals. I veered toward the booth amid male sighs and mumbles and began examining the merchant's offerings. Each bauble bore an intricate design. Some were set in rings like gemstones; others were strung together as ornate necklaces. A few were even attached to the end of cylinders as official seals to be adopted by a nobleman or business.

I picked up one of the ovals, inspecting the design. "What is this, Pateras?"

"You're holding a scarab." The merchant understood Minoan, but his angular features and darker skin were entirely Egyptian. "It bears the image of our god Seth."

"The god of chaos." Admittedly, I was showing off for this man, the first who had acknowledged me as human since we'd docked in Sena.

His toothless grin showed approval. "Yes, but Seth is also the mightiest warrior of all gods. Through chaos, he brings order. Through the storm, he brings life. Our mighty pharaoh and all his officials wear the Eye of Horus as a reminder that when mighty Seth took Horus's eye in battle, it was so the goddess Hathor could restore it—as Egypt is being restored under our great god Khyan's rule."

Our great god . . . Pateras had told me Egyptians believed their pharaohs were the divine embodiment of their patron god, so I formulated my next question carefully. "Is it true that Seth is the only god adopted by the Amu king?"

The merchant's friendly demeanor slipped into tolerance, and I knew I'd made another misstep. "Pharaoh Khyan is as *Egyptian* as any pharaoh before him—except for his Amu blood. He was born in Egypt, guarded Egypt's pharaohs, and now sits on Egypt's throne."

I stood very still, awaiting his wrath. Instead, he pointed to the scarab in my hand. "Why does a Minoan princess care which god Pharaoh Khyan has adopted?" Again he spoke in Minoan-Greek, likely understood by only Pateras and me.

I glanced at Pateras before answering and was encouraged to continue by his approving nod. "I'm an artist and fascinated with faience. How much would a gift like this cost if you knew I purchased it for your pharaoh?" It wasn't the whole truth but perhaps enough to test his willingness to haggle.

He rubbed his chin, studied me, then turned his attention to Pateras. "I didn't expect to see you again until spring, King Rehor. What brings you back to Egypt so soon? And why bring your lovely daughter—who wishes to purchase such a personal gift for the king?"

I turned to Pateras in a panic. "This is why I need Gaios!" My coarse whisper was the same as a shout to the merchant.

"Is Gaios your lover?" The man stood, his pink-gummed smile making him somehow more likable.

"No! He's the one who would know what I should say and do in Egypt."

Pateras chuckled.

"Why are you laughing?"

"Bakari is a good friend, Zul, and the fairest merchant in Sena—but he's also shrewd." He lifted both hands as if surrendering. "I let you bargain on your own so you would realize you're quite capable."

"You don't need this Gaios." Bakari held out the scarab. "You need thirty pieces of silver. Then the scarab is yours."

"I said you were fair, Bakari," Pateras said, all humor gone. "Now you rob my daughter? We'll give you ten pieces of silver."

"No, Pateras." I nudged him aside and met Bakari's gaze. "My pateras seems to respect you though your scruples seem suspect today."

"What? You . . ." His eyes were wide with feigned offense, but his grin proved it safe to continue.

I retrieved Minas's ring from my belt and placed it in his palm. "Melt this bronze ring into a setting for the Seth scarab."

He bent to inspect it more closely, nodded, and made approving noises at the leaping bull I'd fashioned. "Beautiful work. Beautiful."

Pateras patted my back, as proud as the day I'd given the ring to Minas and signed the marriage contract binding Zakros and Knossos.

Bakari finally looked up at me. "I could place the scarab in this bronze. It's pure enough for the king, as fine as all the others King Rehor brings from Crete. But a band for Pharaoh Khyan's finger would require much more bronze, plus the cost of the scarab." He handed Minas's ring back to me, then focused on Pateras. "I sense your fortune has somehow changed, my friend."

Pateras retrieved three bracelets from his waist pouch, and I gasped. "The ones I made for Mitera's birthday! No, please!"

I reached for them, but he shoved my hand away and glared at the merchant. "I took these bracelets from my dead queen's wrist, Bakari. How much silver is grief and yearning worth?"

"Rehor, I didn't . . . I'm sorry, my friend."

Pateras snagged the ring from my palm and held it up to the sobered tradesman. "Take the bronze bracelets in payment for the scarab, and set it in a normal-sized ring. Pharaoh Khyan will appreciate the sentiment."

"Done." Bakari took the ring and bracelets and pulled Pateras into a fierce hug over the narrow scarab-filled table. "May the gods deal kindly with you in whatever purpose takes you to Avaris."

He turned from Pateras to me. "I will answer your original question.

Seth is not the only god adopted by our pharaoh or the Amu in Egypt. Most foreign-born noblemen have adopted the Egyptian deities Seth and Hathor, believing they're simply Baal and Anat, the gods of Canaan, called by different names." He bowed and then offered me a wink. "May you find ma'at in the halls of Pharaoh Khyan's palace, Princess."

I had no idea what ma'at might be, but I was touched by the sentiment. I inclined my head in thanks, then broached the practical. "Your kindness is overwhelming, Bakari. How soon can you have the ring for us? We're about to leave for Avaris."

He chuckled and shook his head at Pateras. "She's as demanding as her abi." He returned his attention to me. "I can finish in two days."

"We leave at dawn," Pateras said. "You know I'm racing receding water levels to get to Avaris and back before the barques need towing." Without waiting for an answer, he hurried me away.

"Such a good deal I've given them," Bakari shouted at our backs. "Barely covers fuel for my furnace."

I glanced back and noted a new customer walking toward his booth.

"At dawn, Princess." He winked at me and then focused on the new client. "Those shrewd Minoans cheated me of today's profit." But I knew it was Bakari's tender heart that had cheated him today.

Our Egyptian guards flanked us, strolling leisurely from the market's frenetic atmosphere. I felt myself relax. The sun had started its slow descent, and shadows would soon begin to lengthen.

"You'll be fine, Zul," Pateras said, his handsome face weathered by sun and recent sorrow. "Our journey to Avaris is only a quarter the distance of our sea journey, but the slower pace will allow you to see the beauty of Lower Egypt."

I cared more about meeting Pharaoh than seeing Egypt's beauty. "You're racing winter storms to return with provisions to Crete. Why sail down to Avaris in four days when the distance could be covered in two?"

"We can't sail it in two days, Zul."

My shoulder muscles tightened with the lengthening silence. "What aren't you telling me?"

He sighed and pulled me to a stop. "We can't travel on the Nile at night because of the crocodiles."

I stared at him, measuring his hesitancy against the stories Gaios had relayed from the Egyptian merchants. My friend had been certain crocodiles were mythical creatures like Greek sea monsters.

"The water level is high enough to sail most of the way," Pateras said. "The oarsmen may need to tow the barque short distances through the shallows. However, it's not safe for them to be in the water when . . . well . . . crocodiles begin feeding at dusk."

My mouth went dry. Crete's most dangerous animal was an angry goat. "Where will we stay at night?"

"We stay on the barque." His eyes held mine. "There's still time to sail home, Zul."

I glimpsed the intense interest of our two escorts and refocused on my plan and purpose. "My decision is final, Pateras. Bakari is melting down some of the most precious treasures we own." I started walking again. "We start for Avaris at dawn." I'd barely finished speaking when our ship came into view. A little gasp escaped. "Are those the Medjays?" It was a silly question. Dressed in animal skins and armed with every weapon imaginable, six very large and terrifying men waited beside our flat-bottomed vessel.

Pateras didn't answer but rather lengthened his stride, then paid our escort with a silver ring each before leaving them on the dock platform where we'd met them. "Come, Zully."

The dockmaster ignored us as Pateras offered his hand to ensure I didn't slip while descending the steps with muddy Minoan boots.

"Wait!" I said, tugging at him to stop our determined march toward the six warriors. "Do you know them?"

He examined the Medjays more closely. "I don't believe I know these particular men, but a contingent of Potiphar's Medjays always escorts me to Avaris when I come to Egypt."

I glanced at the fierce guardians who would lead us into the palace of the world's most powerful king. "I don't trust them, Pateras. They're mercenaries. Pharaoh pays them to kill his enemies."

"They protect Pharaoh and his friends. We're his friends." He lifted a brow. "We have nothing to fear."

Reluctantly I continued the descent. "How do they defend Pharaoh from a port city while he is in Avaris?"

"Potiphar, captain of Pharaoh's bodyguard, stations a contingent of Medjays in every port city and fortress in Lower Egypt as a first line of defense."

When I left the final step, my feet sank into the mud, and I balled all my frustration into a fist. "How can they defend Pharaoh from—"

"Information, my girl. Pharaoh Khyan will know we're in Egypt well before we arrive in his courtroom."

A shaft of fear felt like a spear through my chest. "Why are you smiling?"

"Because Bakari had no idea why we'd come. That means word of the shaking hasn't reached Egypt's shores, and Pharaoh likely has no idea of our need. We've got the upper hand in this negotiation, Zul, and for a trader like me—that's reason to smile." He turned toward the barque and lifted his hand, offering a greeting that sounded different from the dockmaster's Egyptian words.

"What language is that?" I looked at him with more than a little awe.

He grinned. "Swahili. I only know a little." When we reached the barque, he continued his conversation with the Medjay commander in Akkadian. Pateras introduced me and informed him of our delay until dawn. The lead warrior seemed efficient, gave no indication of an opinion, then directed us to the small cabins that would serve as home for our Nile journey.

Egyptian sailors, dressed in linen loincloths and headwraps, scurried around the Egyptian ship, rearranging cargo and placing oars into position, while our Minoan sailors continued their respite on our ship. "Can't they find something to do so they don't feed the Egyptian misperception of Minoan laziness?" I couldn't mask the annoyance in my voice.

Pateras led me to the barque's prow, away from the Medjays' listening ears. "Egypt is a fascinating land, Zul, one you'll appreciate if you let it capture you. The gods water the land—not with rain but with snowmelt from the mountains of Cush. When the water recedes, like it's doing now, Egyptian farmers sow their seed in the fertile silt left behind on the riverbanks and then let their pigs run wild to pound the seeds into the rich black soil. It's been done this way for thousands of years. And now there's a man on Lower Egypt's throne who believes those with foreign blood can and should be treated the same as those with Egypt's pure blood. It is Pharaoh Khyan's will that *all* who come with open minds drink of Egypt's wisdom."

I met Pateras's zeal with silence, searching his expression for what Mitera called a trader's tic. Had the speech been an effort to convince me Pharaoh wasn't so bad? I watched for a twitch of Pateras's lip or nostril. Sometimes he glanced away if he'd exaggerated. Mitera said he could talk the scales off a fish for an extra piece of silver. But he held my gaze unflinchingly, and I knew in the deepest part of me that his freshly unveiled passion was real. Was it Egypt or the giant king he admired more?

"Tell me more about the Amorite pharaoh," I coaxed, although he'd described Khyan's physical uniqueness at least a dozen times. Taller than two men, one standing on another's shoulders. A voice louder and deeper than a trumpet's call. "Why wouldn't the diversity of Lower Egypt make the people more inviting? Surely the danger Gaios warned of is another Greek myth."

"If others recognized the sensibility and benefit of peace, Khyan's efforts would bring unity." He sighed. "Unfortunately, power is a treasure worth more than gold, and diversity draws lines between people clutching for it. A few generations ago, the Amu were pushed south out of Canaan by a wealthy Bedouin prince. The Amu came to Egypt like Inundation but have never receded. Many in Pharaoh Khyan's court secretly call him a Hyksos, yet he doesn't use offensive terms for others. He treats me as Minoan and has never called me a Cretan."

I turned away, hoping he wouldn't see my tears. I'd asked him to describe the essence of the man who inspired him and to explain the danger I might face. Instead, he rehashed politics and how he was treated on trade visits. I needed a portion of his zeal, a transfer of passion to spark hope for my life after he left me alone on Egypt's shores, not a rehashing of the impossible woes of the most powerful nation on earth.

His hands rested heavily on my shoulders, and I shivered, trying to be brave. Instead, I squeezed my eyes shut, sending streams of tears down both cheeks.

"He's frightening at first, my girl, but I've seen him treat his queen, Tani, with a love and respect that rivaled mine for Daria."

I breathed in a ragged gasp. Could it be true? Pharaoh loved his wife? "Do you think he could love another wife?"

"Anyone could love you." He wrapped his arms around me and rested his chin atop my head as we faced the open sea together. I felt his deep sigh. "But he's a soldier, Zully, which means there's a part of him you'll never know."

Pateras's words hung in silence, but my mind examined their deeper message. Minoans were traders. They carried daggers but used them to clean fish. Minas had never killed a man. But a soldier? *A part of him you'll never know.*

"He's evidently one of Egypt's fiercest warriors. He wears the Gold of Praise collar rather than a pharaoh's traditional jewelry."

"Gold of Praise?" My question came out strangled.

"Egypt's highest military honor, awarded for valor to a chosen few—and sometimes for exceptional brutality against a despised enemy." Waves crashed against the barque, and I turned into Pateras's embrace, letting the sound of the sea drown out the words he'd spoken. "We can still go home, Zul."

His whisper, meant to comfort, was an offer that was more torment than possibility. "Please, Pateras. Don't say that again. We both know I can never return to Crete."

FOUR

The LORD was with Joseph so that he prospered,
and he lived in the house of his Egyptian master.

GENESIS 39:2

Joseph grew vaguely aware of silence in the darkness as consciousness seeped into his senses. The carefully measured water in his pitcher had finished dripping from a precisely drilled hole into the copper basin beside his head. A water clock, the Egyptians called it. He called it annoying. But it was effective. He commanded his eyes to open and looked out the only window in his mudbrick home—a one-room chamber in one of the long honeycombed structures shared by Captain Potiphar's slaves. His shutters remained open for a clear view of the stars as they dimmed in the coming dawn.

He'd worked late into the night on the week's livestock and grain inventories, and now his eyelids felt like boulders. He must remember to report the successful negotiation of wool prices when he met with Master Potiphar later this morning. Closing his eyes, he cringed at the memory of his brothers' betrayal and the Midianite slavers who had purchased him. Yesterday the Midianites' chieftain had ground out a curse while counting silver rings into Joseph's hand. As overseer of livestock at Egypt's second-largest estate, Joseph could name his price for Master Potiphar's wool.

His body felt as if it were floating, satisfaction turning to dreamy praise. *Elohim, Your favor goes before me, even with the same Midianites who paid so little to steal my freedom . . .*

He jerked awake, groaned, and stretched tired muscles for another day of service. After rolling to his feet, Joseph grabbed a clean robe and noticed a floral scent while securing his leather belt. One of the new laundry girls must have used the master's oils to prepare him for today's Hathor festival. He splashed his face with water from a clay bowl, then reached for a towel that smelled of sheep. He chuckled to himself and inhaled the familiar earthy scent. Any laundress wishing to win his favor should sprinkle his robes with "oil of sheep" and reject Hathor altogether.

The cock crowed, as if rushing him to duty. He dried his beard, combed fingers through his hair, and grabbed his spear for the morning's jog to Potiphar's villa. Nile waters had receded, but crocodiles still slept atop the dikes and too often were hidden by the swamp grass. Even under a full moon, their dark green scales were hard to distinguish, so with the king's permission, though slaves were forbidden to have weapons, Master Potiphar had allowed Joseph a weapon for the perilous trek to make his weekly livestock reports.

Joseph jogged past the nameless soldiers posted at the slave village entrance, nodding respectfully and keeping his head low. The king often punished men from Egypt's army by assigning them to guard noblemen's slaves. When Joseph arrived in Egypt four years ago, the guards treated human property no better than livestock. A year later, Joseph had delivered a lamb to Potiphar's villa, and the master noticed his bruises.

"Who did this to you, Hebrew?"

He'd considered lying. Would the master think him a troublemaker if he complained? "A frustrated guard in the slave village."

Potiphar paused, measuring him with a penetrating look. "Did you deserve it?"

Another delicate question. "In my opinion, I did not, but only Elohim knows the heart."

"I've heard of this Elohim. Is he your patron god?"

"He is the only God, my lord, and the reason your flocks have prospered under my care." Joseph lifted the lamb in his arms for the master's inspection. "Most of your ewes and some of your cattle birthed twins last spring."

"And the cattle survived?"

"They did."

"Hmm." The master rubbed his clean-shaven chin. "You will now be my overseer of livestock, Hebrew. You will pray your god's blessing continues." He turned Joseph's face roughly side to side. "No bones broken. Though I have no *official* authority over the army, as captain of the king's bodyguard, I have ways to ensure Apophis's soldiers never touch you again."

And they hadn't.

Having navigated the pastures and marshes without using his spear, Joseph snaked through the empty streets of Avaris's lower city. Tarps covered market booths, and rats scurried into dark corners. He avoided the central gutter, where muck flowed in a steady downhill stream. The eastern sky, now amethyst, spurred him to quicken his pace. He dared not shame Elohim by arriving after dawn.

The palace complex rose like a jeweled crown above the lower city's poverty. Joseph arrived at the kitchen gate and greeted one of Potiphar's Medjays. He offered up his spear to the warrior before covering his nose to cross a courtyard full of rotting vegetables and meat. The stench burned his throat and eyes. When he reached the palace's back entrance, he avoided busy kitchen workers, then slipped through an adjoining door to the master's kitchen.

"There you are!" Pushpa, the villa's cook, shoved Potiphar's already-prepared food tray into Joseph's hands. "He'll be hungry and grumpy this morning. He talked with me late into the night after he returned from the palace. Then he refused to eat." Though Pushpa worked like a servant, she'd raised Potiphar since he was thirteen. She'd likely seen sixty Inundations but refused to reveal her age.

"Is there more trouble with the Tehenu tribes?" Joseph whispered.

"No, King Rehor is coming back to Avaris—unannounced."

"Any idea why?"

She shook her head. "Potiphar says his visit is also curious because he's bringing his daughter and it's later than his normal trading season. Now, go." She shooed him away. "That's enough to prepare you. Serve my son well."

He winked at the dear woman. "Thank you for the insight."

Joseph hurried across the hall, and one of the master's chamber guards opened the door. "Careful," the other, Hami, warned Joseph as he walked past. "He'll eat *you* this morning if you get too close." Hami, keeper of halls and commander of the Medjays, was second to Potiphar in the ranks of Pharaoh's protectors. He was an imposing warrior with a generous heart he liked to keep hidden.

Joseph crossed the master's threshold with his usual greeting. "May Elohim's favor continue on this house."

"I'm starving." Potiphar reclined on his cosmetics couch while his longtime steward, Abasi, hovered over him with tools of his trade. "You're late, Hebrew."

Joseph crossed the room and set the master's tray on a table by the couch closest to the courtyard entrance. The eastern sky was just now tinged pink. "Forgive me, Master. I'll pour less water into my clock pitcher next week."

"Humph." A displeased grunt was an unfortunate way to begin their meeting on a festival day.

Perhaps the livestock report would cheer him. "Our shepherds report no livestock lost to crocodiles this week, my lord, even after resuming wider grazing areas with Inundation's receding. I've instructed your shepherds to be especially mindful of the jackals' more aggressive prowling since the crocodiles disrupted their feeding during Inundation. I've trained the shepherds to—"

"How did you know that keeping the livestock in tighter groupings during Inundation would save them? Other landowners have lost hundreds of animals, but I lost only a few dozen."

"You lost six, my lord, and that was because one crocodile attacked a shepherd and four more took down six cattle before the other shepherds could respond."

Potiphar shoved the old steward's hand away and leveled a penetrating stare at Joseph. "The question remains, Hebrew. How did you know what would keep my animals safe? You've experienced only four Inundations yet have already defeated the Nile god, Hapi. Other overseers—true Egyptians—have battled Hapi their whole lives without success."

His steward turned toward Joseph, casting a superior look down his long, true-Egyptian nose. But Joseph ignored the old man's disdain. Joseph was never offended when the master called him "Hebrew." Captain Potiphar proved every day that he judged a man by character, not by ethnicity. He and Khyan had been friends since childhood. Pushpa had raised them to trust each other and fight side by side. They'd joined with Medjays as elite guardians of Egyptian pharaohs until Khyan himself became one.

Still, could Master Potiphar remain gracious if he knew the wealthy Bedouin princes that drove the Amu into Egypt were Joseph's abba, saba, and great-saba, Abraham? "My family's survival depended on multiplying livestock and keeping them alive. Elohim gave Abba Jacob wisdom and passed it on to my brothers and me." Joseph bowed slightly, having kept his heritage vague but truthful. "It's my privilege to use Elohim's wisdom to bless your household."

"Humph." The master closed his eyes.

Abasi exaggerated a sigh and resumed his task. He reached for the small pot of kohl and an angled reed, then started the most important cosmetic—the Eye of Horus. "You must hold still now, my lord." After dipping the reed into the black powder, he began the artistry mandated by Pharaoh for all his officials.

Joseph watched, still fascinated by both Abasi's skill and the reason for Pharaoh's mandate. Joseph had once asked—very respectfully— whether perhaps the Eye might antagonize the nobles forced to wear it. It was, after all, a reminder of the war between Egypt's patron god, Horus, and Seth, the Amu's adopted god.

"It's a reminder to every nobleman in Pharaoh Khyan's court-room—Egyptian and foreign born—of Hathor's power to restore," the master had said. Potiphar never entered Pharaoh's court without the darkened left eyebrow and swirl that proclaimed peace in Lower Egypt.

Abasi shot a cold glance at Joseph. "Don't you have somewhere else to be?"

So much for dwelling in peace.

The master's cosmetic captivity seemed a good time to broach the most difficult matter. "An issue arose in the fields beyond my author-ity, my lord. Vizier Wereni's shepherds are grazing on the pastures you purchased last year. I confronted them, suggesting they inadver-tently—or by habit—wandered onto the familiar land. They responded by threatening me, your shepherds, and your livestock."

Master Potiphar's eyebrows jumped, smearing Abasi's carefully drawn swirl. The steward growled as Potiphar sat up, and both men glared at Joseph as if he, not Abasi, held the offending kohl applicator.

"I'll handle the weasel Wereni," Potiphar said to Joseph with deadly calm. "You will move into the second-story barracks of the villa with the Medjay officers. You will dress as a villa servant. Clean-shaven. Cosmetics. But, like the Medjays, you need not wear a wig."

"Thank you, my lord." Joseph bowed to hide his reaction, but inside he screamed, *What about my friends in the slave village?*

"Can you fix the Eye, or must the Hebrew do that as well?"

Joseph straightened and found the master glaring at Abasi.

"He wouldn't know where to begin, my lord. Now, lie back." Abasi pushed the master's shoulder to the couch and began repairing the errant kohl. After serving Potiphar for two decades, the old steward spoke and acted in ways that no one else would dare. "Vizier Wereni wouldn't have financial issues if it weren't for the Hebrews who drove the Hyksos into Egypt—"

Potiphar bolted upright, having gripped the old man's hand and startled him into silence. "If you ever say *Hyksos* again, I'll flog you myself."

"Forgive me, my lord." Abasi's lips trembled. "I simply meant—"

"Neither the Amu nor the Bedouins are to blame for Wereni's poor character or financial irresponsibility."

He'd used the term *Bedouins* out of consideration for Joseph, but Abasi had been correct. Great-Saba Abraham's quickly growing wealth had displaced whole clans of Amorites from Canaan, a land the Egyptians referred to as Retjenu. Saba Isaac's wealth had displaced even more, and many Egyptian and Amorite nobility—two generations later—still refused to purchase Hebrew slaves or eat food served by them.

"Hebrew!" Potiphar's raised voice startled Joseph from his thoughts.

"Yes, my lord?"

"I called you three times. Where is your mind?"

"Forgive—"

Potiphar waved off his answer. "I'll send a contingent of Medjays to accompany you to the slave village. They'll inform Pharaoh's soldiers of your departure."

"Master Potiphar, I'm concerned—"

"I have regular surveillance on their treatment of my slaves, Hebrew. While the Medjays are with you, find Wereni's shepherds and introduce them to your new personal guards. I suspect the simple warning will keep you *and* my land safe from the vizier's shepherds."

Abasi scooted his stool away from the master's couch. "Finished, my lord." He began tidying the cosmetics.

Potiphar donned the jewelry Abasi had laid out. "Anything else, Hebrew?" It was the question he often asked before abruptly ending their meeting.

A knock on his chamber door prevented Joseph from asking whether the shepherds could be given extra blankets as sowing-season nights grew cooler.

"Come!" Potiphar shouted.

Hami peered inside, unusually cautious. "Another of our guards arrived ahead of Rehor's barque. The oarsmen obeyed the Minoan king instead of your directive to delay."

"How long before they arrive in Avaris?" Potiphar's expression was chiseled stone.

"Tomorrow at the latest. More likely, midday today."

The master sighed and scrubbed his bald head. "Give our Medjays extra rations for their reporting, and have those oarsmen flogged for obeying Rehor's orders instead of mine." After waving away his second-in-command, Potiphar fastened his Gold of Praise collar and strapped on his weapons, muttering something about pushy Minoans.

He strode to the door, flung it open, and shouted orders as he marched. "The Hebrew needs Medjays to accompany him to the pastures this morning."

Hami glanced at Joseph, who blew out a slow breath, grateful to have weathered the master's storm. "I should probably have six men escort me."

"You'll have them." Hami closed the door and left Joseph to face the scathing old steward alone.

"A Hebrew commanding mighty Medjays." Abasi shook his head and spit on the tiled floor at Joseph's feet. "This is not the Egypt of my fathers."

FIVE

*The Midianites sold Joseph in Egypt to Potiphar,
one of Pharaoh's officials, the captain of the guard.*
GENESIS 37:36

Potiphar

Potiphar escaped his chamber with the relief of a prisoner on the run. "Follow," he said to two Medjays at the end of the villa's residence hall.

His thoughts spun in a dozen directions, but Abasi's boorishness shoved aside all else. If the gods had any mercy, they would have freed Potiphar of his vow years ago. He hadn't realized one promise—meant to satisfy Pushpa's overzealous compassion—would turn into a lifetime commitment. Shortly after Potiphar's abi died, Ommi and her husband took in both Potiphar and Abasi, a beggar. The old man was too weak for physical labor, so Ommi nagged Potiphar to take him along as a personal steward during Potiphar's first military mission.

"Maybe I'll give my annoying steward to you Medjays." The guards shook their heads vehemently, a sure sign of Abasi's power to terrify.

Potiphar marched through the villa's hallway adjoining the palace. He could cut through the kitchen, but Pushpa would insist—

"Oh no!" Potiphar stopped so abruptly, he startled his Medjay escort. One guard drew his dagger, glancing around. Potiphar grinned.

"I forgot to break my fast. Perhaps you could slice a fig with that blade, soldier."

The well-trained Medjay almost smiled.

Instead of a fig, the other guard produced a piece of dried venison from the pouch at his waist, and they resumed the march.

Potiphar's mind also resumed its frenzied pace, reciting the topics he'd prepared for the king's briefing after hashing out his concerns with Pushpa last night. That woman was wiser than all Khyan's advisers on their best day.

Most of his thoughts focused on how to make today's Hathor festival more enjoyable for his king and friend. He'd spoken with the queen's brother, General Apophis, yesterday—a boundary he seldom crossed since Potiphar's authority was officially limited to guarding Pharaoh's person. However, since bad news about a Tehenu rebellion could infringe on today's festivities, Potiphar had crossed the invisible diplomatic line and suggested the general dispatch four contingents of Pharaoh's army to quell unrest before sparks became flames.

"Any news of the Tehenu advancing?" he asked as they entered the empty throne hall.

"None since last night." The dagger-wielding guard had been under Potiphar's command since Khyan's inauguration—the day Egyptian kitchen slaves poisoned his abi, King Bnon. "Temehu's drought continues, but only one village is on the move. They haven't crossed into Egyptian territory—yet."

"Good. And Pharaoh's troops?"

"Our man inside says Pharaoh has given no battle orders to march."

"All right. Well done." Potiphar always employed a high-ranking informant inside the king's army to ensure he was never surprised. Potiphar loathed surprises. Khyan would inform Potiphar if he planned to engage, but the captain of Pharaoh's bodyguard must deal in possibilities. If he waited to react after commands and official edicts, his friend and pharaoh would have been killed years ago.

"Anything new on the Minoan king?"

"No, Captain. Commander Hami gave you the most recent news." Potiphar nodded as the three men ascended the platform and walked past Egypt's golden throne. King Rehor's unannounced visit on a festival day was uncharacteristically bold. Bringing his daughter was absolutely brazen. There was only one reason a king presented his daughter to Pharaoh—but Rehor would be sorely disappointed. Khyan was devoted to his wives, and two women created enough complications for any man.

The two Medjays stopped at the tapestry-covered back wall.

"Wait here." Potiphar slipped between the matching blue-and-crimson tapestries to enter the palace's residential wing. He emerged into a narrow tiled hallway and greeted a dozen more guards. Each one saluted, fist to his heart. Potiphar acknowledged them with a nod. The guard at Pharaoh's chamber had already knocked and announced the captain's presence by the time he reached the gilded double doors. Without slowing his step, Potiphar entered and found the king and the great wife, Queen Tani, lounging beside a low table. Their yogurt, bread, and fruit looked as tempting as what Potiphar had left untouched in his chamber.

"No wig?" Pharaoh Khyan shoved half a loaf in his mouth, four bites for any other man.

Potiphar bowed. "Forgive my appearance, Mighty Pharaoh. I came with urgent news."

"You're as handsome without a wig as with one, Captain, but you need a wife to inspect you before you walk out of your chamber." The queen perched her elbow on the table and propped her chin in her hand. "Why don't you marry that pretty dancer who kept draping you with veils at last week's Nehebkau festival?"

"I'm too old to marry," he said. "But I need to tell—"

"Potiphar," said the queen, "you're the most sought-after unmarried man in Egypt. A dozen noblemen's wives would divorce their stodgy husbands to have a handsome warrior like Pharaoh or the captain of his bodyguard."

With more effort than he'd need for a battle charge, he forced a semblance of pleasantry. "Truly, my queen, I thank you for your gracious comments; however, my only personal experience with a family has been with an ommi who chose prostitution over her husband. My abi drank himself to death because of it. A wife is the last thing I desire."

By her sudden pallor, Potiphar knew he'd been less than delicate and turned to his king for rescue.

Khyan patted his wife's hand. "What urgent news, Captain?"

"King Rehor and his daughter are coming to Avaris unannounced. They're likely to arrive as early as midday."

The king's brows rose. "Today?"

"Yes, my king."

"What information has been gathered on Rehor's reason for this unexpected visit?"

"His crew transferred seven small crates of cargo to a rented barque in Sena, and now his men remain with the Minoan vessel." Potiphar lifted one brow. "Presumably awaiting their regents' return."

Khyan nodded. Potiphar knew him well enough to see the thoughts spinning behind his friend's sharp eyes. "Why would Rehor risk a journey with his beloved daughter on rough seas, Potiphar?"

"Is this the daughter married to the Knossos crown prince?" Queen Tani joined the conversation, aiming the question at her husband. "Have you heard of any tragedies on the seas? Any word from our Egyptian traders of a reason the princess might come looking for a new husband?"

Khyan grinned at his wife. "Though I'm flattered by your jealousy, Wife, Rehor mentioned during our negotiations that his daughter and the crown prince would be heavily involved in future transactions. Perhaps Rehor wishes us to meet his daughter before we begin trading in the spring."

Tani glared at him. "Don't lie to yourself or me, Husband. There's only one reason a king brings his daughter to meet Pharaoh." She turned to Potiphar, who marveled that she'd spoken his thoughts aloud. "Tell him, Captain. If that Cretan offers his daughter as a bride, he'll try to negotiate better terms on the agreement already made."

Pharaoh pressed a single large finger against his wife's. "I've made a vow to you, Tani, after I realized what my marriage to Ziwat cost us. I won't marry again."

She pulled her hand away. "I'm sure King Rehor knows nothing of your vow."

The air crackled with tension, and Potiphar wished he could disappear. This was what marriage did to people. Tied them in knots. Changed them from warm and witty to snarling and suspicious.

"Rehor has only one wife." Though Potiphar agreed with Tani, he didn't want this news to ruin the royal couple's celebration of Hathor—the goddess of love. "Why would he give his daughter to a pharaoh who already has two wives?"

Khyan brushed Tani's cheek, then turned with a sigh to Potiphar. "My queen is right. Rehor and I talked about our families when we negotiated the agreement. He knows I have a second wife and may assume I'm willing to—"

"He *assumes* too much!" Tani shouted at Potiphar. "You will determine the reason for his visit before he presents his daughter."

Potiphar hoped Pharaoh would intervene. The queen began rising from her cushion. A pure Egyptian of extraordinary height, she stood beside her seated husband and rested her arm on his shoulder. "You say the Minoan princess might come to learn her abi's trade, but I assure you, Husband, a woman doesn't leave her home unless she seeks another." She raised her chin, making them wait while she swiped at tears. "Keep your vow to me, Khyan. I can't endure another woman in your arms." She kissed him and walked away, every movement a study of elegance.

Pharaoh watched his wife's every step. In moments like this, it was difficult to envision Khyan as Lower Egypt's god on the throne instead of the soldier who fell in love with the former vizier's daughter seven years ago. Potiphar and Khyan had been serving as part of Pharaoh Monthhotep's bodyguard in Memphis. Tani's abi—Monthhotep's vizier—conspired to kill the Egyptian king and then helped place Khyan's grandfather Salitis on Lower Egypt's throne as the first Amu pharaoh. In return, Pharaoh Salitis gave the vizier's daughter to Khyan as his bride, certain she would one day be Egypt's queen.

Potiphar chuckled at his still-besotted friend. "You love her as much as—"

Pharaoh silenced him with an uplifted hand. He waited until the chamber door closed, then offered a weary smile. "You were saying?"

"I don't see many husbands who love their wives like you do, my friend."

"No one has a wife like Tani." He tried to chuckle, but humor died when he leaned forward, his hands clutched in a white-knuckled grip. "I shouldn't have married Ziwat. Why didn't I insist instead that the Medjay chief accept gold or gemstones as proof of my continuing trust?"

The first two Amu pharaohs had been assassinated within three years—with Medjays forming the majority of their bodyguard. When Khyan questioned their loyalty, their chief proved his commitment by executing the warriors who'd allowed the assassinations and presenting Ziwat as his most precious treasure. Khyan held Potiphar's gaze. "Marrying the chieftain's daughter cost me more than all the gold in Egypt."

"You couldn't reject a gift given publicly," Potiphar said to soothe his friend's tortured soul. But Khyan was right. It had been a mistake. The only bad decision his friend had made in four years. His bad marriage was like weeds in a field. No matter how many good harvests, the weeds stole his attention. "We're not certain Rehor intends to offer his daughter as a bride."

Khyan gathered a handful of almonds and tossed a few in his mouth. "He told us she keeps his trade records. Perhaps he is bringing her to—" An unholy rumble interrupted the king of Egypt. He lowered a horrified stare to Potiphar's belly. "Sit down and feed that beast."

Potiphar was grateful for the invitation. His mind worked better when his stomach was full. He stuffed his mouth with bread and yogurt and quickly swallowed. "Go ahead. I'm listening, brother." Only when they were alone would he use such familiar terms.

"If Rehor brought the princess to enlighten her on trade matters, we'll include them in our Hathor celebration and send them home with gifts. If the Minoan king comes like the Medjay chieftain, seeking to make his daughter an iron collar and his trade ships my leash, you will remind him why Lower Egypt is the strongest nation in the world."

Potiphar saluted his pharaoh, fist to chest, and then repeated the vow he and Khyan had made as young soldiers. "My life for your life, Khyan. I'll do whatever is necessary to protect and prosper you all the days of my life."

Pharaoh offered his hand. When Potiphar grabbed his wrist in pledge, Khyan's hand engulfed his forearm. "As I'll do whatever is necessary to protect and prosper you all the days of my life."

Potiphar nodded and released his friend's wrist. He poured himself a goblet full of grape juice and remembered the disturbing news of Vizier Wereni's bullying. "Wereni is harassing my shepherds."

Khyan took a long sip from his goblet. He set it aside. Slowly. Deliberately. "When my family ended the Egyptian's reign in Memphis, I took Wereni from Ra's temple because while other priests trembled and begged, he boldly proposed I use him as a scribe. Then he had the nerve to request I allow his wife to come with him to Avaris. When the man is devoted, he's relentless."

"But his devotion is only to pure-blooded Egyptians and Ra," Potiphar added.

"He's also smart, which is the reason I made him vizier. We keep him close enough to watch and give him a year to change. If he remains a snake in my garden, you'll execute him."

"As you wish, my king." Potiphar wanted to add, *But he could do a lot of damage in a year.*

"You've undoubtedly placed an informant in Wereni's household and in the prisons beneath your villa and his. I trust what happens in your prison, my friend, but I won't let captives waste away under his villa because they're not Egyptian."

"Of course, Khyan. I have informants everywhere." It was almost the truth. Potiphar had informants everywhere—except the prisons. And he'd place a man in Wereni's prison the moment he left Khyan's chamber.

SIX

To humans belong the plans of the heart,
but from the LORD comes the proper answer of the tongue.
PROVERBS 16:1

Zuleika

I'd watched with fascination as our oarsmen fought the Nile's current on our four-day journey to Avaris. Though their straining at the oars had been almost painful to watch, their skill in navigating the receding waters was as wondrous as that of our own Minoan sailors in a mighty storm. And when the river could no longer buoy our flat-bottomed barque, the brave boatmen uncoiled huge hemp ropes—as thick as my arm—and trudged to opposite shores, then tugged us by sheer will toward the great god, Pharaoh Khyan.

Not so inspiring, however, were the flimsy excuses given on the third day for slowing our travel after a Medjay on a small skiff boarded our barque. He engaged in whispered conversation with our guards and the head oarsman before returning to his skiff and rowing south.

Pateras appeared at my side. "They're slowing us down to give Pharaoh time to prepare for our arrival. The Medjay in the skiff will take news to Khyan of our imminent visit."

Though I would have enjoyed the extra time with Pateras, the Nile would only get shallower and travel more difficult as each day passed. "A very wise Minoan king once told me the best traders keep their customers guessing. We shouldn't slow down." I nudged him and gave him a playful grin.

That was the only encouragement he needed. After a short discussion with the Medjays and head oarsman, even though it was dusk, our barque's brave sailors jumped into the shallow waters and resumed tugging. Though horrified that the crocodiles of Gaios's mythical stories were real, I was inspired by our sailors' fortitude and courage and rushed to the barque's prow to help keep watch for the terrifying beasts. We spotted many, but we arrived safely at the Avaris quay with not a single man injured.

When I was ready to disembark, my favorite Medjay offered his hand. "Watch your step, Princess."

"Thank you, Radhi." He embodied the aspect of Gaios I missed most: a personal protector.

"Why is the palace surrounded by huge walls?" I pointed to what looked more like the fortress we'd seen as we sailed away from Sena.

"I've delivered you safely, Blessed of Hathor. May the goddess give you success." Radhi bowed and turned back toward the barque.

"But—"

"Come, Zully." Pateras cradled my elbow, following only two of our Medjays.

"Wait!" I pulled away, looking back at the three Medjays preparing the barque for departure. "Aren't they coming with us?" My voice broke, and Pateras's impatient scowl disappeared.

He drew nearer. "There will be many more goodbyes, my girl." His voice was barely louder than the street noise. "But you've tasted the worst of grief and conquered it. You're a warrior. A queen."

"Pharaoh already has a queen." I swiped at errant tears, refusing to mope about becoming a third wife. "Why did you wait until this morning to tell me Pharaoh already has a second wife?"

"Would it have mattered?"

"What if it did matter? Would you have delivered me to Pharaoh anyway?"

"I've told you, Zuleika. This is your decision until the moment you sign the marriage contract. Then it's done."

I shrugged off his grip. "It's already done, Pateras. I've made my decision."

Marching away from the docks, I emerged onto the tiled streets of Avaris, slowed by a celebrating crowd. A drunken Egyptian stumbled into me. One of our Medjays shoved the man to the tiles, and his headdress toppled off—cow's horns held in place by a woven reed cap. He shouted curses, grabbing for the beloved symbol of Hathor.

The Medjays shooed him away to join the other revelers with similar headpieces, and a niggling suspicion started to rise.

"Are you all right?" Pateras asked.

"Why did Radhi call me 'Blessed of Hathor' as if I had some special—"

"I may have convinced our Egyptian sailors and Medjay escort that you're endowed by Sekhmet and Hathor with special powers." He grinned sheepishly. "I told them you came from destruction, like Sekhmet, and have emerged as Hathor to bring love and joy to Pharaoh Khyan—which was why we needed to arrive for the festival." He leaned down. "It was the only way to convince them to ignore Potiphar's command."

I glanced at the Medjays, trying to recall everything Gaios and Pateras had taught me about Egypt's goddess of love. "Brilliant." Linking my arm with Pateras's, I slipped into the persona of Princess Zuleika and motioned our escort toward the high stone walls. Pateras, too, donned his regal bearing, eyes forward and smiling pleasantly. Our two Medjays flanked us, their long arms extended to clear a path through the mayhem.

The smell of stale beer and vomit was overwhelming. Curious celebrants waved at us, sloshing more amber liquid from their cups than down their throats. I held tightly to Pateras's arm to keep from slipping on the beer-soaked tiles and strained to look beyond the throng ahead of us. We'd need to pass through a mammoth gate to enter the walled palace complex. The gate was more like a tunnel since the wall itself was as thick as a man's height and as high as fifteen men stacked.

Our Medjays cut through the crowd. "King Rehor to see Pharaoh Khyan," one of them announced as we approached the gate. The soldiers at the gate waved us forward.

Pateras guided me through the reeking bodies inside the gate. I kept my head down, trusting him and the two Medjays to be my shield through a crowd of others anxious to join the royal celebration. When we emerged into the palace complex, I noticed the tiles beneath my feet had transformed from plain brown earthenware to shiny, smooth faience. I lifted my head to behold a wonderland of splendor and delight.

Three lofty structures bordered a large rectangular pond filled with a rapturously aromatic blossom. "Are those the lotus flowers you've described?"

Pateras nodded, intent on something straight ahead. I followed his gaze to three long lines of people waiting on the stone steps of the largest of the three buildings. The palace, no doubt.

My heart felt as if it were melting. "Are they waiting for an audience with the king?"

"Yes, my girl, but our fine Medjays will make sure we see Pharaoh Khyan immediately." He spoke loud enough for our escort to hear but got no response.

I no longer cared about flowers or tiles as we approached the towering stairway. The rush of joy I felt when our Medjays led us up the stairs almost drowned out the angry shouts of those we passed. On any other day, I would have at least attempted an explanation for our rudeness, but Crete's salvation demanded that I be as determined as the Egyptian sailors who strained against the oars, tugged hemp ropes, and refused to slow their pace—despite the danger of crocodiles.

We reached the palace halls, and the magnificence stole my breath. More Medjays nodded to our escort before opening the double cedar doors to Egypt's hall of justice.

I halted at the threshold, as rigid as one of my statues. An ostrich squawked on my left. I turned toward a man wrapped—shoulders to ankles—in a multicolored cloth. A tambourine crashed in front of my face, and nearly naked dancers wearing cow's horn headdresses leapt and twirled while musicians played.

Pateras again cradled my elbow, moving me forward. I lowered my gaze and focused on the somewhat-worn crimson carpet lining the center aisle. "Don't be rude." His coarse whisper pierced me.

Mitera would be ashamed of me. She'd taught me to greet royalty with the respect I also deserved. Digging for more courage, I lifted my chin. Then gasped. A hundred paces ahead was something—someone—seated on a throne who appeared more myth than man. Panic rose, filling my sandals with boulders.

"Zully, listen to me." Pateras's calm seemed ludicrous in the moment. "I'm right here with you. Remember Crete."

Crete. I returned my attention to the giant on the throne. *Always stride with your escort. Right foot first.* I hoped to distract myself with the lessons Mitera taught me as a little girl, but with every step, my trepidation grew.

Even while seated, Pharaoh Khyan was taller than the imposing soldier who stood at his right shoulder. Both men wore the Gold of Praise collar. *Awarded for valor,* Pateras had said. I was trying hard to forget the *exceptional brutality* part of the description; however, brutality wasn't hard to imagine when Pharaoh's collar was the size of a blanket, his body a sculpture of chiseled stone.

A group of elegantly clad men stood on a platform, lower than the king's but higher than the marble floor on which I took tremulous steps.

"His royal council," Pateras whispered. "The native Egyptians shave their hair and wear wigs. Foreign-born nobility can be difficult to spot since many adopt Egyptian dress and customs. However, some Amu flaunt their heritage with the square-cut edges of their natural hair and thinly manicured beards."

I noted manicured beards on less than half the council, but how many of the others were Amu beneath an Egyptian facade?

When I returned my focus to the king's dais, I glimpsed two women seated to Pharaoh's left and five paces back, watching the celebration with seeming indifference. Regal in both dress and posture, they were undoubtedly his wives. One was exceptionally tall and lovely, wearing a crown with her purple robe and gold sash. The second appeared to be as Pateras had described the Nehesu, darker skinned and stunning in her white robe with a purple sash.

Pateras and I halted at the end of the crimson carpet and inclined our heads toward Egypt's throne.

"Welcome, King Rehor." I jolted upright at the king's booming voice. "Introduce your lovely guest." Pharaoh's smile soothed me. He didn't seem offended at my thoughtless reaction.

"I stand before you with my greatest treasure, great god and king." Pateras's hand trembled as he nudged me forward. "My daughter, Princess Zuleika of Zakros Palace."

Pharaoh's eyes never left Pateras's. "We've spoken privately about our families, Rehor, and I'm happy to meet your daughter." He waited barely long enough to draw a breath. "But we speak plainly to each other, do we not? Why come to Avaris unannounced?"

Noise in the throne room faded to curious whispers. I maintained a pleasant countenance but held my breath. Would Pateras offer me to an angry king?

"My wife and my daughter's husband were killed in a shaking of the earth that destroyed much of Crete."

A unified gasp swept the courtroom, and Pharaoh winced like he'd been slapped. "I'm truly sorry, my friend." He turned to me, his eyes a deep brown. "And to you, Princess Zuleika, I extend my deepest sympathy. To have lost your husband and ommi in a single tragedy is a heavy burden. But thanks be to the gods, you and King Rehor are safe."

Painful memories clawed up from the dark hole where I'd buried them, closing my throat with emotion. For two weeks I'd been distracted by stormy seas, rude Egyptians, and new adventures. I bowed to hide the rush of pain. *Crete must survive. I'm the only hope.* Gathering courage from desperation, I lifted my head to accept his condolences. "Indeed we thank the gods for our safety, but as you know, Pharaoh Khyan, rulers live for their people. It is the survival of Crete and the Minoan culture I live for now."

Pharaoh studied me, as did the soldier at his right shoulder. The extended silence grew awkward.

"We've come to personally vow," Pateras said loud enough for the whole audience to hear, "that Zakros will rise from the gods' testing to even more glorious heights."

Pharaoh finally turned from me to look at him. "And how will you rise if the shaking destroyed your island?"

"I said *much* of Crete is destroyed, Great Khyan." Pateras bowed at the waist, showing humility if not fealty, and then straightened. "Every district suffered, and many lives were lost. Homes destroyed. Food stores ruined or washed away. If I traded everything of value in all four of Crete's districts, the profits wouldn't purchase enough food and supplies to endure the winter, let alone rebuild. We Minoans will not survive without mercy from Egypt's great and mighty pharaoh."

A wave of whispers rolled through the gathering around us, but I forced stillness and glimpsed the royal wives. They were stoic. Unaffected.

Pharaoh leaned an elbow on his armrest and returned his focus to me. "Why are you here, Princess Zuleika? The Great Sea is rough this time of year. It couldn't have been an easy journey."

"Nothing has been easy since the shaking, Great Khyan." Fear eroded my courage at an alarming rate.

"Zuleika is not only my greatest treasure," Pateras interjected. "She is Crete's most valuable asset. As the wife of Knossos's crown prince and princess of Zakros, Zuleika ruled alongside my wife, Queen Daria, during my seafaring absences. She's educated in ledgers and speaks the language of trade." With his hand at the small of my back, he nudged me forward like a mare at auction. "My daughter is the crowning jewel of Crete and has agreed to serve as your royal wife if your bride-price would include reviving our homeland."

Pharaoh's brows rose but gave away no indication of a reply. I glimpsed the granite countenance of his queen crack, nostrils flaring and lips pursed. The second wife remained placid and distracted.

"You seem like a woman with an opinion," Pharaoh said to me. "If you live for the survival of Crete, Princess Zuleika, how can you become an Egyptian wife? You'll never see your homeland again."

Stunned at the compassion of a man who would consider a woman's longing for home, I opened my mouth and said the only thing that came to mind. "The love between a husband and wife can make anywhere home." As soon as the words escaped, I squeezed my eyes shut, chastising myself. How could a man with two wives know anything of a love like Minas and I shared?

"What do you think of her, Captain?" The king's question startled me.

The imposing guard by Pharaoh's right shoulder bent closer to consult privately with his king. The courtroom hummed, and Pharaoh's queen glared at me with a heat that could have melted bronze. The second wife wore a wry smirk.

"She would be a fine addition to your household, my king." One of the council members offered unsolicited advice, stirring the other noblemen to voice competing opinions.

My palms grew sweaty as the king's whispered conversation with his captain intensified. *Odd that Pharaoh cares what a soldier thinks about him acquiring a third wife.*

When the guard resumed his stance at the king's side, his neck and face were crimson, but his expression had returned to stone.

Pharaoh Khyan aimed an amused smile at Pateras. "You will receive the mercy you've requested, King Rehor. Egypt will aid your little island with enough food and supplies to survive the winter." He turned to me. "And your lovely daughter will marry my best friend, Potiphar, the captain of my bodyguard."

A puff of air parted my lips as the throne room came alive with celebration. Surely he didn't say—

"But, Great Khyan! Great Khyan!" Pateras tried to speak over the noise.

Pharaoh stood, silencing everyone with the sheer power of his size. I stepped back and looked up to see the king, whose head almost reached the great hall's ceiling. "As young warriors, Potiphar and I vowed to do whatever was necessary to prosper the other, even to the point of giving our lives." He turned to the captain, his smile sobered. "You put your life in danger for me every day, but I will not let you die without experiencing the greatest gift the gods ever created. You need a wife. And not just any wife. You need a wife with strong opinions!" His rumbling laughter unleashed the musicians and dancing girls. Jubilation erupted throughout the room, and servants appeared from every corner to refill goblets with beer and offer newcomers their first celebratory taste.

I shot a panicked look at Pateras. Was this some terrible Egyptian jest in which I was both subject and ignorant bystander? Or was I really expected to bind myself for life to the angry-looking guard who stared at a spot on the wall above me?

"But, great king..." Pateras rushed toward Pharaoh. Our Medjays—the same two who had escorted us safely from Sena—leveled their spears at his belly.

Captain Potiphar fixed his gaze on Pateras. "Pharaoh Khyan has spoken. You may reject the entire proposal or accept the decision of Egypt's god."

Pharaoh settled on his throne again, waving his hand to quiet the celebration. "Move the Hathor festival to the courtyard. My council members and I will join you when our business with Crete is done."

Pateras drew a breath to speak, but Pharaoh shot a warning glance at him. The royal wives remained on the dais as the throne room emptied. I kept my countenance pleasant until I glimpsed Captain Potiphar scowling at me. Certain all attention was focused on the departing crowd, I sneered at the proposed groom and lifted my chin in silent rebellion. I need not bend my will and offer practiced pleasantry to a lowly *captain.*

His animosity dissolved into a condescending smirk, and my cheeks flamed. What had I just done? I would have never shown such disrespect to Minas.

"Rehor, you've shown determination to brave the Great Sea and offer your daughter," Pharaoh said, "but I vowed before my council never to marry again." I looked up as his attention turned to me. "Princess Zuleika, I honor you greatly by awarding you to my most trusted protector and friend. Captain Potiphar, though not my brother by blood, has been my brother in war since we were boys. He needs a woman to brighten his world." He grinned at his friend. "She'll be good for you."

"I receive anything from you as a gift to be treasured." Potiphar bowed, and the fire in my cheeks burned hotter.

I wasn't a *thing* to be passed from one man to the other. "Great Pharaoh!" I fell to my knees.

"Zuleika," Pateras whispered, "stand up."

I shrugged off his hands. "I'm honored you deem me worthy of your friend, but how could a Minoan princess satisfy an Egyptian warrior when I know nothing of your culture? I would be woefully lacking and a great disappointment—"

"Would you not have been *woefully lacking* as my wife?" Pharaoh's smile disappeared. "Rise, Princess."

Mind spinning, I realized too late I'd talked my way into trouble again. Movement on the periphery caught my attention—the queen covering a grin. She would be my salvation. "In your household, great king, I would have had your wives to teach me Egypt's ways. I can only assume, since you said Captain Potiphar needed a woman, his household offers no such training?"

Pharaoh's grin returned, and the muted laughter among the royal council brought another angry flush to the fierce captain's cheeks.

"You have a silver tongue like your abi," Pharaoh said, "and a quick mind. I see wisdom in your request for training. You'll spend one week in my wives' care before marrying my captain."

"What? No!" I blurted. A collective gasp from his council and a glare from his captain proved I'd misspoken again. Bowing deeply, I offered respect if not submission. "Please, great and mighty Pharaoh . . ."

Memories flooded my mind—our courageous Minoan sailors

enduring storm-tossed seas, those brave Egyptian oarsmen pulling our barque through crocodile-infested waters. All of it necessary to secure the supplies Pharaoh agreed to give—if I'd simply marry his best friend.

For Crete.

"Because Egypt is such a rich and complex culture," I said, opening negotiations, "a month under your royal wives' wise tutelage would help—"

"Two weeks." Pharaoh Khyan's eyes locked on mine, his ruling final. He turned to Pateras. "Keep the cargo that survived the shaking as seed to begin trading next season. I accept your lovely daughter for my captain and will increase the bride-price. Crete will have an annual shipment of food and building supplies for three consecutive years. By then your island should be functioning again as it did before the shaking took your loved ones."

He stood, bringing his counselors to their feet and concluding the meeting. "In two weeks we'll gather to celebrate the wedding of Captain Potiphar and Princess Zuleika."

Council members filed from their platform to offer congratulations to my betrothed. When I dared to steal a glimpse of Captain Potiphar, he looked as if he'd swallowed a fish bone sideways.

Pateras reached for my hand between the folds of my tiered skirt, hiding his tenderness as he leaned close. "Potiphar is a good man, too, Zully," he whispered. "I know he seems gruff, but I've found him to be fair and honest. He'll take care of you."

As if realizing he was the focus of our conversation, the captain looked my direction and offered a single bob of his head. No smile. No romantic or unspoken messages in his eyes.

Before I could blink, four more Medjays surrounded us. "This way, Princess Zuleika," one of them said. "We'll escort you to the harem entrance. The royal eunuchs will show you to your temporary chamber." He extended his arm toward Pharaoh's platform. Another Medjay strode to the back wall and pulled aside a tapestry, revealing a hidden door where the royal wives had exited.

With my first step, the Medjays formed a circle around me, separating me from Pateras. "Wait! No!"

"Zully, it's all right." Pateras tried to reach through them, but their arms were like iron bars.

"Let him through." The voice was deep but quiet, and the Medjays parted without hesitation. Potiphar stood beside my pateras. "You're not a prisoner here, Princess. There's still time to reconsider. In Egypt a woman has the right to cancel a betrothal made by her family."

I searched his face, wondering whether he hoped I would reject Pharaoh's offer. He turned away, seemingly uncomfortable in the silence.

Pateras took my hands. "The captain is right, Zuleika. You can break the agreement." He gave me a fortifying look. "But if you intend to honor the agreement, I'll wait to witness your wedding before returning home."

"What about the winter seas?" I hugged him before he could answer and held him tight.

"If you can face an uncertain future, my girl," he whispered against my ear, "our sailors and I will do the same."

SEVEN

From the time he put him in charge of his house-
hold and of all that he owned, the LORD blessed the
household of the Egyptian because of Joseph.

GENESIS 39:5

TWO WEEKS LATER

Joseph

"You look pretty today, Joseph." Hami chuckled and elbowed his partner stationed at their captain's door. "The kohl and malachite on your
eyes becomes you."

Joseph dished back the jest. "Maybe your men would look nicer
with a little green powder around their eyes." After two weeks of sharing the villa's second-story barracks, he'd learned most Medjays were as
ferocious in good-natured taunting as they were about protecting Pharaoh Khyan. Though he missed his friends in the slave village, the
camaraderie of the Medjays had been a welcome surprise.

Hami opened the door to the chamber, and Joseph entered with his
usual greeting. "May Elohim's favor continue on this house."

Potiphar paced while Abasi tapped his toe, waiting beside the cosmetics couch.

"I need to get closer to Wereni, but how?" Potiphar muttered rhe-
torically, so Joseph remained silent.

Abasi gestured toward the couch and mouthed, *Get him to lie down.*

Potiphar rubbed the stubble on his head and chin. It wasn't like him to remain in his chamber past dawn. "My lord," Joseph said, "shouldn't you prepare for the day?"

He waved off the question. "Pharaoh Khyan canceled court proceedings to prepare the throne room for tonight's banquet."

"Your wedding banquet, my lord." Joseph waited for the usual growl, but none came. Abasi sneered, apparently still seething that their master was forced to take a foreign bride. But the master's obsessive pacing birthed genuine concern. "Is there anything I could do to help, Master Potiphar?"

He stopped, looked at Joseph with narrowed eyes, and proceeded to the couch.

"Relax now," the steward crooned. "Old Abasi will help you forget whatever's troubling you." He rubbed lotion on Potiphar's head and face to begin the morning's shave.

"Joseph, stand where I can see you."

He obeyed, cringing when Abasi pulled the straight razor across Potiphar's bald head.

"You and Abasi will both help."

"Of course I will," Abasi said, swishing the blade in a copper basin. "I'd do anything for you, Master. You know that." He returned the razor to Potiphar's head for a second swath.

"That weasel Wereni has met with a small group of unescorted noblemen for three consecutive weeks," Potiphar said. "I've paid one of his villa guards to keep me apprised, and he said the noblemen always come under the cover of darkness and on the same night of the week." Potiphar stared at Joseph as if waiting for a reply.

"Is it illegal for noblemen to meet regularly?" Joseph knew little of Egyptian law or politics.

"The noblemen go *unescorted,* Hebrew." He lifted his brow, causing Abasi to caution him and Joseph to feel ignorant. "They don't want Pharaoh's guards to know they're meeting."

Joseph felt the need to clarify. "So, Wereni is planning with other nobles to harm your shepherds?"

"My shep— No!" He waved Abasi away and sat up. "It's the beginning of a coup."

The declaration felt like a boulder dropped into Joseph's stomach. He'd arrived in Avaris only a week after an Egyptian pharaoh was killed in Thebes, Upper Egypt's capital. A few days later, Khyan's abba, King Bnon, was also assassinated. The two events shackled citizens in both capitals with fear until Pharaoh Khyan and Thebes's new king publicized their vow of peace. Still, the looming threat of hostility hung over Avaris like a sandstorm in the distance. "If you know Wereni is stirring a coup, why not arrest him and the others now?"

"The guard has only witnessed a few noblemen visiting the vizier." Potiphar reached up to rub his head again. "We will infiltrate Wereni's inner circle and discover his plan and the names of those involved. Patience will reveal how deeply the roots of conspiracy grow in Lower Egypt."

Joseph didn't like the risk, but he wasn't the captain of Pharaoh's bodyguard. "You're Egypt's best warrior and his most loyal friend, Master Potiphar. I know whoever you choose for this mission will be successful."

Potiphar's grin hinted at returning calm. "I vowed to Khyan he'd die of old age or in battle—as a warrior should." Potiphar clapped Abasi's shoulder. "I need someone I trust to get close to Wereni. Someone who sees him several times a day, gains his trust, and even begins to ask probing questions."

Abasi's rheumy eyes widened. "Me?"

"You, Abasi. I'll give you to Wereni as a goodwill gift—a peace offering—after our hostile encounter over the grazing land. It will appear magnanimous to other nobles on my part and—"

"But who would care for you, Master?" The old man's voice warbled as he tossed the razor into the copper basin.

Potiphar clapped his hands once. "Joseph will become my personal steward *after* you prepare me for tonight's wedding banquet."

"But—"

"I'll pay a few more of Wereni's guards to protect you," Potiphar said. "You're a patriot, Abasi. This is your chance to show your love for

Egypt. Help me rid our land of traitors like Wereni, and I'll grant you freedom—if you so choose."

Abasi's shoulders drooped. "I choose to serve you, Master Potiphar. If it means serving the vizier for a time, I'll obey." He raised his eyes and gave Joseph a withering stare. "But this Hebrew isn't worthy to serve your food, let alone tend your sacred person."

"All right, all right." Potiphar gave him a pat on the back while nudging him away from the couch. "Give Joseph the razor and let him shave me today."

Abasi grabbed the razor and lifted it like a dagger poised to strike. For a single terrifying heartbeat, Joseph thought he'd have to defend himself. Keeping his eyes focused on the old man, he spoke as reassuringly as he could without rousing the master's defenses. "I'm better at delivering lambs and kids and calves, my lord, but I'll do my best until Abasi returns."

The old man's lip twitched before he tossed the blade back into the basin. "Our master is worthy of more than your best." He stepped to the other side of the cosmetics couch to begin his instruction.

Though Joseph knew every step of the master's daily preparation, he followed Abasi's tutelage and bore his cruel remarks. It seemed a small kindness to an old man who was about to risk his life for a master he worshipped.

EIGHT

The soothing tongue is a tree of life,
but a perverse tongue crushes the spirit.
PROVERBS 15:4

Zuleika

The tittering of Avaris's noblewomen grated on my nerves and made the unbearable anticipation of tonight's wedding banquet more torturous. I finished the last stroke of the dolphin's dorsal fin on the wall mural in the harem's common room. "Now do you understand? A dolphin is a fish, but it's much larger than those we eat from the Nile." I turned toward the king's wives and the noblewomen who'd come just after dawn to prepare me for tonight's wedding banquet. Since they'd scorned everything about Crete, I'd painted Malia District's sacred symbol as a lasting "gift" to the royal gathering place but kept my tattoo of Zakros's octopus hidden.

"It looks like a crocodile without scales," said a dim-witted noblewoman.

Ziwat rolled her eyes and refilled her goblet with wine. "I'll admit the colors are beautiful and you have some skill as an artist, but why paint for us things we've never seen when Egypt's flora and fauna are so beautiful?" It was the nearest to a compliment I'd received from Ziwat.

Queen Tani emerged from her chamber, which adjoined the common room. Though she often remained aloof, her strategically placed chamber ensured she was never outwitted, overlooked, or undermined by her rival. "Ziwat makes a good point, Princess Zuleika. You've worked hard to educate us on every detail of your world—the palm forests, the olive fields, the deep gorges and sprawling mountains. How unfortunate your effort to embrace Egypt lacks the same zeal."

Venomous, I thought, *but true.* "And equally unfortunate the women of Egypt seem more concerned about their place in society than true friendship." It was a very unroyal response.

"At least you've learned that." Tani, too, revealed a momentary flaw in her regal veil. She clapped her hands, moving toward the women she ruled. "The sun has risen, ladies. Let's begin preparing Princess Zuleika to wed the most coveted unmarried man in Egypt."

I suppressed a cynical snort. If I'd been given a piece of silver each time I heard how marvelous Potiphar was, I could have rebuilt Crete without a marriage contract. Until now I'd postponed the obligatory preening, instead lingering in the memories of Minas, Zakros, and the sea.

Pharaoh's rumbling chuckle stole my attention, and I sprang to my feet.

Queen Tani and Ziwat rushed past me to greet their husband. Ziwat arrived first and received a peck on her cheek. Tani nudged the woman aside, demanding her husband's embrace. She welcomed him with an impassioned kiss, and uncomfortable silence descended.

An older woman I'd never seen before accompanied the king. She was dressed in plain linen that bore stains common for a servant, yet she smiled at me boldly like Minoan nobility. Portly—but not fat— she was older than Pateras. The woman reminded me of Baba, Mitera's mitera. Though both sets of my grandparents passed into the sea when I was but a child, I remembered the same compassion in the tilt of Baba's head.

"I've brought a gift from your groom." The woman crossed the space between us, gaining everyone's attention with her kind tone. On outstretched arms she offered a pure white linen dress. Exquisite jewelry rested atop it. "My son wishes to shower his beauty with beauty."

Speechless, I ran my fingertips over the delicate linen and sparkling treasures, then regained my manners. "I'm overwhelmed at Captain Potiphar's generosity." I inclined my head, showing customary gratitude, but I was far more intrigued by the woman holding the gifts. "May I ask your name?"

The woman bowed, but Pharaoh subtly raised her to face him. "Ommi Pushpa, you needn't bow to anyone but me." He kissed her wrinkled cheek and turned to me. "Princess Zuleika, meet the woman Potiphar will always love more than any other."

Startled by his introduction, I laughed when she kissed his hand and then swatted him playfully. "Since you're a god now, I can't take a switch to you."

"Indeed you can't." Khyan pulled her into a sideways embrace. "Pushpa has been ommi to both Potiphar and me since our own passed into the afterworld."

I measured the woman with new caution. Was Pushpa like Minas's mitera, the Knossos queen, who had loved to manipulate her son? The only thing my husband and I ever fought about was his mitera's meddling.

Pushpa studied me. "Though I can see my son's new bride has been well cared for by your lovely wives, it would be my great privilege to prepare Princess Zuleika for her wedding banquet in our own villa." She now bowed to me, showing a humility neither Minas's mitera nor the women in Pharaoh's harem would ever have offered. When she straightened, a spark of mischief lit her countenance, and I knew immediately we could be friends. "Others may teach you of Egypt, my dear, but no one can prepare you to meet Potiphar as I can."

The king chuckled. "All right, Pushpa. Prepare her yourself, you sly fox." He turned a gracious smile to me. "Queen Tani tells me you're quite intelligent, Princess. I'll hear more about what you've learned at tonight's banquet."

"Thank you, Great Khyan." I offered a quick nod, excused myself, and started toward my harem chamber to gather my belongings.

Queen Tani halted me at the chamber's threshold. "We'll have a eunuch deliver the paints and brushes."

I stared at the lavish furnishings, baskets of linen robes, and various cosmetics and jewelry. None of it was mine. Everything from Zakros had been taken from me and sent to Potiphar's villa when I entered the harem.

"Come, dear girl." Pushpa's hand gently cradled my elbow, the wedding gifts from her son tucked under her arm. She didn't need to coax. I was more than ready to escape this world of women. I nodded respectful goodbyes, certain—unfortunately—I'd see them all again at tonight's banquet.

The magnitude of this transition settled in as Pushpa led me toward my new life. We walked through open-air courtyards and narrow hallways. Past Medjay guards and scurrying servants. We entered the busy palace kitchen, unnoticed by the ranting head cook. When we crossed to the other side, Pushpa opened another set of double doors. "This is the villa's kitchen. We open the adjoining doors during large events like tonight's banquet to aid the palace efforts."

I scanned her small kitchen with its kneading table, a hearth, and a dozen or so baskets filled with provisions.

"You're Captain Potiphar's cook?"

"I have an important role in my son's home." She grinned. "Who wants to sit idle and become a hateful noblewoman?" She released a mighty chuckle and hustled us out of her kitchen.

I was delighted she saw the true nature of the noblewomen, but I was too cautious to say it. "You don't have time to prepare me for the wedding banquet," I said. "I should be helping you!"

"It's a busy day, to be sure, but I only get to prepare one bride for my son." She puffed a stray strand of gray hair off her forehead as we entered a quiet hallway. Two Medjays guarded a door directly across from the kitchen. "I'm sure a princess is accustomed to a handmaid. I'll send Joseph to purchase one—"

"I'm not!" I stopped, near panic. "Please. I didn't have a maid in Crete, Pushpa. I had *friends* who worked with me to complete tasks." How could I tactfully describe the way those Egyptian noblewomen had wounded my Minoan heart?

She gently lifted my chin. "I see pain in your eyes, my dear. Potiphar told me about your loss, and I'm so sorry. You're safe here with me. Now, come. Let me show you to your chamber." Her arm circled my waist, and she guided me toward the room at the end of the hall-way, where two more guards waited. One of the men opened the door, and both bowed as we entered.

Pushpa took a few steps inside, placed my wedding gifts on a table, and led me into the long, narrow chamber. "Welcome to your new home, Mistress. I believe you can be very happy here with my Poti-phar."

The room was utterly Egyptian but spacious and lavishly furnished. Murals of happy Egyptian families decorated the walls, and an adjoin-ing servant's chamber protruded into the space. Brightly colored couches made the audience chamber inviting, and an elevated bed beyond the meeting space—draped ceiling to floor with sheer linen—gave the whole chamber a whimsical feel.

Past the curtained bed, a large entryway revealed a private court-yard that shared the high walls of Pharaoh's palace complex. I placed my hand against the cold mudbricks, remembering my first sight of the imposing wall from the palace quay. "What's on the other side?" I asked.

"The upper city, where most of the nobility live." Pushpa stepped around two plush couches and stood beside a lovely pond where lotus blossoms floated—beautiful and calming. "You can find more can-vases and paints at the royal market."

My breath caught when I spied the wooden chest that held every-thing I'd salvaged from Zakros Palace. I skidded to my knees beside it, and Pushpa joined me. "I made sure no one opened it until you arrived." She raised her eyebrows, her lips forming a hopeful pout, and I realized she was the one who'd prepared all this for me.

"Pushpa, thank—"

"Zully!" I looked up to see Pateras rushing toward me.

I bolted to my feet and fell into his arms. "You're here!"

He laughed and pointed through my door to the chamber across the hall. "Potiphar invited me to stay in the guest room these two weeks, and Pushpa has fed me well. She's a remarkable cook." He patted his belly.

Pushpa's cheeks bloomed pink. "You're a gracious guest, King Rehor."

After spending two weeks with venomous females, I was overwhelmed by Pushpa's kindness and bowed to my groom's lovely mitera. "How can I thank you enough?"

"Come, come." She wrapped me in a sweet embrace.

Memories of Mitera rushed back without warning, and hysteria threatened. I pushed her away and frantically swiped at tears. "Forgive me. I—"

"You two should have time alone before your handmaid arrives." She hurried out the door.

"Wait, Pushpa." The door closed behind her, and I cast a stricken glance at Pateras. "Did I offend the only friend I've made in Egypt?"

"I believe she's astute, not offended." His brows drew together as he studied me. "Something upset you in the harem."

I'd never been skilled at hiding my emotions, but the truth would only make him worry. "It's always a challenge to discover one's place in a new world of women, Pateras. Queen Tani is forthright and the best among them."

"Hmm." He pulled me into his arms and laid his cheek atop my head. " 'Forthright.' And she's the best of them?"

I wriggled from his embrace and hurried to my wooden chest, needing to change the subject. After turning the latch, I opened the lid and started sorting through my salvaged treasures—a short coat, spices, and a blanket that padded the greatest prize of all. My heart beat faster as I unwrapped my priceless vase. Letting my hands travel over its cool crystal, I remembered my climb up the jagged hills of Crete and the moment I discovered the crystal bedrock. I hauled a large piece back to the palace and began chiseling.

"I didn't think I could ever believe in a god again," I confessed, looking up from my treasure. "But the survival of this vase might convince me there's a higher being who cares."

My finger traced the vase's slender opening, which was barely wide enough to work my hand inside and carve out its soul. I slid my hand over its elegant neck to the collar of gilded ivory discs connected to its beaded handle, then grazed the wide girth that curved gently to its narrow bottom. "When I formed the base, my chisel hit a natural fissure and made it too slender to sit upright. It could never bear the weight of oil or water as it was intended to do, but it was still my treasure—though fated to lie on its side."

Pateras took the vase from my hands and examined it as I had done. "Right before we left for the last trade season, you wanted me to trade it, but I said it wasn't fit for anything."

"No. You said, 'It's not fit for its original purpose, but it's too beautiful to discard.' And then you told me to keep it for the sheer enjoyment of its beauty." The words pierced me as if I and the vase were one. "Is that how Pharaoh saw me, Pateras? I was unfit for his purpose, so Potiphar got the misshapen vessel instead?" Saddened, I wondered whether my misshapen life could bring anyone joy.

"Why do you treasure this vase, Zully?"

"You know why. I climbed a mountain, brought back the stone, then chiseled it into something beautiful. It survived the shaking, storms at sea, and a journey down the Nile. It's like a gift from the gods."

"And *that's* how Pharaoh saw my girl. A gift from the gods, a treasure he presented to his best friend."

I wanted to believe him. "Spoken like a proud pateras."

His smile was brief, and his expression warned me of hard words coming. "I leave tomorrow, Zul."

"No. Why . . ." But I knew.

"The seas will be impassable if we wait longer."

Tomorrow I'd be truly alone in this inhospitable land. I offered the best smile I could and began meandering through my new home. The murals on the walls around me sparked an idea. "What if I could sell my art in Avaris's markets?" I whirled to face him. "They're sending someone with my papyrus and paints from the harem, and surely Pharaoh's heroic captain would purchase more art supplies for his new bride. When you come back in the spring, the profits I've earned could help with Crete's rebuilding."

"It's a wonderful idea, Zul."

I heard doubt in his tone. "You don't think my art will sell in Egypt?"

"It's not that." He hesitated. "You would need to paint enough papyrus to fill this chamber and add murals all over Egypt to revive Crete."

"Then I'll make vases too." And when Crete no longer needed Egypt's wealth, I'd find a way to leave Captain Potiphar and return to the land and people I loved.

NINE

When the Midianite merchants came by, his
brothers pulled Joseph up out of the cistern and sold
him for twenty shekels of silver to the Ishmaelites,
who took him to Egypt.

GENESIS 37:28

Joseph

Joseph stood in the shade of an acacia tree with four of Potiphar's shepherds. "We'll graze the ewes ready for breeding in the south pastures, and after they've been seeded, we'll move them to the north pastures."

"North, south, what does it matter?" A newly acquired shepherd twice Joseph's age made no attempt to shelter his opinions. "Leave them be, and let the gods have their way."

Another shepherd elbowed the man. "The lambs are stronger, with fewer miscarriages, when we help the gods."

"There is but one God—" Joseph began, but he interrupted his own familiar refrain when he glimpsed Hami running toward them. Fear sent him sprinting to meet the Medjay. "What is it? Is Master injured? Pushpa?"

"Pushpa is overwhelmed with kitchen tasks, so she insists you and

I choose five more kitchen slaves." He lifted a disapproving eyebrow. "And a maid for our new mistress. She said to hurry."

Joseph growled his consent and joined the long-legged Medjay at his gazelle-like pace.

"The Midianites will have the most slaves to choose from."

Joseph nodded, painfully aware that the slavers who had sold him to Potiphar four years ago were still the most prolific slave traders in Avaris. Each time he passed through the lower city market, memories of his three-week journey in chains assaulted him.

They slowed their pace upon entering the packed-dirt streets and wound through the mudbrick houses to the central square. The smell of warm bodies, fresh meat, and cloying spices was a harsh contrast to Joseph's life in the open fields.

At the far southern side of the market, they reached the Midianites' stalls and the platform where they displayed their slaves for auction. The next group of women shivered violently despite the burning sun, shackles clanging on their necks and wrists while men called out their worth. Joseph realized he was rubbing his own wrist, remembering the iron's bite, the humiliation, the loss of self.

"Sold!" The chief Midianite's voice jolted Joseph. One of the slavers unlocked a woman's shackles and shoved her down rickety stairs, where a filthy man waited at ground level. More shouting and bidding began on a second group.

"Are you going to bid?" Hami nudged him forward.

Joseph shoved him back. "Give me time to look." He snaked through the gathered buyers and emerged from the crowd in the narrow chasm between captive and free. These five women had borne more abuse than most. He walked slowly past them. Heads lowered, they knelt before a crowd of men, their future holding little hope for anything better than their past.

I can save one as Potiphar saved me.

The last woman in line lifted her eyes. They were golden green, like his, with a hint of life. She looked away. He couldn't. Under all the filth, the matted hair, the pain, was a girl he recognized—Ahira. How had his sister's best friend, the only daughter of Abba Jacob's chief shepherd, been sold to these savages?

"You like this one, eh, Joseph?" The chief Midianite grabbed her hair and yanked her head back.

Ahira winced, but Joseph waved away the comment and moved on, feigning indifference. If the slaver knew of Joseph's desperation to have her, her price would triple. Joseph inspected two other women closely, his stomach in knots by the time he returned to Hami. Neither spoke. As the auction continued, Joseph negotiated for three other women and purposely lost. When it came time to bid on Ahira, the crowd had cleared. Joseph easily prevailed over an oily sailor who seemed more intent on finding a woman than buying a slave.

Hami went to retrieve her while the chief slaver paraded his first stall of male slaves across the platform. "Our first offering of Cretans," he shouted. "The gods finally shook the lazy sheep into the sea, and now we'll teach them to work. Who starts the bidding at six silver pieces for this one?" He shoved the largest of the five men forward.

Silence. It was a good sign. Joseph had seen the Minoans arrive. With their long black hair, rough-spun schentis, and nautical tattoos, they were like the sailors who accompanied King Rehor on his previous trade journeys. The mistress might enjoy slaves from her own land as she adapted to Egypt.

The Midianite placed a hand on the slave's broad shoulder. "This is a healthy Minoan sailor. Do I hear *five* silver pieces?"

"I'll give you sixteen for four of them," Joseph said. "And I choose the four from the five on your platform."

"Give me nineteen and you get all five."

Joseph waved off the offer and turned to go.

"Wait!" the Midianite shouted.

Joseph faced the man who had beaten and humiliated him—a man he now traded with regularly. "I'm your only bidder, and sixteen is fair."

The Midianite sucked air through his teeth and leaned close. "No one wants these lazy Cretans, Joseph. They know only how to paint and sing. You cheat my family out of grain, but I like you. I give you

all five for sixteen." He stood. "Sold to Captain Potiphar's best negotiator!"

Joseph counted out the silver pieces and slapped them onto the
platform as Hami left Ahira to retrieve the male slaves. A moment
later, there was a thud and she was on the ground, unconscious.

"Ahira!" Joseph bent over her and patted her cheek. "I see you still
starve your slaves in transport."

The Midianite snared his payment and tucked it into his belt. "I
deliver them alive. The deal is done." He walked away as the next stall
of slaves came to the platform.

Joseph knelt beside Ahira, cradling her hand. "Ahira, can you hear
me? You're safe now."

Her eyes jolted open. "How do you know me?" She yanked her
hand away.

"You know her?" Hami stood over him with the five Minoan slaves.
"Did you plan to buy this woman and bid on four men but get five?
Or is it more favor from your god, Joseph?"

"Joseph?" Ahira shaded her eyes.

Two slavers approached. "Move along or bid. You're stealing the
bidders' attention."

Hami lifted one eyebrow and took a wide stance.

Joseph stepped between the Medjay and the slavers. "We're finished
here, Hami." He offered his hand to Ahira. "Can you walk?"

She stared at his hand as if it were a viper. "Of course." But when
she struggled to her feet, she stumbled. Joseph reached out to catch
her. "No!" She shoved him away.

Lifting both hands, he let her stand alone and regain composure.
Hami gave him a sideways look and led their small troop to the shade
of a palm. Ahira lagged, and Joseph followed in case she fell. When
they caught up, the Minoans were guzzling from Hami's waterskin.

Joseph offered Ahira his water. "Master Potiphar's villa is too far for
you to keep pace. Either Hami or I will carry you."

"No, I—" She glanced at the Medjay and then studied Joseph, confusion on her face. "The son of Prince Jacob was killed by wild animals. His brothers returned with his bloodstained coat as proof, and

Prince Jacob still mourns his death." Her voice was weak, shaky, as she shoved the waterskin at his chest. "I'll walk."

She was exactly as he remembered.

Hami's eyebrows jumped, and he hid a grin. He turned toward the villa and set off at a brisk pace, shoving the Minoans ahead of him. Joseph extended his hand, directing Ahira to follow on her wobbly legs. As expected, her determination couldn't overcome the reality of a three-week slave journey.

Joseph offered his arm for support and conversation as distraction. "I've often wondered how my brothers explained their treachery. Abba had sent me to check on them in Shechem, where they'd taken the flocks for winter grazing. I checked all the land we'd purchased near Shechem, wandering like a fool. Finally I found an old man who said my brothers had moved the flocks to Dothan."

"Dothan?" Her hand tightened on his forearm. "There's only trouble in Dothan."

Joseph glanced at the shepherd's daughter he'd known as a girl in Abba's camp. What did she know of Dothan's licentious reputation? "I'd betrayed my brothers' poor behavior to Abba earlier in the spring, when they slaughtered one of our sheep for a party with friends. I went to Dothan hoping to mend our relationship and return to Abba with assurance of—" He shrugged. "My brothers sold me to the same Midianites who brought you here, Ahira."

"But you're . . ." She spoke to him in Hebrew.

"Alive? Yes."

"No, Egyptian. You're Egyptian, Joseph."

He grinned and looked down at her. "I'm still Joseph under these paints and lotions." He answered in Hebrew—using the language for the first time in four years. The words sounded foreign and tasted bitter.

"Why would you remember me?" She held out her hand, silently demanding his waterskin. "My abba was one of a hundred shepherds in Prince Jacob's fields."

He gave her the waterskin, noting her steps had become surer. "Your abba was *chief* shepherd, Ahira, and taught me many things."

Abba had made Enoch chief shepherd after Reuben, his firstborn, slept with Abba's slave wife Bilhah. Joseph shoved aside the memory. "Abba's flocks flourished under Enoch's care."

"My abba is the best of men."

Joseph glanced down and glimpsed moisture in Ahira's lovely eyes. He refocused on the street, anxious to change the subject. "I also remember, Ahira bat Enoch, that you and my sister threw rocks at me when we were children."

She swiped at her cheeks. "Because you splashed us while we played in the spring." Though still drawn and weary, her features softened.

"And you were especially kind to my sister after . . ." Joseph still couldn't say the word *rape*. "After Levi and Simeon killed the men of Shechem." Ahira had visited Dinah regularly when she became an empty shell after the brothers took vengeance on Dinah's suitor.

At the mention of Dinah's defilement, Ahira's pace quickened. The water had revived her, but Enoch's determined daughter was stronger than he'd imagined. He understood that any man's touch—no matter how innocent or well intentioned—might feel like a firebrand after three weeks in a Midianite slave train. *Why, Elohim? Why did Ahira have to suffer?*

They caught up with Hami and the Minoans before entering the back gate of the palace complex and moving through the royal kitchen. Joseph greeted the chief baker by name, and a thought struck him like a rock from his sling. "Ahira," he whispered, glancing down at the young woman in his charge, "what if Elohim sent me to the Midianites today to purchase you and show you His favor as He's shown me?"

"Favor?" Her head snapped up. "If pain and humiliation are Elohim's favor, I choose to have no god at all." Her angry eyes flashed more green than gold. Joseph recognized the pain. While shackle wounds still burned, mere words couldn't soothe.

When they crossed the villa kitchen's threshold, the voice that mended many shattered souls welcomed the new slaves. "Finally!" Pushpa puffed a gray tendril off her forehead. "You'll each have a bath, a new robe, and something to eat, but there'll be little time for introductions."

She scurried over to the five Minoans standing in a line by Hami. "What's that?" She pointed at one of the man's tattoos.

"It's an octopus." The smallest Minoan bore a different symbol than the others.

"I've never seen—"

"It's unique to our part of the Great Sea."

Pushpa's brows drew together. "You interrupted me." She glanced at Hami and returned her attention to the new slave. "What's your name?"

"Forgive me, Mistress. I didn't—"

"Your name." Pushpa's steady glare sobered him.

"Gaios."

"You won't last long in my son's villa, Gaios, if you interrupt or insist on your own agenda." She turned from the Minoans and focused on Ahira.

Joseph was suddenly nervous, desperate for her approval. "Pushpa, meet Ahira, the mistress's new maid."

"She's skin and bones." Pushpa scanned Ahira from head to toe, then lifted the slave's chin. "Do you have enough strength to prepare Mistress Zuleika for tonight's—"

"Mistress Zuleika?" Gaios rushed forward and dropped to one knee. "I can attend the mistress if the Hebrew woman can't."

Pushpa planted both fists on her hips, but before she could scold, Hami had clamped the back of his neck and pulled him to his feet. "This one is trouble," he said to Joseph.

"I won't be any trouble," Gaios begged. "I'll obey. I promise."

Hami's eyes narrowed. "Any slave that promises to be no trouble is already a problem."

Joseph exchanged a wary glance with Hami and Pushpa. The Minoan's boldness would cause trouble in Master Potiphar's household. "It's too late in the day now, but I'll trade him tomorrow."

"Joseph!" Pushpa cried. He lunged to catch Ahira as she collapsed. Suddenly holding her in his arms, he looked to Pushpa for direction. "Take her to my chamber," she said and then turned to Hami. "You get the five Minoans cleaned up and find new robes for them."

Hami's spine straightened. "I don't bathe slaves."

"Would you rather knead bread and chop onions?" She motioned toward the palace kitchen. "Take them out to the courtyard, and show them where to wash. They must be clean and working before the palace cook comes looking for his chopped vegetables."

The Medjay paused only a heartbeat and then bowed to the villa's true mistress. Pushpa headed toward her chamber, Joseph trailing behind her. They'd just crossed the adjoining chamber's threshold when Ahira roused from unconsciousness. Her eyes barely open, she instinctively started flailing. "No! Stop! Let me go!"

"Set her down and go, Joseph!" Pushpa pulled her from his arms. "Shh, girl. Pushpa's here. Shh, love."

Joseph backed away, remembering how the old woman's compassion had soothed his brokenness four years ago. Slavers took so much more than a person's freedom. They took everything. Dignity. Identity. Their captive train shattered the human soul. *Please, Elohim, let the balm of Pushpa's compassion heal Ahira's inner wounds.*

Pushpa glanced over Ahira's shoulder with tears in her eyes. "You've purchased the right maid for Mistress Zuleika, Joseph. They'll take care of each other. Now, go. Ahira will be fine after a little food and rest."

Reluctantly he turned and pulled the door closed behind him. He'd find Hami and help with the new slaves—anything to keep his mind off Ahira. *Elohim, please share a mighty portion of Your favor with the shepherd's daughter from Abba's camp.*

TEN

Anxiety weighs down the heart,
but a kind word cheers it up.

PROVERBS 12:25

Ahira

Ahira sank onto Pushpa's wool-stuffed mattress, wounds on fire and body throbbing with every heartbeat.

"Eat this." The old cook took a partial loaf of bread from the bedside table and gave it to her. "You'll have a proper meal after your bath and clean robe. *Ahira*—that's a beautiful name. I'll tell you what you need to know, Ahira, while we get you ready. To save time. Your new mistress is a princess from the isle of Crete, perhaps a little older than you."

Ahira marveled at the woman's ability to talk. Accustomed to quiet pastures and grazing sheep, she was overwhelmed by a chaotic kitchen, strange surroundings, and a chatty cook who spoke Akkadian.

Pushpa handed her a cup. "It will help wash down the bread. Go on. Eat the rest and finish the water."

Ahira obeyed while the cook tapped her sandaled foot.

"Good." Pushpa swept the cup from her hand and pulled Ahira to her feet. "Do you have enough strength to undress, or do you need help?"

"I can do it." Ahira had never even undressed in Abba's presence.

"Put your soiled robe in the corner. I'll burn it." Pushpa crossed the chamber to pour water in a basin, pulled two towels from a shelf, and turned to face Ahira again. "You're still dressed! Get that robe off!"

Ahira turned away and tried to remove the filthy robe but was too weak to raise it over her head. Her trembling increased, as did the threat of tears. She jumped at Pushpa's touch on her shoulders.

"Let me help you, dear." She slipped off the filthy robe and threw it in the corner.

Ahira covered herself, back turned to the old woman, and waited while the sound of sandals slapped the tile behind her.

Pushpa moved Ahira's riotous hair aside and pressed a cool cloth to the base of her neck. Water cascaded down her back, releasing an unbidden groan and unchecked tears. Ahira put both hands to her face, trying to stop the flow. "Forgive me, Mistress." Sniffing, she looked up at the ceiling, vowing to remain strong as she'd done a hundred times since Simeon's betrayal.

"You speak Akkadian very well." The old woman's tone was kind, as was her touch.

"Thank you." Ahira winced when she brushed an abrasion.

"Tell me where you come from and how you learned the merchants' language."

Betrayal had scarred Ahira. How much should she reveal? "My abba taught me to speak. He was a shepherd for a Bedouin prince."

"Bedouin." The cook paused her scrubbing. "You're a part of the tribes that sent the flood of foreigners into Egypt."

Ahira's eyes slid shut. She'd said too much. "Will I suffer because of my heritage?"

She heard only footsteps in reply and glanced over her shoulder. Pushpa poured out the dirty water in a private courtyard and then returned to fill the basin again. Ahira kept her back turned, bracing for whatever punishment she must endure.

"In this house," Pushpa said, "you'll be treated as your character deserves." Ahira heard the cloth plop into the water. "Turn around, dear."

Hesitant to reveal her shame, Ahira swallowed the lump in her throat and let her arms fall to her sides. Facing the older woman, she heard Pushpa's breath catch as her eyes scanned the bruises and bite marks. Pushpa's strokes slowed. Gentler now, she pressed against fresh wounds without commentary or questions.

"Let me tell you about tonight." Pushpa sniffed and swiped at her cheeks. Her compassion seemed real. "Your mistress will marry the master of this villa, the captain of Pharaoh's bodyguard—"

"Your son," Ahira ventured, remembering the woman's comment in the kitchen.

She grinned. "He's the son of my heart, not my body. Potiphar and his abi came to Avaris after— Well, Potiphar's ommi was not a woman of good character. My husband and I invited him and his abi to live with us. When Potiphar's abi died, the boy already felt like a son. He's a very great man now in Egypt."

Then why does he force his ima to work in his kitchen? Ahira kept the question to herself and began humming familiar shepherd's tunes to distract herself from the humiliation of her bath.

"That's a lovely tune."

"Thank you." She began humming again, not interested in conversation. Pushpa must have understood because, by the time they finished the bath, the old cook had learned the simple melody and hummed along. She'd also emptied three more basins of dirty water and scented Ahira's hair with oil.

"There." Pushpa stepped back to assess her work.

"Thank you, Pushpa." Ahira tried to smile. "You've been so kind to me." She'd washed her body and hair to make Ahira clean and given her a beautiful white robe. But the truth was, Ahira would never feel clean again.

Pushpa pulled her toward the only two cushions in the sparsely furnished chamber. She rummaged through a nearby basket and gave Ahira two pieces of dried fish and a handful of almonds. "Eat while we talk."

They settled across from each other, and the old cook lifted rheumy eyes to hold Ahira's gaze. "I can't tend the wounds inside you, dear one, but they will heal. I promise. They may leave scars—ugly ones. But you can choose how those scars affect your future. Will you use the ugliest memories as the focal point, weaving every future event tightly around it with its repetitive themes? Or will you weave your scars into a larger tapestry with more variegated experiences that can comfort or instruct others?"

Ahira swallowed, wishing she could answer the way Pushpa wanted her to, but she couldn't amid her rawness. She inhaled a cleansing breath and attempted a smile. "I want to be brave, Pushpa, and promise I'll be that variegated tapestry, but give me time. Right now I can only feel the shame and pain."

The precious woman brushed Ahira's cheek. "Understandable. I suspect you and your mistress will be good for each other. Oh!" Her eyes widened. "We never finished talking about your wedding duties!"

"Yes, I'm anxious to hear." Ahira hoped the feigned eagerness would hide her dread.

"After the banquet," she said, "Potiphar and his bride will likely return to her chamber for the wedding week."

"Our people also observe a wedding week."

"Good. Then you know you'll remain in your chamber to attend them day and night. Whatever they—"

"In the same chamber?" Ahira's cheeks flushed, and Simeon's angry face flashed in her memory. She'd learned more than a maiden should about wedding nights since Prince Jacob's second-born son levied his ultimatum. She'd refused to become his concubine—then lost her freedom and her innocence to the Midianites.

"It's an *adjoining* chamber." Pushpa's brows drew together. "There's a curtain between you. Have you never been a maid before?"

Joseph had mentioned it was too late in the day to trade the Minoan, but what about tomorrow or the next day? Would Pushpa send *her* back to the Midianites if she knew Ahira had only ever been a shepherdess?

The old woman reached for Ahira's hand. "I'll never punish you for telling me the truth."

Ahira swallowed the lie with the last of the almonds and offered unadorned truth. "I've only tended sheep, but I'm as faithful as a shepherd's dog, and I learn quickly."

Pushpa laughed and shook her head. "What was Joseph thinking? Well, I suppose we should start with the basics." She began the litany of tasks with which Ahira would fill her days. After explaining where to empty the mistress's waste pot, she continued through an extensive list, ending with the bedtime duty of restuffing a sunken wool mattress.

"Whew!" Pushpa's good-natured sigh signaled the end of instruction. She slapped her knees and stood. "Let's go meet your new mistress."

Ahira rose, surprised at the strength returning to her body and soul with a little food and kindness.

Pushpa pulled her into an unexpected hug. "The gods favored you today and gave Joseph great wisdom in choosing you."

Ahira wanted to groan. Must everyone credit a god for her arrival in Egypt?

Pushpa hurried out her door and into the kitchen, grabbed a covered basket, and pointed to a stack of empty ones. "Pick up one, and fill it with enough to satisfy you and the mistress until tonight's banquet."

Ahira slipped a basket over her arm and filled it with a loaf of bread, hard cheese, a few dates, raisins, and more dried fish.

Pushpa paused to inspect the contents and chuckled. "No need to stuff yourselves, dear. The mistress will eat at the banquet, and you can join Joseph and me in the kitchen for leftover banquet delicacies after the guests are served."

Pushpa led her out of the kitchen into a long hallway. Ahira cringed at the thought of eating a meal with Prince Jacob's son. Noticing two guards standing at a door on their right, she realized they'd likely seen her reaction. She ducked her head, cheeks warming. Would she ever escape Prince Jacob's sons? Joseph had visited her dreams as a girl. Simeon had betrayed her as a woman. Now Joseph had purchased her future.

"I'll make sure you have a water clock for your chamber," Pushpa was saying, "to be sure you awaken before your mistress and—"

"A water clock?"

The old woman paused, grinning. "Oh, you Bedouins. Joseph had never heard of one either." Her face brightened. "Say, did your tribe and Joseph's ever . . ." She waved her hand and started walking again. "Pfssht. That's silly. There are Bedouins all over the land of Retjenu."

"Retjenu?"

"I believe your people call it Canaan, dear."

When they reached the mistress's chamber, one of two guards knocked on the door and opened it as Pushpa greeted him by name. "Here we are."

Ahira halted at the threshold when she saw a woman in a vibrantly colored tiered skirt—its red, orange, yellow, blue, and green were as vivid as the sky and sea, fields and wildflowers. She rose from a cushion where she'd arranged items in a sort of stepped altar. "Pushpa! I thought you'd forgotten me." Small in stature, the mistress was both elegant and confident as she approached.

"I see you're unpacking your trunk." Pushpa set aside her basket and peered inside the large wooden box. "Tell me about the treasures from your homeland."

The mistress twirled, arms held aloft. "This is a skirt and short jacket like all Minoan women wear for festivals."

"It's lovely, dear." But even Ahira sensed her hesitation. "How clever to wear it over the robe Potiphar gave you."

"You don't like it." The mistress stopped twirling. "Pushpa, I'm trying hard to make space for both Crete and Egypt in my heart."

Pushpa pressed a comforting hand against her cheek. "It takes time, love." Then she motioned Ahira forward. "I believe your new maid can help. Princess Zuleika, meet Ahira, daughter of a Bedouin shepherd. She's never been a maid before but is eager to learn and serve you well."

Ahira shot a distressed look at the old cook. Why introduce her weaknesses first?

The mistress's lilting chuckle regained her attention. "Come, Ahira. I'll show you and Pushpa my treasures from home." Ahira put down her basket and joined the two women, who knelt on the cushion beside the makeshift altar. "A jar of pink sand from the western beaches." The mistress pointed at the item. "A bag of eronda to spice mulled wine. A purple scarf—dyed with the murex shells from Zakros's seas. And my greatest treasure of all . . ." She lifted a glimmering stone vase from its metal stand. "Pulled from our palace ruins—a small chip the only damage. The survival of this vase proved I, too, could survive the shaking." Her voice quaked, and she bowed her head.

Ahira knelt beside her. "It's the most beautiful thing I've ever seen, Mistress."

She reached for Ahira's hands but halted and turned suddenly to Pushpa. "Why are there shackle wounds on my maid's wrists?"

"Joseph purchased her from Midianite slavers, Mistress."

"Oh, Pushpa, forgive me. I shouldn't have assumed you—"

"I'm proud of you, Mistress." Pushpa spoke tenderly though she had every right to be offended. "A princess who cares about someone below her station is a rare find. Ahira's wounds will heal, and she'll serve you well." Pushpa struggled to her feet and offered a quick bow. "I have much to do in the kitchen before—"

"Wait!" Ahira and the mistress said in unison.

The older woman didn't even slow her steps. "All the items you'll need are in the basket on the trunk." The chamber door closed behind her.

Ahira searched the tiles at her feet, familiar panic stirring in her chest. How could she ever please a princess?

"Look at me, Ahira."

She lifted her head, hands clasped in front of her, and listed her only talents. "I have some knowledge of braiding hair and henna staining from my childhood with a friend."

The mistress stood, coaxing Ahira to her feet as well, and inspected the raw gouges on her wrists and ankles. She straightened and, without a word, retrieved Pushpa's basket. "Sit on the cushion near my treasures. I'll tell you stories about Crete while I dress your wounds."

Ahira obeyed while the mistress opened the basket and removed small pots and bags.

"As I suspected. Pushpa included my cosmetics for the banquet as well as herbs and bandages for your wounds."

"But, Mistress, we must prepare you for—"

The princess lifted her hand, silencing her, and then displayed already-decorated fingernails. "I've been in the royal harem for two weeks—lotioned, primped, and painted. I suspect the captain of Pharaoh's bodyguard won't notice these henna designs."

"Yes, Mistress." Ahira's stomach rumbled. She pressed her hand against it, hoping to quiet the embarrassing noise.

"Are you hungry?" Without waiting for an answer, she hurried toward the second basket, the one Ahira had brought from the kitchen. "I'm too nervous to eat. You can eat all of it." She placed the basket beside Ahira, folded her legs, and sat on the tiled floor beside her.

"May I tell you a secret?" The princess reached for a few raisins though she'd said she wasn't hungry. "I've never had a *real* maid. In Zakros Palace, my pateras's palace, the harem was a place where women took care of each other. Mitera was his queen, and he adored her, but he also had concubines, who bore him sons and a few daughters. His sons were trained as sailors, but his daughters—my half sisters—and his concubines lived in the palace with Mitera and me. Of course, we had our differences, but we learned to trust each other because our lives depended on it. That trust was built, Ahira, by serving each other."

Her story sounded too good to be true, so Ahira shared her own. "The prince of our camp had four wives. Two of them were handmaids of the original two wives but were given wife status when they bore the prince's sons. Though they called themselves 'sister wives' and helped each other with daily tasks, I'm not sure they ever trusted each other."

"Multiple wives certainly complicate a household." The mistress reached for the jar of honey and a rolled bandage and began dressing

Ahira's wounds. "Tell me more about your life in the Bedouin camp. And when we're alone, you may call me Zully."

Cautionary banners flew over Ahira's heart again. She'd already told the mistress about Prince Jacob's wives, and Pushpa disclosed she was Bedouin. Ahira had the sinking feeling the mistress would insist on knowing everything, but how could she share a shattered heart?

The mistress paused her ministrations and met Ahira's eyes. "Don't be afraid. I'll share my captive story if you'll share yours."

ELEVEN

Wine is a mocker and beer a brawler;
whoever is led astray by them is not wise.
PROVERBS 20:1

Zuleika

Ahira and I had spent much of the late afternoon playing with the cosmetics from Pushpa's basket. I felt like I was in the Zakros harem again, preparing for one of our many festivals—except, in the harem, there would have been twenty women laughing and telling stories. I'd applied color to my maid's cheeks, eyes, and lips while she watched the transformation in my polished bronze mirror with the murex-shell handle. It had been the perfect distraction as my wedding banquet approached.

One of the Medjays pounded on my door and announced Pushpa's arrival. She entered with a pitcher of wine. I invited her to stay and was disappointed when she hurried back to her kitchen.

"Tell me more about the sea," Ahira said.

I'd already talked until my throat was sore. "I think I'd rather have a glass of wine."

Another knock at the door, and Pateras barged in without waiting for an invitation. "The royal market is barely a hundred paces outside the palace complex, but without a Medjay escort, I would have been crushed by the crowds." He lifted the scarab of Seth on his necklace and rubbed it like an amulet. "Perhaps the god of chaos likes *both* Minoans and the Amu because, during the two weeks I've been delayed here, I nearly doubled the silver Pharaoh gave me to begin Crete's rebuilding."

When he started to recount his brilliant negotiating, I interrupted his excited chatter. "Pateras, this is my new maid. Ahira, this is King Rehor of Crete's Zakros Palace."

"I'm honored to meet you." Ahira bowed.

"And I you," he said without looking at her, distracted by something he was withdrawing from his waist pouch.

"I'll leave you two alone." Ahira retreated to her chamber, leaving me frustrated by Pateras's indifference.

As I drew breath to scold, he unveiled the item wrapped in roughspun cloth. "I think you'll like the way it turned out." He lifted a bronze scarab ring from its wrapping.

"It matches the one Bakari made in Sena."

Pateras slipped it on my finger. "A perfect fit. The Egyptian metalsmith did a fine job." With a satisfied nod, he released my hand, then noticed the wine Pushpa had delivered. He strode to the pitcher and filled his goblet. "I fear if the Medjays hadn't gone with me yesterday, however, the merchant never would have finished a gift for the *Cretan* bride's wedding." He drank the goblet and poured another. Wine's power over him had grown in recent years—as consuming as his trading.

I retrieved Potiphar's ring from my waist pouch. When we had bargained with Bakari in Sena, we thought the ring would be a gift for Pharaoh—more of a token since we didn't have enough bronze to pay for a Khyan-sized ring. I extended my hand to inspect Pateras's gift in the light of my oil lamps and held Potiphar's ring beside it. "Pateras! Didn't you order Seth as the scarab image?" The images in the oval settings were very different.

"I hoped you wouldn't notice." His shoulders sagged. "Evidently there's disagreement on exactly what Seth is."

I clutched Potiphar's ring in my fist, panic rising. If I believed in the gods, I might interpret the mismatched rings as a bad omen. More likely, it was an Egyptian metalsmith getting the final jab on a pesky Cretan king. "What *is* Seth anyway?" I tried to chuckle, but it came out a squeak. "Is he an aardvark? A jackal-human?" I returned Potiphar's ring to my belt and poured myself a goblet of Pushpa's wine. After downing the first one, I poured a second and joined Pateras on a cushion in the gathering area of my new home.

"I don't have time to find another gift for Potiphar." I held out my hand, inspecting the fine work again. "Why do Egyptians call us lazy Cretans when an Egyptian metalsmith required two weeks to fashion a ring? Was the Egyptian lazy or simply a bigot?" I wanted to rant, anger seeming a better option than fear.

Pateras's goblet was empty, so I snatched it away and poured each of us another goblet full. I drank long and deep, trying to regain calm.

Pateras's hand rested on my arm. "Potiphar is a good man, Zully."

I looked away, staving off tears. "He's not Minas."

"You have to let Minas go, Zul."

I clanked the goblet on the tile floor harder than intended. "Can you let Mitera go?" The lines around his mouth deepened, his silence a sure sign I'd angered him. I didn't care. "You're not the one about to be trapped and alone in Egypt."

"You don't have to be 'trapped and alone' if Egypt becomes home and you realize Potiphar is a man you can admire."

The words sounded simple, but my grief was relentless, like the waves' crashing. I glanced over his shoulder at my shrine of Minoan treasures and took another long draw of wine. "How do you know Potiphar is a good man, Pateras?"

"I've seen the way he treats those closest to him. He's loyal unto death to Pharaoh Khyan."

"He's a soldier. He's paid to be loyal."

He drained his goblet before answering. "It's more than that, Zully. They've been friends since childhood. He knows what it means to commit to someone for a lifetime and take care of them—as he's done with Pushpa."

"She loves him like a son, and he's made her his kitchen slave."

A knock on the door interrupted our debate. "The captain is on his way," someone shouted from the other side.

I nearly vomited. "Pateras, I can't marry him."

"Yes, you can. Do you have his ring?"

I patted my waistband and felt the bump. "Yes." Tears threatened, but I inhaled and blew out a determined breath. "For my people," I whispered, reassured of my purpose.

Pateras helped me to my feet. "You're sure you have the ring?"

"Yes!" He suddenly seemed as nervous as the bride. I clasped my trembling hands, knowing that couldn't possibly be true.

My chamber door opened, revealing two Medjays. A heartbeat later, the stranger I would marry appeared and halted abruptly at the sight of me.

"Where's the jewelry I sent you for tonight's banquet?"

Stunned at his rudeness, I was too offended to respond. Pateras cleared his throat. "I requested Zully wear the wedding necklace I gave Queen Daria instead of the jewelry you provided, Captain."

He took a few steps into the chamber, his eyes sweeping over me. "And the robe I sent. Why have you covered it with that . . . cloth?"

"It's a tiered skirt." My voice warbled. *Steady, Zully.* "I wear it in honor of the Minoan people."

"The robe you gave her, Captain, serves as a tunic beneath the vibrant Minoan colors—a melding of our cultures." Pateras turned to me. "Zully, do you have a gift for the captain?"

My hand went to my belt, but the utter incongruence of the moment overwhelmed me. How could I give a ring—the same symbol of eternal love I'd given to Minas, the prince I'd known since we were children—to a man I didn't trust? Why hadn't I kept Minas at the shoreline with Pateras and me that day? Why had we ever argued or let a day pass without saying "I love you"? Why hadn't we spent every moment in each other's arms, reveling in kisses?

"Princess, don't cry." Potiphar stood before me, hands moving awkwardly and finally resting across his chest. "I'm unaccustomed to tears and thoroughly untrained to defeat them."

"Defeat them?" He sounded so pathetic, I grinned and wiped my cheeks. "Oh, did I smear the kohl?"

"Here, look at me." With a cloth from his belt, he patted and dabbed with surprising tenderness. "You are a beautiful young woman, and you may wear your Minoan costume if you wish."

"Costume?" Though only two weeks had passed since we'd met, it was apparent he was the one wearing a costume. His hair was six inches longer—most certainly a wig. Multiple braids fell like a fountain with intermittent gold beads. The Gold of Praise collar graced his large chest, but he'd added gold armbands and bracelets and completed the glittering ensemble with a jeweled belt and sandals.

His lifted brow warned me to keep silent, but he must learn I would not be cowed. "How very kind of you to escort me to our wedding banquet personally instead of sending me with one of your guards." Judging by his wry smile, he understood my veiled grievance. On the day Pharaoh cast me aside, "gifting" me to a mere soldier, Potiphar had added to my degradation by denying me even a moment of personal attention.

"Were you surprised by the events of that day, Princess? I don't react well to surprises," he continued without giving me time to answer, "so for your protection and mine, I made a tactical decision to delegate authority. Tonight you will become my wife, not because you want me or I want you but because the greatest man in all Egypt wants me to have a wife, and he chose you. He's my king. My friend. My god. What Pharaoh Khyan gives, I would never refuse. This marriage will stand longer than the pyramids of Giza, Princess, not because you or I have any romantic ideas about what marriage holds. We must be practical, you and I. Crete had only one treasure to trade for Egypt's goods and services. I'm simply the pocket that holds it." He offered his arm. "Our wedding guests are waiting."

My cheeks flushed at his emotionless audacity, but I respected the man's transparency. I would grant the same favor. Before taking his arm, I reached into my belt and produced the scarab ring. "I purchased this in Sena for Pharaoh Khyan by trading my dead husband's wedding ring and my mitera's bracelets. I don't know if you worship Seth or one of the other gods, but here it is."

"I don't worship gods, and I don't wear rings. They interfere with the grip on my sword."

"The gods or the rings?" I shook the ring at him, frustration rising. "We're going to a banquet. You won't need to grip a sword."

"I'm always ready to defend—"

"Fine." I fumbled to replace the ring in my belt, but a large hand covered mine.

"Forgive me, Zuleika. It's a very nice gift." He lifted my hand and inspected the ring Pateras had given me. "You bought yourself one like it?" The tightness around his lips softened into a look of wonder.

"Pateras gave me this ring tonight, but the images of Seth don't match."

"Seth is an enigma even for Egyptians." He offered Pateras a respectful nod and returned his attention to me. "Though I don't sacrifice regularly in Seth's temple, Khyan and I pledged him our loyalty on our first mission together as young soldiers. We were part of the military escort for one of Pharaoh Monthhotep's Sinai expeditions."

He looked at my gift, but his expression had grown distant, his thoughts traveling beyond the chamber walls. "I no longer trust the gods, and I serve a better pharaoh." He tucked the ring into his waist pouch, as fierce as the day I'd first seen him, and offered his arm again.

My mouth went dry. There was no escape. I'd endured the most unromantic introduction I could have imagined, but I placed my hand on his arm and started toward a new life. Pateras on my left and a stranger on my right, I was grieving and frustrated yet resolute. *Zully* wanted to remain in my chamber with Ahira and lose myself in paints and pottery and all things lovely, but *Princess Zuleika* would march to Pharaoh's palace on the arm of Egypt's premier soldier, determined to win the battles ahead.

If only I hadn't drunk that wine.

I closed my eyes for part of our trek, relying on the steady presence of my groom to lead me. Despite his tactless, oafish behavior, I felt safe between him and Pateras with the four Medjays who followed.

As I heard sounds of celebration, I opened my eyes, and my steps faltered. We were but a stone's throw away from the cedar doors of Pharaoh's court. I felt myself sway.

"Are you all right?" Potiphar's arm circled my waist, his concern appearing genuine.

Our eyes locked for a moment. His were a deep brown. A little bloodshot and intense but, in that moment, caring.

"Fine. Thank you."

He pulled away to speak with his Medjays privately.

I inhaled deeply and exhaled slowly, a technique I'd practiced many times since the earthquake, but the unrelenting spots in my vision were the wine's addition.

"Zully?" Pateras steadied my shoulders. "Are you ill?"

"No, no." I wiped sweat from my forehead. "That wine must have been stronger than Minoan—"

Potiphar rushed to my side but directed his concern to Pateras. "Does she need to return to her chamber?"

Was I a mouse between two lions? "No, *she* doesn't." I marched toward the palace entry and heard one of the lions roar.

"Princess Zuleika." I stopped but didn't turn to face my groom. "You must have an escort to approach Pharaoh. I suggest you wait."

Inhale deeply. Exhale slowly. I waited for Pharaoh's captain to arrive with Zakros's king and the four Medjays. When the double doors swung open, the scent of flowers and spices mingled with sweat and musk, causing my gorge to rise. I swallowed hard as Potiphar placed his hand over mine and tugged me forward. Only then did I realize I'd been rooted to the tiles, gawking. Conversations faded, and the same nearly naked dancers I'd seen on our first day in Pharaoh's court twirled around us. The music stilled when we reached the crimson carpet.

Potiphar lifted his brow in silent question. Was I ready for Pharaoh's probing questions? The veiled insults of jealous noblewomen? I nodded and tilted my head, returning the challenge. Was he prepared to have a wife? A wry smile lifted one corner of his lips. "Is Egypt ready for you, Princess Zuleika?" The mischief in his tone made him appear younger and sent my heart into an irregular beat.

I turned toward the dais and stepped with my right foot first, as every royal knew to do. Potiphar lumbered, seemingly free of regal constraint. The plush crimson rug muffled our footsteps, making the hushed gasps and whispers somehow louder.

My chin held high, I greeted strangers at each table as we passed. Men and women, seated together, wore strange-looking cones atop their heads. Curiosity overcame decorum, and I leaned close to my groom and whispered, "What are those strange things on their heads?"

"Scented beeswax. Egypt's heat melts it into the wigs to mask odors in large gatherings."

"Are you wearing a wig, Captain?"

My coy question won a low, rumbling chuckle. *He laughs?*

Pharaoh stood at the foot of the dais, awaiting our arrival. "Potiphar, your bride looks flushed. After we sign the wedding document, you can seat her beside my wives. She'll feel better after a goblet or two of my favorite beer."

"Very generous, my king." Potiphar glanced down at me. "I believe she and King Rehor enjoyed the wine I sent to her chamber earlier."

"Indeed." Pateras stepped beside me. I hadn't realized he was trailing us. "The wine was as tasty as I remembered from my last visit. Even better than our Minoan grapes."

"Imported from Retjenu vineyards. The best in the world." Pharaoh turned to me. "Princess Zuleika, Queen Tani informs me you were an eager student of our culture and traditions, so you're aware there are many gods in Egypt and a long history of pharaohs."

"I am, Mighty Khyan."

"Marriage is the most important relationship of gods and kings, and love their greatest power. Love can heal or harm, build or destroy, give life or bring death."

I disagreed but held my tongue.

Pharaoh paused. Perhaps my expression had given away my doubts. But he grinned and continued. "In my kingdom, marriage is to be treasured and nurtured by friends and family. For this reason, the person closest to the bride and groom will sign the wedding contract as a witness to the vows taken at this banquet. King Rehor will sign as your witness, and I will sign as Captain Potiphar's."

A man arrived carrying a waist-high table, gripping papyrus, reed, and pigments beneath one arm.

"Princess Zuleika, the scribe will record your vows, and then you may sign. Potiphar will offer his vows next and sign. Rehor and I will sign last, and we can then celebrate this long-awaited occasion." Pharaoh slapped Potiphar on the back, and then they, with Pateras, looked at me expectantly.

Vows? I glimpsed Queen Tani and Ziwat on the dais, each with her chin raised in arrogant disdain. Not once in two weeks had either mentioned that I'd need to make public vows to my groom. It wasn't only my paintings or my culture they disliked. To them I was Cretan. At last I realized the depths of their malevolence.

Nervous whispers had begun during my hesitation. I bowed to Potiphar, giving my muddled mind time to form something poetic or profound. A glimpse of my groom's dusty feet distracted me. Then I noticed Pharaoh Khyan's. His feet were huge but clean and henna stained. A realization dawned with the observation. I was marrying a soldier. He didn't need poetic or profound.

My eyes met Potiphar's, and I remembered the words he'd spoken earlier. "This marriage will stand longer than the pyramids of Giza, not because you or I have any romantic ideas about what marriage holds but because we're practical, Captain Potiphar." He grinned. Did he recognize the vows as his own words? Would he remember well enough to notice the slight amendment I was about to make? "Crete had only one treasure to trade, and I'm grateful you're the pocket that holds me."

He inclined his head slightly, his grin fading to sober kindness. "I will protect and provide for you in this life and beyond, Princess Zuleika of Zakros. You will never lack anything your heart desires, and should the gods grant us children, I will love them, protect them, and train them to be honorable Egyptians."

I knew he'd spoken of the gods as public appeasement, but his mention of children sent a thrill through me. Though Minas and I had wanted a child, his seed hadn't taken root in my belly. The thought of sharing a child with Potiphar was both intriguing and unsettling.

The startling sound of women's high-pitched ululating joined the men's roaring congratulations. The king's musicians joined the noise, striking their cymbals repeatedly. I covered my ears, thinking my head might burst, while Pharaoh calmly offered my husband a reed to sign the marriage contract.

Pateras reached for my hand, his eyes glistening. He mouthed *I love you* as Pharaoh Khyan nudged my arm to offer me the reed. I signed the binding document. Pateras did too.

Potiphar reached for my hand and kissed it gently. I felt his kindness like a warm blanket on a cold night. He escorted me up the dais steps to where the king's wives waited at the table of honor. Their catty smiles were so forced, they almost purred. I nodded a greeting to them both and sat on a luxurious pillow between Queen Tani and her husband. Potiphar waited until Pharaoh resumed his seat before settling on his own crimson cushion at the king's right. Pateras was given the seat of honor at the groom's right hand. I looked at them longingly, wishing I could be with them instead of my betrayers.

"Let the banquet begin!" Pharaoh's voice boomed over the commotion, releasing a steady stream of servers from doorways beside the dais. Their trays were laden with roasted meats: roebuck, lamb, pork, and duck.

"Make sure the princess gets plenty of my favorite beer, Tani." Pharaoh promptly turned toward Potiphar and Pateras, leaving me in the hands of his quietly hostile wives.

Queen Tani motioned to a servant, who filled my goblet to the brim with the darkest beer I'd ever seen. She, too, turned away, beginning a conversation with Ziwat. I tasted the brew, and my cheeks warmed immediately. Another servant placed a roasted pigeon on my plate, ladled a generous serving of lentils and beans over the top, and drizzled honey over the whole plate. My mouth watered. I sampled the delicacy and wasn't disappointed; however, my appetite dwindled with every behind-the-hand whisper and stolen glance aimed at me.

Potiphar's directness and strong drink had roused my courage. The spurned Cretan princess had been silent long enough. "Queen Tani," I blurted, startling her and the table closest to the dais, "tell me about your family. Are you also Amu like Pharaoh Khyan?"

Ziwat stopped talking midsentence, and the queen turned as slowly as a cobra ready to strike. Even seated, she was two heads taller than any woman in the room. "Why would you think me Amu, Princess Zuleika?"

I realized my error when the three tables closest to the dais grew silent and awaited my answer. "You're a very perceptive woman, and I've heard the Amorites—as descendants of the Rephaim—were given powers of insight from the gods."

"If you must know, Princess Zuleika, I'm of pure Egyptian blood." With practiced elegance, she motioned to the table directly in front of the dais. "My parents are seated with Vizier Wereni and his wife, who are also Egyptian. However, as we tried to emphasize in your training, Lower Egypt is a nation of unity and equality."

I wanted to spit in her eye, but I focused instead on the men and women at her parents' table, who all stared at me with disdain. Each of them wore a half-melted wax cone atop an ornately styled Egyptian wig. "It would appear everyone at the six tables closest to the dais are honored guests—and each person is dressed in the *Egyptian* style. The Amu noblemen with square-cropped hair and manicured beards are seated at the tables in back." I turned to meet my foe. "Where will Minoan nobility sit at future banquets?"

"If Mighty Pharaoh deems your friends worthy guests, they'll sit at the first and second tables." Queen Tani's lips curved into a mocking smile. "My parents and the vizier are Egyptians seated among Amu nobility tonight, Princess Zuleika. Though you proudly wear your heritage, most peace-seeking citizens of Lower Egypt have adapted to a shared culture."

I looked past the queen to ask her Nehesu rival, "Why are there no Medjays seated at the banquet?" Perhaps Ziwat would see my sincerity and answer with the same.

"Medjays' lives and families are in Cush." Ziwat's raspy voice sliced through the banquet noise. She scanned the audience as a hush fell. "A Medjay is Egypt's warrior for a few years, and then he returns to our homeland, sending another in his place. Soldiers who seek no power have nothing to lose but their lives, so they fight fiercely to reunite with those they love. It's why both Egyptian and Amu trust them." She waved with disdain at the room full of faces unlike her own. "It's why Medjays need no honor at banquets."

I then realized the sacrifice Ziwat had made to become Pharaoh's wife. She would never return home like the Medjay warriors who protected him. She must endure the place of honor her countrymen waived. Ziwat was foreign, despised, and alone—like me—but she'd lived here long enough to stop asking questions.

I lifted my goblet to toast Pharaoh's wives, better prepared for my second drink of the dark liquid. It was thick and warm, smelling of barley and the rich black delta soil. With a few long draws, I emptied my goblet and motioned for the servant to refill it. "We'll just see if Pharaoh's favorite beer can make me feel better."

My husband leaned around the king, a twitch pulling at the side of his lips. The humor I'd intended had fallen flat. I lifted the second goblet for a few more swallows before sampling more of the roasted pigeon on my gold plate.

A basket of steaming brown bread was delivered to the table, each loaf in the shape of . . . Was it a dog? Egyptians did the most interesting things with flavors and shapes of bread.

Perhaps bread would be a safe topic for conversation. I saw the queen whispering something to Ziwat and couldn't bear to cross swords with them again. Surely a bride could speak to her husband at a wedding banquet. I emptied my goblet of liquid courage and called the servant for another refill. My head felt as if it might float off my body. Could that have been the type of "better" Pharaoh intended?

When I leaned forward to ask Potiphar about Egyptian bread, I saw my husband snatch a piece of roast duck from one of the king's plates. Pharaoh didn't seem to mind or even notice. But then Potiphar nudged the plate closer to the king and nodded. I realized my husband was approving the food for Pharaoh's consumption. With each item he tasted from Pharaoh's plates, I held my breath in horror, thinking, *What if it's been poisoned?* And each time, Potiphar nodded his approval and Pharaoh ate. Which god should I thank—or curse—that my husband didn't drop dead at our wedding banquet?

With no one to ask but Pharaoh himself, I slammed down my empty gold goblet and saw the king flinch. "Is there no one but your best friend to taste your food?"

My intended whisper sounded more like a growl, and Pharaoh stared as if I'd grown a second head. "Perhaps you've had too much beer."

"Isn't there a slave or prisoner whose death would be less of a loss to your kingdom?" Whispers spread through the hall as the music died.

His features darkened. "You would accuse Pharaoh of thoughtlessly placing my best friend in danger?" He ground out the words in barely a whisper.

Though the room was spinning, I glimpsed Potiphar's angry stare over his shoulder and Pateras's pursed lips. Very soon I would lose the contents of my stomach. "Pharaoh, I must—"

"You must be silent," he hissed and then turned to the audience, lifting his goblet. "Eat. Drink. Continue."

The musicians resumed playing and the dancers twirling while I braced both hands on the table. Servers passed the dais with more aromatic delicacies, and I swallowed repeatedly.

Pharaoh leaned too close. "My friend *volunteered* to be my taster. Perhaps my wives told you of Lower Egypt's history, but let me give you a personal account. The first Amu king, Salitis, was assassinated after reigning only two years. After one year on the throne, my abi, Bnon, died after Egyptian loyalists slipped hemlock into his shoreek, the sweet bread with which he broke his fast each morning. Not a creative weapon of death, but I was much more creative with their executions." Sitting straighter, he clapped Potiphar's shoulder. "Your husband discovered the assassins and their motive to eradicate Amu kings. He insisted no Egyptian would ever poison my food if their

Egyptian hero tasted it first. So you see, Princess Zuleika, your husband's courage and political savvy are concerns you should address with him."

Even in my drunken haze, I recognized the strategic brilliance. But if I opened my mouth, it would not be words that erupted.

Pharaoh Khyan seemed to sense my discomfort. "Potiphar, your wife appears to be unwell."

I shot to my feet.

My husband didn't even stand. "I'll have one of my guards escort you—"

"I'll accompany her." Pateras was already on his feet when Pharaoh nudged his captain.

"*You* will escort your bride and enjoy your wedding week, my friend. I command it."

Blatantly reluctant, my husband lumbered to his feet while I fairly dragged Pateras off the dais and toward the side exit. Two Medjays stopped us at the double doors where we'd entered, presumably so my ambling husband could catch up. But I could stem the tide no longer. I cast a panicked glance for a jar, a pot, a vase—anything to contain what was about to erupt from my roiling belly. I spotted a waist-high vase beside the doors and darted two steps to the left, horrified at the amplifying effect of a vase when I retched into it. The empty hallway increased the echo, and the banquet guests hushed as Potiphar's wine, Pharaoh's beer, and honeyed pigeon made a second appearance on the most atrocious day of my life.

When the eruption ended, I wiped my mouth and rested my head on the oversize vase. A gentle hand rested on my back, and I nearly wept. Pateras had always been the more compassionate of my parents, but he would leave tomorrow. Who would comfort me then?

"Come, Wife. I'll escort you to your chamber." I bolted upright. The comforting voice—and hand on my back—had belonged to my new husband.

"I thought . . ." I captured my words, hoping to prevent a different kind of unpleasant eruption. "I thought you'd never speak to me again."

His expression was sober but not unkind. "You did not think, Zuleika, and your comments tonight embarrassed us both." He pulled me close to kiss my forehead. "We'll get better at this." He released me and extended his hand in the direction of our home.

Head bowed, I swiped at tears. "Forgive me, Husband. I'm sure my actions as your wife reflect on you—that much is true in any culture." Without a war in my belly, regret over my conversation with Tani nearly overwhelmed me. I looked up at Potiphar's chiseled features and noted his flexing jaw muscle. Though I didn't yet recognize his tics and tells, as I'd known Minas's, he was obviously annoyed. "I offer no excuses for tonight's behavior—only my sincere apology and the lessons I've learned. I've learned wine from Retjenu is far stronger than the nectar of our Minoan vineyards. The same is true of Pharaoh's favorite beer. And the mixture of the two on an empty stomach is almost-certain disaster."

He offered a thin smile. "Good lessons." Again he motioned down the hall. "It's been a long night."

I began the journey toward our wedding night and sensed Pateras's presence behind my groom and me. Silence escorted us down the adjoining hallway, through the villa's banquet room, and to the end of the residence hall.

Outside our chamber doorways, Pateras gathered me into his arms. "You'll make a fine mistress of this villa, my girl. Let your sharp mind and creative hands embrace the beauty of Egypt, and the Black Land will treat you well." He kissed both cheeks and turned to Potiphar with an outstretched arm. The two men locked wrists.

"Your daughter is safe in my house, King Rehor."

"I have no doubt." Pateras inclined his head and then headed toward his chamber.

"Wait!" I grabbed his elbow. "You can't leave tomorrow. Please!"

He laid his hand over mine. "We've said our goodbyes, Zul. You must let go." After lifting my hand to his lips, he turned and disappeared into his chamber.

I stared at the closed door, unable to breathe. Alone. I was now alone in Egypt. Why hadn't Gaios come with me? *Only eunuchs are allowed in the harem.* But I wasn't in the harem. It didn't matter now. Gaios would never find me.

My chamber door opened behind me, and I turned to find Potiphar waiting at the threshold. "Would you like a few moments to prepare yourself?"

The same two Medjays waited beside my door, their constant presence suddenly annoying. "Do they follow you everywhere you go?"

"These Medjays have been assigned as your chamber guards." He raised a single eyebrow. "Do you wish me to wait outside your chamber while you prepare?"

I sighed. This was no time to be tedious. Potiphar had been more than patient with me. "Yes, thank you. I won't be long." I offered as much of a smile as I could muster, then hurried past him and was immediately assaulted by the scent of the lotus petals littering my tiled floor.

"Good evening, Mistress." Ahira stood just inside the door. Her eyes widened when she saw Potiphar for the first time. "Good evening, Master. I'll be in my chamber if you need anything." She skittered away as if Potiphar were Anubis himself, the underworld god the Egyptians feared.

I shuffled into the chamber alone, crushing lotus petals and releasing more of their dizzying aroma. At the water basin I splashed my face and grabbed a cloth to dry it. Smears of black and green mingled, propelling me to grab my murex-handled mirror. I quietly giggled and whispered to my reflection, "He might have seen worse on a battlefield—maybe." I returned to the basin to remove whatever pretense remained and then slipped a sprig of mint in my mouth.

With a glance at my treasures from Crete, I bolstered my courage and waited with my back to the door. "You may enter, Potiphar."

I heard the door click shut, sandaled footsteps draw near, and then the distinct sounds of clanging metal dropping to the tile. Curiosity made me turn. The man I'd vowed to spend my life with was shedding his armor like a snake sheds its skin. Off went the bow, the sword with its belt, the sandals, the jewelry, and . . .

"Oh!" I covered a grin. "You're bald."

He ignored the comment, keeping his head bowed. The gold-beaded wig lay at his feet as the receptacle for the rest of his jewelry. Standing in a simple knee-length white kilt, he looked up slowly. His breath caught. "How can you be more beautiful without cosmetics?" He looked away without waiting for an answer, eyes traveling over everything in the chamber—except me. "Pray to your gods you'll conceive during our wedding week, and your old crocodile will never trouble you again."

Old crocodile? Knowing he joined me in the insecurities of the moment somehow emboldened me. I closed the distance between us, examining a body marked by battle. A large gash had healed over his right shoulder. Another down his left thigh. Several shorter scars marred his toned abdomen. He was completely smooth—hairless. I moved around him, circling to find more scars. More evidence of pain. I lifted my hand to trace a diagonal slice across his lower back—but halted a fingertip away. The urge to slide my hands around his waist and cling to him overwhelmed me, to press my body against a man's firm build. Potiphar was smooth like my rock-crystal vase. Minas had been like a bear, furry even on his back.

Minas. I felt the betrayal to the pit of my stomach. How could I give myself to another man only weeks after saying goodbye to the heart of my heart?

Potiphar turned and gripped my shoulders, his breathing ragged. "We need not pretend romance, Princess. You've been married, and I've had many women. Would you like to remove your clothes, or—"

"I'll do it." I turned away, cheeks burning. My body yearned for the pleasure it had known, but my heart would never betray Minas. I slipped off my tiered skirt and the robe my Egyptian husband had given me. But Mitera's Minoan necklace accompanied me to the marriage bed. *I must keep Crete close, or I'll drown in this life by the Nile.*

TWELVE

Do not plot harm against your neighbor,
who lives trustfully near you.

PROVERBS 3:29

Ahira

The newlyweds' heartbreaking words tore open the raw hopes of Ahira's own romantic dreams. What a fool she'd been, fantasizing about becoming Simeon's wife. He'd started flirting with her while gathering her flock report each day. She began inviting him to share her midday meal, and he'd lie on his side while she played her flute. Abba warned her to be careful, but what could she have done? He was Prince Jacob's son.

Ahira covered her ears when the newlyweds' breathing grew ragged. She'd known only the kiss, long and deep, that stirred those emotions but had refused Simeon's demands for more. He had a wife and children nearly her age. She let the visits continue for a while. It was playful and daring—until it wasn't. He changed her flock assignment one morning, placing her in a pasture near the trade route. Midianites asked to draw water for their camels from Prince Jacob's well . . .

Ahira lowered her hands from her ears and now heard long, steady breathing. She recognized the sound of a sleeping man. Abba snored. Perhaps Elohim would spare Zully and make the master a quiet sleeper.

Her mistress's faint whimper was familiar to Ahira. She had held her friend Dinah, Prince Jacob's defiled daughter, for hours after Simeon and Levi killed her husband. Did Shechem rape her? Yes—because he took Dinah to his bed without Prince Jacob's permission. But the brothers' violent rescue left her desolate and without hope of a future. Though Mistress Zully gave herself to a man she didn't love, at least she'd live in a fine villa and have children. A lump formed in Ahira's throat. Perhaps Pushpa was right. She and Zully could help each other.

Ahira's eyelids felt heavy, and her next thought came with a jolt. Rubbing her eyes to clear away sleep, she listened for sounds in the outer chamber. Stillness. It was time to begin her evening duties. She peeked out and found both master and mistress sleeping. Master Potiphar snored softly. The mistress would adjust.

After slipping out of the chamber, she grabbed the water pitcher and padded across the tiles in bare feet. She slowly lifted the latch and opened the door, wincing at the squeaky leather hinges.

Once clear of the chamber, she dangled the pitcher at her side and perused the murals on both sides of the hall. Surely Zully would enjoy Egypt once the initial homesickness ebbed. She was an artist and there was art everywhere. Even the pottery and earthenware dishes were decorated with intricate designs. Any sort of art impressed Ahira. Of course, there were no murals on a Bedouin's tent walls or woven designs in the simple wool cloth she'd used to wrap her food.

The hallway jogged left just before the kitchen door, which stood opposite two more Medjays. She wanted to ask whether the ornate door they guarded belonged to the master's chamber, but Joseph said slaves who spoke without prompting got traded. Instead, she inclined her head respectfully to the sober-faced warriors. So far the mistress and Pushpa were the only people in Egypt she felt she could talk to. Joseph had been kind but was disqualified simply because he was Simeon's brother, another of Prince Jacob's entitled sons.

She pushed open the kitchen door. Lamplight cast eerie shadows in the unfamiliar room. Hopefully, she'd find water left over from the banquet. The thought of trekking into the dark courtyard alone was more frightening than the hundreds of nights she'd slept under the stars guarding sheep—and she'd carried only a slingshot then.

The water jugs Pushpa kept for the villa's use were easy to spot. The first one was empty, but Ahira moved down the line of ten, peering over the rims of the waist-high vessels and finally finding one half-full. Could she lift it by herself to fill the small pitcher in her hand? Why be foolish? She'd find a cup to dip with and fill the pitcher.

Turning slowly, she tried to think like Pushpa. "Where would I put a cup— Ahh!"

The sight of a man not a pace behind her startled her, jostling the pitcher from her hand.

The crash sent the pushy Minoan's hands in the air. "I didn't mean to startle you."

Ahira fell to her knees and gathered broken pottery with shaking hands.

"Here, let me help." The Minoan bent beside her. "My name is Gaios. Did I hear Pushpa call you Ahira?"

"Yes."

"It's all right, Ahira, really. The secret of being a slave is letting our masters believe they're in charge while we find ways to make them do our bidding." Ahira cast a disbelieving look at him and jerked her hand away when she felt his fingers climb her wrist. "Come now, Ahira. You were the Midianites' favorite. I must have a taste."

Before Ahira could cry out, Gaios pulled her against his chest, his hand over her mouth, his cheek against hers. "If you scream, pretty Ahira, I will say you're a conniver and did it to cover your thievery. Zully will believe me. Do you know why?"

Ahira froze, shocked he had called her Zully.

"Because when Zully sees me tomorrow, she'll be so happy I've come to Avaris that she'll believe anything I say. Now, I'm going to take my hand off your mouth so you and I can talk."

Ahira scrambled to her feet and whirled to face her attacker. "Who are you?"

She crept toward the hallway door, but he darted to block her path.

Lamplight danced in his eyes as he examined the length of her. "I'm a man who should never be underestimated."

Ahira had seen that hunger before, but hadn't Gaios seen it too? How could he prey on another when he'd been the target of Midianite abuse only days before? "You deserve every vile thing those slavers did to you."

Gaios's eyes bulged with rage, and his low growl sent Ahira to her knees with a muffled cry. A wail—not her own—rent the air. She scuttled across the floor and hid beneath a table. Peering out, she saw Master Potiphar throw Gaios, like a rag doll, over Pushpa's kneading table. A Medjay stood watch at the doorway while another strode to Ahira, offered his hand, and coaxed her out from beneath the table.

"Did he hurt you?"

Ahira wanted to hug the guard but simply shook her head. "No."

Potiphar loomed over Gaios. "I don't tolerate disrespect of any kind in my house."

Ahira held her breath. One hard blow from the master could kill the Minoan.

"Potiphar!" Pushpa rushed from her adjoining chamber. "What—" She scanned her kitchen, the fallen servant, and Ahira standing beside the Medjay. "Are you all right, dear?"

The maid nodded while Gaios struggled to his feet.

The master pointed at the wobbly slave but spoke to Pushpa. "Tell Joseph to sell him as soon as the market opens."

"Slavers can't *give* Minoans away," she said. "We either send him with King Rehor at dawn or put a bridle on him and tighten the reins."

Potiphar gathered Gaios's collar in his fist. "If I can't trade you for a profit, I'll beat you like the dog you are until you obey." The master cast him to the floor and turned to Ahira. "Why were *you* wandering the kitchen at night?"

"She was doing as I instructed." Pushpa stepped between her son and Ahira. "Joseph chose Ahira especially to serve your wife, and she's done nothing to deserve discipline."

"Come out here, girl," the master said, his tone softening.

Ahira stepped away from the Medjay, keeping her eyes on Pushpa. The woman lifted her chin, the simple act reminding Ahira that the master favored submissive but confident slaves—so Pushpa said. Ahira would have rather crawled into a cave and cried, but she obeyed Pushpa and approached the master, head high.

He studied her as she approached. "Your eyes are the same color as Joseph's. Do all Hebrews—"

"No, my lord." She bowed, annoyed at his observation.

He grabbed her chin and jerked her head up to face him. "Don't ever interrupt me again." Ahira only nodded. Potiphar's eyes narrowed as he continued the examination. "You were angry when I mentioned your eyes. Why? You may speak freely."

He released her chin, and Ahira glanced at Pushpa. "Go ahead, dear. He said you could tell him why it upset you. If he's given permission, he won't punish you for your answer."

"In Prince Jacob's camp," Ahira answered cautiously, "some of the young shepherds said . . ." She paused, not sure how to say the word in Akkadian. "They said I was Prince Jacob's daughter, not my own abba's daughter, since Joseph's and my eyes were the same. But my ima would never—"

He lifted a hand, silencing her. "*Prince* Jacob?" he said. "Joseph's abi was a Bedouin prince?"

Her heart skipped. Joseph hadn't revealed his parentage?

"And you two knew each other as children?"

Ahira's trembling began again, this time in her chest, moving its way through her limbs. "Yes, but I seldom saw him, my lord. I was either in the fields with the flocks or spending time with my friend— Joseph's sister."

Potiphar inspected her wrists and ankles. "Did Joseph tend your shackle wounds?"

"No, my lord."

"Someone tended them." He grabbed her wrist, squeezing. "I think my livestock overseer purchased you for himself."

"Potiphar, stop!" Pushpa wrested Ahira's arm from him. "Your wife tended the girl's wounds. Leave her alone. She's endured enough."

He glared at Ahira and then released a weary sigh. "Anyone could be a spy tonight, Ommi." The master massaged the back of his neck. "Hami just informed me the Tehenu tribes have crossed our western border and attacked villages in the western delta. Pharaoh's troops march at dawn, my guards with them."

"But it's your wedding week." Pushpa cupped his cheek. Ahira had seen imas do the same to Hebrew sons in Jacob's camp. The sign of circumcision made them Hebrew—whether born of Abraham's blood, in the household, or purchased as slaves—but an ima's love transcended borders. An ima's love was boundless. Matchless.

The master chuckled and kissed Pushpa's forehead. "I'll tell Khyan you said I didn't have to go."

She hugged him, and Ahira felt like an intruder. She slipped past the Medjays but didn't see the Minoan. He'd probably crawled into a dark corner. Should she tell Pushpa what he'd revealed about his past with the mistress? But she didn't have time. She had at least a dozen things to accomplish before Zully woke and discovered the wedding week she'd expected would be spent without her husband. She hurried through the hallway door and plowed into what felt like a wall.

"Ahira!" Joseph steadied her. "Are you all right?"

"Fine." Ahira marched around him toward the mistress's chamber.

"Ahira, stop." Joseph grabbed her arm.

She wrenched it away but stopped as he'd commanded. "Must men always use force, Joseph? Did the Midianites teach you that?"

Joseph's mouth fell open, his cheeks paling. Her words appeared to hit him like a fist, and she regretted them. *He's not Gaios.* Joseph had been nothing but kind since the moment he found her in the market.

"We're not in Abba's camp anymore, Ahira." Faint red splotches mottled his neck. "How can I protect you if you won't tell me—"

"Protect me?" Ahira choked out a laugh. "How can you protect me in Egypt when you couldn't protect yourself in Canaan?"

Joseph considered her. "Well. You're still Enoch's mouthy daughter, aren't you?" His expression darkened. "I'm your overseer, so you will tell me why the daughter of Abba's chief shepherd was sold to Midianite slavers."

Ahira would have rather traded insults. She would have rather confessed what Gaios tried to do. But she *must* tell him what she'd allowed to happen.

"I fell in love with your brother Simeon, but when he wanted to bed me, I refused him."

The horror on Joseph's face compounded her shame. "Simeon sold you?"

"It's on my head." Ahira wiped her cheeks. "If I'd listened to Abba and refused Simeon's attention at the start, I would never have borne the consequences of his wrath." She attempted a smirk. "We both know what happens when your brothers bear a grudge."

The humor fell flat and seemed to cut him. She'd been foolish to anger him. "Prince Joseph, I'm sor—"

"I'm not a prince anymore, Ahira."

"Yes, my lord." She bowed. *A slave who speaks unprompted gets traded.*

"Ahira, look at me."

She obeyed.

"Enoch trusted Elohim, and I know he taught you to do the same." Joseph waited for her reply, but Ahira had nothing to say. Elohim hadn't helped her abba nor her ima, who had died when Ahira was five, giving birth to the son Abba always wanted. Yet her abba continued to serve the God of Abraham, Isaac, and Jacob—for what? To have his daughter sold into slavery?

"You're right." Joseph closed the distance between them. "I can't protect you in Egypt, but I'm also right. Elohim wanted you here. Don't assign the sins of men to a faithful God. Elohim will never betray you, and He can protect you in ways I never could. Trust Him, Ahira."

The memory of Potiphar bursting into the kitchen and pulling Gaios away from her reinforced Joseph's words. "I'll try." But trust would come hard to a slave in Egypt.

THIRTEEN

Potiphar left everything he had in Joseph's care.

GENESIS 39:6A

Potiphar

Potiphar searched the room for the Minoan cockroach and found him cowering in a corner. "Get up." He lifted him by his collar.

Ommi inserted herself between them. "I'm sure he's learned his lesson, Potiphar." She turned toward the slave. "Tell my son you'll never bother Ahira again."

"I'll be a perfect gentleman, my lord."

The Minoan's quick answer betrayed his deceit. Potiphar nudged Ommi aside to examine the troublemaker. "King Rehor of Zakros Palace is a guest in my villa."

The slave's eyes widened.

"Hmm, you know him." Potiphar pushed the slave into Hami's custody. "We'll ask Rehor if he's worth training."

Hami caught him with one hand and squeezed the back of Gaios's neck. "Are you sure you can trust the Minoan king?"

It was a valid question. "I'll determine that after I decide on the slave."

The Medjay commander stepped away from the kitchen door, making room for Potiphar to lead him and the captive slave into the hall.

"Potiphar!" Ommi called, and he turned. "Rehor has lived in this villa for two weeks. He's a good man, Son. He's your wife's abi. Trust him."

Potiphar returned and pulled her close to whisper, "Khyan made me captain of his guard because I don't trust *anyone*, Ommi. Not even so-called friends. I'll know if Rehor is true or false by the way he answers my questions." After a quick peck on her forehead, he exited the kitchen and nearly barged into Joseph.

The Hebrew shot a glance at the maid scurrying toward Zuleika's chamber, then turned back to his master. "I stopped her to ask if she needed help."

"Plans have changed considerably for today. Return to my chamber." Potiphar continued toward Rehor's chamber. Hami's steady footsteps slapped the tiles behind him along with the Minoan's nearly soundless swish of bare feet.

As he approached the end of the hallway, Potiphar pointed to the chamber on the left, and one of the guards rapped on the door and opened it.

"What are you . . . ?" The indignation in Rehor's gravelly voice eased when he peered beyond Potiphar's shoulder. "Gaios?" He returned his attention to Potiphar, wisely falling silent.

"Gaios was purchased yesterday as Pushpa's kitchen slave and has already caused trouble. He has no value in trade, King Rehor, so I ask you"—Potiphar watched the king's every blink and twitch—"Can he be trusted to serve honorably in my household?"

Rehor raised a single brow. "Did the trouble involve a young woman?"

"It did."

"Gaios believes himself a ladies' man, but he's harmless—and the best spy on Crete."

Potiphar's chest tightened. "He's a spy?"

Rehor opened his mouth but closed it without speaking. Even in a dimly lit hall, Potiphar recognized fear.

"You need not fear Gaios," Rehor said finally. "He was my *street rat,* discovering information on other Minoan districts to give Zakros trading advantage. When Zully and I left for Egypt, I ordered him to remain on Crete." He turned to Gaios, his forehead wrinkled. "How did you know Zully and I would be here?"

"I didn't know, my king." Gaios fell to his knees. "Merchant sailors captured me in Malia and sold me to the Midianites. Master Potiphar's manservant bought me with four other Minoans." He glanced at one master and then the other. "It's the will of the gods, my lords. How can we deny it?"

"Why would the gods bring him here against your wishes?" Potiphar questioned the king.

"Gaios is brilliant, with a strategic mind, and he's completely loyal to Zully. He's been my daughter's right hand since they were children."

"Are they lovers?"

"Of course not! He's a street rat." The king sneered.

"And your daughter deserves royalty." Potiphar agreed, but Rehor's arrogance still stung.

The king lifted his chin. "Were it not for Crete's destruction, my daughter would have been queen of Zakros and Knossos Districts. She *willingly* sacrificed her position to make Egypt her new home so Crete could be rebuilt."

Indeed she'd seemed willing last night. Or had his instincts been clouded by the most beautiful woman he'd ever seen?

"Please, Master Potiphar." The slave scrambled to his feet. "Surely you see the gods brought me here. I had no idea Princess Zuleika or King Rehor were in your villa—yet here I am."

Potiphar grabbed his throat but squeezed only enough to make a point. "You are my property. I stopped you from damaging the Hebrew maid, who is also my property." Releasing him, Potiphar glanced at Hami. "Take this cockroach to the cellblock, and show him what happens to people who damage property in Egypt."

Hami dragged the pleading slave away, and Potiphar returned his attention to the king of Zakros. "What will you do with him?" Rehor asked.

"That decision depends on how you answer my questions, King Rehor." Potiphar studied him. "If I return your street rat to Crete, is he likely to find his way back now that he knows Zuleika is here?"

Rehor nodded. "He would."

"Hmm." Clasping his hands behind him, Potiphar began pacing the small chamber. "I made promises to your daughter last night, Rehor. Promises I must break this morning." He'd vowed she could trust him to stay with her and to be dependable. Now, before the water clock emptied, he would cut short their wedding week. He couldn't stomach the thought of upsetting her nor publicly admit his own disappointment at leaving. Halting his pacing, he found Rehor staring at him.

"Gaios's arrival will please my daughter, Captain. She sees him as a little brother. A pet."

"Can he be trained to obey *me*, King Rehor? It would be worse to give him to her, then take him away." Potiphar had executed men who were too stubborn to take commands.

Rehor pursed his lips, considering. "I've seen Gaios adapt to many situations. My daughter sees him only as a kind and loyal servant who taught her much about trading while I and the other men of Zakros actually did what he dreamed possible. I've also seen Gaios's darker side, Captain. He's as slippery as they come, but you can train him to do anything you like."

Far from a glowing recommendation. "If Zuleika seems well adjusted to my departure, I'll send Gaios back to Crete. If, however, she's overly upset, I'll keep your street rat and present him as a gift."

"A wise plan, Captain."

"In the meantime, the cockroach will explore the dark corners of Pharaoh's prison." Potiphar strode toward the door, then turned just before he reached the threshold. "I realize you've already delayed your departure for two weeks, but I must ask that you delay a bit longer—at least until we see Zuleika's reaction to my departure."

"You're leaving?"

Potiphar continued into the hallway, instructing Rehor's guards instead of answering. "Make sure Zakros's king has a hearty meal in his chamber this morning." A Minoan king need not know Khyan's plan to attack the Tehenu.

Shifting his thoughts to the rebellion, Potiphar lengthened his strides. With so many details to shore up before leaving, he must shuffle personnel and redistribute responsibilities. The guards opened his chamber door, and he entered without slowing his steps.

Joseph blocked his path. "What did Gaios do?" He bowed as an afterthought. "I mean, as your overseer, my lord, I'd like to know why Hami escorted the troublesome slave to the prison below your villa."

"Pushpa and I handled it." He stepped around Joseph to where Abasi was waiting at the cosmetics couch. "Well, old friend, the gods have given you one more chance to paint the Eye of Horus on my tired face before you go to that weasel Wereni. I'll wear it proudly as I accompany Pharaoh at dawn. How much time left on that water clock, Hebrew?" He lay back on the couch, closed his eyes, and laced his hands over his belly.

"Less than one mark left, Master." Joseph sounded tired. "May I be excused to ask Pushpa what happened between Gaios and Ahira, my lord?"

While Abasi gathered his jars and potions, Potiphar considered his overseer's vigilance concerning the maid. Why hadn't the girl told Joseph the Minoan tried to attack her? Her discretion prevented a stir among the servants. *Admirable.* Perhaps more important was discovering why Joseph hid their shared past. "Describe your training as Prince Jacob's son."

Joseph's lengthy pause proved the question's value. "As you know, Master, my abba was a Bedouin, and—"

"No, no. Your family is *the* Bedouin royalty whose extensive livestock, power, and wealth threatened the tribes already living in Retjenu and pushed Amu clans into Egypt."

"Yes, my lord. I'm the son of Prince Jacob, son of Isaac, son of Abraham, who flourished in Canaan." Another pause. "And it's my firm belief that the same God who blessed my forefathers favors your household because of your kindness to me."

"You're clever, Hebrew." Potiphar covered rising anger with a wry grin. "You threaten your god's vengeance if my kindness ends?"

"Not at all, Master. I meant no disrespect but rather hoped to illustrate that the prosperity you've witnessed since my arrival is similar to what my ancestors experienced."

"Filthy Hebrew," Abasi grumbled. "Silver-tongued serpent."

"Enough, Abasi." Potiphar disregarded the old man's words. Prosperity often seemed unfair to those lacking. "I give little credit to the gods for anything, Hebrew, so I'll repeat my question. What did you learn as a son of the Bedouin prince? Since my flocks and herds now outnumber Pharaoh's, you must have learned a great deal about livestock. What else?"

"Because I was the firstborn of Abba's favored wife, he taught me everything necessary to sustain our tribe: ledgers, supplies, livestock, ratio of hired hands to slave labor, wool sales, shearing. My ima was a midwife, so I even learned how to care for the animals when they were birthing or ill."

Potiphar bolted upright. "Perfect!"

"Master!" Abasi scolded. "Horus's Eye isn't finished."

Potiphar removed the applicator from the old man's hand. "Listen to me, old friend. The Hebrew's training makes my departure, and yours from this villa, easier." He stood, meeting Joseph face to face. "You will be chamberlain of my entire estate, Hebrew. Land, livestock, and villa—you're qualified to manage all of it in my absence."

"But, Master, I . . . I—"

"He may be qualified"—Abasi sneered—"but he's not worthy."

Potiphar ignored the comment. "Abasi, you'll serve Vizier Wereni in his chamber every morning and evening as you've tended me. After you're certain he's sleeping, you'll meet Hami and the Hebrew whenever and wherever Hami commands to report the details you've observed about the traitorous vizier."

Abasi's eyes had become as wide as a camel's. "But, Master, what if we're caught?"

"Hami will be assigned as the vizier's bodyguard while the king's guard is away, so both you and he will have viable reasons to be in

Wereni's villa." Potiphar turned to Joseph. "You can't be seen, but I believe the information Abasi gathers will be worth the risk."

"I don't need a Hebrew scribe to record an Egyptian betrayal." Abasi glared at the new chamberlain. "I can report directly to you, Master Potiphar, when you return."

Potiphar gripped the old man's face with one hand, forcing him to look into his eyes. "Your memory isn't what it used to be, Abasi, and the king's absence makes fertile soil to sow the seeds of treason. You'll do as I say. And you'll obey Hami when I'm gone."

"Of course, Master."

Potiphar resumed his place on the couch. An uncomfortable silence settled over the room while Abasi finished the Eye of Horus. The steward's passion for Egypt would endear him to Wereni, and he'd be the last person the vizier would suspect of being an informant.

Potiphar's mind wandered to his dizzying list of tasks. One, especially sensitive, the Hebrew might have wisdom on how to handle. "As my new chamberlain, you'll work with Hami to choose the appropriate guards for the villa." How could he phrase the command to maintain the Medjay's dignity? "Hami and a few other Medjays have sustained a specific war injury that qualifies them to guard a royal woman's chamber." He paused, allowing his meaning to register.

"Hmm." Abasi's wry chuckle interrupted the moment. "Eunuch by battle."

Potiphar's patience was gone. "Another word, and you leave immediately. Understood?"

"Yes." His tone was clipped.

"Master." Joseph sounded tentative. "How will I know who . . ."

"As chamberlain, you're responsible for all I own, but Hami commands the bodyguard left to monitor the vizier and my villa. He'll choose the Medjays who guard my wife's chamber. The whole regiment need not know why they weren't chosen to protect Pharaoh in Temehu."

"Yes, Master."

Potiphar crossed his ankles and waited, anxious for Abasi to finish. He heard the clay pots shuffling beside him and opened his eyes. "All done?"

The old man nodded but didn't face him. Pouting.

Potiphar sat up and offered his hand in truce. "You can't leave until ma'at is restored."

Abasi locked wrists and held his gaze. "Ma'at can't be restored with a Hebrew as your chamberlain."

"His sentiment will be shared by many, my lord," Joseph said before Potiphar could reprimand Abasi. "Some of your Egyptian servants will likely chafe at a Hebrew overseer."

Potiphar pulled his hand from Abasi's grasp and stood to face his chamberlain. "Then use your abi's training to determine how many servants you replace with slaves. Slaves don't *chafe*, Hebrew. They *obey*. You will use Abasi's chamber while I'm gone." He turned to his long-time steward. "Go, Abasi. A Medjay escort is waiting. Wereni expects you at dawn." The old man bowed deeply and shuffled from the chamber. With his every step, Potiphar felt more shackles fall away.

Shackles. He realized the new chamberlain had never visited the prison he would now oversee. "Follow me, Hebrew." To save time, he'd explain as he walked. "The prison is also under your authority when I leave." After leaving the chamber, he turned, unlocked the seldom-used door immediately on his right, and flung it open.

Joseph gasped.

Potiphar chuckled when the Hebrew covered his nose. "You'll grow accustomed to the smell."

"I hope not."

Potiphar began the trek down the narrow stone stairs, considering what was vital for his chamberlain to know before he left.

"Master, may I ask a rather sensitive question?"

"If you must."

"Why does Pharaoh Khyan sanction a prison? With Amorite heritage and a warrior's heart, why not adopt the more immediate punishments of Hammurabi's Code?"

"Khyan is Egyptian above all else, Hebrew. He follows *Egyptian* law, not Hammurabi." Potiphar ducked under a low doorway at the bottom of the stairs and found Hami waiting in the expansive space, the Minoan cockroach shackled to one of the waist-high tables stained with blood.

"Please, Master Potiphar!" the man wailed. "I'll obey you."

Hami lifted one brow. "I've done nothing but chain him."

Joseph rushed toward the prisoner to intercede. "My lord, how can torture be more merciful than Hammurabi's Code?"

Potiphar exchanged a snide grin with Hami. "I never said Egypt was more merciful. Seven years ago, when Lower Egypt moved its capital to Avaris, our new warrior-kings publicly announced their adherence to all things Egyptian and built two prisons. The modifications were not made public."

The Hebrew scanned the room, his expression screaming disapproval.

The Minoan's incessant whimpering grated. "I've learned my lesson, Master."

"Silence!" Potiphar growled at the slave and turned to his second-in-command. "Hami, I've made the Hebrew chamberlain over my whole estate, and you'll escort Vizier Wereni, as his personal guard, to the palace, to his villa—everywhere. The vizier will rule on petitions in court while Pharaoh Khyan is away, so you must rely on the Hebrew to keep you apprised of what happens in my villa." He glanced at the Minoan cockroach now lying silent. If he believed in the gods, he might have prayed they would take the man back to Crete and keep him there. "We'll discuss further arrangements upstairs. Bring the Minoan."

"Master Potiphar, welcome." The warden's jubilant voice halted their departure.

Potiphar greeted him, another of Pushpa's benevolent recommendations. "Ubaid, you old dog, come meet your new chamberlain." He stepped aside to introduce Joseph. "He'll visit the Place of Confinement each week to record your supply requests."

Ubaid extended his dirt-encrusted hand, offering a smile that boasted few teeth. "I'm anxious to talk about increasing prisoners' rations."

"Watch him," Potiphar said to Joseph. "He's a negotiator."

Joseph locked wrists with Ubaid. "I'll examine the ledgers and decide what the prison can afford."

Ubaid frowned. "Just like the other scribes."

"Come now, Ubaid." Potiphar clapped the man's shoulder, hoping to soothe this forgotten soldier. "Show the Hebrew your kingdom. Perhaps when he sees the conditions, he'll extend some *mercy*." After emphasizing the word Joseph had used so righteously, Potiphar motioned toward the cellblock. "My new Minoan slave should also see what awaits him if he continues to be a problem." A nod to Hami, and the whimpering cockroach fell in step behind the guided tour.

Ubaid grabbed a torch from its leather stirrup on the wall and looked over his shoulder with a lopsided grin. "You're too bright and fancy to visit us snakes in the hole, Chamberlain."

"Sometimes those who are fancy need shade from the sun's heat." Joseph covered his nose and followed, the warden's laughter ushering them down the narrow hall.

Potiphar shoved the Minoan into the cellblock behind Joseph. "Behind these doors are men who will never see daylight again," he said. "You have one chance, Minoan. One. My wife decides if you stay in Egypt or return to Crete. Her decision is final—and obeying her is the only way you survive."

Shrieks and groans rose around them. Some begged to be free. Others threatened Pharaoh's captain. Rehor's street rat looked more like a desert hare about to bolt.

"Silence!" Potiphar shouted, then practically dragged his slave back to the cavernous main room. Every voice had stilled by the time Ubaid replaced the torch in its holster. Hami stood like a granite pillar. In the interest of time, Potiphar shortened the tour, focusing on Joseph. "You've seen the cellblock. Its prisoners await the king's sentencing and are likely not long for this world." He pointed to the torchlit hall on their left. "The second section is called the barracks and holds a greater number of prisoners that Pharaoh Khyan sentenced for a longer stay. This should answer any questions on Egyptian mercy."

"It does, my lord." Joseph dipped his head. "I'll return tomorrow after checking the ledgers and speak with Ubaid about increasing prisoners' rations."

"Thank you, Lord Chamberlain." The warden's enthusiastic nod skewed his wig.

Potiphar started up the stairs. "Hebrew, you have full authority over the estate, but anything my wife wants—within reason—she must have."

"Yes, my lord."

Potiphar stopped at the top of the stairs and turned to assess the two men he trusted most and a slave who no longer dared meet his gaze. "It's of utmost importance that my wife is protected, healthy, and happy in my absence. Understood?"

"Yes, my lord," they said in unison.

"Now I can concentrate on protecting my best friend in battle." He swung open the door and started toward Zuleika's chamber. A slave he didn't recognize hurried into the kitchen. He halted abruptly and aimed his question at Joseph. "Was that one of the other Minoans you bought yesterday?"

He nodded, and before he could speak, Potiphar shoved Gaios into Hami's custody. "Take the cockroach to Rehor's chamber; then bring the other Minoans to Zuleika's chamber immediately."

"Yes, Captain." Without hesitation, Hami gripped the street rat's arm and thrust him down the hall toward Rehor's chamber.

"We'll hope the other slaves from her homeland bring enough joy to help my wife forget the broken promises," Potiphar mumbled to himself more than Joseph.

"Did Pushpa explain why we can't trade Gaios?"

Potiphar released a cynical huff. "You need to catch up, Hebrew. Gaios is my wife's childhood companion and King Rehor's informant." Joseph's expression showed the anticipated shock. "If my wife seems upset by my departure, I'll present the troublesome Minoan to Zuleika as a gift. If she's indifferent to my absence, Rehor will take his street rat back to Crete."

The Hebrew's tight features eased. "I pray your wife is saddened by your leaving, my lord, but a man like Gaios could wreak havoc on our household."

"He'll be more compliant after this morning's encounter." Potiphar started toward his wife's chamber again and remembered the Hebrew maid. "Don't get too involved with Zuleika's servant. A woman can blur your focus. You must run my household without fault while I'm away."

"I'll strive to be worthy of your approval, Master Potiphar." Joseph bowed when they arrived at Zuleika's door and remained in the humble posture. "Just as I've tried to be worthy of Elohim's favor."

"If you're so favored, why were you in a Midianite captive train?" He waved off Joseph's answer when one of his wife's chamber guards pounded a spearhead on her door to announce his arrival. "Open it!" He was her husband and master of this house. He didn't need permission. Potiphar marched inside and found Zuleika and her maid sitting at a low table, bent over something he couldn't quite make out.

The girl shot to her feet, as if caught stealing from Pushpa's kitchen. When his wife remained at her task, he moved closer. She was painting a lotus on a small piece of papyrus.

Perhaps she hadn't heard him enter. He cleared his throat, but she continued to ignore him. Anger rising, he started counting silently to calm himself. When he reached twenty, he stepped toward her, anything but calm.

"There!" Zuleika leapt to her feet and showed him the papyrus. "What do you think? I could paint the various flora of Egypt and then sell them in the market to raise more silver for Crete's rebuild—"

"No!" His harsh response made her flinch. He sniffed, regaining composure. "It's a lovely painting, Wife, but Egypt has sent ample provision to your homeland."

She faced the courtyard's amethyst glow. "I only want to help."

Potiphar's ommi had offered the same excuse to Abi when she resumed her priestess duties for profit because he couldn't provide enough silver for her expensive tastes. She abandoned them a few years later. "You may paint, sculpt, and create whatever you like, Zuleika, but you will not sell your wares in the market like a beggar whose husband can't provide. No arguments."

He stared at her back in the interminable silence. "I leave with Pharaoh at dawn," he said. "The Tehenu tribes have crossed into the delta's western border."

"What?" She whirled to face him. "Why?"

"Zuleika, I'm captain of his bodygua—"

"No, Ahira told me you were leaving. I meant, Why did the Tehenu tribes cross? There must be a reason."

He grinned. "You are obviously a king's daughter with an interest in policies and politics." Her tense pout softened with the compliment. He'd remember to praise her more when he returned. "Tehenu lands have seen decades of drought. Their tribes occasionally raid our delta villages. Pharaohs of the past, who ruled from Memphis, allowed it, but Great Khyan protects all his people with equal justice."

"Thank you for explaining." Her cheeks pinked, and she cast an awkward glance over his shoulder. "Who's this?"

Joseph stepped forward.

"This is my estate chamberlain. He administrates everything I own—the household and the fields."

"But I can do that. At Zakros Palace, I inventoried supplies, balanced ledgers, and helped Mitera rule on villagers' complaints while Pateras was trading abroad. I assure you, Potiphar, I'm quite capable of—"

"As I said before . . ." He cleared his throat, giving himself a moment to calm his tone. Must everything be a battle with this woman? "You will do all the things you enjoy. Painting. Sculpting."

"*That's* how I'm supposed to fill my days?" She looked as though he'd sentenced her to Ubaid's cellblock. "If I can't sell my art, why create it? If I make no contribution to this estate, why not return to Crete with Pateras?"

Her obsession with returning home must end. "You will learn to be an Egyptian noblewoman. *That* is your contribution to this estate."

"Captain, the new slaves." Hami entered, his timing impeccable.

As Hami led the four Minoans into the chamber, Potiphar said,

"The villa's keeper of halls will continue to oversee the Medjays I assign to Avaris, but he'll become personal guard to Vizier Wereni. Joseph, as chamberlain of the estate, will oversee the servants."

Zuleika stared at the slaves. "They're Minoan," she whispered. "Thank you, Potiphar. I know you must leave, but please come home to me. Remember your promises, and don't abandon me."

Tears wet her long, thick lashes, piercing him like a dagger through his heart. "You needn't be lonely, Zuleika. These additional slaves will allow you to entertain as often as you like without worry of overtaxing Pushpa."

She scoffed. "Egypt's noblewomen want nothing to do with me, nor do I wish to waste time on them."

"But, Zuleika—"

"Without you as mediator, I'll have no one to help me brave this new world." Her lovely face twisted in sorrow.

Potiphar cast a defeated glance at Hami. "Bring in Rehor and the other slave."

"Pateras is still here?"

"I asked him to stay until—"

"Oh, Potiphar!" She pulled him close for a quick kiss. "You're proving far more agreeable than any crocodile."

"And my Minoan mare is harder to leave behind than expected." He tilted her chin up for another kiss, reveling in the taste of her. The sound of footsteps signaled Hami's return with the two men he hoped would calm her. Potiphar stepped aside to reveal the surprise.

Her gasp gave way to gaping wonder. "Gaios! How did you find me?"

Awkward tension rose in the chamber, all eyes darting warily from Potiphar to the slave his wife so eagerly welcomed.

"Mycenaean sailors captured me at Malia."

"Captured you?" She lunged toward him, as if to embrace him, but halted—scanning him instead from head to toe. "Why were you in Malia, Gaios? Are you injured?"

Potiphar had seen enough. He stepped in front of his wife with a warning glance to both the cockroach and Rehor. "We need not color hard goodbyes with a slave's sad stories." He kissed his wife's cheek. "King Rehor must sail, and I've already kept Pharaoh waiting too long."

His wife's focus shifted. "When will I see you again, Pateras?"

"Only the gods know, my girl." He pulled her into his arms. "They seem to have overruled my command that Gaios remain on Crete, so I'm sure there's a purpose for his presence here."

Zuleika broke away. "Gaios will teach me how to win the favor of Egypt's noblewomen."

"Anything you need, Princess." The cockroach bowed.

Potiphar felt a niggling sense of dread, but dawn's brightening glow from the courtyard was like a battle trumpet. "I must go, love. Pharaoh is waiting." He pulled his wife close for another kiss.

"Remember your promise," she whispered. "Come back to me. I have no desire to lose another husband."

His chest ached as he etched every detail of her form into his memory. "This is not goodbye, Zuleika. I will return to you."

FOURTEEN

*Joseph was well-built and handsome, and after a
while his master's wife took notice of Joseph.*

GENESIS 39:6B–7

Zuleika

Potiphar's kiss had been overwhelmingly tender, and his departure
troubled me more than I wanted to admit.

Hami motioned the slaves to exit.

"Gaios stays."

My command seemed to surprise both the Hebrew chamberlain
and the Medjay, but it was Pateras who took me aside to speak privately. "Zully, it's not proper for a male slave—unless he's a eunuch—
to be alone with you, an Egyptian noblewoman."

"I *need* him." Desperation made the whisper a soft shout.

Pateras feigned a smile. "Gaios has been like a brother to her since
they were children."

Before he could scold me, I addressed the gawkers. "Gaios and I
worked together to improve Zakros District's trade, and he will work
with me here to smooth my transition to Egyptian society. You will
not betray me with sordid gossip. Is that understood?"

"Yes, Mistress." The chamberlain bowed, but the Medjay turned his back and herded the other four slaves from the room. I would confront his disrespect after saying goodbye to Pateras.

"Be careful, Zul," Pateras whispered as he embraced me. "Gaios is still devoted to you, but his captivity changed him. He's more dangerous than before."

Dangerous? I pulled away, expecting a wink. Instead, I saw only concern.

"You may be the most courageous person I know." He kissed my forehead and strode away.

The door closed behind him. Pateras was really gone this time. *They're all gone.* Minas. Mitera. Pateras. Even the husband I'd expected to hate, gone after a night of surprising pleasure. I had only Gaios now. Ahira. And a disturbingly handsome chamberlain who stared at me. "May I bring you anything, Mistress?"

I gulped back a sob. This man had no idea who I was or what I needed.

Ahira rushed toward me. "Mistress, come and lie down."

Gaios stepped between us. "You look unwell, Ahira." Only then did I notice her gray pallor.

"Ahira, are you unwell?" The chamberlain seemed overly concerned.

My maid's eyes darted from one man to the other, then landed on me. "Might I lie down for a moment, Mistress?"

"Of course. Go."

She disappeared into her room.

"Zully." My name on Gaios's lips drew me. In four strides, he was before me. "You're strong. You're capable. You'll improve this villa in ways Egypt can't imagine. Decide your first project and attack it with your talent."

Yes, this was my Gaios. I inhaled deeply, regaining calm. "Together, Gaios, we'll do it."

"I am, as always, at your service." He bowed but winced as he rose, holding his side.

I noticed shackle marks like Ahira's on his wrists and ankles. "Gaios, your wounds need tending."

Joseph stepped forward. "I'll see to it myself, Mistress."

"Thank you, Chamberlain, but no. I'll tend to my friend."

His expression screamed disapproval. "Have you some training as a midwife or healer?" His green eyes flecked with brown reminded me of a tarnished bronze bowl Mitera had kept at her bedside.

"I'm well trained in many things," I said. "Bring me Pushpa's basket of remedies."

He hesitated. "Forgive me, Mistress, but I cannot allow it. As chamberlain, I'm responsible for everything on Master Potiphar's estate. Your husband instructed the keeper of halls to use only eunuchs as your chamber guards, so I would be remiss to leave you alone in your chamber with a man who isn't one."

"Both you and Gaios are with me now. Are you a eunuch, Chamberlain?"

His cheeks flushed and his eyes narrowed. "*I* will tend Gaios's wounds."

"Ahira!" I shouted.

After a moment's shuffling, she emerged from her room. "Mistress?"

"Is the chamberlain the same Joseph you mentioned as one of the twelve brothers in the Bedouin camp where you grew up?"

Her eyes widened, and she shot him a panicked glance.

"Look at *me*, Ahira." I spoke with the calm sureness of authority. "Consider your loyalty and speak the truth, because a lie ends your service as my maid." I needed to prove my control over the one person Joseph valued in the villa.

His features softened when he looked at her. "It's all right, Ahira."

"I'm sorry, Joseph." Ahira straightened and returned her attention to me. "Yes, Mistress Zuleika, this is Prince Joseph, one of the brothers in the captive story I *confided* to you." Her voice dripped with venom.

Couldn't she understand why I did it? "Gaios is the only one who can rescue me from captivity."

"Mistress, were you forced to stay here?" The chamberlain's pity was humiliating. "I thought you agreed to—"

"I agreed to save Crete!" I was shaking now, and the silence after my shout amplified its impropriety. I had stooped to marrying a soldier, but I was still *Princess* Zuleika. "Am I correct to assume you've never led a household, Joseph?"

"I've been trained to manage an entire camp, Mistress."

"I'm a Minoan princess who's ruled Zakros District with Queen Daria while King Rehor was away. I'm sure you're capable, or my husband wouldn't have made you chamberlain."

"Thank you, Mistress." Joseph bowed. "I believe, working together, we'll make this estate prosper."

I exchanged a victorious glance with Gaios. Diplomacy was always preferred to force when negotiating. "In Potiphar's absence, I'll command Ahira and the five Minoan slaves."

"You'll command Gaios only."

So much for diplomacy. "I command all five Minoans and Ahira, and I'll maintain the villa's financial ledgers. It's not a request, Chamberlain. It's a command from your mistress, Princess Zuleika of Zakros!" My voice had risen with each word and brought the chamber guards charging into the room. "Get out! All of you." They looked to Joseph for his approval before obeying, which infuriated me more.

The chamberlain's countenance was chiseled stone. "All *five* Minoans must serve in the kitchen for any banquets you host. I concede to you authority of your friend Gaios and *my* friend Ahira—since she was purchased as your maid. However, if Ahira is harmed in any way, Gaios will be removed from the villa immediately." He bowed, strode from the chamber, and quietly closed the door behind him.

The fear on Gaios's face planted a seed of hate. How dare that arrogant Bedouin threaten my friend? How dare he show more composure than me? "When Pharaoh leaves with his troops," I said to Gaios, forcing calm, "you, Ahira, and I will go to the royal market and purchase supplies to tend your wounds. We don't need Pushpa's basket of remedies or the chamberlain's interference."

"You're magnificent, Zully." Gaios applauded but winced again with the effort.

"And you are a great gift from the gods. Come. You must rest until we go to the market." I led Gaios toward the courtyard.

"Your Akkadian has improved in such a short time."

"Thank you, Gaios." Though small affirmations, hope rose in me with each of his compliments, like a new day's waking.

Ahira followed us dutifully, silently. Was she truly unwell or pouting because I'd betrayed her trust?

"Help me lower him to the couch," I said.

She did as she was told, wrapping his left arm around her neck.

He was nearly settled on the cushions when she inadvertently bumped his side. "You clumsy cow!" he roared.

"Gaios!" I stood over him like a scolding mitera. "I've never spoken that way to servants, and neither will—"

"Leave me alone, Zully." He lay on the couch, curled into a ball, and covered his head. "I hear the slavers' taunts in your reproach."

"Gaios, I . . ." Was this the danger of which Pateras had warned me, changes lurking inside my friend? I'd heard rumors, but I'd never seen him lash out or withdraw. He'd always been my rock.

Ahira had retreated to the pond and stared at the mudbrick wall surrounding us. The two people I'd lean on most were both in this courtyard. Yet their similar horrific experience separated them from me. If forced to choose, however, I must pick my trusted guide who'd proven faithful since the first day we met.

I knelt beside the couch where Gaios lay, desperate for a way to reach him. *A code.* Something only we understood. I leaned over him and whispered, "Does a leaping bull's calf keep his pen clean when an octopus is gone so long?"

He turned over, and our noses nearly touched.

I moved back. Stood quickly.

"No, Zully. Prince Kostas hasn't started rebuilding Crete." He curled into a ball again. "In fact, he locked himself in Knossos Palace with the last barrel of wine on the island."

I ached at the report. If Crete's destruction was already sealed, my marriage to Potiphar meant nothing. I reached for Gaios's hand. "You're here now, my friend. We'll find a way to return and—"

He sat up, staring at my ring. "Seth? Have you so quickly pledged your allegiance to the Hyksos god of chaos?"

I shushed him, pointing at the wall. "Potiphar's Medjays patrol regularly on the other side."

His brows rose. "Is he so afraid you'll have suitors climbing the wall to steal your virtue?"

"No." I gave him a good-natured swat. "My wall is part of the palace complex."

He sobered, and his thumb gently stroked the back of my hand. "Did Captain Potiphar give you the ring?"

Had we not been friends so long, I might have thought him jealous. "Pateras gave it to me before our wedding. It matches the one we had made for Potiphar in Sena."

"You mean a ring made for *Pharaoh* in Sena." He shook his head. "Why did you let them discard you, Zully?"

"No one *discarded* me." I pulled my hand away. "You weren't there, Gaios. You didn't hear—"

"I know the queen of Zakros and Knossos deserves better than a decaying old man who couldn't find his own wife."

I shot him a glare. "You know nothing about Potiphar."

I took one step toward the chamber before Gaios bolted off the couch and caught my arm. "But I know *you*, Zully."

I scowled. If he were truly injured, he couldn't have leapt off that couch. "Maybe I don't know you at all, Gaios."

His hand fell to his side. "Of course you do. And I know, if you've chosen Seth as your god, it's him we should thank for bringing me to this villa. Until that arrogant chamberlain purchased me, I still thought you'd married Pharaoh."

A shiver coursed through me. "Perhaps you're right. Something greater than human effort summoned both you and Ahira to this villa." I called my maid, and she approached with her head bowed. "Are you truly ill, or are you pouting because I used our private conversation to prove my point with Joseph?"

She glanced at Gaios, then turned her attention back to me, her hands clasped and trembling. "Neither. I need to tell you what Gaios—"

"I found Ahira crying in the kitchen this morning." Gaios's voice seemed to startle her. "When I lifted my hand to wipe her tears, your husband came in and thought I meant to strike her." He shrugged. "My ribs will heal, Zully. It doesn't matter. He's gone now."

"Potiphar hurt you?"

"He's a liar, Mistress." Ahira glared at him. "He said he'd spent years manipulating those in authority, and he wanted my help to do the same here. He knows you'll believe whatever he says because you're so happy to see him."

Embarrassed by the shades of truth, I mocked her. "Will you believe whatever Simeon's handsome brother tells you?"

Her weepy eyes took on a hard glint. "If you don't believe me, Joseph and Pushpa will."

"Joseph and Pushpa?" The woman I'd thought loyal had drawn her battle line. "You're *my* maid, Ahira, not Joseph's or Pushpa's. If you have something to tell, you tell me only. Then I decide to believe my friend who's protected me since childhood or a maid who seems determined to protect herself."

"I'm trying to protect you from him." She spit on the tiles at Gaios's feet.

The next moment was a frightening blur as Gaios locked his arm around Ahira's neck. "Zully and I will return to Crete before Potiphar comes home," he hissed at her, "and you'll tell no one—or I'll kill you."

"Gaios, no!" I clawed at his arm. "Let her go!"

He released her. "Zully is your only protection, Ahira. If you betray us to Pushpa or Joseph, you and they will pay."

"Stop it." I shoved him away, then knelt beside her and pulled her into my arms. "Don't listen to him, Ahira. Gaios isn't himself."

Ahira trembled. Didn't answer. Gaios paced the courtyard, and my dread rose. "Gaios, you heard Joseph. If you hurt Ahira, he'll sell you." For the first time, I questioned my decision to keep my friend in Egypt. Perhaps the slavers' abuse had damaged him beyond repair. "I can pay for your passage to Crete, my friend. You need not feel responsible for me if returning to our homeland would be more restful—"

He stopped pacing and stared at us. "Zully. Why are you on the floor?" He rushed over and helped me to my feet. "What happened? Did I do something awful?"

Weeping, Ahira escaped into her room.

"Gaios?" I watched his vacant expression change to something more alarming—a wry smile.

"I needed to be rid of her so we could be alone."

"You *threatened* her." The Gaios I knew would never . . .

"Zully, you know I wouldn't really harm her." He moved closer, and I stepped back. "But she was spewing lies about me."

"Was she lying, Gaios?"

"Have you noticed her eyes are the same unique color as Joseph's?"

What did that have to do with his bullying?

"They grew up in the same Bedouin camp, Zully. Joseph was the master's son."

"Ahira was a shepherd's daughter." The details of her story blazed through my mind.

"Look at her eyes, Zul." He scoffed. "Ahira isn't a shepherd's daughter."

"She would have told me if she and Joseph were related."

"Would she, Zully?" His tone was equal parts condescension and compassion. "You've known her less than a day. Who is more likely to protect you here? And who can help you escape to Crete before your husband returns?"

"Gaios, I can't just leave."

Dark emotions shadowed his features. He was too volatile to hear truth.

"Of course, I want to return with you, but we can't until Crete has been rebuilt." I dared not tell him my wedding night had been unexpectedly pleasant.

"Pharaoh won't chase you if you desert his best friend. Egypt's ships are built for the Nile, not the Great Sea." Eyes narrowed, he sneered. "You're beautiful, Zully, but not enough to cause a war."

My cheeks warmed. I preferred his affirmation to his mocking. "They may not declare war, Gaios, but without the three years of funds secured by my marriage, Crete can't be rebuilt." I folded my arms.

"You may leave now. I'll send Ahira to the kitchen to fetch you when we're ready for our venture to the royal market."

Instead of leaving, he extended his hand. "Forgive me if I hurt your feelings. My whole life is devoted to you, Zully. It always has been and always will be."

I wanted to trust him. I needed to trust *someone*. But this Gaios seemed unreliable. Still, he'd been an exceptional resource all my life. "Thank you, my friend." I accepted his hand, and he pulled me into a hug. Though it felt awkward, I allowed the blurring of the line between royalty and street rat. Perhaps some kindness would heal the wounds of his captivity and bring the old Gaios back.

FIFTEEN

Joseph

Joseph heard the last drop of water land in the copper basin and leapt off his reed mat. After donning his knee-length tunic and leather belt, he raced to the kitchen, frantic to be there when Ahira arrived for her morning chores. He burst through the kitchen door.

Pushpa yelped. "Seth's toenails! Joseph! What's nipping at your heels?"

"Where's Gaios?" He searched the torchlit room and saw only four of the five Minoan slaves busy with tasks.

"I let him sleep late this morning."

"Why?" Joseph snapped.

She cautioned him with a look and kept kneading.

"Forgive me." If she'd seen Ahira's silent pleading yesterday, the compassionate older woman would have sold Gaios despite the master's wishes.

"He worked with Zully all day—"

"Zully?"

"Her family and friends in Crete called her Zully. The familiar name will help her feel more at home. I seem to remember a Hebrew boy being homesick when he first came to Egypt."

"I'm not questioning Mistress Zuleika's need to build a home here." Joseph noticed that the four Minoans had stopped working and were leaning attentively toward their conversation. He sent them to the kitchen courtyard with a list of tasks to complete, then found a stool and placed it near Pushpa's kneading table. "The mistress admitted knowing Gaios at Zakros and said only that they'd worked together to improve Zakros District's trade."

Pushpa kept kneading. "Did you reveal your whole story to the first person who asked?"

"That's different, and you know it."

She paused, sinking her hands into the brown dough. "I know Gaios is a jackal, but Zully feels safe with him. In the meantime, we must protect Ahira." She started kneading again. "Perhaps you should marry her, Joseph."

"Pfssht. She was my sister's best friend."

The squeak of leather hinges saved him from the topic. "Good morning, dear."

Ahira passed without returning Pushpa's greeting.

Joseph left his stool and met her at the water jugs. "Let me—"

"No!" She clutched the pitcher to her chest, shaking like a palm frond in the wind. He offered her a cup as a peace offering. She snatched it from his hand and began filling the pitcher.

"Are you still angry about yesterday's conversation?"

She ignored him.

"I thought you'd be comforted by the knowledge of Elohim's presence with—"

"Don't." She slammed the cup back on the shelf. "I'm not angry with you, Joseph. Leave me alone." She strode to the hearth and began preparing the morning meal tray with two bowls of honey-spiced gruel.

Pushpa added a small bag to the tray. "Have your mistress chew on one of these anytime her breath needs freshening."

Ahira held the bag against her nose, closed her eyes, and inhaled. "Cloves and mint." The taut lines on her face relaxed into a sad smile.

"Thank you, Pushpa." She kissed the old woman's cheek and hurried out the door.

Joseph glared at the kindhearted woman. "Why will she talk to you and not me?"

Pushpa looked at him as if he were simpler than a child. "She's just spent three weeks in a captive train, and you're a man, Joseph. Figure it out." She worked the brown dough, lifting, turning, and pushing it again. "Give her time. Show Zully kindness. That's how you'll win Ahira's trust."

Showing the mistress kindness seemed as impossible as winning Ahira's trust. "Has the mistress given you any idea of when she'd like to host her first banquet?"

"Next week." Pushpa chuckled, but Joseph felt nothing but panic.

"How can we—"

"She and Gaios will instruct us on how to create a *Minoan*-style banquet." The sparkle in her eyes dimmed. "Why did you allow him to be in her chamber alone, Joseph? He's already found a way to make himself irreplaceable to her."

"In the end, Pushpa, she is the mistress of this villa, and I am a slave. Master Potiphar made me chamberlain, overseer of everything—except his wife." He searched the wrinkled face of one who gained power through service. "If you command me to be rid of Gaios, I'll do it now."

Her delayed response betrayed indecision. "She's lost too much already, Joseph. We can't take Gaios too."

"But he's—"

"Her husband and ommi were killed in the earthquake. Rehor and Potiphar left the morning after her wedding. Gaios is all that's familiar. Maybe when she sees what a treasure Ahira is, she won't need Gaios anymore."

It was a good point. "How much will this banquet cost?" Joseph had spent yesterday reviewing prison ledgers. He hadn't yet checked the villa's accounts.

"I'm not sure, Lord Chamberlain. That's no longer my concern." She winked.

He gave her a playful growl, dreading another day amid the dusty stacks of papyrus in Master Potiphar's library. Joseph's livestock reports were the only thing resembling an organized system. He'd found the prison ledgers scattered in various piles and scribbled on scrolls shoved into niches. "Will I have to renege on extra rations for Ubaid's prisoners to finance the folly of a spoiled princess?"

Pushpa slammed her fist into the dough. "I managed this household's finances for many years and always found sufficient funds to maintain my son's impeccable reputation and feed the prisoners."

"Have you ever visited the prison?"

Her hands stilled. "I'm relieved you've taken over the record keeping, Joseph, but don't think extra rations will save those prisoners."

"Good morning." Gaios entered, his greeting overly chipper.

Joseph kept his eyes on Pushpa, waiting for her conciliatory smile as proof she'd forgiven his rude comment about the "spoiled princess." *Elohim, forgive me.* He would ask for Pushpa's pardon later today.

"How are you feeling this morning, Gaios?" She pointed toward the palace kitchen doors. "You'll start chopping vegetables for—"

"Forgive me, Mistress Pushpa." He bowed.

"I'm not the mistress of this villa."

"Of course. How could I forget?" His patronizing smile launched Joseph from his stool.

"Don't forget that Pushpa is our master's ommi, born to nobility, and must be treated with utmost respect."

"Nobility?" Gaios offered an exaggerated bow. "It is with utmost respect, then, that I relay the news that Princess Zuleika plans an outing to the royal market this morning. She'd hoped to go yesterday, but Master Potiphar's departure was too devastating. She's ordered Ahira and me to accompany her." Turning to Joseph, he asked, "Since this is our first foray into Egyptian commerce, how should she go about purchasing art supplies as mistress of this house? Am I to be entrusted with a waist pouch of silver, or can I assume this household has established accounts with the merchants to pay for purchases at later dates?"

This slave was clearly no ordinary kitchen worker. "How exactly did you serve King Rehor in Crete?"

"I served the royal family of Zakros Palace," he said. "When King Rehor was away trading, I served Queen Daria and Princess Zuleika."

An evasive answer. "But what did you *do*, Gaios?"

His right cheek twitched. "Whatever needed doing, Lord Chamberlain." His eyes bored into Joseph's—something a lifelong slave would never do. "This morning, Princess Zuleika commanded me to accompany her to the royal market, and I will obey. Is there someone else I should ask about the payment process?"

His defiance was more than the notorious Minoan cheek. The other four slaves had worked diligently for Pushpa and shown their gratitude. "You may return to your mistress, Gaios, and tell her *I* will escort her to the royal market this morning."

"As you wish, Lord Chamberlain." He strode from the kitchen without a bow or permission.

Elohim, why is he here? Joseph didn't believe in chance.

"Could he be a spy?" Pushpa whispered.

"Why would you say that?"

"Before Potiphar left for Temehu, he said, 'Anyone could be a spy.' " She returned to her kneading table. "I don't know, Joseph. Maybe Gaios isn't a spy, but you were right. He's a rotten cucumber."

"Then let me sell him—or at least put him in prison."

"No!" Her smile quaked. "We must believe Ahira can win Zully's trust. Besides, Gaios can be useful while planning the Minoan-style banquet."

Someone burst through the kitchen door, jolting Joseph to his feet.

Before he could speak, the mistress waved her finger in his face. "*Gaios* will escort me to the royal market, Chamberlain. I sent him to ask a simple question. How do I pay for purchases?"

"Good morning, Mistress." Heart pounding, Joseph stepped back to bow and give himself time to think.

"Would you like a fresh loaf of warm bread, Zully?" Pushpa offered.

Joseph straightened and saw the same softening in Zully that he'd noted in Ahira. "No thank you, Pushpa." She tensed again when her focus returned to him. "Answer me, Joseph."

The older woman's kindness was a powerful weapon. He needed to hone that skill. "Please allow me to accompany you, Mistress." *Elohim, please give me favor in her sight.* "The merchants of the royal market know me as Master Potiphar's representative, so I can arrange terms of payment for your future visits."

Her shoulders relaxed though she eyed him with suspicion. "You may accompany Gaios and me, but he must come along to see which booths sell the supplies I favor so he can return later in my stead."

"If you trust him to do so, I bow to your wishes."

Elohim, protect Mistress Zuleika, and guide her heart toward Ahira's friendship—and both their hearts toward You.

PART II

Joseph was well-built and handsome, and after a
while his master's wife took notice of Joseph.
GENESIS 39:6B–7

SIXTEEN

[Jacob's] love for Rachel was greater than his love
for Leah.

GENESIS 29:30

ONE WEEK LATER
Zuleika

I stood before my reflection in the full-length bronze mirror, feeling
more like myself than I had since the shaking. The octopus crest on
my short royal coat proudly designated Zakros District. I twirled like
a little girl, fluttering my tiered skirt to show off its brilliant reds,
blues, and greens.

"You're radiant, Zully." Gaios stepped to my side, joining me in the
reflection, and placed his hand at the small of my back.

My breath caught.

He stepped away quickly, head bowed. "Forgive me, Princess. I
should never have—"

I reached for his hand and cradled it in my own. His were Minoan
hands. Light brown and gentle. "You're my friend, Gaios, not just a
servant."

"I hoped you felt the same."

I pulled away, glimpsing in his eyes a desire for more.

Ahira waited beside my display of Minoan treasures and held up

Mitera's necklace. "What other jewelry, Mistress?" She hadn't called me Zully since Gaios threatened her.

"No other jewelry. Today I'm purely Minoan."

"And Egypt's noblewomen will be awed by your natural beauty." Gaios offered me a fan I'd painted, a piece of folded papyrus with a leather string tethered to one end. "They'll envy you, and the gifts at each place setting will whet their appetites for the paintings they'll see later this week in the market."

If only I could share his confidence. "They hated my mural in the harem." I lifted my murex-shell hand mirror and touched each faience bead of Mitera's necklace, remembering the colors of the sea, the feel of my body sliding through the waves. It was freedom. Life giving. Gone.

Gaios stole the mirror, forcing me to look at him. "Prepare yourself for their criticism of today's Minoan paintings beside their place settings, but remember this: the paintings we sell at the market are Egyptian themed—and as magnificent as anything you've ever created. The difference in style will ensure the nobility's gossip channels don't travel to the Tehenu battlefront and betray our profits to your husband. Now, come, Princess Zuleika." He offered his arm to escort me. "Show them the elegance of Zakros Palace."

I ignored his arm and pecked his cheek with a kiss. "Thank you, Gaios." I slipped into the hall, my face flushed. I'd kissed him on impulse, but how else could I have refused his escort without hurting his feelings? If I'd left the chamber on his arm, my credibility as the villa's mistress would have been damaged. The old Gaios would have known that. The wounded Gaios was moody at best and shocking at worst. His love for me had always been playful and harmless. Now it was like tares amid wheat. How could I uproot unrealistic infatuation without destroying cherished friendship?

I heard two sets of footsteps behind me. Ahira and Gaios knew their roles for today's banquet, and I knew mine: establish at least a civil relationship with the wives of Avaris's most prominent noblemen, and repair the damage to Potiphar's reputation inflicted by my drunken departure from the wedding banquet.

"Mistress! Mistress Zuleika, wait." Joseph's voice halted me. He'd mended my first impression with helpful suggestions for the banquet, but I had no time or patience for his counsel now. "Mistress, may I make one suggestion before the oranges are served?" He stood before me with a single orange and a paring knife in his hand.

"No, you may not." I continued toward the banquet hall.

"Mistress, wait." He blocked my path, tilting his head with a confident smile.

I was startled by how handsome he was. Of course, I'd noticed before, but that smile . . . "Your charm may impress servant girls, Chamberlain, but it doesn't delay my guests. They'll be here any—"

"I need only a moment, Mistress. Please."

"You're as stubborn as my husband."

"Master Potiphar can be headstrong."

My breath caught. I'd meant Minas—but . . . "Gaios and Ahira, go into the banquet hall, and alert me when guests begin to arrive." The inner storm raged, but I forced a calm tone. "Speak, Chamberlain."

"Oranges are a good choice for your menu, but your guests won't want to peel the fruit themselves."

"But it's a Minoan tradition, a competition." I took the knife and orange from his hands and demonstrated while I explained. "Minoans try to peel their oranges in a single coil at our feasts, Joseph. Whoever removes the rind in an unbroken coil quickest wins the place of honor at the host's right hand." I finished the feat and let my perfectly coiled rind fall to the floor.

Instead of giving me a congratulatory smile, the chamberlain still appeared as if he'd swallowed a fish bone sideways. "It's a lovely tradition, Mistress, but please let us prepare and serve the oranges on platters. Pushpa said—"

"Princess!" Gaios appeared at the dividing tapestries. "Your first guests have arrived."

I returned the knife and peeled orange to the chamberlain, then wiped my sticky hands on my skirt. "Now you've made me late to greet my first guests. Serve the oranges exactly as Gaios and I described." I stomped away but consciously slowed my pace, refusing to greet

Egypt's finest like Knossos's leaping bull. The thought of my husband's district symbol sobered me. I inhaled deeply and exhaled my purpose on a calming breath. "For the people of Crete."

As I breached the tapestries, Gaios caught my arm. "I sent Ahira to welcome the king's wives and told her the chamberlain's life depended on her charm."

"His life? Gaios—"

"You should join her." He nodded toward the villa entrance. "Or she might win their favor over you."

I strode toward my two most honored guests, who had paused at the doorway with Ahira. "Great royal wives, I'm honored you've come to our villa."

"Not honored enough to greet us personally." Queen Tani's practiced smile returned to my maid. "However, I've found Ahira to be a delight. Perhaps I'll steal her."

Revealing Ahira's Hebrew heritage would undoubtedly sour the queen's opinion of her, but I had no desire to hurt my maid again. "No stealing, my queen. You're in Potiphar's villa, and I've heard there's a prison beneath us."

My humor fell like a boulder in the sea. "Come, Ziwat." Tani motioned to her sister wife, and two of our Minoan slaves escorted them to the cozy table we'd prepared for them in the northeast corner.

"Forgive me," Ahira whispered. "Please don't punish Joseph for my failure." Head bowed, she clasped her hands in a white-knuckled ball.

As the next guest approached, I whispered reassurance. "You tamed the barracudas from Pharaoh's palace." Her wrinkled brow reminded me a shepherdess would know nothing of barracudas. "I'm thanking you, Ahira."

Her hands relaxed a little, and she even smiled—the first since Gaios's arrival. It was the best gift she could have given me.

Vizier Wereni's wife huffed as she appeared beside me. "If your maid requires that much attention, beat her and send her back to the market."

"Thank you for your concern, Mistress Sanura, but Ahira serves me well." I motioned toward the corner table. "You'll be seated beside

Pharaoh's wives, the only women at my banquet who match your character." She had no idea I'd compared her to whale dung.

I greeted seven more noblemen's wives, each carefully chosen for her connections in Lower Egypt's gossip pyramid. When everyone had been seated, I addressed my guests. "Thank you for gracing my villa with your presence, renowned women of Avaris. As you so cordially instructed me in the ways of Egypt before my wedding, I'm honored to share with you some of the customs from my beautiful homeland."

"Is there no music in Crete?" Queen Tani aimed reproach like an arrow, and awkward whispers changed to chortling.

I signaled the slaves to serve the food. "Women of Crete make our own music with pleasant conversation. Why battle noise when a friend's voice is so much sweeter?"

But my guests had already begun private chats, ignoring me completely. I motioned to Ahira. "Fill their goblets with the mulled wine." I'd given Pushpa the recipe and a small supply of the dittany mint I salvaged from the Zakros ruins. Dittany was an herbal treasure unique to Crete. Egyptians imported it occasionally, calling it *eronda,* and used it to cure everything from open wounds to faltering libido.

I watched the women sip the sweet brew. Sniff. And sip again. "What do you think of your mulled wine, ladies?"

The vizier's wife sneered. "It's mint, Princess Zuleika, a common herb in Egypt."

I wanted to claw her eyes out but ignored her rudeness while my Minoans served the first platters of food. "Please enjoy the dakos before you. It's a barley bread baked at low temperatures to remove all moisture and then soaked in Egypt's lovely olive oil. Pushpa has prepared a deliciously tart olive paste to spread on the dakos."

More mocking conversation and laughter followed, warming my cheeks. I signaled for the main dish—lamb with greens and a fennel-mint sauce. This time I omitted the commentary, guzzling a goblet of mulled wine.

The paintings I'd worked hard to complete lay unnoticed. Why had I allowed Gaios to raise my hopes when I'd experienced nothing but heartache from these women? Without the lively spirit of Minoan people to replace Egypt's musicians and dancers, my intimate banquet was becoming another public humiliation.

I offered up my empty goblet for Ahira to fill, thankful Pushpa had chosen a wine barely stronger than grape juice. I needed my wits about me. Enjoying the plentiful olive oil in all my homeland's recipes, I'd remain content and silent until the peeling of oranges.

However, halfway through my meal, the silence grew excruciating. Egypt's most frightening women did nothing but glare at me. Ahira knelt beside me. "Mistress, how can I help?" she whispered.

Pushing away my plate, I asked, "Are we ready for the best Minoan treat?"

One of the women mumbled something, but I spoke over her. "Tell the chamberlain to serve the oranges himself. I'd like my Egyptian friends to experience the effects of eronda for themselves."

"Mistress, I . . ."

I slammed my fist on the table at her hesitation. "Joseph will serve the oranges."

"Yes, Mistress."

The vizier's wife watched Ahira go. "That one would return to the slavers if she were mine."

"Well, she's not yours." I glimpsed a grin from Queen Tani.

Ahira returned with Joseph, who carried the tray of oranges. Scowls faded. Noble postures improved. Eyelashes batted at a servant handsome enough to entice. Eronda was doing its work.

"I love oranges," Ziwat said, motioning Joseph to serve her first. Suddenly every guest vied for my chamberlain's attention.

It was then I realized *he* could be better entertainment than musicians or dancers. "Joseph, regale us with stories of your family. How did the son of the Bedouin prince come to be Potiphar's slave?" I refilled my goblet with wine. "I'm sure the most powerful women in Egypt would love to hear of your beautiful mitera and jealous brothers."

"You're Hebrew?" The vizier's wife dropped her orange as if it were infested. "My husband would not approve—"

"Our husbands need not know," another woman said, a conspiratorial glint in her eyes. "My family has had Hebrew slaves since the first Bedouin prince came to Egypt during a famine over a hundred years ago. Pharaoh simply said we can't eat with them. Isn't that true, Queen Tani?"

All eyes shifted to the most honored guest who scanned Joseph from head to toe. "Let him tell his stories." Then she sneered at me and lifted her knife. "But why must we prepare our own food, Zuleika?" Laughter rose again.

I'd reached my limit. "Take that knife and—"

"It's entertainment." Joseph's calm silenced me. "In Princess Zuleika's homeland, in the splendor of her beloved Zakros Palace, the women could wield spindle and dagger with equal skill. The first event of every feast was the celebrated tradition of peeling an orange—which requires both agility and speed. Today the one who is the first to remove the rind in a perfect spiral wins my admiration and the seat of honor at our lovely host's right hand." He motioned toward the empty seat beside me and bowed.

I nodded, blinking back tears of gratitude. He'd spoken more regally than any king, and now every woman at my table madly peeled her orange. I drained my goblet, ashamed of how I'd treated the man who was about to recount the most painful parts of his life as entertainment for my guests.

"Abba fell in love with my ima the moment he saw her," Joseph began. "He worked as a shepherd for seven years to earn her brideprice. On the night of their wedding, her abba deceived him by sending her sister into the wedding tent when my abba was too drunk to notice."

"What a crook!" one woman cried.

"Pharaoh Khyan would have cut out his liver," Queen Tani added.

Joseph grinned. "I suspect my abba considered Pharaoh's solution, but he finished the first wedding week with Ima Leah and agreed to work another seven years for my ima—Rachel. They shared their wedding week immediately after Ima Leah's."

Quiet whispers fluttered among the women, but I concentrated on my orange rind with practiced skill. "How sad for the first wife," I said without lifting my head. Joseph had grabbed our hearts with the mastery of a king's scribe.

"Ima Leah was sad for many years, but Elohim—the Creator of all things—opened her womb because He knew she was unloved."

Ziwat cackled. "Well, your god must have opened Rachel's womb as well."

"True, but years later. As she waited, Ima Rachel grew desperate and gave her maid to Abba so her maid could bear children for her. When Ima Leah stopped bearing, she too gave her maidservant to Abba as a wife."

Tani chuckled. "Sounds like the harems in Upper Eshypt." Easy laughter rolled like ocean waves at the queen's slurred speech.

Odd. Even my senses seemed a little dulled by the eronda. No more wine. I was almost finished with my perfectly spiral orange peel.

"When Ima Leah conceived for the seventh time," Joseph continued, "Abba Jacob had ten sons, and Elohim finally opened Ima Rachel's womb. I was born only a day after Ima Leah's only daughter, Dinah. Though Abba's wives were very different, he once told me he loved them both—Ima Rachel with a burning like the sun and Ima Leah like the beating of his heart."

The lovely sentiment brought tears to my eyes as I finished my perfect spiral rind and—

"Bandages, Ahira!" Joseph shouted, jolting the knife in my hand. I felt no pain but stared at a trickle of blood running down my thumb. *These knives must be sharper than—*

"Get bandages!" Another shout. Distant. Muffled.

I raised my head. People had swarmed my banquet table. Pandemonium. Where had they come from?

"Mistress?" Ahira bent over me. "Let me see your hand."

"What's happening?" Panic gripped me, the room spinning.

"My baby!" A woman writhed on the floor, gripping her belly. "Save my baby!" I forced focus and recognized the wife of Pharaoh's physician.

Queen Tani staggered toward me, screaming, "What have you done to us?"

"Me?" I leapt to my feet. "You did this! All of you have driven me mad!"

The queen stumbled toward the door as Joseph wrapped her bloody hand with Ahira's cloth belt.

Gaios appeared. "Mistress, calm down."

Faithful, dear Gaios. "Did you see how they treated me?"

"How much eronda did you tell Pushpa to put in the wine?" he asked.

I squinted amid my haze, trying to remember. Women were fleeing the villa, weeping and bloodied. Half-peeled oranges lay on the table, my carefully crafted paintings stained with my grand failure.

"Leave me alone, Gaios." I shoved him away but bungled my indignation by tripping over his foot. My legs carried me past nondescript faces and muted sounds. I needed a hole to hide in, a grave to die in. I reached for the detestable image of Seth in my belt and hurled him at the wall as I passed through the tapestries and into the residence hall.

"Mistress Zully, I followed your instruct—"

I ran past Pushpa. Something had gone terribly wrong with the wine. But what did it matter whose fault it was? It was my banquet. My reputation. My life that had been ruined.

The Medjays opened my door. I ran across the threshold and straight to Ahira's adjoining room, preferring cramped, dark isolation to the trappings of a life I despised. Pressing my face against her lamb's wool headrest, I muffled my demand. "Kill me now, Elohim, god of slaves and princes. If you opened a desperate woman's womb, you could end my misery." The room spun around me.

"Shh, Zully. Shh." Gentle arms cradled my shoulders and knees, then lifted me and carried me into the light.

"Leave me to Elohim." I passed Ahira. Was she a dream? I reached for her hand.

"Leave us!" Gaios's angry voice startled me. "I'll answer questions later. Go to your chamber . . . Don't be afraid, Zully." He spoke softly now. "I'll take care of everything."

Blinking, I tried to clear the haze. "Where are you taking me?"

He laid me on a couch. My couch. In my courtyard.

"There now. Relax." He sat beside me and then leaned close. Very close.

A rush of fear cleared my head. "Gaios—"

"Shh. Do you trust me, Zully?"

My mind raced through what had just happened. "Those women. The wine."

"I'll take care of all that." His head tilted. "Do you believe me?"

"Gaios, it was so—"

"Zully." He brushed my cheek. "Do you trust me?"

His presence calmed me. This was Gaios. *My* Gaios. "Of course."

"Then know everything I do is because I love you." He brushed his lips over mine.

I pulled away, gasping.

"Shh. It's okay." His lips curved into a tender smile. "I love you, Princess Zuleika." His next kiss covered my mouth, leaving no room for misunderstanding.

I pushed against his chest. "Gaios, stop!"

He seemed angry at first but inhaled sharply—and exhaled eerie calm. He hovered over me. "I'll protect you, Zully, if you do exactly as I say." His hand traveled down the curve of my hip.

"No, Gaios. Wait." I tried to sit up, but he pressed my shoulders against the couch.

"No more waiting, Zully."

Even in my delirium, his intention was clear. "Gaios, you're my dearest friend, but—"

"And I couldn't bear to lose you, Zully."

"Lose me? What do you—"

"There was too much eronda in the wine. The vizier's wife slipped while cutting her orange and sliced her wrist. And eronda is an abortive, Zully. The physician's wife may lose her unborn child."

"What? No! I gave Pushpa the precise quantities—"

"Since I work in the kitchen, I could testify that our Hebrew chamberlain had access to the wine. I could also accuse any of the Minoans. But Pushpa is the more sympathetic target. I'll swear she was overwhelmed with banquet preparations and overmeasured the eronda." He brushed my cheek with his lips and whispered, "I protected you from such ugliness in Zakros, my love. In Egypt we'll protect each other." When our eyes met, the darkness in him chilled me. "I found a supplier of eronda in Avaris, Zully. I bought all he had. Soon we'll leave this place; then you and I will never be parted again. You're mine now."

Gaios's kisses were no longer gentle, his touch no longer a friend's. Evil covered me like a blanket. Horrified, I let my mind slip away. My body was an object, detached from self. As if in a freakish, unholy dream, he stole what wasn't his. I endured. I wept.

His weight lifted, and I curled into a ball. He dressed while I lay in the aftermath. *How could this have happened?* In the haze of confusion and shame, I glimpsed the sacred Minoan treasures in my chamber. Was my determination to return to Crete worth *this* price? But I had no one else to turn to. As terrifying as Gaios had become, he was still my only hope of returning home.

"Don't be frightened, Zully." He sat beside me on the couch. "Pushpa was already wringing her hands before the last guest fled, afraid she'd used too much of an unfamiliar Minoan spice. No one would dare charge 'the great Potiphar's ommi' with willful wrongdoing."

He leaned down to kiss me, but I recoiled, whimpering. "Please, Gaios. Go." He loomed over me, but I couldn't look at him.

"Be careful, Zul, or Egypt's noblewomen will believe your madness is real—since you confessed it at your own banquet."

I bolted upright, my head swimming, and met his mocking smile. "Gaios, I was upset. Angry. I said *they* had driven me mad."

"With the incestuous lines of the pharaohs, no one jests about hysteria in Egypt, Zully." He bent to one knee, drawing too close. "Those women will blame you for the wine—claiming hysteria as the cause and revenge as your motive. You could be imprisoned or executed or—possibly worse, Zully—treated by one of their magicians or physicians."

Gaios's face blurred, and the sky above me seemed to swirl. My breaths came in quick gasps. Gaios's face was suddenly hovering over me.

"I said I'll fix it, my love." Another gentle kiss. "Asking Joseph to entertain them was brilliant," Gaios said, sitting beside me. "I may even be able to implicate him. The noblemen will be gracious to kind-hearted old Pushpa, but they'll show no mercy to a Hebrew."

My sluggish mind tried to keep up with his words, which felt unnecessarily complex.

He kissed me again before hurrying out of the courtyard. "I'll check Pushpa's notes with your original wine recipe, Mistress." It was a contrived goodbye for the guards to hear. "I'm sure she never intended to harm anyone."

The door slammed. My body melted into the couch, and I gazed at the cloudless sky. Did the invisible Hebrew god see a despicable Minoan princess? Had he watched me sell myself to rebuild Crete? Betray Ahira to establish control of a slave who now controlled me? "If you're there," I whispered, "either strike me dead for my faults, or prove to me you exist."

I watched the sky for any sign of the Hebrew god, who supposedly held the world in his hands yet knew the thoughts of every heart. *Nothing.* In that moment, I was more alone than ever.

Not even death could restore my dignity.

SEVENTEEN

I will put enmity
  between you and the woman,
  and between your offspring and hers;
he will crush your head,
  and you will strike his heel.

GENESIS 3:15

Time stood still in Ahira's windowless chamber. She had recognized the dangerous glint in Gaios's eyes, that of a predator with its prey as he carried the mistress toward the courtyard. But how could she have helped?

Elohim, where are You when I need Your protection?

Sandals slapped the tiles outside her chamber. "I'll check Pushpa's notes with your original wine recipe, Mistress." Gaios was leaving. "I'm sure she never intended to harm anyone."

Would Gaios blame Pushpa for the tainted wine? Ahira's breath caught. An accusation like that could become a criminal complaint—at least in Prince Jacob's camp. Replaying the day's events, she rolled them around like a hand mill, each memory crushing. Then the realization . . . *I poured the wine!*

Would she be named an accomplice? The sound of weeping crashed through her fear. Ahira cracked open her adjoining door, listening. The crying came from the courtyard, so she left her little chamber and padded across the tiles to peer outside. Her mistress huddled on the couch, nearly naked.

Ahira ran toward her. "Mistress, did he hurt you?"

The mistress covered herself and wiped her face. "Ahira. Leave me." Her voice broke.

Ahira recognized the shame left behind when a man takes a woman's body—and her spirit with it. Ahira moved slowly to the other end of the couch and sat down.

"You don't have to be nice to me," the mistress whispered. "I've been horrible to you."

She had, but Ahira knew better than to speak unadorned truth to the mistress now. "Those women were horrible to you, Mistress."

Slowly she lifted her tear-streaked face. "I didn't think Gaios would hurt anyone until . . ." Her face twisted with emotion. "Pateras was right. He's dangerous. He'll blame me for the tainted wine unless I do whatever he asks. He's not the same man I knew in Crete, but he's the only one who can help me return." She looked away. "He loves me—in his own way."

"Mistress, no! Love doesn't humiliate or hurt." The words struck her like a blow. Abba had shouted the same wisdom when she'd declared her love for Simeon. "Think about those whose love is patient, kind, and gives without demands—like me and Pushpa—and let us help you." Ahira offered her hand.

The mistress pursed her lips and stared at Ahira's hand as though standing on the edge of a cliff. "Gaios is the only one who can protect me. He's always been my defender." She shook her head and turned away. "He'll discover who tainted the wine and make sure I'm safe."

Ahira tried to hide her shock. Would the mistress allow Gaios to do *anything* to ensure her safety? "Are you sure it was the wine?"

"It had to be. I gave Pushpa the bag of eronda from my shrine with explicit written instructions to use only the size of a ring in each pitcher. To cause the kind of overdosing we saw, she must have used the entire bag."

"Pushpa is not careless, Mistress, and she would never intentionally—"

"I know!" She slammed her hands into her lap with a frustrated sigh.

Ahira scooted off the couch and bowed quickly. "Forgive me, Mistress."

"No, Ahira." The mistress caught her hand. "Forgive *me*."

Ahira stiffened, too prudent to swoon at a simple apology.

"Do you believe in Joseph's god, Ahira? This Elohim, the Creator of all things?"

"My abba taught me of Him, Mistress, and I believe He lives and blesses those He favors." She swallowed the lump forming in her throat. "I am not so favored."

"Which humans are favored, Ahira?" Her tone dripped with cynicism. "Who escapes the gods' sick games?"

Hopelessness echoed between them.

"Of this I'm sure, Mistress: there is only one God."

The mistress lifted one brow. Was she intrigued?

"Elohim made a promise to one man," Ahira continued. "He vowed that through Abraham ben Terah and his descendants, all nations of the earth will be blessed."

"What do you mean *blessed*? Could he help rebuild Crete?"

Ahira tried not to grin at her mistress's singular focus. "You must think much larger, Mistress. To *every* nation, the blessing is given. The blessing will arrive in a man who will crush the ancient deceiver and restore communion with Elohim, but until then . . ." Ahira remembered Abba's words each time a stillborn lamb was born. "Until then we live and die with pain."

Her mistress stared at her. "It's a nice story but similar to other legends of the gods."

"Abba said all the most convincing lies have a seed of truth at their beginning. Elohim is the truth at the root of every god's deception."

"You sound quite committed to this god, Ahira." She left the couch to sit beside the pond and swirled her finger amid the closed lotus blossoms. "He didn't strike me dead, so perhaps he'll carry me to Crete."

"Why would He strike you dead, Mistress?"

"I want you to call me Zully." She lifted a lotus blossom from the pond.

Ahira must obey. "Of course—Zully."

"They're fascinating, aren't they?" Zully inspected the bloom in her hand. "Opening to release their lovely fragrance each morning and closing to protect themselves from burning afternoon sun. Did you know they refresh themselves overnight so they can do it all again when morning comes?"

"Yes, Mis—Zully. Pushpa told me about the lotus—"

Zully crushed the flower violently, shredding it with both hands. "In the end, it's only another fragile plant, easier to destroy than an ugly thistle." She let the pieces fall and the fragrance rise.

Ahira knelt beside her. "But only the lotus is so treasured, Zully. A thousand thistles can irritate or wound, but the lotus is sacred because it's unique."

"Beautifully phrased, Ahira. You should have been a scribe." She brushed her hand across the pond's surface, raining water over the sunbaked tiles. "I'm parched. Go to the kitchen, and see if any tainted wine remains." She paused. "I'll need it if Gaios's seed takes root in my belly."

Ahira's heart broke at the sight of the Minoan lotus sitting by her pond. Her mistress carried the weight of two worlds on her shoulders. Could she help lift the burden? *Elohim, You are the one true God, and only You can protect me in Egypt. Would You protect Zully too?*

Ahira hurried out the chamber door but pressed her back against the wall when she saw Potiphar's guards and Pharaoh's soldiers gathered outside the kitchen. Joseph emerged from the small room he used for keeping the estate records. She used their tribe's shepherd's signal to gain his attention, a burst of air between her front teeth, and he turned.

He rushed toward her, guided her into the guest room, and closed the door behind them.

Panic started to rise. Memories of Simeon and the captive train launched her toward the door.

"Ahira, no. Wait." Joseph blocked her path. "They're questioning Pushpa."

"Who's questioning her?"

"Vizier Wereni. He came immediately after his day at court. His wife told him about the banquet, still hysterical and bleeding. Hami escorted him here and suggested I be questioned first."

"Why you?"

"I'm the chamberlain." His features hardened. "Gaios testified next and said that I distracted the noblewomen with stories while they lost themselves in drink."

"Joseph, no!"

"He told them Potiphar made me chamberlain because Pushpa's record keeping had shown signs of memory issues. He implied it was Pushpa who likely used too much eronda in the mulled wine."

"But Pushpa is as sharp as obsidian. I watched her measure—"

"No!" Joseph grabbed her shoulders. "You saw nothing."

Instinctively she twisted from his grasp, unable to bear a man's confinement.

"Ahira, you're safe. Shalom, Ahira. Shalom."

Shalom. The Hebrew word for "peace" breathed with the scent of cloves and mint . . . Ahira opened her eyes.

"Are you all right?" he asked. "I need to know you're all right."

"Fine, yes. May I go?"

"I don't want them to question you. Gaios is cunning, and I believe he knows more about the wine than he's saying."

"Did *he* taint the wine?"

Joseph's tense pause was answer enough. "Pushpa tried to take responsibility, but none of it made sense. She pointed out to the vizier how much Minoan mint remained in the bag, proving she'd used the correct measurement in the wine."

"So it couldn't have been the wine."

Joseph lifted his brow. "It couldn't have been *Pushpa*."

The door was suddenly flung open, revealing a hallway full of soldiers and a wiry Egyptian with an angry glare. "You Hebrews multiply
like desert hares." Ahira backed deeper into the chamber.

"That's the maid, Vizier Wereni." Gaios stood beside him. "She
served the wine."

Egypt's acting pharaoh grabbed her arm and pulled her into the
hall. "Is it true? Did you pour wine for every guest?"

Was it *every* guest? "I think so, my lord."

"You think so?" He scoffed. "Will a beating make you more certain?"

"No, my lord. I served the wine, but some women refilled their
own goblets." Soldiers surrounded Wereni, while four Medjays separated them from Pushpa, guarding Potiphar's ommi like a treasure.

The vizier gripped Ahira's face. "Are you sure the king's *Medjay* wife
didn't slip something into the pitchers or goblets?"

"Vizier Wereni!" Pushpa cried.

He shoved Ahira at Joseph. "If you and your Hebrew lover conspired to shed pure Egyptian blood, girl, Queen Tani herself won't be
able to save you."

"Vizier Wereni." Pushpa's tone was restrained fury. "If my son
returns to find his property damaged—be it human or field or flock—
he'll regret having given you his beloved Egyptian steward. Betray my
son's kindness once, as your shepherds did in the pastures, and he may
forgive. Betray him twice, Lord Vizier, and Potiphar's wrath is very
unpredictable."

Wereni turned slowly to the brave woman. "Are you threatening
me, Mistress Pushpa?"

"I would never." She straightened her shoulders, holding his gaze.
"I'm only aiding your investigation. Perhaps you should question the
women who attended. Your wife tells me shaming Princess Zuleika has
become a new game among the nobility. What better way than to ruin
her first banquet?"

The vizier didn't seem surprised at Pushpa's connections or her accusation. "We're done here." He glared at Gaios. "You're a useful little rodent. What are you?"

"My lord?"

Pushpa laughed. "He's a Cretan, Wereni, and if you make him your pet, he'll bite you."

The vizier scoffed and waved Gaios away as the sea of soldiers parted for him and then followed him out of the villa.

Joseph leaned close. "Be certain of this, Ahira: Gaios had something to do with the wine. This war is just starting."

EIGHTEEN

Whoever derides their neighbor has no sense,
  but the one who has understanding holds their tongue.
PROVERBS 11:12

SIX MONTHS LATER
Joseph

Joseph closed the office door and stretched his arms toward the ceiling. It had been a long day, and an even longer night lay ahead. His weekly meetings with Hami and Abasi felt like swimming the Nile with a millstone on each leg. The old steward begrudged every word of his reports on Vizier Wereni's treason. Thus far he'd given no solid proof of a conspiracy against Pharaoh Khyan.

Joseph's bigger concern was Mistress Zuleika. He hadn't seen her since the disastrous banquet, and she hadn't been at today's akhet festival—the largest celebration of the year. Vizier Wereni, speaking as the king's mouthpiece, had declared the Nile's paltry Inundation to be indicative of the gods' displeasure. His next remarks were thinly veiled treason, inciting pure-born Egyptians to sell goods only to one another. The festival had devolved into riots, and Hami spent most of his day dealing with death threats against the vizier. Today's events would, of course, reach Master Potiphar without needing to be recorded in Abasi's secret reports.

But how would they affect the master's wife?

Joseph glanced right toward the kitchen, where Hami and Pushpa waited to share a cup of mint tea with him. He glanced left toward Mistress Zuleika's chamber and was filled with rising dread. His feet started moving before his mind could overrule them.

One of the chamber guards knocked on her door. "The chamberlain to see Mistress Zuleika."

Joseph waited.

The guards exchanged a concerned glance and knocked again. "The chamberlain to see—"

Gaios flung open the door. "Yes, yes, come in, Lord Chamberlain." Dispensing with the pretense of a bow, he swept his hand toward the chamber. "It's rather late, and Zully was finishing one of her paintings."

Zully. His familiarity with her grated. Joseph entered a veritable showplace of paintings, pottery, and faience jewelry. "Mistress, did you do all this?" Silence answered, and his concern deepened as he approached a small table where Ahira sat across from her mistress. "I was concerned when I didn't see either of you at the akhet festival."

"Your concern is unnecessary." The mistress remained bent over her painting, but her hands were clasped in her lap. No paints at the ready. No brush in her hand.

"Ahira, are you well?" Joseph asked. They'd grown comfortable in each other's company since she sometimes joined Hami and him for evening tea with Pushpa.

Her smile was genuine, but he sensed more sadness than usual. "Isn't Hami waiting for you in the kitchen?" she asked.

"I've seen you and Hami leave the villa together each week." Gaios spoke before Joseph could answer. "Is he teaching you to fight?"

"Unfortunately, no." Joseph moved past him and crouched beside the mistress, fears confirmed when he saw her sallow complexion and the dark shadows beneath her eyes. "Mistress, you're not a captive here. You need not limit yourself to your chamber or the potter's wheel on the roof. Ahira or I could escort you to see the lambs in the master's pastures. They're only a few months old."

"Why would you drag our mistress into danger?" Gaios stood over him like a scolding tutor. "After Vizier Wereni's blatant display of bigotry at today's festival, why would you parade Zully—the *foreign* wife of Egypt's beloved hero—into the boiling cauldron of revolt?"

"Pharaoh's army restored order, and the festival continued, Gaios." Joseph stood, overshadowing the spindly servant. "If foreign-born citizens hide when Wereni declares Inundation level their fault, he's won the war before the battle—"

"No, no, enough!" The mistress covered her ears. "Leave, Joseph. I don't want to hear about Wereni."

"Mistress, you're safe." Joseph tried to reassure her, but Ahira waved him away.

"She asked you to leave." Gaios sounded more like a sentry than a slave.

"Go, Joseph," Ahira said. "It's better if you leave us."

Saddened and horrified, he strode out the door and marched to the kitchen. Hami and Pushpa looked up when he barged in. "We have to get rid of Gaios."

Pushpa's brows rose. "And a good evening to you, Chamberlain."

Hami met him before Joseph reached the steaming cup. "You're too late for tea. We shouldn't keep old Abasi waiting." The Medjay pushed Joseph out the door.

"Gaios goes," Joseph called to Pushpa over his shoulder.

In the hallway, Hami donned the detached mystique of a Medjay, but Joseph pressed him. "Master Potiphar entrusted us with Mistress Zuleika's well-being before he left, Hami. Have you seen her?"

"Yes."

"Why didn't you tell me she was withering away?"

"There was nothing to be done. Pushpa won't allow Gaios to be sold."

"Has Pushpa seen her?"

"Pushpa trusts Ahira's loyalty to the mistress more than she distrusts Gaios. Much like Captain Potiphar trusts Abasi's loyalty to Egypt more than he distrusts Vizier Wereni."

"This isn't about Wereni and conspiracies," Joseph protested. "It's about rescuing an innocent woman from unnecessary pain."

Hami scoffed. "No one is innocent, Chamberlain, and pain is the best teacher." He swatted Joseph's head. "Now, concentrate. We must go into the night and meet with the bigoted steward."

Joseph followed the Medjay closely, hugging the shadows of the three-story wall surrounding the palace complex. They passed the centerpiece of Pharaoh's royal complex—the lotus-filled pond—lit by shimmering moonlight. The barely stirring waters, fed by Nile tributaries, provided a cool respite from Egypt's daytime sun as Pharaoh's visitors, guards, and nobility strolled the pristine grounds. But at night the complex was as deserted as a burial cave.

Hami pressed his back against the wall, then looked left and right. The next twenty paces were the most dangerous. Since there was no cover, they had to sprint from the shadows to a hidden entrance used only by the vizier's personal guards. The area was completely exposed to the watchmen on the palace walls. Every week, Joseph remembered Potiphar's instruction to his chief Medjay: *If you're caught and questioned, my friend, you'll know how to deflect suspicion.* What possible reason could Hami concoct for leading Potiphar's chamberlain into the vizier's private entrance at night?

Hami thrust his arm forward, his signal to move ahead of him. As Joseph took his first step, a trumpet blast split the silence. He pressed himself against the wall, heart pounding, and glanced sideways at Hami. Guards on the wall above showered fiery arrows on something—or someone—outside the palace complex. Hami gestured wildly toward the vizier's villa. Go! Go! Go!

Joseph ran. Didn't look back. He counted the twenty strides. Flattened himself against the vizier's wall. *Breathe. Slowly. Quietly.* He released his breath and glanced around the corner. A lamp burned in the window beside the entrance. A soft thud, and Hami beside him. The Medjay whistled softly, the call of a nightjar.

The door opened and they slipped inside.

"It's about time." Abasi's new wig bobbed as he scolded.

"Tell us quickly, Abasi, and we'll be gone." Joseph unrolled the waiting scroll on a chest-high shelf near the door and dipped a quill in the pigments.

Abasi held his oil lamp higher, his hand trembling, forcing a smile. "If I wished to inspect your previous reports, *Joseph,* where would I find those scrolls?" His voice squeaked.

"You've never called the Hebrew by his name." Hami stepped closer. "A crocodile hides its teeth only to lure prey."

"No, I would never betray—" He glanced at Joseph, then Hami. "I merely wanted the scrolls because . . ." In the hesitation, the steward's countenance changed. He glared at Hami and raised his chin. "I refuse to divulge any more secrets about Vizier Wereni, and I want the previous scrolls destroyed. The vizier is a good man. Loyal to Egypt."

Joseph's heart leapt into his throat. Had Abasi betrayed them? Would Pharaoh's soldiers burst through the doors and arrest them? Joseph had questioned Abasi's loyalty last week when he denied knowledge of Wereni's rulings against Egypt's foreign citizens and described the vizier as "a good man at heart."

"You must choose, Abasi." Hami advanced on Abasi like a predator on prey. "Obey Captain Potiphar, the man who saved you, provided for you, and asked for your loyalty in return or . . ." He moved closer. "Or I will kill you."

"I'll be loyal to Master Potiphar *always.*" The steward whimpered. "That is my choice."

"Then give your report, old man." Hami crossed his arms.

Abasi removed his new wig and wiped sweat from his brow. "Vizier Wereni asks me to paint the Eye of Horus on his face each morning, and his few favors for Egyptian noblemen and merchants seem harmless to one such as me."

Joseph sighed, weary of the man's games. "Explain why three booths in the royal market belonging to Amu merchants closed last week and new businesses—Egyptian merchants—filled the spaces yesterday, the day before the festival."

"Egyptians are ambitious and offer better merchandise." Abasi's lip curled, obnoxious even in dim lighting. "Record all you wish in your little scroll, Hebrew, but if that Hyksos king arrests Vizier Wereni, I'll testify he's a loyal Egyptian and obedient to his pharaoh."

"And who is *his pharaoh*?" Hami's blade was suddenly at Abasi's throat. "I'm tired, old man."

"The merchants are from On." Abasi's eyes closed with the confession. "I don't know their names or the vizier's contact in On."

Joseph barely stifled a gasp.

"Recite for Joseph every nobleman's name involved in Wereni's conspiracy." The Medjay ground out the instruction.

In a shaky voice, Abasi dictated, and Joseph wrote furiously. It was more information than they'd heard in the six months since Potiphar left. And it was gold. The city of On, home of the sun god, Ra, held many connections for Wereni, Ra's former priest.

Abasi spoke the last conspirator's name. "I know nothing else, Medjay." He winced and dabbed at a drop of blood on his neck when Hami released him.

"Your loyalty to Egypt is noble," Joseph said. "And your loyalty to Potiphar commendable. However, Wereni's treachery will get good Egyptians killed. He won't help unite Lower and Upper Egypt, Abasi. He'll drive a deeper wedge between two pharaohs who have agreed to live at peace. By helping Master Potiphar, you save Egyptian lives and preserve peace. For that, I commend you."

"He's a croaking toad." The Medjay rolled up the scroll and pointed it at Abasi. "Next week, I use the dagger first."

Joseph followed his friend into the darkness and paused at the wall until he received the signal to cross the divide into shadowed safety. From there, he continued in the Medjay's carefully placed footsteps until they reached the master's chamber.

When Hami turned to face him, Joseph saw his own concern reflected in his friend's expression. "We must send another message to Captain Potiphar."

"I didn't know you'd been in contact. When did you last hear from him?"

"Today." Hami pulled a small folded papyrus from his waist pouch. "Sometimes I have Pushpa read them. It's not good for any one person in the villa to know everything."

Joseph read the missive: *Tehenu tribes stronger than expected.*

"Don't tell me where you've hidden the scrolls." Hami's stare was still friendly but intense. "Captain Potiphar trusts you. He trusts Pushpa. He trusts me. But I tell you, my friend: no one should know everything about anything."

"Understood." Joseph relaxed into the logic, but his concern for the mistress reemerged and intensified. "Ahira said the mistress hadn't received any messages. Has the master not written to his wife, or has Gaios kept the missives from her?"

"There have been no messages for the mistress. And, Hebrew . . ."

"What?"

Potiphar's guard scowled. "The captain's marriage is not our—"

"Mistress Zuleika doesn't leave the villa. She seems diminished. She sees only Ahira and Gaios, and Gaios seems to hold sway over her. At least mention to Master Potiphar that his wife needs him."

Hami barked a laugh. "I will *not* mention to a soldier that his wife needs him when he's a week's march away and there are twenty healthy men living upstairs."

Joseph hadn't considered that. "All right, Commander. I trust your judgment, but you shouldn't laugh. You sound like a jackal."

He gave Joseph a good-natured shove. "Keep the scrolls well hidden, and tell Ahira to cheer the mistress with a daily stroll around the palace pond." Sobering, he pointed to the message in Joseph's hand. "The timing of the Tehenu rebellion and Vizier Wereni's connections with the priests of On hint at treachery reaching both west and south. The Tehenu's unexpected strength could have come from Upper Egypt and might have been stirred to lure Pharaoh and his protectors from Avaris. Be watchful, Joseph, for yourself and your mistress."

NINETEEN

The righteous lead blameless lives;
blessed are their children after them.

PROVERBS 20:7

Potiphar

Avaris perched on the horizon like Lower Egypt's crown on Khyan's head. Beckoning. Coaxing the men through the warm, marshy delta, which had tugged at the army's sandals for two days.

"Nearly home . . . my king." Potiphar kept his words few on the grueling trek.

Theoretically Khyan had taken fewer strides since his legs were longer, but even the great god was wilting like a human in the midday sun. General Apophis and his army stretched behind them, guarding cooks, supply carts, and Tehenu captives, who had spent their last drop of courage to march into slavery.

The return journey after nearly a year of battle was more circuitous than their march to face the western border rebels. Pharaoh's army had started for home a week previously, sailing down one branch of the Nile and up another since, in his last message, Hami was still unsure whether the zealots were taking orders from Thebes or an Abydos governor rumored to claim Ra's divinity.

"You seemed uncomfortable . . . in the Bubastis temple." Khyan's words came in short bursts, his breath as shallow as Potiphar's.

"I'm uncomfortable . . . in any temple."

While sailing the Tanitic branch, Potiphar had sent scouts ahead to Bubastis to ensure the city dedicated to the cat god was safe for their overnight rest. Khyan insisted on sacrificing in their temple to honor the Egyptian soldiers' bravery, which helped save the western border.

"Also uncomfortable . . . because . . . I hate cats," Potiphar added with a wry grin.

They'd set sail immediately after the sacrifice, debarked at an undisclosed location, and marched without rest for two days. With every step, Potiphar's mind replayed the assassin's spear in flight. "Let me kill Wereni."

Khyan's dry, cracked lips curved into a grin. "Patience. We need names. Coconspirators."

"Let me torture him."

The grin disappeared. "My decision . . . is . . . final."

"Forgive me . . . Great Khyan."

"Halt!" The king leaned over, hands braced on his knees, and looked up at Potiphar. "You earned a lifetime of forgiveness when you saved my life. How's your shoulder?"

The sling Potiphar wore on his left arm was more nuisance than cure. "A mere scratch." But when he lifted it to demonstrate, a sharp pain stole his breath.

"That scratch nearly cost your life. A few finger widths over, and I would have delivered your heart in a canopic jar to your widow."

Potiphar knew what he said was true. The injury had sobered him. He glanced around to be sure no one could hear and lowered his voice. "I should thank you for this injury. I've realized my marriage isn't a millstone around my neck. Zuleika and I need children to care for us in the underworld. My soldiers have vowed that they and their children will provide for me, but what of Zuleika? I vowed to provide for her, but only children truly tend the souls of eternity." Providing for his ancestors was the only annual offering Potiphar made in Seth's temple, the only reason he appeased gods—if they existed at all.

"Have you told her of this new commitment?" The mischief in the king's voice drew his attention. "Surely some of those messengers I saw traveling back and forth carried greetings to your wife."

"Most were from Hami." He tried to deflect the king's question, but Khyan's stare was relentless.

"Did you write to her?"

Potiphar's guilt slowed his steps. "The battles were fiercer than we expected. A month went by. Then two. Then it had been so long, I didn't know what to say."

"You're in deep trouble, my friend." Khyan wagged his head.

"This is why your captain never wanted a wife, Pharaoh Khyan. My whole focus should be devoted to your protection." He withdrew the papyrus message from his belt and held it aloft. "Such as this message from my informant in Sobekhotep's palace. Need I remind you that Thebes could be an ally, not an enemy, in this fight?"

"Or it could be a trap." Khyan gave him a sidelong glance. "Tell me again why my captain trusts a priest of Ra in Pharaoh Sobekhotep's patron temple."

Potiphar had told his friend only some details of his past, but now *Pharaoh* needed them all. "My ommi became enchantress of Ra's temple in On. Monthhotep heard of her skills and stole her away to his temple in Memphis."

"Becoming the enchantress of Memphis is a great honor."

"Except when the enchantress never worshipped the sun god. She only wanted men to worship *her*." His revelation was met with silence, the great Khyan's face expressionless.

"By the time you and I marched on Memphis to destroy Monthhotep's reign, my abi had already died."

"I don't remember seeing your abi sober."

"Now you know why." Fending off pity, Potiphar continued, "When we destroyed Ra's temple, I recognized one of the surviving priests from my childhood in On. He showed me where my ommi lay dead and then begged me to spare his life. I put him on a barque to Thebes and told him someday I'd ask a favor in return."

"The priest you trust from Pharaoh Sobekhotep's patron temple."

Potiphar nodded.

"I'm sorry you never said goodbye to your ommi."

Potiphar set aside the bitter memories. "My ommi waits for me in Avaris."

"She is ommi to us both, brother."

As they neared the Pelusiac shore, the threat of danger increased, but Avaris and their families waited on the other side. "Alert now!" Potiphar shouted, life surging through him. "My king, I would ask you to *get small,* but that seems a *tall order.*"

Khyan unsheathed his sword. "Your jests are getting old, my friend." The two stood back to back as they'd done a hundred times in battle. Medjays formed three concentric circles around them: those in the first and third circles with arrows nocked, and those mid-circle with spears on their shoulder ready for launch.

"First battalion advance!" Apophis gave his order, and Pharaoh's regular army marched past his royal guards.

"Circle right, my king." Potiphar moved first, eyes darting every direction for signs of ambush. Hami's last message said their enemy used the Pelusiac for all communication.

"Second battalion, advance!" The king's brother-in-law approached the wall of Medjays. "The second battalion will use barques to form a bridge for you, Great Khyan. I'll ensure the rest of your army provides sufficient rear guard." He paused. "I think we've made it home, my king."

"No!" Potiphar growled. "We don't stop defending, General, until your king is inside his chamber."

"Yes, Captain!" Apophis slammed his fist against his chest and rushed toward the shoreline. "Get those barques in place!"

"I think we've made it home too." Khyan's low rumble was full of mischief, but Potiphar wouldn't let himself relax.

Potiphar leaned his head against his friend's back. "You're the one who always said, 'One mistake ends it all.'"

"One mistake did end it all." Potiphar heard the pain in his voice. Khyan likely still blamed himself for his abi's death, but King Bnon had refused a food taster.

"You couldn't have stopped a kitchen slave's poison."

"You can't guard every kitchen slave either, my friend. If the gods will it, Wereni will end me."

"Let me arrest Wereni *now.*"

Pharaoh paused. Was he considering it—or giving them both time to calm? "We must get to the root of hatred, Potiphar, so those worthy of respect receive it. Egypt's king should deserve the throne, not have it handed to him because he's Egyptian."

"Come, great king!" The general waited on the first of the barques that formed the makeshift bridge. "Return to your people, O Great Khyan, mighty in wisdom and power, born of the storm god, Seth, and blessed by Hathor, goddess of love. Let your people gaze on your presence and refresh their withered souls by the beauty of your mighty countenance."

The king sighed and sheathed his sword.

Potiphar did the same, wondering whether his friend ever tired of the endless pomp. "Let's move." At Potiphar's quiet directive, a sharp contrast to the general's shout, his Medjays advanced in perfect formation. Potiphar, however, resumed his position at Pharaoh's right side. "Remember, the danger doesn't end inside the palace complex, my king."

Khyan glared down at him. "Could we please enjoy our processional? I intend to concentrate on my family for the next week. Lock me in the harem if you must, but—" His eyes widened. "You should do the same. You still need a wedding week with your bride."

"Oh no." Potiphar huffed. "There's way too much danger for—"

"I command it. Hami is well trained and more familiar with what's happening in Avaris than you are. Let your shoulder heal. I don't want to see you for a week, Captain. Is that clear?"

"I—"

"Say, 'Yes, my king.' "

"Yes, my king." But Potiphar's mind was spinning at the sight of crushing crowds lining their path to the palace complex. "Hold formation all the way!" he shouted at his men.

The people roared with excitement, casting flowers before them.

The scent of lotus filled the air as they rushed toward the complex gates. The massive entrance closed behind them, and now the nobility closed in. Potiphar scanned every hand, schenti, and sandal. Did anyone conceal a weapon?

"Look, Potiphar." Khyan pointed toward the palace steps. "There they are."

"Wereni?" Potiphar found the man, and white-hot hate surged through him.

Pharaoh laughed. "No, Tani and Ziwat. They're actually talking to each other. Tani is holding our new son. See them? Your wife and Pushpa are standing beside them."

The sight of them near Wereni felt like a boulder in his gut. "Has Ommi ever stood publicly with your wives, Pharaoh Khyan?"

His friend's smile faded. Though both Pushpa's parents were Egyptian nobility, she preferred the villa kitchen to displaying her position in public.

"Wereni." A razor's edge in the king's tone proved he understood.

"Ommi is a shield between that weasel and my wife."

"Hami is behind them," Khyan said in a coarse whisper. "Your women are safe, Captain. Focus."

"Of course, my king." He was focused—on Zuleika. Soft curls fell over her shoulders, and she wore a simple white robe with a single necklace. His wife was even more beautiful than he remembered. Princess Zuleika of Zakros Palace. And she was his.

"Do you see it?" Khyan asked.

See what? Potiphar immediately shifted his attention to Wereni and noted his left eye glaringly naked. "No Eye of Horus."

Khyan's pace quickened as they neared the palace steps. "We conquered the foreign rebellion and returned to even bolder rebels at home."

"So it appears." Potiphar moved as one with the king at his right while Medjays followed them up the steps, shoving the nobility aside.

"It's good to be home!" Khyan shouted at the confounded crowd. "Every nobleman in Avaris will report to my courtroom by the time I finish my first glass of wine." He leaned toward Potiphar. "And then we get an uninterrupted week with our wives."

Potiphar nodded. "Clear!" he commanded his guards.

Amid shouted questions and greetings, the Medjays cleared a private path for Pharaoh to approach his wives. After slipping an arm around each one's shoulders, he led Tani and Ziwat into the palace without a backward glance.

"To the throne room!" Potiphar shouted after them, intending the command for his Medjays; however, the whole crowd seemed to follow the order. Everyone but two women who waited on the steps.

"Ommi." He held out his right arm, inviting her to his uninjured side.

Pushpa rushed down four steps and grabbed his waist, nearly knocking him over with her enthusiasm. "Are you all right? What happened? Is it serious? Let me see." She started to untie the knotted sling at his shoulder, but he nudged her away and chuckled.

"Ommi, I'm fine. I'll show you my wound later." He turned to Zuleika, who remained planted, head bowed, where she'd been when the processional arrived. Heart in his throat, he aimed a silent question at Pushpa.

"It's been hard for her while you were away. She needs you, Son." Ommi squeezed his hand and continued down the stairs. "I'll wait at the pond to escort Zully home."

Potiphar glanced at his wife and then turned back to Pushpa in confusion. "She can come with me into the courtroom. The other wives will be there, and—"

"No!" Zuleika started down the stairs, taking a wide path around him.

He reached for her hand. "Wait, Zuleik—Zully."

Her head snapped up, eyes wide as a frightened doe's. What had happened to his spirited princess?

He descended a few steps to meet her at eye level. "Pharaoh Khyan has given me a second wedding week with you, Wife. When he finishes meeting with Avaris's nobility, I will sit at your feet for seven days and learn who you are, Princess Zuleika of Zakros Palace. I'll discover what makes you happy. Is it wealth? Your art?" He paused, looking deeper into the eyes that still seemed distant. "Perhaps children?"

A flicker within them gave him hope. "Yes," she said. "Maybe children."

TWENTY

Zuleika

I stared down at my hand in Potiphar's, his touch gentler than I remembered. Gentler than Gaios's. A slight squeeze, and I looked up at this husband I barely knew. He wasn't wearing a wig today. His head was shaved and tanned. The green malachite above his eyes sparkled in the sun. "Should I continue to call you Zuleika, or may I call you Zully?"

"Zully." It came out in little more than a whisper.

"I'll see you later this afternoon, then, Zully." Potiphar smiled and lifted my hand for a kiss. "Duty first." A brief bow, and he was gone.

Duty. It shackled us all.

He left me standing alone on the palace steps of this nation filled with secrets and shadows—some of them mine.

What secrets had Queen Tani been hiding when she whispered to me during our husbands' arrival? *Potiphar should begin tasting your banquet food too. Only his heroics can save you.*

My reputation or my life? Fear gutted me. More banquets and shadows and hate.

Gaios had told me not to come. *It's not safe to be near Wereni, Zully.* He was right. Wereni's stare had been hotter than Egypt's sun, and I felt more like a Tehenu captive than the nobility surrounding me. After the disastrous banquet, Gaios had kept me safe. *Safe?* Well, *hidden* from noble predators, narrowing my world to one familiar stranger.

Gaios claimed we'd focus our efforts on the one thing I longed for—returning to Crete. So I worked continually to create salable art in my safe chamber or at my rooftop potter's wheel, and Gaios satisfied himself with my body—when I gave up trying to deny him. I knew only longing for my true home—Crete and the sea.

But . . . *Perhaps children?* Potiphar's tender question had stirred a yearning long dead. Minas and I had tried—and failed.

"Come, dear. You look flushed." Pushpa met me on the steps. "You're not accustomed to leaving the villa. Are you feeling faint?"

"It's rather warm for a winter day, isn't it?" We started toward the villa.

"The great power of Ra is a mystery, Zully. He burns hot when it pleases him."

I had no response. I'd abandoned Egypt's gods after Seth betrayed me at my banquet.

"Ra isn't just powerful." Dear Pushpa filled the silence with kindhearted prattle. "Oh no. He's also the most faithful of the gods, appearing every morning after his journey through the underworld to brighten a new day."

Hopefully, she'd notice my indifference and embrace the silence. I wanted my chamber. Paints and papyrus. The cool shade of my rooftop shelter with the rhythmic whir of my potter's wheel. I linked my arm with hers so I could close my eyes and let another lead me. Blocking out the world around me, I imagined my hands on cool, wet clay, sliding up and then down, molding gently with my fingers and thumbs.

I'll discover what makes you happy. Potiphar's unexpectedly tender words invaded the moment. How? I could never be truly happy in Egypt.

"Zully, what did Queen Tani say to upset you so?"

My private world shattered when I opened my eyes. "Another hurtful comment." I appreciated her concern but dared not open my heart to explain and risk unleashing a year of constrained emotions.

She kissed the back of my hand. "I'm sorry Tani was unkind. Her ommi would be ashamed of her." We arrived at the villa, and the guards bowed, not to me but to the villa's cook, who was more respected than most noblemen in Avaris.

"Let's not speak of Queen Tani. I did as you asked and publicly welcomed Potiphar home. I did it for *you,* Pushpa." Tears threatened. "You've been very kind. Thank you."

We walked through the empty banquet hall in silence, echoes of shouts and cruel words from the awful banquet and its aftermath torturing my wounded soul. I'd been horrified when Gaios forced his desires on me, my mind clouded by eronda, my emotional defenses weakened by noblewomen's hate and all I'd lost. Each time he took my body, he chipped away at my soul and gave me a cup of eronda—his supply lasting only a month—to be sure no child redeemed the horrible act. I was almost certain he'd told me he purchased a merchant's entire stock of eronda. How could he have run out so quickly? He replaced the eronda with a harsher Egyptian purgative—so he said.

Clinging to Pushpa's arm, I asked the question that had vexed me for months. "Did the vizier's investigation uncover who tainted the wine?" Days after the banquet, Gaios told me one of the noblewomen had done it to ruin me. I wanted to believe him. Yet—what had Gaios done with a merchant's whole inventory, if not taint the banquet wine or purge his seed from my womb?

"Wereni's wife, Sanura, said no one was seriously injured, so her husband ended the investigation."

"But Gaios said the magician's wife lost her unborn child."

Pushpa's abrupt halt stopped me too. "Gaios isn't privy to all the details of noblewomen. She *almost* lost the baby but delivered a healthy son six months ago." Her warm, dark eyes held mine. "I know he was your friend in Crete, Zully, but this isn't the first lie I've caught him telling."

Defenses rising, I shrugged. "Gaios can't be responsible for hearing faulty gossip."

"Please be careful, Zully. Potiphar is home now."

We began walking again, and I feigned ignorance. "I don't know what you mean."

"I know Gaios has been a"—she paused—"familiar comfort who helped you adjust to your new home when Potiphar left so abruptly. But your husband is here now. *He* must be your comfort."

A lump lodged in my throat, making words impossible, and though I blinked rapidly, tears were inevitable.

Pushpa stopped at the dividing tapestries before entering the residence hall. "Today is a new start for everyone. The past is forgotten. Your kitchen servants would welcome news that the master has returned safely. They should hear it from their mistress."

"I'm not truly the mistress of this villa." I sniffed back my emotions and let resentment dry my tears. "Joseph has taken responsibilities that could have been mine. Tasks I excelled at in Crete."

Pushpa frowned. "He's your chamberlain, Mistress. He deserves our gratitude, not your scorn. This estate has flourished during Potiphar's absence."

"Proof that I'm neither mistress nor needed." I escaped through the tapestries.

"Please, Zully." Pushpa stopped me when we reached the kitchen door. "Joseph and the Minoan slaves remained at the villa rather than attending the welcome processional out of consideration for you. I can tell them my son has returned, but it's important you prove your sharp mind and pleasantness." She pulled me into the kitchen before I could question her.

"Pushpa! Mistress! Welcome." Joseph scrambled to his feet. We seemed to have startled him and all five Minoans, who had been scrubbing the kitchen floor. Gaios cast silent daggers at me. I couldn't remember seeing him scrub anything in all the years I'd known him. Ahira rose from a stool in a corner, where she'd been sorting vegetables.

Joseph threw his bunch of bound hyssop into a bucket and wiped his wet hands on the cloth tied at his waist. "Is the master well?"

"The rumors of Potiphar's injury are true, but the wound is not serious," Pushpa reported. "To reward Potiphar for his brave service, Pharaoh Khyan has given him a full seven days of rest with Mistress Zuleika to compensate for the wedding week they missed."

"May the octopus dance till the ink flows." Gaios's snide comment was lost on the others, but I'd understood exactly what he meant and ducked my head to hide my fiery cheeks. Zakros's sacred symbol sprayed its ink only when a predator came near.

My lover laughed at his own wit, raising my ire enough to overcome my dismay. I released my pent-up offense on the villa's chamberlain instead. "When your master finally comes home, after fulfilling his *duty* to the king, he'll undoubtedly wish to meet with you to discuss your *duties* on his estate. Since he abandoned me the day after our wedding, leaving me with no duties of my own, I'm the last person Captain Potiphar needs to see in this villa."

The merriment stilled to uncomfortable shock. I glanced at Pushpa with remorse. So much for the mistress displaying a sharp mind and pleasantness.

But Pushpa's gaze never wavered. "By the end of your wedding week, I hope you'll know your value reaches beyond duty."

Unable to bear her kindness, I started toward the door. Ahira fell in step beside me, and Pushpa began instructing the Minoans on the day's tasks. Gaios, however, rushed toward me instead of obeying the cook.

"How may I serve you, Mistress?" His intensity held an unspoken threat. After nearly a year, our secrets now far outnumbered the eronda-tainted wine. Pushpa obviously knew of our affair, but only Ahira knew my art would pay for our passage back to Crete.

"Follow Ahira and me to my chamber, Gaios. I'll dictate a list of things needed from the royal market." After moving out of the kitchen, I greeted the Medjays at Potiphar's chamber. Why hadn't I learned their names? I'd known the name of every person in Zakros District. Joseph likely knew the name of everyone on Potiphar's estate. Why didn't I? *Unacceptable, Zully.*

"Gaios, I want flowers from the market—if there are any left after Pharaoh's welcome."

"Why flowers?"

I cast him a sideways glare. "There will be fresh petals strewn across my chamber floor as they were for my wedding night. And I want colored sheets for my bed."

His face reddened; his fists clenched.

I ignored his seething and spoke loud enough for my chamber guards to hear as we approached them. "Ahira, scent the new sheets with myrrh, aloe, and cinnamon, and refresh them each day when my husband and I retire to the courtyard. Make sure I have plenty of healing herbs and a supply of bandages to dress his shoulder in the chamber." They were the most commands I'd spoken in a long time. I was exhausted by the effort, but the authority tasted like honey on my tongue.

I hadn't wielded control over anyone—including myself—since the awful day Egypt's noblewomen ran screaming and bloody from my villa. When Gaios pretended to care for me, I'd become a walking mummy, placing my heart in a canopic jar. My chamber and rooftop potter's wheel had become my tomb.

Only when Gaios left the villa did a spark of life return. Colorful paints, papyrus, and pottery decorated my world, while Ahira replaced my graveclothes with stories of a god who cared. She was peace. Breath. Restoration.

But Gaios always returned. Early on, I'd hoped he would somehow heal from the slavers' abuse. But there was no "old Gaios" to resurrect. So the mummy Zully survived in isolated regret with a single focus: find a way home.

The Medjays opened my chamber door for the three of us, and I wondered for the thousandth time, *What if I'd alerted them at Gaios's first unwelcome advance?*

The door clicked shut behind us. "You were magnificent, Zully. Like the princess of Zakros Palace."

I faced the jackal who still feigned complete devotion. "The Zully of Egypt is your creation, Gaios. Is she so repulsive?" Before he could appease me or blame my comment on one of my *moods*, I turned my attention to Ahira. "I'll wear my light blue robe this evening."

Gaios grabbed my arm. "You are everything to me." He pulled me into a kiss, his show of affection more power than passion.

I pushed him away and wiped my mouth. "I let you bed me because you promised you'd help me get back to Crete."

"You let me bed you then because you were scared." His lips curved into a wicked grin. "I bed you now because you like it."

"No!" I choked on a sob. It wasn't true, was it? I covered my face to hide my confusion. How could hate and need exist in one heart? I hated the man in my chamber, but I needed my *friend,* the one who knew me and stayed when others abandoned me.

"You said you loved me."

"I do love you, Zully." His hands slid up my arms, and he pulled me close. "But I won't allow your moods to endanger us. We don't have enough silver to return to Crete, because your art doesn't sell in the *royal* market. A lower city merchant has sold plenty but very cheaply, so it could take months before we have enough for both passages to Crete. But I think I've found a way to earn extra silver."

I felt Ahira's gentle touch on my back. "Would you like a cup of watered wine, Mistress?" Her kindness was always a calming presence on the edges of my life.

"Get it for her, Ahira, and then go to your chamber." Gaios's threatening tone raised the hair on my arms.

Everything in me wanted to run. But I wasn't yet brave enough to escape from Gaios's embrace or call out for help. To appease his recurring fury, I laid my head on his shoulder.

But Potiphar would come.

I almost smiled at the irony. Would I transfer my hope to an Egyptian husband I barely knew? "I don't need wine, Ahira. Go rest in your chamber until Gaios goes to the market. Then you and I will begin preparations for my second wedding night."

I heard the soft shuffle of her sandaled feet and knew, when Gaios led me toward my bed, she'd disappeared into her room. "Did you say 'my second wedding night' to hurt me?" He lay beside me and propped his head on his hand. "You know it will drive me mad knowing you're in his arms, Zully."

I stared at the ceiling, ignoring the circles he drew on my chest. *My husband is Pharaoh's captain because of his skill in exposing schemes and lies.* "Gaios, you must stay away from me for a while."

"No, Zully. I love you. I can't leave you unprotected. He's a butcher." He hovered over me for two heartbeats and then brushed my lips with his. "I could never forgive myself if something terrible happened to you."

I searched the dark windows of his soul. Was it a veiled threat? "Gaios, I don't believe Potiphar would harm me."

"But he can't love you the way I do," Gaios said. "No one can." Before I could respond, he smothered me with a revolting attempt at passion, pawing and demanding.

"Stop! Gaios, stop!" I pushed against his chest and sent him to the floor. "Are you mad? Potiphar could walk in here any moment."

A wry grin pulled at one side of his lips. "Perhaps your madness is contagious."

My blood ran cold, and I remembered Pushpa's comment. *It's important you prove your sharp mind and pleasantness.* "Have you started rumors about me, Gaios?"

"No!" His immediate answer seemed sincere. "I would never—" He knelt beside my bed. "I know you love Crete more than you love me, Zully, but I'm working hard to earn extra silver so you can have us both. I received a message last week that Crete has garnered funds from another benefactor. Crete may be rebuilt and your marriage reversed sooner than expected."

"Gaios! That's wonderful." But I stared into the abyss of his repeated deceptions and faced my reality. "Potiphar has returned, and—"

"Shh." He pressed his finger to my lips. "I'll have one of the other slaves purchase your sheets and flowers from the market while I finalize my deal with . . ." He pecked my cheek with another kiss. "I won't bother you with details, my love."

His thin, lithe frame hurried from my chamber, and my thoughts turned to the powerful warrior who had treated me so tenderly on the palace steps. Why must I place my future in any man's hands?

Elohim, god of my friend Ahira, can you restore life to a mummy princess in a foreign land?

TWENTY-ONE

Their malice may be concealed by deception,
  but their wickedness will be exposed in the assembly.
PROVERBS 26:26

Joseph

"I'll speak with you privately, Chamberlain." Pushpa motioned Joseph to a quiet corner of her kitchen while the four remaining Minoan slaves went back to their floor-scrubbing project.

Though Joseph had wanted to join the crowds and welcome the processional in person, his brief interaction with the mistress that morning—a simple request to clarify a purchase Gaios made—proved the mere sight of him caused her distress. He didn't wish to detract from her reunion with Master Potiphar.

"I thought you stayed in the villa to spend more time with Ahira." Pushpa's scolding began before they reached their discreet nook. She looked over Joseph's shoulders, nodding toward the slaves, who had returned to scrubbing tiles. "My Minoan slaves are hard workers. You had no need to oversee their work."

"I stayed to ensure Gaios remained at the villa." He locked eyes with Pushpa. Months ago, after discovering Mistress Zuleika's frail condition, he'd begun checking on her daily—and soon believed

Gaios had manipulated the mistress into an affair. Certainly, his power over her was palpable. Pushpa agreed with Joseph's conclusions but refused to let him sell the Minoan, confront the mistress, or even ask Ahira whether their suspicions were true.

"Now that Potiphar has returned, it may be time to be rid of Gaios," Pushpa whispered, "but I worry Zully is still so fragile, she may break when we take him away."

"The mistress is fragile because she's living a secret life."

"Don't give me that self-righteous look, Joseph." She jammed her fists to her hips. "It's more than that. The law may say she committed adultery, but the law wasn't abandoned one night after the wedding. A few weeks before, she'd lost not only her husband and ommi but also the vital role of caring for her people in Zakros. The way she described her island—the mountains, the sea, and the pink sandy beaches— Gaios alone could share those memories. If we'd taken him from her, she might have—" She cleared her throat. "You see how thin she is, Joseph. Her ka is damaged, and we must restore her ma'at before she's too far gone."

"We can only help restore her peace if she's willing, Pushpa." He didn't wish to sound harsh, but allowing evil in the hope of bringing good had never been Elohim's way. "We must sell Gaios and let the mistress lean on Ahira. Egyptians are purchasing Minoans at the slave market now. Master Potiphar will approve of the sale as long as I can get a fair price."

Pushpa shook her head.

"Ahira told me yesterday the mistress asked how adultery was punished in our Hebrew camp."

Pushpa looked surprised. "What did she say?"

"The punishment for adultery in our camp is death by stoning."

She nodded soberly. "Similar to Hammurabi's Code—death. In Egypt there is mercy. The king may set aside death and offer maiming."

Remembering the torture chamber, Joseph cringed. "I'm not sure maiming is merciful. The mistress told Ahira punishment in Crete is a fight between the husband and the accused. The winner gets the woman."

"Then in Crete, Gaios would be dead." Pushpa grinned. "It sounds like she wants to be with Potiphar."

Joseph wasn't smiling. "My point is, I wonder if discussing the punishments means our mistress has weighed the cost and is prepared to be caught. We can't let that happen—for her sake and ours. How will the master react when he discovers you and I knew of the affair, did nothing to stop it, and then hid it from him when he returned home? I'm not willing to find out. Are you? And he'll punish Ahira too. You know he will."

She sighed. "Sell him during the wedding week so she doesn't notice."

"I will."

"Will you tell Potiphar the bad news about Abasi before the wedding week or after?"

"I'll tell him right away. We can't bring a traitor into the villa." Joseph snorted cynically.

A Medjay pushed open the kitchen door. "The meeting at the palace adjourned. Captain Potiphar and Commander Hami are on their way." The guard retreated into the hallway.

Pushpa's features brightened. "My hungry household has returned!" She clapped to get the Minoans' attention. "After we greet Potiphar," she told them, "I'll need all of you to help me carry food from the market. My ravenous Medjays eat like lions when they return from battle."

Leading the villa's welcoming processional of Joseph and the Minoans, Pushpa entered the banquet room just as Potiphar emerged from the palace hallway.

"Welcome, my lord!" Joseph's greeting echoed in the large, empty room.

"Hebrew!" The word from his master's lips, warm and familiar, carried none of the rancid undertones Joseph had endured from Abasi during their clandestine meetings.

Potiphar rushed to Pushpa. She grinned up at him. "We're on our way to the market to get all your favorites for tonight's meal. Roasted pigeon with raisins and honey, almond bread, and—"

"It sounds wonderful, Ommi." He braced her shoulders and kissed her forehead. "Is there anything you haven't told Hami?"

"No. I've told him every—"

"Good." He started toward the residence hall. "We'll talk more later."

As he walked away, her bright countenance faded, replaced with the wrestling of pain and pride—something Joseph had recognized in the four imas who'd borne Abba Jacob's sons.

"Come, Hebrew!" Potiphar shouted over his shoulder. "I want you and Hami in my chamber with all the reports—now! My wedding week begins when your briefing ends."

Joseph scrambled to keep up. "I'll retrieve the scrolls and meet you in your chamber."

Joseph hadn't told anyone where he hid Abasi's weekly reports. With the kitchen deserted, he need not use his normal stealth. He grabbed a lamp, then lit the wick with a torch before climbing down the winery ladder. The cool air prickled his cheeks as he descended, a welcome relief from this season's unusual heat. After setting the lamp on the floor, he unloaded wineskins from the pegs on the farthest end of the long, narrow shaft. Behind the skins, he'd dug a hole in the wall and placed nearly a year's collection of scrolls documenting Abasi's testimony against Vizier Wereni. As he reached to stack the third scroll on his arm, he heard a hushed voice above him. After replacing the scrolls and a few wineskins, he blew out his lamp, then hid in a darkened corner.

A man descended the ladder in a small circle of lamplight. "I have the silver," he shouted to someone above. "I always pay my debts." *Gaios.* As he leapt from the bottom rung, Joseph noticed blood trickling from a cut on his forehead. Gaios strode to the other side of the cool, dark space and shoved aside two wineskins, then pulled a small bag from a hole behind them.

He returned to the ladder but hesitated, speaking to the one above. "I hope you'll tell Vizier Wereni that I would be honored to provide information from Captain Potiphar's villa. As Mistress Zuleika's personal attendant, I could be very useful to the vizier now that the captain has returned."

A low chuckle came from above. "If you spy like you gamble, Cretan, the vizier has no use for you."

"I'm a much better informant, soldier." Gaios searched through a small bag of silver. "For instance, I've paid a boy to keep watch near your house. If I don't give him a silver coin tonight, he'll deliver a message to your wife." Silence stretched between the ladder and ground level. The man must be one of Pharaoh's soldiers, not a Medjay, if his wife lived in Avaris.

"My wife doesn't read," he said finally.

"Neither does the boy," Gaios said. "I told him to simply say, 'Your husband doesn't always sleep at the vizier's villa.'"

"What do you want, Cretan?"

Gaios attached the parcel to his belt and began his climb up the ladder. "Only what I said before, my friend." He disappeared into the kitchen. "I want to help the vizier achieve his goals . . ." His voice faded.

Joseph felt a chill down to his bones.

Elohim, why do You allow such darkness in people? He'd been its victim when his brothers sold him. He wouldn't allow the mistress to be Gaios's prey any longer.

Without a lamp, Joseph reached into the musty, dark hole and withdrew every scroll. Cradling them as tenderly as an infant, he climbed the ladder, then peeked into every corner of the kitchen before emerging and hurrying across the hall to the master's chamber. Once inside, he pressed his back against the closed door, panting and staring at Hami and Potiphar, not sure how to relay the startling scene he'd witnessed.

The two men halted their conversation.

The master grinned. "Is Anubis chasing you?" He sobered when Joseph had no answer. "What happened?"

Elohim, how much do I tell him? Must he confide Mistress Zuleika's unfaithfulness at the same time he revealed Gaios as a spy? He looked down at the pile of scrolls in his arms, knowing they would prove the guilt of a man Potiphar had trusted for more than twenty years. Joseph had painstakingly documented the testimony of a hateful old man who had ultimately shifted his loyalty to the traitorous vizier. Joseph couldn't deceive the man who had trusted him with everything he owned. Master Potiphar had shared everything with him—except his wife. Joseph owed him the truth.

"I don't know what Hami has already told you, but—"

"Abasi is a traitor," Potiphar interrupted and began pacing. "I'm saddened but not surprised. Hami says if I fawn over him and make him believe he's too valuable to us as a spy, he'll be happy to remain as Wereni's steward." He paused and faced Joseph. "Do you agree?"

"I agree, Master, but I have two things to reveal that aren't found in these scrolls, that Hami doesn't know. A very wise man once said no one should know everything about anything. Should your chief Medjay leave the chamber before I confide these two things?"

Potiphar's eyes narrowed, the weight of his stare bearing down on Joseph like the cargo of two barques. "Hami, leave us."

He obeyed without hesitation, leaving Joseph to deliver news that would change his master's future. "I just came from the winery, where I'd hidden these scrolls, and I heard Gaios, the Minoan slave—"

"Yes, I remember him." Potiphar's hand twirled like he was rolling a ball of string. "King Rehor's cockroach—or street rat."

"I just overheard a conversation in which Gaios volunteered to become Vizier Wereni's street rat, providing information from your villa to one of Pharaoh's soldiers."

The master searched Joseph's face. "There's something you're not telling me."

"He was your wife's personal attendant while you were away."

A moment of reckoning, and then his eyes widened. "Her personal attendant and what else?" Now came the gathering storm.

"Mistress Zuleika hasn't been herself since you left—she longs only for Crete—and we . . . *I* waited to sell Gaios until you returned for fear she might not survive another loss. With the new information of his likely role in the vizier's plan, I felt you should know everything and be the one to determine Gaios's fate."

"And my wife's fate?" Egypt's fiercest soldier hurled his javelin into the far wall and sat down hard, trembling. "I saw her at the palace. She's still the most beautiful woman in the crowd, but she's frail. I thought she wasn't herself because she was standing beside Wereni."

Joseph lowered himself as well. Silent. Potiphar rubbed his injured shoulder, then removed the sling.

Joseph glimpsed a wound, three finger widths. It must have been a clean thrust—a spear. Now wasn't the time to ask.

"Before Pharaoh's 'gift,' I hated the idea of marriage. A wife makes a man old, Hebrew. A woman at home slows a soldier's thinking, makes him hesitate. I'd never hesitated before the conflict in Temehu."

"Were you injured because you hesitated?"

"No. I took a spear intended for Pharaoh." He lifted piercing eyes to Joseph. "And I'd do it again, even if it meant my life."

"I know you would, Master, but I'm glad you and Pharaoh Khyan *both* came home to your wives."

"Humph." A cynical huff conveyed his doubts. "I didn't want to marry because it meant the end of my freedom. I couldn't have the women I wanted or travel to the southern nomes on a whim. I didn't want to marry *her* because she was Cretan. I was as bigoted as Abasi but too proud to admit it."

"You've never shown any aversion to me as a Hebrew, my lord."

"You'll never bear my children."

"Indeed." They shared a grin.

"Has your opinion of marriage—of Mistress Zuleika—changed?" Joseph asked.

The master's pleasantness faded, his gaze wandering toward the javelin in the wall. "Much has changed since Pharaoh's processional entered the palace complex." A soldier's answer—guarded. The master had finished confiding.

Joseph stood and offered his hand. Potiphar gripped his wrist, and Joseph widened his stance to help the weary warrior to his feet. Unable to silence the niggling voice inside, Joseph held fast when Potiphar tried to release him. "I'm only a slave, Master Potiphar—and a Hebrew at that—but I must speak the truth. Elohim is a God of justice *and* mercy. He creates streams of justice in a desert of wrongs for those who value mercy."

Potiphar pulled his hand free, glaring.

Joseph waited, not daring to look away. *Elohim, protect me.*

"Sell the Minoan," Potiphar said finally. "If I see him, I'll kill him."

"And the mistress?"

The master's cheek twitched; his nostrils flared. "Get Hami in here to review the reports."

Joseph bowed to hide his fear. Would there be no mercy for Mistress Zuleika? "Yes, Master." He started toward the door as the master began shuffling through the scrolls on the floor.

"Hebrew, stop!"

Joseph halted, his hand on the door's latch.

"You said '*We* waited to sell Gaios.' You're the chamberlain. Who else did you consult on the matter?"

Surely he knew. "The only person in this villa you trust more than me."

Hami entered and marched past him. "Which reports would you like to review first, Captain? Or do you want a summary?"

Potiphar scrubbed his face, attacking cosmetics already smeared by sweat and dread. He turned to Hami. "Let's do this quickly. I have a wife who needs my attention."

TWENTY-TWO

Better is open rebuke
than hidden love.
PROVERBS 27:5

Zuleika

Ahira silently applied my cosmetics. I didn't mind. My thoughts drifted to the husband I'd met on the palace steps. Queen Tani's whispered threat. The way I'd embarrassed myself in front of Pushpa and the slaves. And Gaios's promise to earn more silver. I glimpsed the pink sand in my shrine and shivered in horror at the thought of returning to Crete *together* with Gaios. He must never wear a crown.

"Mistress Zully, should I skip the kohl around your eyes?" Ahira pressed away the moisture with a scrap of linen.

I sighed and looked up, blinking furiously. "No, Ahira. I must be presentable for my husband."

She dried my eyes once more, and I closed them. "He seemed kind," I whispered as her steady hand lined my lashes. "What if it was pretense because Pushpa was watching?"

A knock at the door startled me. "Yes?"

"Captain Potiphar has been delayed." The guard's report hung in the air, confirming my fears.

"The master was thoughtful to send word, Zully."

Her hand was poised to apply sparkling green malachite, but I shoved it away. "I hate green, Ahira. Everything in Egypt is either delta green or desert brown. Crete and her people span the colors of the rainbow, vibrant as wildflowers and restless as the sea."

Ahira pursed her lips, patiently enduring my yearnings as she had for months. "Whether you wear malachite to greet your husband or not," she said, "you've proven wildflowers can survive Egypt's desert."

"Why try to please a man who never wrote me a single message while he was away? Minas wrote me dozens of times when he went trading. Pateras wrote Mitera. I realize Potiphar was fighting a rebellion, but . . ." *Dare I voice my most shocking realization?* "I saw his arm in that sling and couldn't bear that he might have been killed, Ahira."

Her features softened. "He's your husband." She calmly pressed my shoulders back against the couch. "Give him a chance to love you."

"But I don't *want* to love him."

"I remember how that felt."

Ahira hid her face and offered me the hand mirror, then began applying Egypt's precious green powder. The kohl liner would serve as boundaries to the windows of my soul. It was as barren as drought-ridden Temehu, but I'd offer Potiphar what I could.

"All done." Ahira took the mirror and offered her hand to help me stand. "Would you like to wait in the courtyard?"

I nodded. We linked arms and strolled toward the pond as though I had no cares in this world. However, when we entered the courtyard, muffled male voices grabbed my attention. "That's Potiphar's courtyard," I whispered, pointing at crooked tapestries covering a poorly hidden door.

"Are you hungry?" Ahira's volume and forced brightness reminded me those in Potiphar's courtyard would hear us too.

The first day in my chamber, I'd noticed the blockaded connecting door and asked Pushpa what lay on the other side. She'd confessed that Potiphar had tried to hide the portal to prevent his new wife's unannounced visits.

Ahira followed as I meandered to my favorite couch tucked beneath a copse of palm trees. "In all the months I've lived in the villa," I said,

"I still haven't glimpsed my husband's chamber." Staring into the blue sky, I finally answered her question. "I'm not hungry, but I'd like some wine. Bring a pitcher." I curled around a pillow on the cushioned bench like a cat around a ball of wool. Perhaps a nap before Potiphar arrived would prepare me for a crocodile or a stallion. I'd glimpsed both in my warrior husband. I closed my eyes, and let the warm breeze take me away.

". . . grateful you returned safe." On the edges of consciousness, I heard Ahira's voice. *Wine. She was supposed to bring me wine.*

"Where is my wife?" Potiphar's voice brought me to my feet.

"Potiphar!" Suddenly I faced him. Barely two paces away, he raised a brow as if waiting for me to say more.

Ahira carried a tray with a silver pitcher and two silver goblets. *Too late.* I stood as silent as a villa pillar.

"Leave the wine. Pushpa will bring our evening meal." His instructions were for the maid, but his gaze held mine.

"Of course, Master. Is there anything else?"

"The chamberlain has found somewhere else for you to stay during the wedding week. Leave us."

Ahira hesitated, and I cast a panicked glance her direction. "But she's—"

"Leave now." His voice was a low growl, raising the hair on my arms.

"As you wish, Master." Ahira bowed, casting a concerned look at me before she fled.

I glimpsed Hami waiting at my open chamber door. He met Ahira, coaxed her into the hallway, then closed the door.

Hami knows about Gaios too. Potiphar must know. Everyone knows. I couldn't look at my husband, certain he was about to kill me for my betrayal. *I don't want to die in my lovely courtyard!* Without looking at Potiphar, I scooted past him into my chamber. He didn't try to stop me but instead wandered inside, his uninjured arm leisurely tucked behind his back.

He lingered beside my Minoan treasures, knelt, and poured some pink sand into his hand.

"No, don't!" I grabbed the jar, knelt beside him, and bowed my head. "I'd rather you kill me than destroy what little I have left of my homeland. Only two beaches on Crete have pink sand. It's precious . . ."

Without a word, he moved on, perusing my paintings and pottery. "I see a striking improvement in these pieces over the palace mural, Zuleika. You seem to have found a special sort of inspiration during my absence."

Special inspiration. My ragged breaths quickened. I was too terrified to conjure a lie. Amid the quiet sputtering of oil lamps, he returned to lift me to my feet, and I met the hard stare of a man betrayed.

He lifted a brow and nodded toward the rock-crystal vase in the shrine—my most prized possession. "It's different from anything we have in Egypt." He took it from its metal stand and inspected the pointed base. "Undeniably lovely, but a vase unable to perform the task for which it was created seems rather . . . worthless." He shrugged his good shoulder.

"I was created to rule Zakros District but was sold for a different use. Am I now worthless?" The shock I intended raised his brows. "This vase is the only piece of art I brought with me from Crete. After the shaking, Pateras and I picked through the ruins of Zakros Palace, and he found it lying near the courtyard, only a slight chip on the slender face above the neck."

He turned the piece in the light, examining the fault I'd mentioned. "Hmm, I see it now. To be pulled from destruction whole and largely untouched—"

"Nothing was untouched, Potiphar."

He gazed at me as intensely as he'd studied the vase. "Perhaps the most unique treasures need special care."

I recognized the coded words, not so different from the way Gaios and I communicated. Could Potiphar and I use the vase as a bridge to mercy? I offered a tentative smile, pressing my body against the vase and the vase against him. "With your promise of special care, I give you this vase."

"You would give me such a treasure?"

I searched the deep lines of his enigmatic expression. Was he scrutinizing or scowling? Would he let me live—at least long enough to find a way back to Crete? Other noblemen allowed their wives to dally with servants if they did it privately. Would Potiphar allow Gaios to remain in the villa? Then we could still trade my art. *And* it would allow me to threaten Gaios with Potiphar's jealousy and refuse his advances.

I gave my treasure one last perusal and decided it was a fair trade to stay my execution. "I strung the handle with rock-crystal beads on bronze wire." I lifted it for further inspection. "It's beautiful but impractical to bear its weight full of wine."

"And this?" He cupped the vase's slender bottom.

"I saw imperfections in the stone and kept chiseling until it was smooth—by then it was totally useless." I shook my head, remembering my conversation with Pateras about its worth. "Though my creation made no sense, it was so beautiful I couldn't discard it. Then Pateras found it amid the palace rubble after the shaking, and I knew it must accompany me to Egypt." I cleared my throat of rising emotion and focused only on the husband Pharaoh had chosen for me. "I give it to you, Potiphar. Just as my vase was pulled from the ruins of Zakros Palace, you pulled me from the ruins of a destitute life and made a way of salvation for my people." Our eyes held, and the weight of my actions crashed down on me. "I ask that you take all that's misshapen and somehow make it yours."

"Don't." He stepped back, teeth suddenly clenched. "You—rather, your *vase*—can remain in my villa without pretending your heart is mine. It may live in this chamber as my guest. No one need know. Though others deem your Minoan flair misshapen, Zuleika, I will treasure you. But make no mistake—the 'vase' will meet its end if it is ever given to another."

His jaw muscle jumped, and I recognized the crocodile. Yet a true crocodile could have devoured me. *I* was the one who had betrayed *him*. He could have condemned me in Pharaoh's court. Shamed me publicly and ordered my execution. Potiphar was neither crocodile nor stallion. He was a man, as rife with conflicting emotion as I.

A wave of nausea overtook me. I steadied myself by reaching for the table and sent the vase's metal stand tumbling.

"Zully?" He reached for me with his uninjured arm. "You're not well. I shouldn't have—"

Awed at the concern, I whispered, "How can you be kind to me?"

He steadied me but didn't remove his arm from my waist. "I've thought of you every day since my injury. I returned home to find many challenges—both at the palace and here—but I want you as my wife." He nodded toward the walls of my chamber. "These bright Minoan colors, your paintings and pottery—they're a part of you. I find you both an enigma and a fortress, Princess Zuleika of Zakros Palace. I want to untangle you and breach your walls."

"I'm so relieved you like me," I blurted.

"Like you? It's more than *like*. I wholeheartedly accept your gift." A wry grin became a low chuckle and turned into a lion's purr. His kiss was urgent but gentle. Hungry yet restrained.

The man I'd feared was both fierce and tender. My body responded without permission, betraying all the boundaries I'd set before he walked into my courtyard. "I don't want to want you," I whispered.

"But you do. I sense it."

Startled by the truth, I pressed against his chest. "Pushpa will arrive soon with our meal." Shaking with desire, I replaced the vase in its metal stand. His kisses, full of tenderness and promise, had stirred longings far deeper than physical pleasure.

His presence loomed behind me. "The vase is truly remarkable, Zully."

Did all men flatter to get their way? I turned to search his eyes and found no trickery. Only sincerity.

"As are you, Captain Potiphar." My words pleased him. "May I show you other things I've created?"

"I'd like that very much."

I guided him around the chamber, explaining my craft. "The early pieces focused on Minoan gardens and Egyptian florals. Then I learned to make faience beads." Lifting my necklace for his approval, I noticed his eyes wandering downward. I tilted up his chin, my angst returning. "People seem eager to buy anything bearing the symbol of life."

His pleasantness fled. "They're eager to *buy* the ankh?"

"I—"

"Here we are, dears!" Pushpa's happy greeting silenced me.

"We'll speak of this later," he whispered and walked away. "Ommi, thank you."

Pushpa glanced my direction. I couldn't move. Had I just confessed my last secret to the man whose mercy had already stretched beyond reason?

"Come, dear, before the food gets cold." Pushpa glanced at Potiphar. Tension crackled as I moved toward a woman who read people like a scribe reads a scroll. The sight of food reminded me of Gaios, likely fuming in the kitchen. The vase had saved my life, but what about his? As much as I had grown to detest him, a part of me still loved the Gaios I once knew.

Nausea threatened again. I pressed against my stomach, willing myself to remain in the moment.

Pushpa reached for the knotted sling at Potiphar's shoulder. "I want to check on your injury, dear."

"Ommi, no." He retreated, waving away her attention, and tripped over a table.

"Potiphar!" I rushed toward him as he landed on a nest of pillows. He and Pushpa belly laughed, but I raised my trembling hand to my mouth. Another shaking was beginning. Not the earth beneath me but a cracking and crumbling within. Jumbled emotions erupted in a low moan with tears I couldn't restrain and quaking I couldn't control.

"Zully, it's okay." Potiphar leapt to his feet. "I'm not hurt."

"I need to know," I whispered, daring to beg for the jackal who had saved me. "Will you save the other vase, Potiphar?"

I knew he'd understood my code when he stepped back, his expression changing to a warrior's detached mask. "Neither vase will be broken, Princess." With that, he turned and inspected Pushpa's tray. "All my favorite foods, Ommi. Thank you."

"Come, dear." The woman extended her hand to me, ignoring her son's diversion. "It's important that a warrior's wife know how to dress her husband's wounds."

"I'll dress it myself, Ommi." Potiphar appeared as reluctant as I.

"You can only know the value of duty when you know its cost," she said to her son and then turned to me. "And perhaps during your wedding week, Zully, you'll discover that some duties can be enjoyable."

Duty. I breathed in the word and breathed out a calming breath. Breathed in the mercy Potiphar had shown me and exhaled my memories of the sea. Holding Pushpa's gaze, I offered a single nod.

She nudged her mountainous son toward the couch. "Lie down, boy. The sooner we finish, the sooner I'll leave you two alone. After tonight, I'll simply knock and leave your meals at the door so you two can eat at your leisure."

With a defeated sigh, he lay down, and I knelt by Pushpa. "It's nearly healed," he said as she untied the sling. "There's no need to—"

Pushpa gasped when she saw the wound. "Oh, Potiphar!" I looked away. I'd never seen such a large wound.

"Khyan's physician said it's mending nicely," Potiphar whispered. "Ommi, don't fuss. It's a clean shot through the muscle." Even my inexperienced eye could see that the weapon had indeed pierced his shoulder from front to back in a wide gash.

"It does look clean. Zully. You must apply honey, turmeric, and fresh bandages twice a day."

"I understand." But I felt woefully unprepared. "I've never bandaged such a serious wound."

"I've done it a few times." Potiphar held my gaze. "You'll have a whole week with only me to teach you." His lazy grin seemed more playful than mocking, and I marveled anew at the mercy of Egypt's fiercest warrior. How could he even look at me after I'd asked him to spare my lover's life? *Neither vase will be broken.* But would Gaios be sold? I kept that question to myself.

Potiphar's quick breath captured my attention. He needed a distraction as Pushpa applied a mixture of honey and turmeric powder to his wound.

"How were you injured?" I hovered over him.

He focused on me, wincing. "We had secured Egypt's borderlands. The nearest Tehenu rebels were a day's march to the west. Khyan left garrisons along the border, but a small rebel contingent had infiltrated one of our delta villages. On the day of our withdrawal, I caught a glimpse of a spearman launching his weapon. I ran toward Pharaoh Khyan, planted my foot on a large stone beside him, and hurled myself in front of the spear that would have pierced his heart." He waved away my increasing horror. "Instead, it was an inconsequential wound to my shoulder."

"It could have pierced *your* heart!" Mine beat like a thousand horses racing. "What would happen to Pushpa, to me, to everyone who depends on you if you and Pharaoh were killed? Vizier Wereni would—" Panic threatened again as the thought of more loss, more hate, more treachery overwhelmed me. I bolted toward the courtyard. *I must get back to Crete.* I knew the rules there. I knew the people. The land. The sea.

But Gaios . . . Could I trust him to take me home?

"Zully." Potiphar's whisper raised prickly flesh all over me.

"No. I can't . . ."

I felt his presence behind me. "Why won't you let me love you?" His strong arm slid around my waist and pulled me tightly against him.

I groaned, a mix of frustration and longing. "I don't want to *need* you."

"I feel the same, but what if there are gods who have a different plan?"

The gods. I broke from his embrace and peered into the chamber. Pushpa was gone. I cast a longing look at my treasures from home before I refocused on my husband. "I admire your bravery, Potiphar. Truly. But you must allow me to return to Crete if something happens to you. I have no reason to stay in Egypt if—"

"You stay with Pushpa." His features hardened. "She's a wealthy noblewoman who cooks because she wants to cook and helps others because her heart floods deeper than the Nile."

"What about what *I* want, Potiphar? What about the Minoan people I want to help?"

"You married an Egyptian, Zuleika. Our children will be Egyptian. *You* are now an Egyptian."

"You can't be so naive!" I shouted, but he didn't flinch—like a statue but less pliable under my chisel. "I'm an artist, Potiphar. Minoan or Egyptian, it's who *I* am. At least let me open a booth in the royal market to sell—"

"Zuleika, I forbid it! You can do anything—buy anything, give away anything—but you will not be a common street harlot." His right eye twitched, and I sensed something deeper in the verdict.

"Were you swindled by a market prostitute and now consider all merchants to be criminals?"

"My ommi abandoned Abi and me when she earned enough silver to leave us."

"I'm sorry, Potiphar." The irony that I shared his mitera's intention stoked my compassion.

"Zully." My name softened his tone. "Pharaoh Khyan has challenged me to be a better husband. I'm responsible for your safety, not just Pushpa's. Wereni's hostility toward foreign nobility can't touch you inside this villa or when you're accompanied by me or my Medjays. You need not be afraid." He placed his huge hand on my cheek with remarkable tenderness. "As long as you never share your *vase* with another."

I hesitated—unintentionally but irrevocably—and his hand fell to his side.

"No, wait." I studied every line and callus on his hand while contemplating how to begin our week of captivity. Finally I found the courage to look into eyes hardened by my indecision. "Thank you for making me your wife, Potiphar. You are a truly courageous man in more ways than on the battlefield. You are more than a soldier. You are a dutiful and loving son, and I'm honored that you care enough to speak with your king about becoming a better husband."

"Are you more than an artist, Zully?" He lifted one eyebrow. A challenge.

"I'm trying to be." It was the truth. "Art has been my constant comfort and purpose. Perhaps I'd feel more *useful* if people could purchase my art."

"Don't." His eyes sparked with warning. He began to pace, rubbing his bald head. "You are a fortress, Princess Zuleika."

He had no idea what a compliment that was after I'd become such a mummy under Gaios's demanding supervision. I didn't want my Minoan friend harmed, but even a partial day of freedom from his influence had given me a new perspective on my life and future.

Potiphar halted his pacing, staring at something in the chamber, then looked at me with a mischievous grin.

"What?" Would I face a sandstorm or a cool breeze?

"You may never *sell* your art, Zully, but you'll give it as gifts—as you've done for me. We'll inaugurate your talent by hosting the lotus festival."

I would never invite anyone into the villa again. "No, Potiphar. I tried giving a banquet—"

"Pushpa told me, but it wasn't your fault. Wereni stopped investigating when he discovered one of the Egyptian noblewomen tainted the wine to shame you."

"And you want to invite them into your home?"

"I do." He crossed the divide between us. "Because you're better than them and you'll show your courage with mercy."

Mercy. Like he'd shown me. Was that his game? I searched his expression for the same manipulation Gaios showed. A twitch or sideways glance. But the deep crags on my husband's face were relaxed. Hopeful even. "How long do I have to make these gifts for the whiny, spoiled cows of Egypt?"

He laughed. "I'll speak with Khyan. The lotus festival is as distinctive among our celebrations as the flower is to Egypt. We can celebrate it anytime we wish—as long as the Nile is high enough to carry our greatest dreams to the gods."

"I don't understand."

"Joseph will take great care with the details. You need only create a gift for each woman who attends. I'll suggest we celebrate after the next Inundation, giving you nine months to prepare." He brushed his lips across my forehead and down my cheek, lingering by my ear to whisper. "Enough talk. Even my favorite of Pushpa's dishes can't compare to feasting on the wife I've dreamed of for months." His hand slid down my arm, tenderly grasping my fingers to lead me toward my bed.

My stomach churned more than it had on my wedding night with Minas. Or was it more than nerves? Nausea worsening, mouth watering, I felt the gorge coming. I broke from his grasp. I fled to Ahira's chamber and aimed my sparse stomach contents at her waste pot, grateful she'd emptied it before she left. I sat back on my heels and wiped the sweat from my brow. Why was I so nervous? I'd given myself to him before.

What if it wasn't nerves? What if . . .

A baby.

Trepidation and wonder filled me. Minas and I had tried but never conceived. Gaios always provided a purgative after we were intimate. Could it have failed? But why now? I froze.

Surely Gaios wouldn't have—

Terror hit me like a hammer. Had Gaios purposely allowed me to conceive? I tried to remember the days I'd bled with the moon's cycle— and couldn't. Ahira would know.

"Should I call for Pushpa?" Potiphar stood outside Ahira's room. "Are you ill?"

I swallowed my panic, forcing calm into my tone. "I think I'm a little nervous." More than a little. If I was indeed with child, I must be able to convince Potiphar the child was his when my belly began to swell. I would deliver a fully developed baby weeks before it was due, but perhaps I could blame its size on Potiphar's bulk.

"Zully?"

I leapt to my feet and emerged from the closet-sized room, then went straight to the tray of food and chewed on a sprig of parsley to freshen my breath.

Potiphar filled two goblets with wine and handed one to me. "You need not be nervous. We have seven days together. I'm a patient man." He lifted his goblet, prepared to wait.

"Your kindness overwhelms me." It was true. I'd never expected to enjoy being in his presence. I set aside my goblet and closed the space between us. "I'm nervous about the festival, Husband, but about my future, I'm quite determined."

Let him interpret my words as he wished.

Perhaps Pharaoh's captain wasn't the crocodile I feared, but if I carried Gaios's child, I must convince Potiphar he was a stallion—while Gaios planned for *three* return passages to Crete.

TWENTY-THREE

The man said,
  "This is now bone of my bones
    and flesh of my flesh."
GENESIS 2:23

Each morning of her weeklong stay in Pushpa's chamber, Ahira had asked Elohim to wake her before the stone water clock ceased its flow into the copper basin. To her delighted surprise, He'd graciously done so. Was it coincidence? Perhaps, but she wanted to believe He was as personal as Joseph promised.

Pushpa's strict morning schedule felt a little like stiff new sandals to a Hebrew shepherdess; however, on this morning before Ahira returned to Zully's chamber, she watched Pushpa with a wistful grin.

The old cook charged at one of the Minoans, towel waving. "Get away from the gruel. I'll add the spices." She lifted a spoonful to taste it and noticed Ahira watching her. "Have you seen Joseph yet this morning?" During the last seven days, Joseph had joined Pushpa and Ahira to help prepare the morning meals and shared a cup of tea or mulled wine every evening. Ahira's heart had never felt so full.

"I haven't seen him yet," Ahira said. "Maybe he's already preparing Master Potiphar for his return to palace duties."

Pushpa swiped her hands over the gruel to add the cinnamon. "If I know my Potiphar, he'll be at Pharaoh's side before dawn."

As though her words conjured him, the master burst through the kitchen door. Donned in full military regalia, he also wore something new—a smile. "My wife will have a small bowl of gruel with a few raisins, Ommi. She also likes a little honey in her yogurt and a bit of fruit—doesn't matter what kind." He marched around the table to kiss Pushpa's forehead. "I've told Zully I'll need to work more than usual. Many weeds infested the garden while we were away, so don't expect me for midday or evening meals."

"Is your shoulder at full strength?"

Potiphar placed his right hand on his left shoulder and rolled his arm around with almost full motion. "Not completely, but I suspect after a few weeks of sparring, I'll be fine."

"You will return for the evening meal with your wife—won't you?"

Pushpa stirred the gruel, trying to look busy. The question wasn't really a question. He'd already told her he wouldn't.

"I've been away from Avaris for months, and although Hami has admirably protected our pharaoh for the past seven days, he reports chaos in the palace, among the nobles, and in Pharaoh's heart. Ma'at must be restored to Lower Egypt, Ommi, and I begin that work today. I'll discern which of the Tehenu prisoners must be executed for their stubborn allegiance and which can become a loyal part of Egypt's labor force. I'll dig deeper into the investigation of Pharaoh's noblemen to discover who might kill me or my best friend with our next breath or bite of food. So, no, Ommi. Unfortunately, I won't enjoy tonight's meal with my beautiful wife."

Pushpa raised her chin. "Did you at least assure Zully that you won't always be so busy?"

With a bronze-tipped spear in one hand and a bronze-bordered shield in the other, Master Potiphar was a frightening figure—until a lazy grin appeared. "My wife was still sleeping when I left. Joseph has my permission to relay that information." He turned his attention to Ahira. "He also has my permission to bed you, but you will not marry my chamberlain. His duty is to this villa and my estate. You would only distract him."

He strode out of the kitchen, leaving Ahira's cheeks burning. She heard the Minoan slaves laughing. Mortified, she glanced at Pushpa.

She chuckled. "You Hebrews are too shy about the pleasures granted by the gods."

Humiliation turned to anger. "I won't be shy about such pleasures when I have a *husband*." Ahira regretted the hurt she saw in Pushpa's pinched expression. "I'm sorry, Pushpa. I shouldn't have been rude to you. Elohim gave that unique pleasure to share with only one person—a man who loves me enough to sacrifice his desires for my needs. A man who knows me more intimately than anyone else." The Midianites had tainted that oneness for Ahira, and Gaios had stolen it from Zully. Checking to ensure she wasn't overheard, she lowered her voice. "If the mistress could have saved that pleasure for her husband alone, this morning's news wouldn't be so grave."

Pushpa's features softened. "Are you sure you should tell her? Why not let Joseph? He's the chamberlain, after all—and he doesn't have to see Zully all day every day."

"She wouldn't believe him, Pushpa." Ahira gathered spices for Zully's mulled wine into a small cloth and tied it into a pouch. "I'm the only one Zully trusted with the truth of her relationship with Gaios. I'll be the one she trusts with her sorrow when I tell her he's been sold."

After placing the pouch in the bottom of a small pan, Ahira poured wine over it and set the pan in the glowing coals to steep. The villa had been unusually quiet since Joseph sold Gaios the day Potiphar returned. So far neither Ahira nor Pushpa had heard any gossip about him among the Medjays or kitchen slaves. Maybe they were all so relieved by his absence that they pretended he'd never been there. Careful not to let the wine boil, she extended her hands over the fire and remembered Zully's terror when the master confronted her about Gaios. Ahira had alerted Pushpa, and even she had been surprised at the seven days of laughter and pleasure from the wedding chamber. *Thank You, Elohim.* It was a miracle the mistress hadn't been accused publicly to face maiming or death.

"Ahira?"

"Ah!" She jumped when Joseph gently rested his hand on her arm.

"I didn't mean to startle you." Concern deepened the lines between his brows.

"It's all right. I was . . ." What could she say? *I was thinking about our owners' wedding week?* "I was waiting on the mulled wine, but it's ready now." She grabbed a cloth, doubled it over, and pulled the small pot from the embers before pouring the wine into a cup.

Joseph stood beside her. "I can tell the mistress about Gaios. You need not bear this news."

"No, Joseph." She set aside the empty pan. "I must tell her so I can be the one to comfort her."

A flush bloomed on his cheeks.

"Joseph, are you well?"

He released a self-conscious puff. "I wondered if Master Potiphar told you that he granted permission—"

"Yes!" Her rush to stop him came in a shout, drawing Pushpa's attention as well as that of the other four kitchen slaves. Ahira's cheeks flamed into a color likely matching Joseph's. She lowered her voice. "We need not discuss it—"

"But I need to know if your heart is open to marriage. Then we can pray for Elohim to change the master's heart."

She was astonished. "But, Joseph, you know what happened to me in that captive train."

He drew near, so close she felt his breath on her cheek. "And you know the proud and self-righteous Prince Joseph before Elohim's mercy made me its slave. Can you forgive my past and love me for who I'm becoming?"

Ahira stared into the face of true humility. "Perhaps you've been right all along, Joseph ben Jacob. Maybe Elohim really did look on me with favor when He brought me to Egypt."

Joseph placed a kiss on her forehead. "We'll pray for Elohim's favor to spill over into Master Potiphar's heart so we can marry." When he released her, his countenance brightened. "Set your water clock for two lines after dark. I'll meet you in the kitchen each night with Pushpa as our chaperone—until we're married and have a chamber of our own."

Ahira watched him go, her throat too tight to speak.

Pushpa appeared at her side. "Married or not," she said with a wry grin, "you two are one vessel—whole only when you're together."

Ahira nodded, Abba Enoch's teaching never more meaningful than in this moment. "Elohim created the first woman from the man's rib, and when our God presented her to him, the man called her bone of his bones and flesh of his flesh. Do you see now, Pushpa, why a woman was intended to give herself fully to only one, a man who treasures her as he cares for his own flesh and bones?"

Pushpa's playful grin waned. "Your mistress awaits her morning meal." She abruptly returned to her chopping table, picked up her knife, and began cutting leeks and onions for the evening's stew. Silence meant she was pondering.

Reminding herself that Pushpa never held a grudge, Ahira ladled gruel into a small bowl, then prepared Zully's yogurt as the master had ordered. Her heart warmed, realizing he'd learned his wife's favorite foods and cared enough to request them before beginning his day. It was a small kindness but worth telling her mistress—especially after she'd heard of Gaios's departure. After placing a sprig of parsley beside the handful of raisins, Ahira picked up the tray and started toward Zully's chamber, thinking that the mistress probably would expect Gaios to serve her this morning as he'd done every morning since Joseph bought him from the Midianites.

As she approached the guards outside the mistress's chamber, Ahira didn't recognize them. "I'm Ahira, Mistress Zuleika's—"

"We know. Captain Potiphar said we're to treat you with respect." He inclined his head as the other guard knocked on the door.

"Come!" Zully answered quickly as if she'd been awaiting the arrival.

"Thank you." Ahira bowed to the Medjays and sent up a silent prayer. *Give me courage and favor, Elohim.*

"Ahira." The mistress met her and glanced over her shoulder as the door clicked shut. "Where's—"

Ahira darted past the low table in the chamber, where Zully and Gaios normally shared their meals. "I thought you might enjoy watching the new day arrive," she said, continuing toward the courtyard. Her voice was brittle with forced cheer. She placed the tray on a table between two couches and turned.

Mistress Zully stood at the threshold. "Is Gaios still in the kitchen?" She pulled a blanket tighter around her shoulders though the harvest morning air was warm. "How long till he comes?"

"He's not coming, Zully." Ahira moved to guide her mistress to one of the couches.

Zully sat stiffly and accepted the cup of warmed wine. "Why?"

Ahira knelt beside her, inhaling courage. "Gaios has been sold."

Zully stared into her cup, remaining perfectly still.

Ahira removed the cup from her hand. "Master Potiphar ordered your favorite foods in the kitchen before he left. He was so happy."

The mistress blinked. Barely breathing. Then blinked rapidly. She launched to her feet. First clasping her hands. Then fisting and opening them. She paced like a wild beast in a cage. If only she would scream or flail. Instead, her body spasmed with silent protests.

Ahira watched helplessly. "Mistress, come. Eat something."

"Was it Joseph? Gaios told me Joseph hated him. Ask your Hebrew prince where Gaios is. Gaios alone knows where our profits are kept and—"

"Joseph discovered Gaios retrieving a hidden pouch of silver from the winery to pay gambling debts." Ahira purposely spared Zully the worst—that Gaios had offered villa information to Wereni, the man her mistress feared most.

Zully stumbled back and fell onto her couch. "Gambling? Was gambling the way that fool hoped to hasten our return to Crete? What will I do now? I don't even know which merchants he dealt with in the lower city."

The mistress didn't seem overly saddened by the loss of Gaios himself. "Perhaps it's for the best. Master Potiphar appeared very much in love with you."

"Gaios may have been sold, but I know the man. He promised to return me to Crete, and Gaios has never broken a promise to me, Ahira. He'll come back for me." Her stomach growled loudly and she pressed against it.

"Eat something. Please." Ahira knelt beside her and offered the bowl of gruel with a spoon.

Zully reached for the spoon but suddenly leapt from the couch and raced into her chamber. Ahira followed and found the mistress emptying her stomach into a waste pot. When she lifted her head to face Ahira, she was the color of Egypt's mudbricks.

Please, Elohim, no. Ahira helped her stand. "I'll get frankincense from Pushpa."

"Frankincense won't cure this sickness." She lumbered to her bed and fell onto the mattress. "You know, don't you? How long since you washed my menstrual rags?"

Ahira's heart hammered in her chest. "We don't *know* you're with child. You've never been regular with the moon cycles."

"I'm carrying Potiphar's child, Ahira."

"Zully, it has to be Gaios's—"

"I'm carrying *Potiphar's* child," Zully hissed, "and it will arrive a few weeks early."

"Mistress, no! Even if people believe the child's delivery is premature, Gaios looks nothing like the master."

Her eyes narrowed. "We'll decide if the risk is worth the reward after we determine if I'm actually pregnant or have simply been ill for a week. Bring me a small onion with my midday meal. At Zakros harem, we inserted a small onion inside a woman. If the taste traveled to her mouth by the next mealtime, she was proven to be carrying a living seed."

"Our camp used the same test." Ahira didn't mention it was Joseph's ima, Rachel, who brought the practice to Canaan.

Zully pulled her into a tight embrace. "We'll know by sunset if a child grows in my belly."

TWENTY-FOUR

*Better a dry crust with peace and quiet
than a house full of feasting, with strife.*
PROVERBS 17:1

How long had it been since Potiphar had enjoyed a cup of mulled
wine with Ommi? *Soon,* he promised himself. Sleep had come easier
last night after the covert arrest of two collaborators in Wereni's coup.
Potiphar escorted them to his prison, documented their collusion in
the traitorous scheme, and then suggested Pharaoh announce the
noblemen's disappearance as a sudden trade journey to Cush. Wereni
wouldn't realize he'd been betrayed. By using the information from the
traitors, the would-be pharaoh in Abydos would believe Wereni had
skimmed silver from his pockets. Perhaps putting Wereni on the
defensive would decrease his not-so-subtle threats against foreign-
born nobility in Avaris. Amu noblemen had become hesitant to leave
their homes.

During his four-month investigation of Wereni's conspiracy, Potiphar had left everything he owned in the Hebrew's care, and his chamberlain had proved himself faithful. That morning, however, Joseph
had been unusually sullen, his facial features closed as if he were hold-

ing something back. After nearly three decades of interrogating prisoners, Potiphar knew what secrets looked like. Something was
bothering the Hebrew—but did he want to know?

"You slept soundly this morning." Joseph applied Horus's swirl
beneath Potiphar's lower lashes. "I hope that's a good sign, Master."

"Make sure you draw the Eye of Horus bolder than yesterday," he
said. "It must last into evening."

"So, you'll be late again tonight?" The Hebrew's steady hand continued applying the kohl, providing a good reason for silence.

Potiphar knew he'd neglected his wife, but it couldn't be helped.
When he left the villa the morning after their wedding week, he'd
returned to a hornet's nest of issues at the palace. After working day
and night for three weeks—without seeing Zully—he'd finally
returned to his wife's chamber, expecting his Minoan princess to berate
him for breaking more promises. She inflicted cool indifference
instead, offering as much affection as a dead fish.

"How are my fields, Hebrew?"

"Excellent harvest this season, my lord."

"Your god's favor remains on my house."

No response.

Potiphar checked his reflection in the mirror. "Red ochre? Am I so
old and pasty that I require color on my cheeks?"

"I've added red ochre to your cheeks since your efforts to protect
Pharaoh Khyan keep you inside the palace or prison. Perhaps your
restful sleep made your mind even sharper, my lord."

Carefully worded and astute as always. Potiphar realized on most
mornings he likely wouldn't even have noticed the Hebrew's detached
mood. For the first time in months, his thoughts had space for something other than protecting his best friend.

"Finished."

Potiphar grabbed his wrist before he could walk away. "Out with it,
Hebrew."

"I don't wish to pry, Master." He met Potiphar's gaze without hesitation.

"I've given you permission to speak."

"How long since you've seen your wife?"

Potiphar hovered between anger, shame, and curiosity. "Why do you ask?"

"You may wish to see her soon."

A chill shot through him. "Is she ill?" He bolted to his feet.

"Ahira said she's feeling better."

"She was nauseous during our wedding week." Potiphar stopped; his hand stilled on the latch. Turning slowly, he aimed a menacing glare at his chamberlain. "Has she been ill all this time, and no one told me?"

"She's not ill, my lord. She's with child."

"She's . . ." Potiphar felt the blood rush from his face and tried to control his breathing. "She's with child? She's with child." He repeated the words, tasting them, mulling them, processing the weight of the revelation. "My wife is with child."

Joseph chuckled. "I'm sure you'll find her on the roof."

"On the roof?" Again he asked the Hebrew for an answer he should know.

"Working on her potter's wheel."

"It's before dawn."

The Hebrew's features sobered. "She appears as diligent as you, my lord."

"But she should be resting. She's with child."

"Perhaps she's as determined to show her worth to you as you are to save your king." Joseph bowed after offering the insight.

Potiphar scrubbed his head and growled. "How can I see a conspiracy so clearly and be so blind to my wife?" He flung open his door, not waiting for an answer. "I'm going to be an abi!" he shouted and glimpsed grins from his stoic Medjays. After blasting through the door to the rooftop stairs, he bounded up two at a time. "Zully! Zully!"

At the top he found her standing beside the spinning potter's wheel, hands covered in clay. "Are we under attack?"

She was pale as a sheet, and he inwardly kicked himself for frightening her. "No, Zully. Nothing like that." His eyes traveled to her belly.

A pottery apron, tied above her slight bump, proved his hope true. "I just heard." Anticipation thrust him forward, hand extended to welcome his child.

Her glare held the warning of a viper. "You race up those stairs after ignoring me for nearly a month, and you pretend to care about a child?" She marched back to the stool behind her potter's wheel and kicked the lower plate to resume her work. "Break promises to me, Potiphar, but I'll not let you break promises to our child."

Nearly a month. How could he have stayed away so long? "I've come to apologize." He could count on one hand how many times he'd said those words.

"Why apologize?" She scoffed. "You'll only do it again." His wife didn't look up.

Drawing breath to list the vast responsibilities that kept him from her—chief among them protecting the king of Egypt—he glimpsed dozens of colorful hand-sized vases. "Those are stunning." He stepped toward the shelves lining the waist-high rooftop wall. Stacked like fancy earthenware soldiers, all the vases bore Egyptian gods and symbols, yet each one was uniquely alive with vibrant Minoan colors.

Suddenly awed, he saw his wife anew. *You are distinctively Zully.* Even the robe she wore under her apron had been dyed from its traditional natron white to a sun's-glow yellow. "You've brought Crete to Egypt, my love."

Her foot slowed the wheel, and she began rinsing her hands in a water basin. "Who told you I was with child?"

"Joseph."

A cynical chuckle brought her to her feet. "Of course. No one is as good as Joseph pretends to be, Potiphar. He's manipulating you."

She dried her hands and stood silhouetted in dawn's light. A leather tie held her hair back, allowing long tendrils to frame her natural beauty. She wore no cosmetics, yet her smooth skin was a sun-kissed auburn. The small bulge beneath the apron drew him a step closer.

Potiphar would ignore her comment about Joseph. She'd been angry from the beginning that he ran the villa instead of her. "Your vases are truly remarkable, Zully. There are enough on your shelves for the high-ranking noblewomen and Pharaoh's two wives. We'll keep the guest list small, so you need not continue working at your wheel. I'm sorry I've neglected you." He offered his hand. "It's time now to care for our child. Please. Let Pushpa spoil you with cinnamon baked pears, and your Hebrew maid will decorate your nails."

"Why would I want to become one of the whiny, spoiled nobleman's wives you and I hate?"

"No, I didn't—" Yet what he'd prescribed for her life was exactly what spoiled noblewomen did. Frustrated, he rubbed his bald head again. Why hadn't he made time for her? She was right. How could he add a baby to his life if he couldn't even be available to his wife? Potiphar had watched Khyan laugh and play with his children and enjoy meaningful conversations with his wives. Why couldn't the king's protector live out the same legacy?

Potiphar looked up and found his wife standing beside the short wall, scanning the city below. Beyond her, the rising sun cast startling colors into a brightening sky—looking very much like his wife's artistry.

"I've cheated you, Zully, asking you to make these gifts for a festival I didn't fully explain."

"I've seen Hathor's festival, Potiphar, and heard the riots of akhet. I'm sure the lotus festival will be—"

"No, Zully. The lotus festival is as unique as the flower itself. People will flock to the Nile, whenever and wherever a lotus festival is declared, from both Upper and Lower Egypt. Nobility and beggars. Highborn and low. They converge at Hapi's feet, god of the Nile, giver of life, granter of dreams."

"You said you didn't believe in the gods," she whispered.

"I believe in dreams."

She didn't answer.

"Everyone floats their heart's dearest dream into Hapi's Nile with a burning candle in a lotus-shaped votive. The wealthy make their votives of silver. The poor weave them with papyrus. But Hapi considers every lotus dream as though borne on Pharaoh's gold."

Zuleika faced him. "Must we share a votive, Potiphar? Or can I have a heart dream of my own?"

"Married couples share one heart, Zully, and, therefore, one votive." He recognized her continuing distress and pulled her away from the rooftop wall. "Something more than my neglect troubles you." He lifted her hair off her neck, inadvertently brushing her skin.

Her breath caught.

She was like a frightened bird, jittery and eager to flee. He'd been a fool to break the promises he made during their wedding week. "You're safe with me, Zully."

"If you don't believe in the gods, Potiphar, why do you float a candle?"

"For the same reason I'll provide all the silver votives for our guests."

"You must explain."

"Because our invited guests must come to our villa first, collect their silver votive and candle, and proceed out the door to light their candle from Pharaoh's flame."

Her understanding came with a single nod. "Pharaoh will look each guest in the eye and become the god who gives birth to every dream."

"You are incredibly adept at politics, Princess Zuleika." His compliment softened the hard lines around her mouth. "It doesn't matter what *I* believe about the gods. It matters only that the people believe their dreams are heard and that Pharaoh Khyan is the center of their lives."

"He's the center of your world, Potiphar. Everyone else still lives a life of their own." Expressionless, she started toward her pottery wheel.

Potiphar grabbed her arm. "I'm responsible for his life, Zully!"

She wrenched away and steadied herself against the wheel.

"I'm sorry. I didn't mean to—"

She pierced him with a glare. "You taste his food. You take a spear meant for his heart. You investigate a coup against him. What will be your excuse to stay away when I deliver this child?" Her chin quaked, but she shed no tears. "You returned from Temehu promising to be a better husband and demanding I reserve my *vase* for you alone. You've broken your promise, Potiphar. Must I keep mine?"

"Yes!" He raised a hand to strike her but halted.

Her arms shot up in defense. When she lowered them, his hand was still poised and condemning. Her shock mirrored Potiphar's horror.

"I would never hurt you," he said. But the words were hollow. He'd heard his abi say the same thing to Ommi and then seen him strike her many times in the heat of anger.

"You said you loved me," she spat—an accusation, not a statement.

"I love you as much as I'm capable."

"You know nothing of love, Potiphar, because it requires sacrifice."

"Don't talk to me about sacrifice!" He pounded his scarred shoulder.

She scoffed, no longer flinching. "More proof of your twisted love." She sat behind her wheel and thrust her foot against the kickplate. "You protect a king in his palace, surround him with hundreds of Medjays, but you leave your wife alone in a villa while a vizier seeks her destruction."

Fear shot through him like an arrow. "Wereni threatened you?"

"His politics threaten me. Wereni threatens foreign nobility in Avaris, and Pharaoh pretends ignorance."

Potiphar swiped a weary hand down his face. "Who has filled your mind—"

"You should have been here, Potiphar. Warned me. Talked to me. I'm the daughter of a foreign king. I understand power struggles and political games." She wrapped her arms around her waist. "If Wereni can't get to Pharaoh, he'll aim at others close to him. If he can't harm you, he'll attack . . ." She looked over the rooftop wall, the fears she left unspoken as real as the child she now carried. Her cheeks were as gray as the clay on her wheel. Why hadn't he considered that his wife might be afraid?

"I would never leave you or Pushpa in danger, Zully. This villa is as well defended as the palace, day and night. Wereni knows I'd cut his heart out if he or his spies crossed my threshold. I've broken promises and wronged you with my absence. I see that, Zuleika, and I'll make it right somehow. But I've kept my vow to protect you as I protect Ommi. You're safe . . . my love."

She covered a sob at the endearment he'd chosen carefully. He needed to hold her, to assure her. He moved closer, as if approaching a shy colt, and first brushed her arm with a single finger. Then tucked a tendril of hair behind her ear. She didn't recoil, so he gently coaxed her to stand and pulled her into his arms. The warmth of her soaked into his soul. She was trembling, her hands limp at her sides. How could he prove he was trustworthy and make her feel safe? "I wish I'd known you were so frightened."

"Should I have sent word through your chamberlain?"

Potiphar's eyes slid shut, and he let her go.

She returned to her pottery wheel.

"Zully, please."

She kicked the lower wheel and dipped her hands into the water basin before gathering another lump of clay and slamming it onto the wheel. Not a tear. No emotion at all. She seemed as formless as the lump in her hands—and he had no idea how to shape her.

"I'll return to share a meal tonight." It was the first of many promises he must honor. Perhaps he could dismantle the wall between them brick by brick.

She gave no indication she'd heard him. Her empty stare brought the rumors of her madness to mind. He'd ignored them with all the other whispers about her infamous banquet and its tainted wine. He retreated down the stairs, reluctantly accepting his own advice: *There's a seed of truth behind every rumor.* He marched past his guards, entered his chamber, and found Joseph cleaning. Careful to close the door first, he kept his voice low. "When did Zully's hysteria begin?"

"She hasn't been diagnosed by a physician, Master Potiphar." The chamberlain's soft tone acknowledged awareness.

"But you've witnessed it: the unfounded fear and despair." The treatments for madness in Egypt were often more heinous than the malady.

He paused, hesitant, and then nodded.

"When did it start, Hebrew?"

"Soon after her banquet. But not all her fears are unfounded, my lord," he added quickly. "Three foreign noblewomen were attacked in their villas last month."

"Did you tell her that?"

"No, Master. I believe she hears the palace kitchen's gossip from the rooftop."

Potiphar paced as the morning sun screamed its condemnation through his courtyard. "I'm late for court." He reached for his weapons and started toward the door. "Tell my wife's maid to watch her carefully. If Zully's mood worsens or her fear grows, send for me." Khyan had shared his personal physician to tend Potiphar's shoulder. He'd request the king's best healers for Zully if her condition worsened. Potiphar paused. "Thank you, Joseph, for suggesting I see my wife this morning. You were courageous to speak as more than a slave."

He hurried out of the chamber and passed the kitchen with barely a glance. His first thought on waking was how long it had been since he shared a cup of wine with Ommi. He hadn't even considered how he'd neglected his wife. Family guilt weighed more than warrior's armor. He still wasn't sure Khyan's gift was a good idea, but now the thought of a life without Princess Zuleika was worse than falling on his own sword.

TWENTY-FIVE

*The angel of the LORD found Hagar near a spring
in the desert; it was the spring that is beside the
road to Shur. . . .*
   *She gave this name to the LORD who spoke to
her: "You are the God who sees me."*
GENESIS 16:7, 13

Zuleika

The cramping had wakened me before dawn, so I'd climbed to my
rooftop hideaway, lighting torches and lamps as I went. Sitting at my
potter's wheel, I kicked the lower plate and felt a stronger twinge in
my abdomen. *It's pain from last night's lentil stew.* But flatulence didn't
come at regular intervals as these pains had all morning.

When Potiphar bounded into my private world, I'd tried to hide
my pain, tried to deny it in either my belly or my heart. I wanted to
rush at him, beat his chest with my fists, but then kiss him long and
deep. Perhaps then he'd understand a tiny measure of the chaos inside
me. His promises were as empty as my heart. I could never feel safe in
his villa—or anywhere in Egypt. Potiphar had abandoned me, and
Gaios had vanished.

"Oh!" The tightening worsened. I grabbed my belly, and a shaft of
fear surged through me. Would my child abandon me like all the men

I'd known? *Please, little one, you must be strong. Stay with me until Gaios, your pateras, comes to take us home.*

Was I being ridiculous? Four months without a word from him. Joseph had sold him to the Midianites, and Ahira said they had likely sold him to a land far away. What if he had died in a captive train?

The cramping eased, and I massaged my belly, wishing I knew Ahira's god better. From her description, he seemed too prudish to save the baby of my affair.

I stared at the lump of clay on the wheel and felt my creative urge drain away. I'd sat on this rooftop at every time of the day and night, throwing hundreds of little vases and decorating each with a unique design. Potiphar said there were plenty for the lotus festival guests, but he had no idea the ravenous demand for them in the lower city market.

After I'd heard that Joseph sold Gaios to the Midianites, I used Ahira's pity to convince her to make a clandestine journey to the lower city market and find the merchant to whom Gaios sold my art. She told me that when the vendor saw my vases, he returned my unsold paintings and stocked only the hand-sized treasures. They later sold like water in the desert. At least that's what the merchant said. I could hardly believe it at first, but the numbers didn't lie.

I cupped my hands around the child rounding my belly. "Your pateras wasn't always a bad man, little one, but you'll grow up believing Potiphar is your pateras, an Egyptian hero who loves you very much."

Even so, we couldn't stay in Egypt. We'd return home. I sighed, tallying how much profit I'd need now that I was the only one saving for two passages. And Potiphar would never let me go if he believed the child was his. When I arrived safely home, I'd write and tell him the child was Gaios's. By then I'd be too far away for a Nile-bound soldier's revenge.

Another pain tore through my abdomen, this one stealing my breath. Pressing one hand to my belly, I hissed through clenched teeth and leaned forward. When the cramping ebbed, I moved the wheel with my hands so as not to strain my abdominal muscles further, then dipped my hands in the basin of tepid water and sprinkled a few drops on the drying clay.

"Egypt is a furnace," I grumbled to no one. It wasn't the only thing I loathed about the country—nor did I entirely hate the Black Land. I'd discovered lovely things about it—as Pateras predicted—though I'd rather cut out my own tongue than admit it.

I kicked the bottom plate, spinning the clay into workable speed. My hands moved up and down, pulling, shaping. I pressed a thumb into its center and carefully angled a tiny lip barely larger than the neck. Intent on my new creation, I breathed deeply but didn't even pause through the cramping that followed. I couldn't stop creating. It kept me alive. "And I will teach you someday, little one."

The pain in my back became constant. I stretched my arms overhead while slowing the lower wheel with one foot. Slipping a strand of horse's mane between the wet clay and the wheel, I separated my new creation cleanly. It would wait on a tray with the others for baking later that day. Pushpa had been eager to help with the festival gifts, so I taught her to adjust her bread ovens to safely fire pottery. If there was a kinder soul on this earth, I had yet to meet one.

The sound of sandals on the stairs reminded me I was hungry. "Ahira, I'm famished. I hope you brought extra honey for the gruel."

She appeared at the doorway, tray in hand. "The Medjays ate all the gruel again. It's rather a light meal this morning." After placing the tray of fruit, yogurt, and bread on the table beside me, she tilted my chin to face her. "Zully, you're flushed."

I pulled away and directed her attention to the vessel in my hand. "This one will be the last vase I make for our festival guests. It deserves a scarab beetle carving, Egypt's sacred sign of renewal. Can you imagine, Ahira? Making a dung beetle sacred? Potiphar said it's because they seem to appear out of nothing, like the sun god, Ra. I'd say if nasty little dung beetles can create themselves from nothing, perhaps anyone has a chance to start fresh, to be transformed."

My own words condemned me. Though Pateras had challenged me to make a new life here, I didn't want to start fresh or be transformed. I used my carving tool to etch the disgusting bug into the wet clay. Let the dung beetles start over. I wanted my old life, my first love—Crete.

"Neither Ra nor a scarab beetle created the new life inside you,

Zully." Ahira knelt beside me, begging for my attention. "These vases will be gifts for people who launch a floating candle with their deepest desire—to a god who can neither hear nor answer. Only one God hears when we pray, Zully. What is your heart's dream?"

I couldn't look into her searching eyes, couldn't believe there was truly a god who heard my cries. What if he, too, abandoned me or disappointed me with a *no*? "You know the answer, Ahira."

She stilled my hand, placing her own over it. "Say it."

Exhaling an unsteady breath, I obeyed her. "My heart's dream is to return to Crete."

She moved her hand to my stomach, and my gaze met hers. "Why must you return to Crete?"

"To raise my child among his own—" Another cramp seized me, low and tight. My hands squeezed the newly formed vase. "Uhh," I growled to endure the pain.

Ahira shot to her feet. "How long have you been in labor?"

"No!" I barked. "Not labor . . . Ohhh!" I felt a gush between my legs. Despair rose and gave birth to panic. "Ahira!" I stood, and a trickle of blood rolled down my legs.

"Come with me." She slipped her arm around my waist and supported me down the stairs. My legs wobbled, and I felt as if I balanced on someone else's limbs. We crossed the hall and passed my chamber guards.

"Mistress," both whispered respectfully, then closed the door behind us.

"Only a little farther." Ahira guided me to my elevated mattress and gently lifted my legs so I didn't have to use my tender stomach muscles. "I'm going to get a midwife."

"No!" I grabbed her arm. "She'll tell Pushpa—or Potiphar." *Oh, not Potiphar.* He'd been overjoyed at the news of the baby. He probably hated me after the way I'd treated him, but I didn't want him to know about the pains. "I can't allow myself to love him, Ahira. He'll fail me again. All men fail." I faced the wall, letting the tears come.

"Focus on resting, Zully." She smoothed stray hair from my face.

"You need a midwife. Pushpa and the master must know. This isn't a secret we can keep." She turned to go.

"I don't want to be alone." I bolted upright, and the effort felt like a rending of my middle. I doubled over, seized with pain.

"Shh, all right. I'll send one of the guards."

"Nooo! Stay."

She pried my fingers away and left me.

But before panic set in, I heard, "I'm here, Zully. I'm back." She positioned a pillow behind me. I turned from one side to the other but couldn't find a comfortable position.

Another cramp attacked me. I curled into a ball and cried, "Pray to your god, Ahira."

Her hand found mine and gripped it as tightly as I held hers. I squeezed my eyes closed, waiting for the pain to end. Why had I ever allowed Gaios to bed me? Why would I trust herbs given by a man to keep a woman's womb empty? Even as the tightening in my abdomen eased, a terrible backache remained.

If my calculations were correct, I'd missed six moon cycles, which meant my child couldn't be fully formed and live outside my womb. I'd seen one of Pateras's concubines miscarry. The baby's translucent eyelids and furry body had haunted my dreams for months.

As the cramping eased, I realized Ahira hadn't prayed. I relaxed my grip and opened my eyes, finding her head bowed and lips moving without making a sound. "What are you doing?"

She lifted her head. "Praying to Elohim as you asked."

"Does he hear your thoughts?"

"I've seen Joseph pray this way, and I'm sure Elohim hears him."

Joseph. "Would your god hear me if I were kinder to Joseph? Or perhaps your Elohim requires a bigger offering to save a child. What if I—"

"Elohim doesn't bargain like imaginary gods, and He doesn't always answer as we would like. I promised Him anything to save me from the slavers, but His plan for me was Egypt."

Another pain started, and I gritted my teeth. "What if I don't like your god's plan?"

She squeezed my hand. "Then we trust Him together for a future we don't understand and perhaps see His goodness when we recount our past."

I released a calming breath after the brief cramp and was distracted by the sound of birdsong in my courtyard. "Would your god hear me if I spoke to the sky? I always felt closer to the Mother Goddess while in the ocean or in the palace garden." Without waiting for her opinion or permission, I scooted off my bed and walked toward the courtyard on shaky legs.

Ahira followed a step behind and helped me to the couch. "Though most in Joseph's family believed Elohim dwelled only in Jacob's camp, God's favor on Joseph in Egypt proves He works anywhere." Her smile held hope and mischief. "I think He could have heard you from your chamber."

I was suddenly overwhelmed by what a treasure she was. I'd focused so long on the men who abandoned or betrayed me and utterly over-looked this woman, who had served me so selflessly. "Thank you, Ahira."

She seemed as surprised as a slave should be at a mistress's gratitude.

"I'll try to be kinder to Joseph," I said, "whether your god is kinder to me or not—even though Joseph's perfection annoys me."

"He's less perfect than he used to be." She grinned and propped pillows behind my back while I breathed through another light cramp.

Our humor faded as I looked into the cloudless sky. "If you hear me, Elohim," I said, daring to address the Hebrew god, "I beg you to save my child."

I waited. Scanned the sky. Waited more. Looked at Ahira.

"He doesn't speak aloud, Zully."

Undaunted, I spoke to the sky again. "I'll never be unkind to the chamberlain again." A bird fluttered from my palm tree and soared into the blue sky. My heart leapt. "Was that a sign, Ahira? Will he save my child?"

As if in answer, another cramp seized me—the most severe yet. I glared at my maid. "Your god is deaf to a woman's cries."

I squeezed her hand, and she wiped my brow with a cloth. "Not true. Elohim spoke comfort to an Egyptian woman when she cried out for her dying child."

"Tell me," I said between gasps.

"Prince Abraham was called Abram before he became 'the father of many,' and his wife, Sarai, was barren. She'd given her Egyptian maid-servant, Hagar, to Abram so the concubine's son could become her own. But when Hagar conceived, she despised Sarai, so the first wife mistreated her, and Hagar fled into the wilderness. The angel of the Lord appeared to Hagar near a spring on the road to Shur and promised the seed within her would be a son to whom she would give the name Ishmael."

"The mitera of the Ishmaelites?"

"Yes, but she wasn't royalty or elevated to a place of honor. She wasn't sent to a safe place to raise her son. Elohim commanded she return to serve her mistress willingly."

"Not to be mistreated."

"He commanded she return." Ahira stroked my hand. "Hagar then called Elohim by a new name: El Roi—'the God who sees me.' It didn't matter how Sarai treated her when she knew with absolute certainty that El Roi truly saw her, an *Egyptian* slave—not even a Hebrew. He saw a foreigner, Zully. I believe He sees you too."

"Zully?" Pushpa bustled into the courtyard without warning or invitation, a harried-looking woman following close behind. "This is Halima, my dearest friend and the midwife for Hathor's temple and Pharaoh's wives."

The midwife didn't carry a basket, pots, or unguents—only a cup of steaming liquid, which she handed to me. "Here, my dear. Drink this down. Your pains will increase for a little while, but it will be over soon."

The pungent scent of eronda burned my nose. "No," I said, pushing the cup away. It sloshed on my robe as another pain doubled me over. "Ahh . . ." I reached out for Ahira but felt the clammy, bony hand of a stranger.

"Lie back, and let your body do the work." Halima gently pushed my shoulders back against the armrest of the couch. "It would be unkind to give you false hope," she whispered, leaning close, "so I tell you the baby is already dead, my dear. You've left a trail of blood from the rooftop stairs to your bed and to this couch. You must drink the purgative tea to ensure nothing of its life remains inside you to fester, or you will die with it—and I simply can't allow that."

Nothing in her words was threatening, yet the eyes that seemed to bore into my soul terrified me. "I want nothing from you." I shoved her away, strength renewed with the ebbing pain.

"I'm telling you, Princess, you will die if you don't drink this tea."

"Then let me die." I rolled to my side.

Sandals shuffled behind me, receding into the chamber. Had Ahira left me too? I was too frightened to look. Another cramp threatened and the pain mounted. "Ahiraaa . . ."

Strong arms scooped me off the couch. I couldn't force my eyes open or unfurl my body to fight.

"Out!" my husband roared. "Everyone!"

"You will not die." He swayed, rocking me like a newborn. "You will live, Zully, and we will have more children."

I quieted as the pain ebbed. He laid me gently on my bed, and I turned toward the wall.

He sat on my mattress. "Zully, look at me."

I squinted at him and saw kohl running down his cheeks. Black tears had stained his robe. "You must live, Zully."

He took the cup of dreaded tea from my bedside table, where the midwife had placed it before her hurried retreat. "We'll have more children." He lifted my head and held the cup to my lips, pouring the tea down my throat. After placing the empty cup on the table, he scooted me over to lie beside me and propped his head on one hand. He wiped his cheeks and laid his hand on my tortured belly. "I won't leave you."

Until the baby is gone. I wanted to finish his sentence, but another cramp tore through me. I pursed my lips through the pain, shaking but refusing to cry out. My anger made me stronger. Without my child, nothing could keep me in Egypt—except a lack of information. How would I know when Crete no longer needed Pharaoh's funding? I needed a street rat. If Gaios ever returned for me, I'd never again trust his loyalty, but I'd wager my life on his greed.

TWENTY-SIX

The human spirit can endure in sickness,
  but a crushed spirit who can bear?
PROVERBS 18:14

Joseph

Though his water clock still dripped into the copper basin, Joseph lay awake in the small, dark chamber adjoining his master's. Surrendering to wakefulness, he pulled on his white schenti and cinched the braided gold belt. He slipped through the narrow opening of his door without letting the leather hinges creak, then padded silently on bare feet to check on his sleeping master.

His bed hadn't been slept in—again. Joseph pulled his fingers through thick, dark curls and tried to release his mounting concern to the only One who could salve the inner wounds festering in the master and mistress. *Elohim, I see real changes in the master's heart. Please, heal Mistress Zuleika's inner wounds so she can accept the love he's offering.*

Certain he'd find his master in Mistress Zuleika's chamber, Joseph would go to offer solace. Since the miscarriage, Potiphar had spent more time with his wife, guarding Pharaoh only while in court and leaving the investigation of Wereni's conspiracy to Hami.

At the mistress's door, Joseph greeted the guards, who knocked quietly, then waited in silence. The latch lifted, and Ahira appeared, her eyes brightening when she saw Joseph. He crossed the threshold and saw Master Potiphar sprawled on the elevated mattress, snoring. The mistress sat on the bed beside him. Her appearance startled him. Though Joseph had seen her the previous week, she looked even thinner now, like skin stretched over bones. Her complexion was sandy gray, her eyes as empty as Nile tide pools at harvest.

"Master?"

Potiphar bolted upright, and the mistress flinched.

"Shh." Ahira knelt beside her.

"Forgive me, my love." The master reached for his wife's hand. "I didn't mean to startle you. Shall we break our fast together this morning since it's early? I have time before leaving for the palace."

Joseph regretted disturbing them. "I'm sorry I woke you, my lord. I—"

"Both of you can go." The mistress slid her hand away from the master's, glancing up at him and Joseph. "I'm not hungry." She scooted against the wall and covered her head with both arms. Her sleeves fell away, revealing deep scratches on her forearms. Ahira had mentioned self-inflicted wounds.

Potiphar swung his legs to the floor. "Bring your mistress's meal, Ahira. I'll break my fast in my chamber while the chamberlain prepares me for the day."

When he pushed himself off the bed, the mistress lunged at his hand. "Wait! Potiphar. Will you come back?" She pressed his hand against her forehead, silent for two long heartbeats before gasping with a sob. "Why did you make me drink the eronda? I could have festered with infection, and you would have been free of me—and I could be free of a life I never wanted."

His shoulders sagged. He reached for her and placed a kiss amid her tangled hair. "I'll return to share our evening meal." As he passed Joseph and Ahira, he growled, "Both of you in my chamber—now."

The mistress curled onto her side. "Ahira will leave me someday too."

"I always come back, Zully," Ahira called from the doorway, her eyes filling with tears. "I tell her that at least fifty times in a day," she whispered.

Joseph's chest ached as they walked down the hall. The mistress had worsened considerably, and though Egypt's treatments for hysteria were harsh, what else could the master do?

"This can't continue," Potiphar said the moment they entered his chamber. "I've requested Khyan send his best healers to evaluate Zully today."

"No!" Ahira's panicked reaction drew a dangerous glare from their master. She immediately bowed but wasn't dissuaded. "Forgive me, my lord, but I've heard Egyptian remedies for . . . symptoms like those Mistress Zully is experiencing can be more devastating than the condition itself. Truly, my lord, I believe she's improving. Or she can improve—" Her voice broke, and she ceased the hopeless attempt.

"She isn't improving." His tone was surprisingly gentle. "Ommi said she eats no more than a crust of bread a day and drinks only mint tea or honeyed water. Have you observed the same?"

Ahira hesitated, head still bowed. "Yes, my lord."

"You've served my wife well, Ahira, but Zully needs more than you or I can give her. Return to her chamber, and don't leave her. Ommi will deliver food, and Joseph will escort the physicians when they arrive."

"Yes, my lord." Ahira glanced at Joseph, her eyes swollen and weary with concern.

When Potiphar started pacing, Joseph brushed Ahira's cheek, a gentle reminder of his growing affection. They'd spent no time together since the mistress lost her child. The whole household had rested little and worried much. Joseph watched her until the door closed behind her, aching for a quiet moment alone—or even a cup of tea with Pushpa and Ahira, his two favorite women.

"Isn't it odd that King Rehor hasn't tried to contact his daughter since he returned to Crete?" Potiphar halted on the tiles discolored by his pacing and stared at Joseph. Though his armor and weapons still hung on the wall pegs, his shoulders rounded with heavier burdens.

"Did Zully receive any messages from him while I fought the Tehenu rebellion?"

"She did not." Joseph watched the master resume his anxious habit. "I wondered about King Rehor's silence myself and asked Ahira if I should send a missive asking the king to send a message of comfort to his daughter. Ahira discouraged any contact."

Potiphar halted abruptly. "Why discourage a message to inform a man his daughter needed to hear from him?"

"Ahira said Mistress Zuleika felt abandoned and an *unanswered* message from her abba would be worse than no word at all."

"Humph." Potiphar marched to his cosmetics couch and lay back. "Begin." Without further conversation, Joseph prepared the master for the day. He silently dressed him and helped him don his jewelry and weapons.

As the master strode toward the door, he said only one thing. "Don't tell Zully the healers are coming. We need not add to her hysteria." He opened the door and was gone, leaving the terrible word hanging in the dawn's light.

Though Joseph knew nothing specific about Pharaoh's healers, Pushpa had warned him that Ahira and Potiphar must somehow stop the mistress's increasing mania before a physician was called. Over their nightly cup of mint tea, she'd described some of Egypt's remedies for the malady of hysteria: cutting the patient's flesh, consuming animals' blood or crushed bones, humiliating sexual acts in Hathor's temple. "Zully must never be seen by a priest, magician, or physician," Pushpa had whispered though she herself still professed belief in Egypt's gods. Evidently she hadn't been able to convince Potiphar that the healers were worse than the mania.

Joseph tidied the cosmetics, swept the chamber, emptied the waste pots, then set out a fresh robe for the master's evening visit with his wife. He'd planned to monitor the shepherds today but would busy himself with villa tasks instead so he could be available when the healers arrived.

He'd collected the prison's supply list yesterday, and— *Ubaid's cough.* Joseph had forgotten to return to the prison yesterday afternoon with the promised remedy after noticing that the old goat's chesty cough had returned. Ubaid protested any treatment, but Joseph refused to let him die in that dark, dank hole in the ground. He'd get the necessary herbs from Pushpa while collecting her weekly request for nonperishables and equipment.

Exiting the master's chamber, he greeted the Medjays with a nod and received the same in return. The kitchen was abuzz as usual.

"Make sure you add extra honey to the two bowls of gruel for our mistress and her maid," Pushpa ordered her slaves, using the same tone Potiphar used with his Medjays. "Today we pamper them."

Joseph approached her kneading table.

"Make yourself a tray, Chamberlain. I don't have the time or heart to think of anything except Zully and those awful healers." She slammed an innocent lump of dough onto the table and pounded it with her fist.

"May I hug you?" he asked.

"Absolutely not." She wiped her wet cheeks on each shoulder and kept kneading. "I'd completely fall to pieces. Stay on your side of the table, and don't talk about it."

Joseph obeyed, honoring the woman's tender heart and the hard shell that covered it. "Do you have any fenugreek in your basket of remedies?"

"Why?"

"Ubaid has a cough."

She wiped sweat from her brow. "Fenugreek is in the remedy basket under my bed. Bring it to me so I can show you how many seeds to use in a cup of hot water."

Joseph obeyed, hurrying to her adjoining chamber. He found the basket where she'd said it would be and sorted through four bags to find the one with the brown seeds he needed.

He returned and Pushpa studied him. "How is it you know fenugreek is for cough, Chamberlain?"

"My ima was a midwife, remember?" He grinned. "I learned quickly."

"Then why aren't *you* treating the mistress?"

"*I'm* not a midwife." What a ridiculous suggestion.

She jammed her floured fists to her hips. "You must be there, Joseph, when the healers come. You must protect our Zully."

"What can I do? Your midwife friend, Halima, couldn't help her."

"She wouldn't let Halima touch her."

"She only tolerates me in hopes of winning Elohim's favor."

"Your midwifery knowledge will be better than Egypt's healers, Joseph. Potiphar wouldn't let me call another midwife because he feared she would contradict Pharaoh's men—and he was right."

"How can you be sure? If they're healers, perhaps they—"

"You've managed the flocks and this villa brilliantly, Joseph, but you know nothing of Pharaoh's court. Khyan will send his magician, the priest of Seth, and his physician. All compete to maintain Pharaoh's favor. The magician's incantations must prove as powerful as the priest's god. The priest's temple needs Pharaoh's silver. And the physician's morbid curiosity is veiled torture in the name of science. All three are butchers who attended Ziwat's miscarriage last month—that young, otherwise-healthy woman who will never have another child." She held his gaze, waiting as the weight of truth landed like a boulder in his belly.

"Pushpa, I'm only a slave."

"You are more than a slave, Joseph. You're chamberlain of Potiphar's estate, and Pharaoh's men must respect your directives. You can be Zully's defender."

Courage began to rise as her mercy challenged his logic. "All right. I'll go."

"You may hug me now." An impish grin brightened her features.

Joseph showed her the bag of fenugreek. "Not until you tell me how many seeds to use for Ubaid's cough."

"Wet your fingertip and dip it into the bag. What sticks is the right portion of seeds. Grind them first, place the grounds in a cloth, and steep them to make one cup of tea for your oily warden. He won't like the flavor, but make the old goat drink it anyway. He'll breathe better and his cough will dissipate."

She opened her arms, welcoming him to her side of the table, and hugged him tight. "Deliver the seeds, and hurry back upstairs to wait in your office. I'll send one of my kitchen boys when the healers come."

Joseph made the steaming cup of fenugreek tea with the pot of boiling water Pushpa always kept on the cook fire. He carried it down the prison stairs, hearing Ubaid's cough as he descended.

"Warden, I've come with an order from the villa's commander." Joseph's words bounced off the walls in the torchlit main room.

Eerie voices erupted from the dark hallway of cells.

"I'm dying!"

"Let me out!"

"I'm innocent!"

"My waste pot's full."

Ubaid's cough mingled with the prisoners' complaints. "You said 'the villa's commander'? Hami?"

"Pushpa." Joseph thrust the steaming tea into his hand. "I'm to watch you drink it and return her cup."

He sniffed it, and his face contorted. "I'll not drink something that smells worse than my feet."

He handed it back to Joseph, but the chamberlain pushed the cup toward Ubaid's lips. "You *will* drink it or face my wrath and Pushpa's."

Ubaid raised an eyebrow. "Your wrath doesn't scare me, Chamberlain, but Pushpa's fury is fiercer than death itself." He downed all the tea in a gulp and shivered as he returned the cup to Joseph. "I might rather face death than do that again."

"Prepare yourself. My ima treated coughs like yours with fenugreek tea three times a day. I'll return with your second dose at midday."

"Oh no!" Ubaid's grumbling followed Joseph up the steps.

Joseph returned the cup to Pushpa's kitchen, retrieved the water clock from his chamber, and set it up in his small office as a reminder to give Ubaid his second cup—that is, if he wasn't occupied with the mistress and Pharaoh's healers.

Why had he agreed to Pushpa's outrageous request? Though the mistress had been civil since Master Potiphar's return, she would undoubtedly feel even more uncomfortable with him in the room while being evaluated by three Egyptian men she didn't know. *Elohim, please protect her and strengthen her for whatever lies ahead.*

After removing the estate ledgers from a shelf, he opened two scrolls and used polished stones to keep them open while he transferred the month's figures. He had plenty to keep him busy while he waited for Pushpa's summons.

The sound of running feet in the hallway came well before midday, and his office door burst open without a knock.

"They're coming." The Minoan slave's words were clipped, his eyes wide.

Joseph shot to his feet to catch the three men before they reached Mistress Zuleika's chamber. "Welcome, my lords!"

They halted and turned to appraise him. The tallest man wore a beaked headdress. Undoubtedly the priest of Seth. The healer, a short, plump man, wore finer robes than the king. "Your master's direction to his wife's chamber were clear," the third said. "We need no escort and have no time to waste. Captain Potiphar's wife needs immediate care." They continued down the hall, leaving a whiff of frankincense in their wake.

Joseph strode into their path and assumed a wide stance. "I appreciate your urgency," he said, "but allow me to introduce myself." The jingle of Medjay armor rang behind him, and the master's chamber guards flanked the healers. Remembering Pushpa's declaration—*more than a slave*—Joseph continued, "I'm Captain Potiphar's chamberlain, and the entire estate is in my care. My master has entrusted me with every decision, and as you see by the Medjays congregated around us, my decisions will be enforced. Every soldier and servant cares deeply for our mistress, so, my lords, I will ensure your treatment is in her best interest."

Pharaoh's healers exchanged mocking grins. "Lead us, then, O Great Chamberlain."

Joseph inclined his head and turned toward the mistress's chamber, heart thudding. *Elohim, give me wisdom and courage.*

One of the mistress's chamber guards pounded a spearhead on her door, and a weak voice bid them enter. Joseph lifted a hand to delay the healers. "I'll go in first and inform her—"

"We must see her reaction to the unexpected." The frankincense-scented physician barged past him as the guard opened the door. "It's part of the evaluation."

Elohim, help her.

Ahira sat with the mistress at the low table. Both women jumped to their feet as the three men entered, and the mistress whimpered. Ahira's arm wrapped her like a mother hen's wing.

Joseph stepped around the men, hoping to instill calm in the mistress. "These men are Pharaoh Khyan's premier healers. They've come to help you feel better."

"I'm fine," she said, trembling from head to toe.

The priest shoved Joseph aside before the others could object. "Come, Princess Zuleika. You must lie down so we can assess your needs." He led her toward the elevated mattress. "This won't take long if you fully cooperate."

The mistress obeyed but cast pleading glances at Ahira when the three men gathered around her.

"Do something," Ahira whispered, her fingers digging into Joseph's arm. "Get Pushpa."

"Pushpa can't stop them." He hoped his eyes communicated regret. "She sent me to listen with the knowledge I gleaned from Ima Rachel."

She released a tortured breath. "Then go." She nudged him forward and followed close behind.

"How long since you've made an offering at Seth's temple?" The priest stood over his patient, arms crossed. "The god of chaos can manifest in hysteria if he's been neglected."

The storm on the mistress's face broke. "Your god has no—"

"Captain Potiphar makes regular offerings," Joseph interjected. "My records prove Captain Potiphar's faithful offerings to Seth's temple."

"You've already gotten your silver, Priest." The magician moved him aside with his protruding belly and leaned over Mistress Zuleika. "Do you see or speak to the spirits of those lost in the shaking?"

"No." She attempted to scoot away, but the wall blocked her escape.

"You don't trust."

"Well, I—"

"You've stopped eating, haven't you?"

"Yes, but—"

"One of your dead relatives has taken up residence and torments you from within." In a single, swift motion, the magician unsheathed his dagger and gripped her wrist.

Joseph lunged for his arm. "Get away from her!" He shook the blade from the man's hand and pushed him away, then stood between the mistress and the men. "Leave. All of you. Now." He fully understood what Pushpa had meant by "butchers."

The physician distanced himself from the other two, sneering. "Send the two imbeciles away if you wish, Chamberlain, but don't exile Princess Zuleika's only hope of recovery. Greed makes them overly zealous because they're only paid if their treatment marks the patient. I have steady income from the king and merely record my findings for ongoing research in the ancient papyri." He produced a small item from his waist pouch and unwrapped its rough-spun covering.

Joseph recognized the overwhelming scent of the wax. "Frankincense."

The physician gave an appreciative nod. "You're familiar with healing herbs, Chamberlain. My methods are as reliable as the sun and moon."

The magician lifted his chins. "You're a fool to listen to the physician. I've been royal magician for six pharaohs. Princess Zuleika is tortured by a wandering ka."

"And I've been Seth's priest since the Amu took Egypt's throne. She's angered Seth."

The physician waved off their comments like pesky gnats. "Princess Zuleika suffers from hysteria—as has been rumored for months. Its cause in women is always rebel female parts, likely a floating uterus. Correct the uterus, and we correct a woman's mind."

The mistress whimpered, and Ahira shouldered through the healers to cradle the frightened woman. Both looked to Joseph, pleading silently.

"How do you treat hysteria?" Joseph asked the physician.

The man cast a triumphant glance at his competitors. "I fumigate the uterus, and it returns to its proper position, balancing the ka into perfect peace. We repeat the simple treatment every day for six weeks and restore ma'at to Princess Zuleika and this household."

"No, please!" the mistress cried out. "Joseph, please!"

Ahira whispered something to her mistress. "No! You can't tell him!" Mistress Zuleika's panic soared until Ahira's promise to remain silent settled her.

"You can always trust me, Mistress." Ahira gathered her into an embrace, piercing Joseph with a look he didn't understand. She lowered her head again to whisper and then laid her mistress gently on the bed before walking past the healers to pull Joseph aside. "She needs you to fight for her," she whispered. "Please, Joseph. She's afraid of these men. Is that madness?"

"It's the floating uterus that makes her afraid." The physician had overheard.

"Tell me." Joseph's eyes locked on Ahira's.

"Ahira, no," the mistress called from her bed.

Joseph glanced at the desperate woman and turned his focus back to Ahira. "How can I protect her if I don't know . . ." The words died on his lips, the irony of the moment hitting him like a fist. Hadn't he said the same words to Ahira on her first morning at the villa? Joseph turned again to examine the woman who had lost so much. Her husband and ima—killed in a single tragic moment—and then she left all she held dear to marry a king but instead married a soldier who had never wanted a wife.

Joseph glimpsed the Minoan shrine near the low table where the two women ate their meals. Disorganized and neglected, it declared the truth they'd all missed. The mistress had lost hope.

Whatever the secret she and Ahira held—it was all she had left.

Joseph returned his attention to Pharaoh's three healers and extended his hand toward the door. "Mistress Zuleika has no need of your treatments, my lords. I'll escort you out of the villa."

The physician's eyes narrowed. "Chamberlain, you may recognize frankincense, but the human body and its ka are mysteries you can't fathom."

Joseph let the healers' indignation feed his own. "That's the first sensible thing any of you have said. I remember seeing the results of a Canaanite healer's fumigating treatment. My ima treated a woman's serious burns after a Shechemite physician scalded her legs and buttocks." Joseph ignored their derision. "Guards!"

The healers jumped at his voice and looked cowed when four Medjays entered the room.

"Return Pharaoh Khyan's healers to the king," Joseph said, then turned on the men. "Thank you for your time, my lords. I believe your diagnoses have revealed a clear path to Mistress Zuleika's recovery."

The hint of a smile curved one guard's lips. Seething with rage, the noblemen marched out the door and stillness fell.

Joseph released the breath he'd been holding. He would answer to the master for offending them.

"Thank you, Joseph." It was barely a whisper, but the mistress's eyes held a spark he hadn't seen in months.

"You were wonderful." Ahira's arms circled his neck, and the warmth of her body soothed his concern.

Burying his face in the bend of her neck, he allowed his hands to rest on the curve of her hips and inhaled the scent of lotus blossoms in her hair. "*You* are wonderful, my love." The whispered words startled them both.

She stepped back, her cheeks flushed a lovely shade of pink, and returned to her mistress. "You see, Zully? Joseph wants only what's best for you. And did you notice the Medjays? Your guards were ready to drag those men out of your chamber if needed."

The mistress's eyes held Joseph's with new warmth. "How can I thank you?"

"Thank me by eating, Mistress."

Ahira transferred their food tray from the low table to her bed. "Pushpa included some broth for you this morning." Ahira nudged the bowl toward her, and the mistress sipped it. "Yes, good!"

Joseph turned to go. "Master Potiphar will be relieved to hear you're eating again, Mistress."

"I'm eating only to regain my strength and leave this vile country, Joseph."

He exchanged a concerned glance with Ahira. *Is the mistress truly mad?* Couldn't she see that Master Potiphar loved her? He would never let her leave Egypt. "I hope you'll feel differently, Mistress Zuleika, when your health is fully restored—body *and* mind."

TWENTY-SEVEN

How useless to spread a net
  where every bird can see it! . . .
Such are the paths of all who go after ill-gotten gain;
  it takes away the life of those who get it.
PROVERBS 1:17, 19

The day I'd dreaded for months had arrived. Potiphar and I stood at the head of a long line, waiting at the doorway of our banquet hall until palace and villa servants distributed the silver votives and candles to the lotus festival guests behind us. Each couple received only one, forced to share their greatest dream.

Potiphar held our candle. I held the silver votive in my left hand and rested my right on his forearm. He whispered something to Pharaoh Khyan. No doubt they spoke of some coup or a would-be assassin lurking around a corner or beneath a lotus blossom in the royal pond. My mind wandered to the Minoan treasures in my chamber. I'd ignored my circle of memories during the months hysteria tormented me, but the threat of Pharaoh's butchers and the proof of Joseph's protection had given me hope. I wasn't sure how I'd make it back to Crete, but my pink sand, purple scarf, murex-shell mirror, and rock-crystal vase bolstered my courage.

Pharaoh's booming laughter ended my musings, and Potiphar smiled at me. "You're not even trembling, my love. I'm so proud of you."

"You need not worry about me, Husband. I've even started painting again."

His eyes widened. "Perhaps after tonight's banquet, you'll offer me final proof of your complete recovery." A lusty grin conveyed the meaning. "You must admit I've been patient."

Tonight was the first time I'd really left my chamber since tainted wine sent noblewomen fleeing from these walls over a year ago. How could he not understand what I'd overcome to stand with him tonight? "Is a turn on my sheets the heart's dream you wish to float down the Nile, Potiphar?"

His playfulness evaporated, and I regretted my too-pointed dig. For nearly two months, I'd built my husband's confidence in me with softer words and a stronger body. Why risk the freedom I yearned for with this moment's frustration? "Forgive me," I whispered. "As you can imagine, I'm a little nervous. Perhaps we could dream of a child to fill my womb, Husband."

The suggestion softened the severe lines between his brows. "A child would be my heart's dream as well, Zully." He kissed my forehead.

"I'm happy to see your health returned, Princess." Pharaoh Khyan's rumble startled me, but his smile was reassuring. "I offer you both a happy life and the blessing of your dream fulfilled." He held out his votive, offering the flame of his candle to ignite ours.

I bowed as Potiphar tipped the wick of our candle to catch the king's flame. "Thank you, my king," we said in unison and crossed our threshold to begin the processional toward the palace quay.

At that moment, Vizier Wereni and his wife arrived. "Forgive our tardiness, Great Khyan."

"You'll follow my captain and his lovely wife," Pharaoh said. "If you can't arrive on time, Wereni, you'll forfeit your position as second in line—and perhaps as second in my kingdom."

The vizier's glare sent gooseflesh up my arms. I watched over my shoulder as he and his hateful wife snatched their votive and candle from our servants and fell in line behind us. "Are you sure Wereni won't thrust a dagger in my back?" I whispered to Potiphar.

He motioned toward the six Medjays flanking us and gave me a crooked grin. "The vizier values his life more than he hates us, Zully."

I hoped it was true. I distracted myself with our guests' earlier reaction to the vases I'd made. I refused to let fear steal the satisfaction I'd felt when Egypt's noblewomen had examined the vases at each place setting as if they were gold, not clay. They'd huddled in little swarms, buzzing about my gifts. Even Pharaoh's wives seemed pleased with the vases I'd chosen specifically for them.

"Are you all right?" Potiphar asked.

I glanced behind us, reminded that I was surrounded by my noble enemies. "Stop asking, Potiphar. I can't bear a whole evening of your hovering." How could I explain to him the terror growing inside me with each step away from my chamber? Until this evening, I hadn't even ventured back to the rooftop after my child died. Ahira had salvaged the vases I made that day, and Pushpa fired them. We had exactly the number needed for the banquet guests, but I had no passion to create anything else after my womb destroyed the greatest creation I'd ever begun.

Pharaoh and his wives arrived at the river's edge, and the line of nobility halted behind them to offer privacy while they whispered their dream and floated the votive. My heart's dream was still to return to Crete, but if I couldn't sell my art, I had no way to earn the passage. I'd begged Ahira to at least collect the profits from the merchant in the lower market. She refused, and I had no wish to force her. I'd used all my strength to convince Potiphar that both my ka and my uterus were happy and healthy to avoid another encounter with Pharaoh's butchers.

As Egypt's king and his wives walked away, Potiphar led me to the water. "Children, then." His expression was full of hope and kindness. "Is that our hearts' dream, Zully?"

A twinge of guilt held my tongue. The man before me had transformed from a surly soldier to a devoted husband since I lost the baby.

Every evening, he was with me to share a meal and then hold me tenderly without forcing the passion he so clearly desired. I gazed into his yearning eyes and spoke the sincerest words I'd said in months. "Any woman would be honored to have you as her husband, Potiphar."

His hopeful countenance clouded. I should have known he would see through my compliment. "I want only *one* woman to be honored."

I moved toward the water with our votive. "May my womb be filled with children that bring honor to their pateras."

He lingered beside me before setting the candle afloat. Had he noticed my vague wording?

I glanced over my shoulder. "There are others waiting. Shouldn't we finish?"

"Of course." We released our divergent dreams into Hapi's hands—a god neither of us believed existed.

I turned quickly, anxious to return to the villa, but Potiphar tugged me off the path. "What are you doing?"

When I looked up, his eyes were intense. Pleading. "Will you ever love me, Zully?"

Overcome by his vulnerability, I opened my mouth but had no words.

The kind and compassionate husband I'd come to know disappeared behind the surly soldier I'd first met. "There's my answer." He took my wrist and started back to the villa.

We walked in silence until we'd almost reached the entrance. "I love only Crete." Finally the truth. Only a whisper, but it was like a boulder rolling off my chest.

Potiphar said nothing. He kept walking. Had he heard me?

"Potiphar, I said—"

"Don't ever say it again." The threat in his voice chilled me.

We continued into the banquet hall and greeted the guests who, like us, had set their dreams afloat on the Nile. How many couples were as divided as we? How many women wished for a dream of their own, and how many men wished their wives loved them more?

I followed Potiphar to the head table, where we sat on crimson pillows, side by side. I'd asked to sit by Potiphar and not be seated beside Tani and Ziwat tonight. After my confession and Potiphar's icy response, however, I wished for a table alone in the corner. Scanning the room as people trickled in, I noticed Vizier Wereni and his wife seated at the table directly in front of us. Queen Tani's parents sat with them, along with the core group of vile women and their husbands who had treated me so shabbily when I'd tried to become one of them. In the process, I not only forfeited their favor but also lost myself.

Construction workers and artisans had transformed our adequate banquet room into a lavishly adorned gallery with sculptures and floral arrangements that would please every taste. Two hundred guests now filled the room. Musicians played, dancers entertained, beer flowed freely, and borrowed palace servants carried silver platters full of Pushpa's most delicious recipes. Perhaps after tonight, new rumors would replace the ones about my hysteria and focus on the outrageously successful lotus feast given by Captain Potiphar's Minoan princess. Perhaps that was the dream we should have floated.

Potiphar leaned close to be heard over the noise, his smile never dimming. "The servers will refill your goblet with *only* honeyed water." His tone was sharp as a blade. "And you will eat because everyone is watching." He raised his goblet at the shouts of praise for our feast while my cheeks burned with humiliation.

"I don't need you to regulate my drinking."

He laughed. "The only two banquets you've attended ended disastrously with strong drink. I told Joseph to watch you."

Of course. Joseph. He stood behind the tapestries, surveying the banquet he'd so adeptly organized.

Potiphar returned his attention to Pharaoh, who was seated on his right. He tasted the king's food as always, and a cupbearer stood behind them, sipping each goblet of wine or beer before serving it to captain or king. Pharaoh's wives sat at the far end of our head table, heads together in conversation. When had Pharaoh's wives become friends? Perhaps after the second wife lost her child.

Losing a child changes us.

My own darkness threatened to swallow me. I reached for my goblet and returned my attention to Joseph. He'd tried to involve me in planning the feast, but as the time drew near, decision-making and details grew overwhelming. He was leaning now against the doorframe, still behind the tapestries but peering at me. He lifted his wooden cup, toasting me—with honeyed water, no doubt. I shouldn't be angry with him. Though I couldn't trust him with secrets, he was a good man. Ahira loved him, and I recognized more than lusty longing when he watched her. When Potiphar looked at me that way, my skin crawled.

"You could at least smile," my husband whispered through his own forced pleasantness.

"Or I could return to my chamber." *Where at least a little bit of Crete waits for me.* Joseph had suggested Ahira wait there as a safe place for me to flee if something went wrong.

Potiphar lifted his empty goblet to the slave serving his favorite beer. The man filled both Potiphar's and the king's goblets. My husband took a long draw, then wiped his mouth with the back of his hand.

I wanted to toss my honeyed water in his face but picked at the roasted meat on my plate instead. What was it? Something brown with cheese. I shoved the plate away and noticed two more contingents of Medjays march into the room. One unit formed a line in front of our dais, and the other mounted the platform to stand behind us. Music stopped and dancers retreated.

"Potiphar, what's happening?" Fear shot through me like a spear.

My husband seemed as surprised as I, his eyes darting silent questions to both Hami and the king.

"Vizier Wereni." Pharaoh's big voice quieted the crowd and drained all color from the vizier's face. "I grow weary of the whispers between our wives. If you wish to challenge Captain Potiphar, do it publicly. If you believe him to be a threat to my kingdom, stand and accuse him, Vizier, or pay the price for collusion against one of Pharaoh's officials."

A collective gasp sent Wereni to his feet. "I wouldn't call my concerns *accusations,* my king." He offered a pretentious bow to Potiphar. "Who would dare accuse Captain Potiphar? He is a faithful and courageous Egyptian, Pharaoh's fiercest protector, and a clever investigator. However, I would ask the captain a few simple questions. For instance, why did he send his Hebrew chamberlain to threaten my Egyptian steward, demanding information on my private life?"

Whispers rippled through the gathering. "And was Princess Zuleika's two weeks in the palace harem as spontaneous as King Rehor wanted us to believe?" Wereni pressed another pebble of doubt into Pharaoh's sandal. "Or did he and Potiphar conspire to have the princess gather information about the king and his court, thereby strengthening Upper Egypt's claim to Pharaoh Khyan's throne?"

"Ha! You're a fool, Wereni." Potiphar's mocking stifled the speculation. "Anyone in court on the day Rehor and Zuleika arrived can witness to Pharaoh Khyan's and my surprise when the *princess* suggested she go to the harem for two weeks before living as my wife."

Wereni drew a breath to argue, but Potiphar roared over him, "And why would I send my estate chamberlain to collude with your steward when I could simply ask the steward for information—a man who had served me faithfully for twenty years before I *gave* him to you?"

I glanced at the tapestries, from where Joseph watched the unfolding scene. Had he really carried information between the two villas?

"Where did King Rehor stay during the two weeks his daughter lived in the harem?"

Potiphar met Wereni's question with unrelenting calm. "Rehor stayed in my villa's guest chamber while Princess Zuleika painted a mural on the harem wall and endured the mocking of Egypt's noble wives."

Wereni huffed, then held out his hand to his wife. She gave him the small vase and looked at me with a victorious smile.

"No . . ." I breathed. She knew. Somehow she'd discovered I sold similar vases in the lower city. Though they bore very different designs—she knew.

"These vases are lovely, Captain Potiphar." Wereni held it up for all to see, giving my husband a moment to cast a silent question at me.

I shook my head. How could I prepare him for the truth about to be spoken?

"Why did your wife try to disguise the pottery she sold in the lower market?" Wereni's question silenced the hall.

A small breath escaped my husband. His fingers clenched, released, then stretched.

"Was she trying to hide the profits for some reason, Captain?" Wereni pressed. "Why doesn't she sell them in the royal market, where nobility would pay a higher price?"

Potiphar's stony half smile froze in the silence.

"Captain? Your answer, please."

"My wife chose to give her treasures as a gift to my friends tonight and sell her art at a price people in the common market could afford." Potiphar's face and neck grew splotchy. "I've heard you speak of equality for pure-blooded Egyptians, both lowborn and nobility, Vizier, but my wife made her art available to *all* Egyptians regardless of heritage or station. Would you condemn me for Princess Zuleika's generosity?"

Had I not known my own betrayal, I might have been moved by his sentiment. Potiphar was clearly better at deception than I had been.

Wereni's smile was as false as my husband's when he returned his attention to Pharaoh. "Thank you, my king, for the opportunity to pose these troublesome questions in a public setting. Now you've heard Captain Potiphar's answers directly and can proceed with further investigation if you deem it necessary." He offered a compulsory bow and resumed his seat.

Pharaoh turned to his captain, his voice a low rumbling. "I learned things I didn't know about my friend." The king stood, bringing the entire audience to their feet, and raised his golden goblet. "It's time to honor tonight's host."

I stood beside my husband, feeling his tension like radiating heat.

"To Potiphar, my friend, the greatest man I know," Pharaoh began. "The whole world knows of your fierceness in battle and the courage that saved my life more than once. But I also want them to know your strength of character."

"Please, my king," Potiphar said between clenched teeth, "this is unnecessary."

"It *is* necessary!" Pharaoh's shout sent a nervous pall over the crowd. Then his eyes traveled to me. "These people will know the strength of character that dwells in this villa—both Captain Potiphar's and that of his wife."

What? Was he accusing me or lauding me?

He turned back to our guests, and I held my breath as the lines on his features deepened with growing disapproval. "I've heard rumors of Princess Zuleika's hysteria, and because many of you have whispered behind your hands, I sent my best healers to assess her condition."

I swallowed the threat of an impending gorge rising. By the gods, I wouldn't vomit at another royal banquet.

Pharaoh lifted the queen's vase, displaying it to the crowd. "My captain confided months ago that his wife worked day and night on special gifts for each woman at this festival. I'm sure it was modesty that prevented him from revealing she made them available to those in the lower market." He scanned the audience, letting the tension grow in silence. "Every woman with a vase in your hand drove Zuleika to madness with your gossip and hate," he shouted.

I sniffed back tears, refusing to add to my humiliation. Pharaoh leaned over to whisper something to Potiphar. My husband nodded once, his expression unaffected.

"Despite his wife's hysteria," Pharaoh continued, "my friend has confirmed that he tended his wife every night since our return from Temehu, treating her as mercifully and gently as an ommi with an infant child."

That's not true! He abandoned me after Temehu. Only after the miscarriage—

"How many of you would have shown such mercy to your husband or wife?" Pharaoh was reshaping the image of his great warrior into a great prince. "Or would you have used such a malady as an excuse to divorce or take a lover?"

Silence stretched for two long heartbeats. "Pharaoh hears all, sees all, knows all." Pharaoh spoke with terrifying calm. "Hammurabi's justice has bent to Egyptian leniency for too long. Some of you deserve the maiming punishment for adultery, but I give you a gift greater than the vases tonight. Every noble couple in this room is declared innocent of adultery—now. But my mercy ends when you leave this feast. In my kingdom, husbands protect their wives, and wives honor their husbands. If marriages fail, Egypt fails." He raised his goblet again. "To marriage."

"To marriage." Every goblet in the room was raised.

"I declare this lotus feast ended." Pharaoh poured out his drink, signifying the evening's end. "Return to your homes. Adjust your lives. Or bear my wrath."

The guests hurried away from half-eaten meals, snatching the pottery gift but leaving the potter trembling. "Please, Potiphar," I whispered. "Let me go to my chamber." I could bear my husband's wrath if I had Ahira's reassurance and focused on my Minoan treasures.

Potiphar's body was as rigid as his smile. "You will remain at this table until the last guest leaves." He glanced at Hami. "Make sure she stays." Potiphar descended the dais to escort our guests to the door, offering the hospitality expected of Egyptian nobility.

Hami stood over me like a falcon on its perch.

"My husband is quite taken with you." Queen Tani's silky voice startled me.

She and Ziwat stood beside the king, all three waiting for me to say something regal and appropriate. I bowed, giving myself more time to think, and in that blink of a moment determined to address only the king. "Thank you for your kind words, Pharaoh Khyan." I tried to smile. "But I fear your benevolence may have made Potiphar and me Wereni's prime targets."

"Surely you're not afraid, Princess." He lifted a single brow as if challenging me. "You're married to Egypt's fiercest warrior. Only deception can destroy true love and friendship." Eyes fixed on Potiphar as he crossed the banquet floor, he added, "A true friend never keeps secrets."

Potiphar leapt onto the dais without using the steps. "True, my king, which is why I would never keep anything *of importance* from you."

The two men's eyes locked in challenge. Dread slithered up my spine. I wasn't sure what secrets Potiphar had kept from his friend and king, but Khyan's displeasure was a clear sign of their importance.

"We'll weather Wereni's storm," Potiphar whispered. "He's trying to divide us."

"He's trying to divide you and your wife as well, Captain." The king nodded in my direction. "You should be very proud of her. She handled herself well tonight—as did you, my friend." He turned and walked away, resting a hand on each of his wives' backs.

We watched Pharaoh and his wives walk away, and the door clicked shut behind them.

My husband turned slowly to meet my eyes, his feigned smile gone.

"I haven't sold anything since the miscarriage. Can you forgive me?"

A burst of light, and I was on the floor. The blow had come without warning. The left side of my face throbbed, and spots danced before my eyes.

"Take my wife to the guest chamber, and bring me her maid. I will discover how deep this root of deception grows in my household."

TWENTY-EIGHT

You have set our iniquities before you,
  our secret sins in the light of your presence.
PSALM 90:8

Ahira

Ahira hummed her favorite shepherd's song and tidied Zully's chamber. *Elohim, give my dear mistress courage to face those awful women and peace in her husband's arms.* She lifted the beautiful rock-crystal vase from its metal stand and turned it in the lamplight to inspect Zully's workmanship. To imagine that this beautiful creation was once a piece of rock on a mountainside was astounding. She never questioned her mistress's talent, but would Zully ever see beyond her creations to worship the Creator of all?

Joseph burst through the door. "Did *you* know?"

"Did I know what?"

He grabbed her shoulders, eyes wild with fear. "Did you know she sold vases in the lower city?"

The walls seemed to tilt. "Joseph, I . . ."

Shock softened his grip. "Did you *help* her?"

"Yes." Though her response was barely audible, Joseph's slack jaw proved the confession would change her life.

"How could you deceive . . ." He released her and backed away as if she were a leper. "How could you sin against Elohim?"

"I did it to help, Joseph. Gaios started to earn their passage back to Crete. After he was sold, I refused to help her, but when the master was away so much, she felt abandoned again."

"You must go, Ahira." He glanced at the open door. "Run to the kitchen. Tell Pushpa I ordered you to the fields to retrieve a lamb."

"Wait." She reached for him, pausing his frenzy. "Do you forgive me?"

"Ahira, my forgiveness is the least of your worries. Master Potiphar knows. Wereni challenged him publicly, including the mistress's secret sale of vases in the lower city."

"I must go to her." Ahira started toward the door.

Joseph grabbed her waist and pulled her close. "You can't, my love. I know the master. Though he publicly pretended to know about his wife's pottery sales, he'll punish her and anyone else involved." He fell silent at the sound of footsteps. He dropped his hands and looked at her with resigned defeat. "It's too late. They're coming for you."

As if the words had summoned the chief Medjay, Hami stood in the open doorway. "Ahira. You must come with me."

Behind him, two soldiers were escorting Zully into the guest chamber across the hall.

"Mistress?" Ahira rushed toward her, but Zully didn't respond.

When the Medjay reached for Ahira, Joseph rushed in front of her, blocking him. "Let me take her to the fields, Hami. I'll assign her to shepherd the master's flocks until he calms down. You know she stands a better chance—"

"Lord Chamberlain, be silent." Hami stepped aside, allowing three other Medjays to enter the chamber. "Captain Potiphar wishes to question the maid—and you."

Ahira's legs turned to water. "Joseph knew nothing!"

"Silence!" Hami's impassioned shout was more terrifying than the Medjays who bound her wrists with leather ties. Hami never showed emotion. *Is he angry or frightened for me? Will I die today?* A roar in her ears grew loud, and her vision tunneled until light vanished.

When she opened her eyes, she was on the floor, surrounded by Medjays.

"Leave her!" Joseph shouted at the four large guards hovering over her.

She blinked a few times. "I fainted?"

Without warning, Joseph slipped a hand beneath her head and pulled her into a tender kiss. "That is our first kiss, Ahira bat Enoch, but not our last."

Breathless, she looked into the golden-green eyes that reflected both love and fear.

He cradled her, letting the moment linger. "Hami will escort you to the banquet room for questioning while I wait in the master's chamber."

"No!" She scrambled to her feet. "Hami, I'm the only one who helped Zully deceive her husband." Still light-headed, she swayed.

Hami caught her, his expressionless gaze restored. "Stay with him in the captain's chamber," he ordered the two guards nearest Joseph. Without awaiting a reply, the gentle warrior escorted Ahira to their aggrieved master.

He slowed to match the pace of her wobbly legs. Pushpa stood at the kitchen door, tears streaming down her cheeks. Ahira mouthed a silent *I'm sorry.* The dear woman disappeared into her private kingdom, returning to the tasks that kept her world ordered, predictable, and constant—no matter what happened in Egypt or to her son. Grain always needed grinding. Bread always needed baking. Recipes required the same measurements no matter whose life fell apart.

When Hami and Ahira breached the dividing tapestries, Master Potiphar was seated alone on the dais, shoulders slumped, face buried in his hands. He looked weak. Vulnerable. And in that moment, Ahira pitied him. Her guilt turned to shame, and she realized Joseph was right. She'd deceived this good man and, in the process, sinned against Elohim. Unintentionally, she'd mocked the favor Elohim had showered on her. It wasn't Joseph's forgiveness she should beg—or even her master's. *Elohim, is there forgiveness for one as vile as me?*

As if hearing and scoffing at her prayer, Master Potiphar lifted his head and stood to face her. Smeared kohl combined with his rage, transforming the weak and vulnerable into a horrifying beast. "You knew!" With three lunges, he reached her, his hand like a vice on her throat.

"Captain!" Hami seized his wrist. "She will tell you everything."

The master's feral eyes barely blinked. He cast Ahira away. "You helped her." A statement. Three little words offering escape if she denied them.

But a lie would compound my sin against You, Elohim. "Yes, my lord."

The master straightened. "Prison." A single vein in his forehead bulged as he walked away.

Hami grabbed Ahira's arm, hurrying her at the master's pace.

"It was Gaios!" she cried out. "He found a merchant in the lower city when you left for Temehu."

The master whirled on her, grinding out the words between clenched teeth. "You will remain silent until I give you permission to speak." He stalked away, and Hami's grip tightened again.

Ahira's vision dimmed, the threat of unconsciousness a welcome alternative to the prison awaiting her. Joseph had told her of the dark place where an old warden dwelled. Damp and lonely. Sparking memories of his nightmare in the cistern where his brothers abandoned him.

Master Potiphar flung open the door adjacent to his chamber. Hami rushed Ahira through, and they began the descent down steep, narrow stairs.

The stench intensified with her fear, and an uncontrolled whine escaped when she saw the prison's main chamber. Three waist-high tables stood in a neat row, each equipped with six leather restraints: one at the head, one at the chest, two for hands, and two more for feet. Bloodstains and deep gashes proved their purpose to be too much like Pushpa's butcher block.

Ahira's knees buckled. Hami pinned her arms at her sides, and she began the fight for her life. Screaming, kicking, flailing, she was no match for Egypt's royal guard. He cast her roughly onto the wooden pallet. She tossed her head, still fighting, panting, and moaning with panic.

Master Potiphar's hands were the most terrifying restraint. Holding her head like a melon, he hovered over her. "How long has my wife deceived me?"

Ragged breaths drew out her hesitation.

He grasped her hair with both hands. "How long?" he shouted.

"Since the day I came." She closed her eyes and let the tears come. Surely death would save her soon. Instead, the master released his grip.

"Leave us!" the master shouted. Ahira opened her eyes and saw Hami and two more Medjays climbing the stairs. An old man disappeared into an adjoining chamber.

Master Potiphar waited at the stairway, watching until the door above them slammed, then walked toward her again. She struggled against wrist and ankle tethers. "Elohim, help me. Help me, El Shaddai."

"No god will hear you." He leaned over, blocking every sight but his fury. "How many ways has Zuleika betrayed me? I know about the Minoan lover. I know she sold the vases. What has she done that I don't know, little Hebrew? And what have *you* done with Joseph? Have you turned my loyal chamberlain against me?"

"No, no! Joseph is still loyal to you. He knew nothing about Zully selling vases."

He studied her, peering into her eyes as if digging out her soul with a shovel. But revealing *all* seemed unthinkable. An immediate path to certain death. Shaking like a palm frond in a storm, she closed her eyes. *Elohim, You set our secret sins in the light of Your presence. If I'm utterly transparent, will You show mercy at the resurrection Joseph speaks of?*

The question brought a steady trickle of peace that lessened her trembling and infused her with courage to open her eyes again. "I can't erase the wrongs I've committed against you, Master Potiphar, but I vow to confess the truth before you and my God."

He straightened, seeming confused by her cooperation. "Don't think you'll avoid punishment. Your fate is sealed, girl."

Peace, Ahira. She felt more than heard the inner whisper and knew she didn't face the master's judgment alone. "You'll decide what's just for my crimes."

"Tell me," he said, folding his arms.

Ahira stared at the rock-hewn ceiling. "Mistress Zully's heart has always been devoted to the people of her homeland and rebuilding Crete. On the first day we met, she'd endured two weeks of torment by the noblewomen in Pharaoh's harem but was still the fiery Princess Zuleika of Zakros Palace. More determined than ever to save her people, she was easily convinced when Gaios vowed he could sell her art to pay for both their return passages to Crete. But after the awful banquet in which Gaios tainted the wine—"

"Gaios?" The master's roar made her flinch.

Ahira turned her head, preferring to look at the wall to speak of the shameful things she must say. "Gaios used her fragile state to bed her against her will and began manipulating her to his gain. He made her world small, increasing his demands on her body and her art, limiting her world to her chamber and the potter's wheel on the roof. He convinced her that he was the only one who could protect her from those who would investigate the tainted wine. He filled her mind with terrible possibilities, threats of Wereni's violence against foreign nobility that made her afraid to leave her chamber. Mistress Zully feared prison and death, so she gave him what he desired. He made her believe he was her only protector and—most importantly—her only passage back to Crete."

"She planned to leave me?" The pain in the master's tone was as agonizing as a tear-streaked face.

"I'm sorry, Master. Yes. After Gaios was sold, she was even more desperate to leave Egypt."

"She loved him that much?"

"No, Master! Zully doesn't love Gaios." How could Ahira explain a woman's heart to a man who had never been as alone as her mistress? "Your wife has no one here, Master."

"She has me!" He was suddenly hovering over her again, eyes wild. "Why can't she—" He shook with fury, the vein in his forehead bulging with the same tangled emotions that held his tongue.

"A woman needs more than a man to be happy, Master Potiphar. She needs other women—true friends. A home she can call her own.

A city and culture where she's invested and eager to leave a legacy. Zully's heart has always belonged in Crete, Master Potiphar. Joseph, Pushpa, and I are her friends. Gaios is wicked, but he was her passage home. And you . . . you, Master, are her captor—reluctant to care for her at first and now so kind she grows bitter at her own betrayal."

A cynical snort. "By the gods, I'm a fool. Who else knew all this was happening?"

Ahira closed her eyes. She'd dreaded that question. "You should ask Pushpa and Joseph how much they knew. Perhaps the Medjays who guarded Zully's chamber. I will confess only the truth I know, Master Potiphar."

"I will ask you one more time, then, little Hebrew. Is there anything else you haven't told me? If I discover later that you knew something and didn't—"

"The child Zully carried wasn't yours."

He drew a sharp breath.

"Gaios never knew he sired a child," Ahira rushed to add, "and she hasn't seen him since the day you returned from Temehu—the day Joseph sold him. When I told her Gaios was sold, I thought she'd fall apart. She didn't. Her only concern was continuing to save profits to earn her passage back to Crete. I didn't agree to help right away. After I saw how happy you were that first morning after your wedding week, I was sure your marriage would grow stronger."

Ahira hesitated. Dare she be as transparent about what caused Zully's despair? "When a full week passed and you didn't return to her chamber, your wife grew despondent. I feared she might harm herself, Master, so I agreed to find the merchant Gaios had used to sell her art. The vendor sold many of her little vases. When I returned with Zully's share, she realized Gaios had likely lied and cheated her out of her profits. She began saving for two passages to Crete—hers and the baby's—and planned to write you when she arrived safely to tell you the truth. After the miscarriage, she lost herself and her will to create. I never returned to the merchant again, but I believe Zully still holds out hope to return to her homeland."

"She told me as much tonight," he said with a defeated sigh. "Where does she hide the silver?"

"You'll find the silver in the unused waste pot in my chamber."

He nodded and let more silence pass. "What about Joseph? Did he know—"

"Joseph knew nothing about selling the vases. He hated Gaios as much as I did."

"I believe you, girl, but the truth doesn't erase your offenses. Ubaid!"

Startled at his shout, Ahira whimpered instinctively. "Please, Master, send me to the fields. I'm a good shepherd."

A gray-haired man emerged from the adjoining chamber near the foot of her pallet. "Yes, Captain?"

"How much did you hear?" The master lifted his brows.

"I hear everything, Captain. You know that."

"And you will never repeat any of it, not even to Pharaoh, or divulge the name of this woman, who will live in your cellblock."

"I vow it on my life." Ubaid bowed. The warden was just as Joseph had described him: toothless and foul smelling but remarkably calm considering his home was a prison. He glanced at Ahira while untying her tethers but didn't speak.

Master Potiphar pulled Ahira off the table, and her wobbly legs carried her toward a dark hallway. Ubaid snagged a torch from the main room, and the master shoved her inside the only open door.

When it slammed shut, Ahira sat on slimy, prickly straw. Lost in total darkness. Something scurried over her foot, and she bolted to her feet. Screaming, she crashed into a corner after only two frantic steps. A soft click on the opposite side of the door deepened her despair.

"Remember, Ubaid. No one knows she's here."

"Yes, Captain."

Shaking violently, Ahira listened to footsteps shuffling away.

"Are you Joseph's love?" A low voice spoke outside her door.

The impossibility of such tenderness brought a smile. "I . . . was." She hiccupped through barely controlled emotions.

"Don't give up hope, little Hebrew. Joseph can charm the scales off a fish. Captain Potiphar will relent for his favorite servant."

She slid down the wall and landed in the putrid straw. "Thank you, Ubaid. May Elohim bless you for your kindness."

And may the favor of Elohim move their master to unprecedented mercy.

TWENTY-NINE

A king's wrath is a messenger of death,
but the wise will appease it.
PROVERBS 16:14

Potiphar

The Medjays opened Potiphar's chamber door and slammed their fists against their chests. "Pharaoh Khyan summoned you, Captain," one said. "Commander Hami went in your place to assure the great Khyan you'd come promptly."

Joseph was no doubt anxiously waiting in his chamber, but there was no time for another interrogation if Khyan needed him. "Well done." Potiphar tapped his fist against his chest and strode away to attend his king. Potiphar had never needed to keep secrets from Khyan until his friend gave him a wife who shamed him. Hami would know to be discreet. Potiphar trusted his chief Medjay as much as Joseph.

He paused at the thought. Could he still trust Joseph? His steps slowed. Could he still trust Hami? Potiphar had given his Medjay commander the full responsibility of Wereni's investigation after Zully's miscarriage. If the two men Potiphar trusted most had betrayed him, they could sway Khyan to distrust his best friend.

He broke into a jog, waved off concerned Medjays in the connecting hall, and slowed only when he approached Khyan's chamber in the palace.

The guards at Pharaoh's residence blocked the door, and Hami stepped into Potiphar's path. "Forgive me, Captain, but I have orders to take all weapons before anyone enters Pharaoh's private chamber." Potiphar reached for his belt, and four nervous subordinates drew their swords.

With their blades poised a finger width from his throat, he glared at Hami. "Are these men prepared to kill me, Commander?"

"Without hesitation, Captain. No one defies our king's orders."

"Good." Potiphar unlatched his weapons belt, glimpsing the relieved expressions of his men. "Did our king offer a reason for his added caution?"

"He did not. The king usually shares his reasons only with the captain of his guard."

Potiphar listened for an inconsistent tone and watched the man's eyes for any hint of falsehood. Hami displayed neither tell. Either Potiphar had trained him too well, or he spoke truth. *How unfortunate I didn't watch my wife for those same signals.*

Slamming fists to their hearts, his guards bowed and let him pass. Potiphar returned their salute as he entered Khyan's chamber. Though the hour was late, Queen Tani and Ziwat lounged on the king's bed, tempting him with sweet treats left over from the banquet. All three sobered when they saw Potiphar.

"Leave us." Khyan's quick command was obeyed without protest. Unusual.

Potiphar turned his back while the women rose and covered themselves. When the door slammed shut, he turned to find the women gone and his friend's expression hard as stone. Foreboding grated at his already-raw nerves. "What offense have I committed, Khyan, that I am stripped of my weapons?"

Pharaoh left his bed, pulled on a tunic, and poured himself some wine. An empty goblet sat beside the pitcher—which his friend left empty. Normally Khyan poured both goblets full. When the king occasionally overlooked the courtesy, Potiphar made a rude joke and poured his own.

Not tonight.

Potiphar stiffened to attention before Egypt's king. He hadn't been summoned as a friend. Not even as the captain of his guard. He was summoned by an angry pharaoh.

"I saw your reaction when Wereni asked his questions," Pharaoh said, measuring him. "I don't believe you're a traitor, Potiphar, or I would have killed you at the feast. But I've known you long enough to discern when you're lying. We both know your chamberlain did, in fact, collude with the steward you gifted to Wereni. I've interrogated my wives about the two weeks your princess spent with them in my harem. No information was worthy of Rehor's spying, and we both know your tantrum about marriage was authentic. So Wereni's accusations were unfounded."

Potiphar heard the doubt in his tone. "But?"

Khyan sat on his favorite red cushion. "That leaves only one thing for you to lie about—your lovely wife."

If Potiphar was forced to discuss Zully, he wouldn't do it without wine. He filled the empty goblet and sat on his customary pillow across from Pharaoh. "I didn't lie about anything I told you." He took a quick sip, calculating how transparent he should be. "I simply did not tell you everything."

Khyan lifted a single eyebrow in challenge. "So, tell me now, Captain."

Heart rate quickening, Potiphar stalled again. "Do you tell me everything about Tani and Ziwat?"

"I am Pharaoh!" He slammed his goblet down. "Tell me what you're hiding."

"I'll protect you with every drop of my blood until they bury my bones, but some parts of my marriage are not yours to command." Potiphar leaned across the table and lowered his voice. "I confess that my heart is held prisoner by a wife who doesn't love me. More than that you need not know."

"You declare your loyalty and then insert a clever emotional twist. You're hiding something important, Potiphar. If you won't tell me, I'll summon your wife to the prison and find out."

"Aahh!" Potiphar slammed his own goblet onto the table. The wine sloshed as he bolted to his feet.

Three Medjays burst into the room, but Khyan waved them away, wine dripping from his nose. "Leave," he said, maintaining focus on his friend. "Your detachment training has failed you on this topic, Potiphar. Your heart is truly her captive, which puts you at a severe disadvantage."

This was a dangerous game. Potiphar had confided Zully's hysteria but nothing about her lover or miscarriage. Both would expose his failure as her protector. The adultery could mean her execution or maiming. *But Khyan offered clemency to adulterers tonight.*

"Tell me what she's done, my friend. I can see she's humiliated you." The latent fury in Khyan's eyes made clemency moot.

Why should Potiphar care about what happened to Zully? She'd betrayed him, deceived him. She'd tried to leave him since the day she'd entered his life.

Khyan shoved their goblets aside and gripped Potiphar's wrist. "Remember our vow: I'll do whatever is necessary to protect and prosper you. If she's harmed you or dishonored you, I'll kill her myself." His eyes watched Potiphar's intently, measuring him the way Potiphar measured his Medjays.

Potiphar dared not lie. "I never told you what caused her hysteria." No matter how angry he was, he couldn't bear the thought of Zully's death. "During the wedding week after Temehu, I promised to be a better husband, but then I always placed palace duties above her and neglected her. When my chamberlain told me Zully was pregnant, I tried to mend the damage, but the divide was too great. The day I tried to reconcile, she had a miscarriage. We've never fully recovered, no matter how attentive I've become." Potiphar pulled his hand free of his friend's grasp. "You can sheath your dagger, Pharaoh Khyan," he added, trying to lighten the mood. "My wife need not be executed tonight."

Khyan relaxed for the first time that night. "Though I'm sorry for your loss, my friend, I'm relieved it's something time can heal. You'll win her heart, and Zully will conceive again." His brow furrowed. "Wereni's accusation about King Rehor was ridiculous, but it made me wonder. Has the princess had regular contact with Rehor?"

"No, she hasn't." Potiphar shared the unease he'd been feeling. "He seemed devoted when he brought her here well over a year ago. It's strange that he wouldn't at least send an occasional message."

"He's sent *me* plenty of messages asking for more building funds." Khyan swirled his goblet, sneering into the dregs. "But he didn't visit personally when we returned from Temehu. That, too, is strange. Rehor doesn't miss a trade opportunity—especially when, by all merchant reports, Crete is still rebuilding."

Potiphar finished his wine. "Should I send spies?"

"No need, but"—Khyan pointed his empty goblet at him like a weapon—"your wife is a gifted artist, Potiphar, so make sure she has plenty of supplies to do what she loves. It's vital you give her plenty of attention and keep her out of the markets and away from banquets. No matter how much I threaten the nobility, Princess Zuleika is gossip fodder."

Thankfully, he knew only half of it. "I'll obey your every command, my king." Potiphar stood and bowed, then lifted his head and grinned. "Is there anything else we should discuss before I return to my chamber and fall exhausted into my bed?"

Khyan was studying him, their usual banter still affected. "In the future you need not tell me everything about your marriage, my friend, but I want to know if King Rehor contacts his daughter."

"Of course, my king."

Potiphar left Pharaoh's chamber, grabbed his pile of weapons, and passed his guards without acknowledging them. Sticky with dried wine and pummeled by his friend's suspicions, he marched toward the next battle.

In a single evening, he'd been ambushed and stumbled into a war. Now he wasn't exactly sure for whom or what he fought. How much had Joseph known and kept from him? Had his chamberlain used the same "don't tell, don't lie" logic he'd adopted with Khyan? The nuances between truth and transparency had never been more real than they were tonight.

The Medjays opened his chamber door without his command, and Potiphar slammed fist to chest with new appreciation. These were men he trusted.

Joseph rose from his stool at the cosmetics couch but didn't speak while Potiphar dropped his weapons in a pile. He continued to his water basin and washed the stickiness from his hands and arms. The Hebrew hovered like stink on dung. Potiphar snatched the towel from his hands and nudged past him. "Sit. Give me space to breathe."

The chamberlain plopped down on the tiles at Potiphar's feet. "Is Ahira safe, my lord? Is she alive?"

Potiphar glared at him. "Have you betrayed me, too, Joseph?"

The Hebrew startled. Potiphar had used his given name to unsettle him.

"Did you know my wife's child wasn't mine?"

The Hebrew's eyes widened. "No, my lord. I'm so very sorry."

Potiphar sat on his cosmetics couch, fighting for calm. "Did you help Zuleika sell the vases?"

When Joseph paused, Potiphar felt as if the room tilted. Had he misread his Hebrew chamberlain all these years?

"No, Master Potiphar, I did *not* help your wife, but I did fail you. A worthy chamberlain should have known—and I had no idea."

Too relieved to rail, Potiphar said, "How could you not know?"

"Love wants to trust, Master. I love Ahira, and though I knew she and the mistress shared a secret, I trusted she'd never keep anything from me that might threaten our future together." The hard set of Joseph's jaw proved he felt equally betrayed. "I'm deeply sorry for my neglect of duty, Master Potiphar. I'll bear any punishment you deem fit. But I beg you, my lord, please . . ." His voice broke, and he looked down at his hands and cleared his throat before looking up again. "Let me bear Ahira's punishment too. And if I may be so bold, I plead with you to show mercy to Mistress Zuleika. Both women have wronged you terribly, but let mercy and forgiveness become the ruins on which a stronger house is built."

Potiphar grimaced. "You're as skilled a wordsmith as I, Hebrew, so I'll grant the mercy you beg. Your little Hebrew will live—in the cellblock—because of her courage and transparency. She confessed to hiding my wife's profits in her chamber. You'll retrieve the silver from the waste pot and add it to my estate earnings."

Joseph's relief was palpable. "May I visit her, my lord?"

"Did you hear me, Hebrew? Your woman will *survive* in a dark cell. Alone."

"She's not alone, my lord." Tears welled in his eyes. "Elohim is with her, and I would be most grateful if you'd allow me to deliver her a meal from Pushpa's kitchen once a day."

Ommi loved the Hebrew maid. Perhaps sending a meal each day would salve her broken heart. "Very well."

"Thank you, my lord." Joseph bowed with his face to the floor. "And Mistress Zuleika? How may I help you show mercy to her, my lord?"

"Pushpa will deliver my mercy to Zully—tomorrow morning. Tonight she waits and wonders. Princess Zuleika will live the rest of her days in my guest chamber. She is exiled from my presence. Hami will assign new chamber guards who will bar her door and remain aloof from her wiles. If she ever tries to escape or deceive me again, she'll share a cell beside her Hebrew maid."

The Hebrew lifted his head, the dismay Potiphar expected distorting his features. "She'll be a captive. The guest chamber is so small and furnished for a short stay—"

"Not to worry, Chamberlain. Pushpa will take care of the furnishings when she visits Zully in the morning."

THIRTY

Folly is an unruly woman;
  she is simple and knows nothing.
PROVERBS 9:13

Zuleika

Awakened by hideous scraping on the chamber door, I pushed myself upright on a mattress not my own. Pain exploded through my battered face. Cradling the left side, I lifted the guest chamber's hand mirror and saw the reflection of a creature I didn't know. My left eye was nearly swollen shut, the translucent flesh around it crimson and purple. The damage of Potiphar's single blow extended from cheek to brow, proof of my husband's combat skill.

"Good morning, Princess Zuleika." Pushpa's formality came with averted eyes and no smile. She set my food tray on the tiled floor and turned toward the slaves who had followed her into the chamber. "Everything goes except the waste pot. Bring in the reed mat and wooden stool."

I sat on the bed in silence. The throbbing in my face increased with every heartbeat as I watched them dismantle the room.

"Excuse me, Mistress." A Minoan slave stood over me.

He expected me to move? Would he remove the mattress on which I sat?

"Pushpa?" I huffed, slowly moving toward her. "Will you make this chamber a slave's quarters? If Pateras returns—*when* he returns—he'll need to stay here. Across from my chamber."

"*This* is your chamber now, Princess Zuleika." Her eyes glistened.

"What? No . . ." I glimpsed the wooden bar on the exterior of the door. That had been the awful scraping that woke me—and the reason for the pounding last night on one side of the door while I pounded for release on the other. Fear sent me to my knees at Pushpa's feet. "Please, don't do this. Tell Potiphar I'll never sell anything again." *Can I keep such a promise?*

"It's too late." Pushpa cradled my chin in her hand. "My son says you're to be stripped of every comfort he tried to give you so you'll realize what you've discarded." She walked away.

"Wait, Pushpa!" I scrambled to my feet and followed her. But two Medjays I didn't know blocked the door the moment she passed through. "Let me pass! I'm the mistress of this villa."

Their dead eyes stared through me.

"How long, Pushpa?" I shouted over their shoulders. "How long must I live in this Egyptian underworld?"

No answer.

One of the Medjays pushed me aside so the Minoan slaves could remove more finery from my new chamber. "Please," I begged my Minoan brethren. "Don't let Potiphar do this to me! Send a message to King Rehor of Zakros Palace that his daughter is being held captive. Tell Pateras to come for me!"

But my countrymen ignored me as they continued marching in and out of the chamber—as lifeless and cold as my husband's trained Medjays.

I grabbed the one piece of furniture they left for me—a three-legged stool—and sat in the now-barren corner as they stripped the rest of the room. "At least get me some paints and brushes or my pottery wheel from the roof with some clay."

As the last Minoan carried the final table toward the door, a shaft of panic speared me. "My circle of treasures! I must have them! Please!" I clawed at the Medjay who filled my doorway. I couldn't bear a world without any hint of my homeland.

The guard's expression showed more disdain than pity. "Have you no concern for the other lives you've destroyed?" He shrugged off my pleas and let an avalanche of shame crush me.

The door closed. The bar scraped across it. *Other lives I've destroyed?* Hami had been with Ahira last night in my chamber when she called my name. They couldn't blame her. They mustn't . . . A chill raced down my spine and set my fists pounding on the door. "Where is Ahira? She only did as I commanded." I kicked the thick cedar barrier. "Get Joseph. He'll tell you. Ahira had to obey my orders."

A sudden realization silenced me, draining the fight. *What if Potiphar has killed them?* I crossed the small chamber and ran into the tiny courtyard. Tilting my face to the sky, I screamed, "If any god is listening, I hate you!" I fell to my knees while sobs racked me.

Time was lost. The sun burned down. My soul poured out. Potiphar had been right to strip my chamber bare.

When the tears finally ebbed, I felt—empty. I glimpsed the puddle my tears had made in the dirt and scraped together a tiny ball of mud. I added a little spit to make it more workable—like clay—and then flattened it in the palm of my hand. I carved a rough image with the sharp corner of my fingernail. A punctured dot here. A straight line there. An arc to give texture and depth. As tiny as the real pest, the image of a scarab beetle emerged on a piece of mud the size of my thumbprint.

"No." I squished the little scarab in my fist, funneling fear and hate into the destruction of Egypt's sacred image. "I'll never sell my soul to Egypt again."

I opened my hand and spit on the mud ball again, then reworked it into a newly flattened canvas. The oval matched the size of the scarab insets in rings and pendants, but my carving was sacred to me. Primitive but recognizable. The Zakros octopus. The noble creature stared at me, filling me with a sense of self. I was Princess Zuleika of Zakros Palace—whether in Egypt or Crete—and no one could take that from me. And *Zully* was mine to protect. No matter what they did to me. I would create my own Minoan world in the emptiness of Egypt.

My stomach grumbled, reminding me to eat, so I placed my octopus scarab in the dust to bake while I escaped Egypt's punishing sun. I crossed the threshold and thrilled at a simple yet life-altering treasure on my food tray. "You certainly can make more mud than spit and tears," I said to the water pitcher. Like Pateras's best trade or Mitera's prized necklace, this would be my greatest treasure. Since the pitcher would be replenished at each meal, it would provide a steady supply of water to fill my empty days with the joy of creating. It didn't matter that the scarabs and I were trapped. I was Zully, and I would create. It's how I would survive.

THIRTY-ONE

Hope deferred makes the heart sick,
but a longing fulfilled is a tree of life.
PROVERBS 13:12

Joseph

Applying the master's Eye of Horus was more difficult this morning than expected. Joseph's whole body still trembled from last night's ordeal. After being interrogated by Master Potiphar, he'd lain awake on his reed mat, anxiously awaiting the water clock's final drip. Now, hovering over the man he'd only yesterday considered master and friend, he was afraid to speak a word.

"Will Horus's Eye look more like Seth's beak today?" The master's snide question betrayed his dark mood.

Of course, Joseph didn't dare reply with the friendly jest he once would have. "The Eye of Horus will be as sharp as I've ever drawn, but I'll never match Abasi's skill, my lord."

Potiphar answered with a grunt.

Steadying his elbow against his knee, Joseph carefully touched the pointed wooden applicator to the base of the master's lashes, creating a relatively straight line. After finishing the master's cosmetics, Joseph tidied the pots and brushes. Potiphar rose from the couch, and Joseph

followed to aid with his wardrobe. They continued morning preparations in silence. Jewelry next. Then weapons.

Joseph straightened the bow across the master's back as he smoothed
its leather strap over his chest. "You haven't worn a wig since your
return from Temehu," Joseph said. "I assumed you lost the habit and
never regained it."

Potiphar glared at him. "Wigs itch, Hebrew, and I have no one to
impress." He strode toward the door. "I'll be gone for a few days." That
was all. He gave no destination. It wasn't like him.

Joseph glanced at the messy chamber and decided to clean it later.
He hurried across the hall and found Pushpa's kitchen unusually quiet.
"Where are your Minoans?"

"They're putting the guest room furnishings in storage." She looked
up from chopping onions, eyes red and watery. "I know Zully did a
terrible thing, but he shouldn't have hit her. Why must she be locked
in that room with no hope of release? And our little Ahira—in that
terrible prison." She dropped the knife and braced herself against the
table, shoulders heaving with sobs.

Joseph pulled her into his arms—without asking permission.

"Potiphar is not himself, Joseph. He told me he was leaving but
wouldn't say where he was going or when he'd return."

"I know." Joseph rested his chin atop her gray head. "Master Potiphar must grieve in his own way."

"But I've never seen him grieve like this, Joseph. He didn't even tell
Hami where he was going."

That revelation concerned Joseph more than any, but he dared not
show it. Pushpa was already worried. "We entrust Potiphar to Elohim's
continued favor and trust Him to show mercy to those in our care."

"Yes, yes." She pulled away, swiping at her cheeks. "Have you seen
Ahira?"

"Not yet. That's why I've come. The master said I could visit her
once a day with food from your—"

"Oh!" Her eyes brightened, and she grabbed a basket. "The daughter of my heart gets the best my kitchen offers." She flitted from tables

to bins to cook fire, gathering bread, hard cheese, dates and raisins, dried fish, and a small bowl of honeyed gruel. "Ahira must eat whether she has an appetite or not. We can't let her fall ill in that wretched place."

"Pushpa, stop." Joseph chuckled, taking the ample provisions.

"I've sent enough for you both." Her busy hands stilled. "Are you prepared for what you'll see, Joseph?"

"I've visited Ubaid in the prison dozens of times."

"You know what I mean. Have you ever seen inside the cells?"

A lump formed in his throat. He'd walked the dark hallway but purposely avoided the tiny rooms that were too much like the cistern that had imprisoned him before his brothers sold him. "I've prepared myself to be strong for Ahira." His tone was far braver than his quaking insides.

"I've seen it only once," she said. "It was before my husband died. He begged me to go with him to tend Ubaid's cough. The warden's fever had become so high he fainted in the dark hallway near the last cell. My husband and I had to venture into that underworld of suffering—barely a stone's throw from the belly of Anubis—to retrieve him and carry him back to his chamber. I vowed never to go there again." She resumed chopping her onions. "Give Ahira my love, and tell her I'll see her when my son comes to his senses and frees her."

Joseph nodded, forcing a smile. He would pass along her love to Ahira but could make no promise about her freedom. *Elohim, only You can give me courage to enter the cellblock and see the woman I love imprisoned there.*

His heart rate increased with every step. Across the hall and to the left of the master's chamber, he asked one of the Medjays to open the door, then began his descent, arms full of Pushpa's provisions. The fetid air thickened as he went, stealing his appetite. How could such a place exist beneath Potiphar's lavish villa? *Elohim, mend the master's heart and guide his thoughts.*

Eerie silence met him in the prisoner exam chamber—an innocuous label for the torture area. Unlit torches rested in their holsters, while a dozen oil lamps sputtered in wall niches. Faint shadows danced over shackles and weapons. Joseph's gaze settled on one of the horrible tables. The image of Ahira stretched between the bindings sent a shiver through him. *Elohim, save her from this place!*

Remembering the master's comment on her courage, Joseph adjusted the food to one arm, grabbed a lamp from a wall niche, and headed down the narrow, dark hallway, where heavy cedar doors lined both sides. Each door had a small opening at the bottom, allowing the stench of hopelessness to escape and the prisoners' rations to be given once each day.

"Is someone there?" came a gravelly male voice from behind a door. "Help me. Please. I didn't poison my son. Tell the king it wasn't me!"

The shout wakened others in the wing—those awaiting Pharaoh's final judgment. Their cries began in earnest, more like what Joseph had heard on his weekly visits to Ubaid. But he'd never *known* anyone behind one of these doors. Even now, no female voice cried out.

"Ahira?" he shouted above the noise. "Ahira? Where are you?"

No answer. Panic replaced the revulsion he felt. "Ahira!" he screamed.

"Joseph?" A soft female voice. A whimper.

"Ahira?"

"Joseph."

He moved toward the voice he'd longed for —and dreaded—his throat too tight to respond.

"Joseph," she said a little louder. "Is it you?"

Swallowing his despair, he forced calm into his reply. "Yes, my love. Keep talking so I can find you."

"No!" she shouted. "Leave me here. Go."

At her declaration, all other voices stilled. He couldn't move. "What do you mean?" Silence. Why would she want him to go? "Ahira, talk to me. I need you to speak so I can—"

"Leave, man," a gruff voice interrupted. "I wouldn't want my wife to see me here."

"Nor me," another man added. They began speaking of their families, the horrors they wouldn't want them to see. The punishment they deserved and the false evidence against them.

Joseph walked farther down the hallway, listening carefully. Only one cell remained silent. He set the basket and lamp on the floor, kneeling on the filthy straw in the dark hall, and then leaned down to peer through the opening at the bottom. Though he couldn't see anything in the utter darkness, he heard quiet weeping. Ahira's weeping.

"Ahira, my love, I would surely fall under Pushpa's wrath if I left before you ate the food she sent."

"I can't eat, Joseph."

"But you must."

"Lord Chamberlain." Ubaid lifted his torch as he approached. "I expected you sooner."

"You must open this prisoner's door immediately."

His bristly gray brows drew together as he began sorting through his keys. "You are a strong young man, Lord Chamberlain, and I've seen nearly sixty Inundations. I'll *give* you the key to this cell." He lifted a single wooden key, letting the others dangle on an iron ring. "But I ask you to give me a considerable bump on the head so I can assure Captain Potiphar and his Medjays you took the key by force. I won't tell anyone—unless I'm called to testify against you."

With all his heart, Joseph wanted that key. Master Potiphar was gone. Who would know? Ahira could sleep in Pushpa's chamber—at least until the master returned. Ubaid was under Joseph's authority, and he trusted the old warden to be discreet. But last night's confrontation flashed through his mind. *Have you betrayed me, too, Joseph?* Potiphar's stricken countenance would forever be etched on Joseph's heart. If he accepted the wooden key and released Ahira from her cell—no matter the brevity or reason—it would be a betrayal of his master's trust and a sin against Elohim.

Joseph clasped Ubaid's shoulder. "Thank you, my friend, but I must leave Ahira's key in your hands. She is the one I hold most dear, but Captain Potiphar entrusted her imprisonment to you, not me."

The warden lifted a single brow. "You're a better man than I." He unlocked her door, pulled it open, and walked away, leaving Joseph dizzy at the glimpse of Ahira's reality.

Ubaid's torch had lit the cell for an instant. The oil lamp remained on the floor at Joseph's feet, casting a dim glow barely past the threshold. *Elohim, give me strength.* He reached for the lamp and held it aloft, illuminating Ahira's dark world. The woman he loved cowered in the corner of a space not large enough to lie down. She shivered on a stone floor covered with soiled straw.

"Leave the basket and go. But first—is Zully safe?" She squinted into the dim light.

"She's safe." Why give her details that would worry her?

Ahira hid her face. "Tell Pushpa I'm grateful, but I don't want you to come again. And I don't want you to attend my execution."

"Execution?" The word was a dagger to his heart. "There will be no execution. I have permission to visit you every day. You can't give up, Ahira."

She looked at him, squinting at the light but with a strange calm on her features. "I haven't given up, Joseph. I've given *in* to Elohim's perfect plan. We both know no one is freed from the cellblock."

"That's not true." He stepped over the threshold, and sudden panic overwhelmed him. He was in the cistern again. Betrayed by blood. Shouting to silent captors. The walls in the small space felt like they squeezed closer. The floor seemed to tilt. His breathing quickened. "Ahira?" Her face became blurred and distant.

"Joseph, go!" She shoved him, and he stumbled back into the narrow hall.

The impact helped clear his head. He lowered the lamp to the floor and braced his hands against his knees, trying to steady his breathing. "I'm sorry, Ahira. I wanted to be strong for you, but the cistern. It still haunts—"

"You're the strongest man I know, Joseph ben Jacob." Ahira's tone was that of the feisty shepherdess he knew, but in the silence after her declaration, he felt the darkness seep into them both. "We learned when I first arrived in Egypt—*you* can't protect me. Only Elohim can be in this cell with me. There's no room for anyone else."

Ahira stood silhouetted in the lamp's dim glow, and Joseph was awed at the woman she'd become. Even in the grime and stench of Pharaoh's prison, she was the most beautiful woman he'd ever seen. "Someday I *will* marry you," he whispered.

She laughed. "I want to . . . marry you too." Shared sorrow filled the silence. "But it seems Elohim has other plans for us, Joseph."

"I need to see you every day, Ahira."

"Let him come, girl," one of the prisoners said.

"If she doesn't want the food, I'll take it," offered another.

Through the prisoners' bickering and name-calling came Ahira's soft chuckle. "Perhaps I was too hasty, Joseph. I would welcome your visits and Pushpa's sweet offerings. You can teach me more about Elohim. Recently I've become especially interested in the topic of the resurrection from the dead."

"Ahira . . ." He started to scold, but her levity was contagious, the morbid humor drawing several prisoners' laughter.

"I'll come every day," Joseph said, opening Pushpa's basket at Ahira's threshold. "Let's break our fast."

In the lamp's glow, Ahira looked weary but no longer seemed despairing. "I love you, Joseph." She looked down for a moment, then met his gaze. "I wanted to say it before . . ." She sobered at the unspoken possibility of death, yet her eyes shone.

"And I love you." He leaned over his crossed legs to brush her lips with a kiss. "Until our master's temper calms, you must eat what Pushpa sends and lean into Elohim's presence."

She nodded. "You must trust Him, too—no matter what happens to me."

"I will trust Him to do the impossible because I've seen Him do it before. Elohim promised my brothers would bow before me someday, but they threw me in a cistern and planned to kill me. I prayed a hopeless prayer in that pit, and the next voice I heard was my brother Judah suggesting they sell me instead. It wasn't good news, Ahira, but it left room for God to work."

"Joseph, I'm so sorry. I felt the stab of Simeon's betrayal, but you felt all your brothers twist the blade."

It was an apt description. "But I'm alive, Ahira. And now I have you. Sometimes God's favor is simply a spark that keeps hope alive in utter darkness. Elohim gave us each other to keep hope alive. Trust His presence in the dark, but never stop hoping for light."

She took a small bite of bread as she blinked away tears. Joseph also forced himself to eat, trying to apply his own advice. It was easier to deliver speeches and share his beliefs than to live out the truth. *Please, El Shaddai, turn my words into action and my fears into triumph.*

They ate as much of Pushpa's offering as they could. Joseph divided the rest among the other prisoners, pushing their portions through the opening at the bottom of each door. He stood at the threshold of Ahira's cell, but he couldn't pull the door closed. "Ubaid!" he shouted and then returned his attention to Ahira. "I'll see you again tomorrow morning, my love."

Joseph turned sideways to pass Ubaid in the narrow hall. Fleeing like a man being chased, Joseph climbed the prison stairs two at a time. Panting, he paused to regain his composure before opening the door. Perhaps tomorrow would be easier.

He entered the kitchen to return Pushpa's basket and empty bowl. She was preparing a tray with as many foods as she'd included for Ahira. "If Zully must endure an empty chamber, she'll not suffer an empty stomach." The compassionate woman jabbed her fists to her hips. "But I can't bear another confrontation, Joseph. You must deliver her tray."

"No. Send one of the Minoans."

She lifted her brows, challenging his thoughtless suggestion. *And tempt fate with another Gaios situation?*

"Must I be kind to a woman whose thoughtless deceit harmed the love of my life?" He grabbed the tray and started to walk away.

"She asked about you and Ahira this morning." Pushpa's words stopped him. "I couldn't tell her about Ahira. I only managed to say *she* was quarantined to that empty guest chamber indefinitely. I left before she saw my tears. Why couldn't Potiphar tell her—" She pursed her lips and shook her head.

"Because he couldn't look at the damage he'd done," Joseph said. "How badly was she hurt?"

"She's talking, so her jaw isn't broken. The left side of her face is badly bruised. I've included a cup of poppy tea. She'll have a nice afternoon nap." Pushpa chopped parsley and moved it into the pile of prepared leeks and onions. "Stay and talk with her. I'm sure she's lonely and frightened—but sit at the threshold. Keep the door open. I still don't trust her, Joseph. Make sure the Medjays hear everything you say."

Life had been so much simpler before Mistress Zuleika entered their world. Joseph marched down the hallway, obeying the woman ruled by her compassion. Right now he felt more like a kitchen slave than the chamberlain of Lower Egypt's second-largest estate. He didn't have time to feed this ungrateful viper. He had to sort through a pile of invoices and pay for the food, drink, and services from last night's banquet.

He approached the unfamiliar Medjays at the guest chamber door. "Alert the mistress that I've come with her midday meal."

Neither moved. One sneered. "Who are you?"

Every injustice of last night and this morning spewed out in a command. "I'm the chamberlain of this estate. Now, announce my presence immediately, or I'll put you on a barque back to Cush before sunset!"

"Hebrew!" Hami approached with purposeful strides. "When were you appointed commander of my guards?"

"I'm commander of this villa, and these imbeciles—"

"Stand down, Chamberlain." The chief Medjay spoke in a measured tone. "You're understandably upset, my friend, but you must compose yourself, or I will remove you from the situation."

Joseph's knuckles grew white as he gripped the tray. Had he ever so completely lost his temper? He inhaled sharply, unable to muster the humility he'd need to address the Medjays properly. *Elohim, help me!*

Pounding broke the silence. "Joseph? Is that you?"

"Be careful, Joseph," Hami said. "You defended her against the healers. Don't become her protector. She's desperate now and will use anyone or anything to get her way."

Stunned at his friend's venom, Joseph saw his own resentment mirrored in Hami's eyes. "I'm angry with the mistress, too, but I don't think she intended—"

"You've been warned." Hami turned to his Medjays. "You will allow the chamberlain to deliver food trays to the mistress." He nodded at Joseph and walked away.

The Medjays slid the bar aside and opened the door. "Thanks be to your god, Joseph. You're safe," the mistress said. "And Ahira?"

He slid the tray across the threshold. "She's safe, too, Mistress."

Her relieved smile faded. "You're not leaving—are you?"

"I have work to attend to."

"Please!" She rushed at the door. Pushing Joseph aside, the Medjays became human barriers between them. "Please, Joseph. I never meant . . ." Her anguished cry was like salt in a wound.

One of the guards snorted softly.

Joseph was struck by his arrogance. Why were these men so unlike every other Medjay he'd met? "I apologize for treating you disrespect-fully earlier," Joseph said. "I don't wish to be your enemy, but neither will I lick your sandals to be a friend."

The mistress reached between them. "Please, Joseph, stay for just—"

The Medjay shoved her inside, and kicked her tray, scattering the food across her chamber floor.

"I'm sorry," the mistress whimpered. "I wasn't trying to leave. Please don't hurt me!" Eyes filled with terror, she backed farther into her chamber.

"Mistress, it's all right," Joseph said. "I'll get another tray for you." He glared at the guards but heeded Hami's and Pushpa's advice and remained in the hall. To cross her threshold would invite a desperate woman into his arms for comfort—a woman who'd proved deceptive. "Well, men. My job is to bring the mistress a new tray. Since Medjays never leave their post and the mistress has no maid, your duty is to both guard her room *and* clean it." Joseph strode away, their sputtered objections salving his wounded pride.

THIRTY-TWO

The plans of the righteous are just,
  but the advice of the wicked is deceitful.
PROVERBS 12:5

I sat on my three-legged stool in the moonlight and considered my oil lamp. The sputtering flame of the little clay vessel had changed my world. With it adding light to the moon's glow, I could fashion my Minoan-style scarabs long into the night. Joseph had brought the lamp with my midday meal and two new chamber guards on my second day of captivity, proving his friendship and protection. The friendlier Medjays had provided amiable conversation while Joseph and I sat at my threshold to share the meal, but Hami's continuing silence still stung.

I poured a little more water into the dust and made another handful of mud. *Why couldn't Joseph have been Pharaoh's captain of the guard?* His gold-flecked green eyes were much like Ahira's, brimming with compassion and goodness. And love. The spark of passion that lit Joseph's eyes when he spoke of Ahira was the same that had burned in Minas's eyes for me. Different from lust, his gaze was tender yet strong. Intimate and selfless, revealing someone who wanted only to please. I lifted my face to inhale deeply. "Belonging," I whispered. "That's what I miss most, Minas. I miss *belonging* to someone and knowing that same someone belongs only to me."

I searched the night sky. "Are you there, Elohim, Creator of all things? Or are you another legend conjured by strong men to bend the weak?" Silence echoed as it did whenever I asked questions of the Hebrews' god.

Joseph brought word of Ahira each day, breaking my heart yet soothing my worry with reports of their unflappable trust in Elohim. How could they trust a god who had no priest to speak for him and no image to represent his form? My hands returned to shaping the mud.

I was tired of my whispered questions and circular thoughts.

The busy world outside my courtyard walls was deserted at night. A bug or mouse could scurry over my north or west wall into the palace's kitchen waste piles. My east wall abutted an alleyway that divided the palace complex from the lower city. Since I was neither bug nor mouse, hated heights, and couldn't climb, I sat under my lone palm on the three-legged stool, creating dozens of scarabs. Each oval bore a kiss of Crete: an octopus, a dolphin, a murex shell. I even carved a leaping bull into a few—to honor the husband I missed more with every breath.

After completing another dozen, I stood, groaned, and stretched. "You've got to move around more, Zully girl." I talked to myself now since there was no one else to talk to. I'd tried shouting to those on the other side of my wall, insisting I was being held prisoner. Whether I called out pleas or polite conversation, nothing I said mattered. I assumed my captivity had become more gossip fodder, proving the healers' diagnosis. *Captain Potiphar's hysterical wife.*

I'd asked Joseph yesterday, "What kind of man imprisons his wife in her own home?"

"I can't discuss the master with you, Mistress." He'd bolted to his feet and hurried away.

"No, wait! Please! I won't speak of Potiphar!"

Joseph had sent my food tray with someone else this morning, and

I feared I'd angered him beyond forgiveness. When he arrived with the midday meal, I'd never felt such relief. "I brought something to keep us occupied so you're not tempted to ask questions I can't answer," he'd said. "It's the master's favorite game. I'll teach you to play, and when he returns, I'll mention your skill at it."

I'd laughed, thinking he was teasing. "How can you boast of my skill when I'm just learning to play?"

"You're an intelligent woman, Mistress. You'll learn quickly."

My eyes traveled to the gift he'd brought me: the Egyptian board game senet. His matter-of-fact confidence in me was as stunning now, at the moon's zenith, as it had been at midday.

With three steps, I crossed my small courtyard to the corner where I'd placed the game with my pile of completed scarabs. I traced my fingers over the clay game board, five cones, and five spindles, the memory of Joseph's compassion overwhelming me, shaming me for the way I'd treated him for so long. I could love a man like Joseph. Not Joseph, of course, though I certainly liked him better since realizing his confidence was based more on his trust in the Hebrew god than arrogance. As I lightly touched the still-tender bruise on my face, longing stirred for a gentle man, kind and good. A man worthy of respect and favored by his god.

I had no desire to play senet with Potiphar. The entire game replicated the journey of the ka to the afterlife—the obsession of their culture. I scooped up a handful of my Minoan scarabs and inspected them one by one. Though a scarab was a thoroughly Egyptian bauble, I'd made each of *my* scarabs entirely Minoan. I'd chewed my fingernails into points, added water to Egypt's dust, and carved each oval with a sweet memory of Zakros. It had grounded me in who I was— not who I could never become. I picked up one of the senet spindles and studied the craftsmanship. I could easily replicate it with mud from my courtyard and make the game board as Minoan as my scarabs. But what alternate journey could the game signify?

Startled by a strange scuffling noise at my east wall, I set the scarabs aside. I heard a man's low grunt and another. *The alley!* A scratching sound—like someone climbing. I backed away, looking for a weapon.

Has Wereni sent someone to kill me? Or Potiphar? Panicked, I backed into my chamber, searching for an object to use in my defense. *My pitcher or stool.* Swinging them at an attacker was better than hiding in the dark like a helpless fish. I raced into the courtyard to retrieve them.

"Zully?" The coarse whisper stopped me.

Who would call me Zully?

"Zully, are you all right?"

"Gaios?" I said in a matching hushed tone. "Is it you?"

His deep chuckle was unmistakable. He appeared atop the wall, shimmied over, and landed on his feet—arms extended as if waiting for applause.

I was too stunned to speak—and then I laughed. "You look ridiculous. You look—Egyptian."

Dressed in a dusty white robe, he was clean shaven and wore Egyptian cosmetics. Brushing dust off his robe, he seemed more interested in his attire than in me.

"Where have you been, Gaios?" My voice broke—a jumble of emotions conspiring to undo me.

"Oh, Zully." He rushed closer to inspect my partially healed face in the moonlight. He was nearer than anyone had been in a week. "Potiphar is a brute. I'm well acquainted now with a few assassins in Avaris. Your husband will pay." His mouth covered mine with a deep kiss as though no time had separated us.

I shoved him away. Shocked. Furious. Confused. "But where have you— I thought Joseph sold you!"

"Shh!" He grinned. "Yes, my love, to the same greedy Midianites that brought me to Egypt. I told them Vizier Wereni would pay dearly for my release, and they were happy to be rid of me."

"Wereni?" The name tasted like dung on my lips. "You've been in Avaris this whole time?" My throat tightened around almost a year of hideous memories.

"I gather information for Wereni as I did for you and King Rehor. I blend into the ranks of Egyptian servants and have earned more freedom as I've built the vizier's trust."

"No! You—"

He silenced me in a crushing embrace, his lips close but not for passion. "The market is filled with news of Potiphar's wife, the gifted artist who won't leave his villa." With a sharp breath, he stepped back, and his gaze lingered on the pile of scarabs. "What's this, Princess Zuleika?"

He started toward my treasure, but I snagged his arm. "Leave, Gaios." Our eyes locked.

Sober, he brushed stray hairs off my forehead, and I slapped his hand away. I wouldn't be so easily manipulated this time.

"Forgive me." He bowed. When he straightened, his wounded look cracked my resolve. "Do you think I would ever betray you, Zully? Who has turned you against me? I've already saved up enough silver for one passage to Crete, and I'll send you back tomorrow if you want to go."

My breath caught. "Gaios."

He gestured at the wall. "I'll help you climb over right now. You'll be free of Egypt. Free of *me*—if that's what you want. I've only ever lived to serve you, Princess Zuleika."

Was the man in my courtyard the boy I'd known and trusted? Or was he the manipulator who had imprisoned me as surely as Potiphar kept me in this chamber?

During my silence, Gaios returned to stand with barely a hand-breadth between us. "Every moment away from you has been torture, but I've had only one purpose. We belong in Crete. Together. Have you so completely forgotten who I am, Zully?" He lowered his head as if to kiss me, but I pulled away.

"You would give me enough silver for the full passage to Zakros?"

His expression grew harsh, his eyes cold as he stepped back. "Of course. Passage on a barque from Avaris to Sena is relatively inexpensive following Inundation. However, fares from Sena to Crete change since merchant ships negotiate price with each passenger. You'll likely find a merchant ship all too willing to board an unescorted woman on the Great Sea." His veiled threat was valid. Without a guard or husband, I'd be at the mercy of a ship full of men and likely sold to a captive train.

"You need me." Gaios glared at me, moonlight casting a silver glint to his dark eyes. "It looks as though you've created something we can sell to help us return to Crete together." He nodded toward the corner stacked with scarabs.

"That may be the first time you've told me the truth since you arrived in Egypt." I led him toward my enterprise. "They're only mud scarabs with Minoan designs, Gaios. Nothing you can sell."

"They're unique, Zully," he said, inspecting them.

"You mean worthless?"

"No." His tone was filled with wonder. "They're unlike anything in the market. If we make it known Potiphar's wife created them, they'll sell like—"

"Are you mad?" I slapped the scarabs out of his hand. They rained onto the dry earth. "Potiphar would cut my throat."

"People are trading your vases like silver, Zully. If we reveal these Minoan scarabs as your newest creation, Pharaoh himself will purchase them." He braced my shoulders, giddy with greed. "Potiphar won't dare touch you."

Fear coursed through me as I relived the jolt of Potiphar's slap. I touched my cheek. "He may not kill me, but—"

"Potiphar's gone, Zully."

"Where?" Joseph *had* been vague about Potiphar's absence.

"Wereni's informants say he went to On and met with Ra's priests—the very center of Upper Egypt's plot against Pharaoh Khyan."

"You're lying, Gaios."

"I'm not lying this time, Zul." He scoffed. "I'd rather your husband stay on Khyan's side. The attack on Avaris will hit fast and hard—and my blade will be aimed at your husband, no matter who he calls Pharaoh."

"Don't be ridiculous, Gaios. Potiphar is a trained soldier." I turned away, hiding my fear. "When will the attack—"

"I've already said too much, Zully, but I want you to trust me."

"Wereni's informants are wrong," I said. "Potiphar must be searching for information to make arrests in On. He would never betray Pharaoh Khyan."

No answer. I turned to find Gaios bending to retrieve my game board from the corner.

"You've acquired the game of senet." He waved it in my face. "It requires two players, Zully. Who are you entertaining in your chamber now that your husband is gone?"

I held my tongue, realizing our conversation had taken a dangerous turn. He likely suspected one of the other Minoan slaves. I dared not hint at my growing friendship with Joseph and make him a target. The Gaios who stood before me was more dangerous than I'd ever imagined. "The game board came with my food tray. I'd planned to create a Minoan version of the game just like I've made the scarabs Minoan."

He lowered the game board and scrutinized it, then traced all three rows of ten squares, lingering on the five spaces with special carvings. "Anyone can draw the empty squares in the dust, but few artists could accurately depict these five squares that represent the most significant journey of the Egyptian religion." He lifted his eyes to meet mine. "Zully, you can replicate these five squares that players can place amid a game board drawn in the dust. Anyone could then afford a version of senet that provides only five pieces, spindles, and throwing sticks for two players."

"It's the game of passing," I reminded him. "I don't believe in the journey this board represents. Why create something that has nothing to do with who I am?"

All attempts at pleasantness disappeared as he placed the game board on my shoulder and moved it back and forth against my neck in a sawing motion. I was horrified at his allusion, and shivers overtook me.

"You can be Princess Zuleika and create fashionable and profitable pieces of art, or you can be the lunatic wife of Captain Potiphar who Pharaoh mercifully sends on her own journey of the ka because your ma'at was hopelessly unbalanced in this world."

He lowered the game board to his side, moonlight casting eerie shadows across his face. "We need not believe in their gods to take their silver, Zully. I'll supply potter's clay, a little copper—maybe even some gold and gemstones if I can get them at a good price—and you'll carve beautiful Egyptian game pieces and special squares for a senet game even lowborn Egyptians can afford." He discarded the game board carelessly on my pile of scarabs. "We can try to sell your little mud scarabs too. Who knows? Perhaps they'll strike gold like your vases."

"And you'll cheat me out of the profits as before?" I spit the words, daring him to deny them.

His shock seemed so convincing. "I *never* cheated you. I gambled to increase my portion and sent a large sum with merchants I trusted to help rebuild Crete. Joseph sold me before I could replace the silver." He straightened. "Haven't you wondered why your pateras never sent you a message, Zully?"

"Of course. I told you how it saddened me."

A derisive snort raised my defenses. "When I moved into Vizier Wereni's servant quarters, I sent a message to King Rehor asking why he'd never contacted you. I received a message from him within a month. He *had* tried to contact you. Many times. His missives never reached you in this fortress your husband commands." The flush of anger on his cheeks was visible even in moonlight. Could he feign the color in his cheeks, or were his accusations true?

"That's when I discovered how desperate Crete had become," he continued. "Merchants still refused to trade with Rehor after the shaking, believing it was judgment from the gods. The quantity of food and supplies Pharaoh Khyan sent last year—the second year of his three-year agreement—barely supplied two districts. Khyan cheated King Rehor, and Potiphar holds you captive. That's why I'm working with Wereni, Zully. To free us both and help save the home we love."

I was breathless in the wake of the revelations. "Pateras sent messages?"

His features softened. "Yes, and it was the chamberlain who intercepted them."

"Joseph? But why?"

"At the master's order, no doubt." Gaios sneered and waited for my reaction. He'd always hated Joseph. So had I—then.

I tried to untangle all I'd heard. All I knew to be true of both Gaios and the chamberlain I was learning to trust. The untangling stirred more questions.

"If you could send money to Crete for rebuilding, why didn't you take me home instead? Show me one of Pateras's messages. I want to see proof he's contacted you."

His lips pursed into a disapproving scowl. "After all I've done, you would question my loyalty? I can leave now, Zully, and you need never see me again. Is that what you want?"

My heart skipped, and I hugged my waist. *Is* that what I wanted? Was he only a street rat, sniffing out spoiled morsels for the one who rewarded him best? "No!" The word escaped while my inner battle raged. I feared him. But I would never blindly follow a man again. Though desperation made me bow, my necessity gave me power. "We both know you need my profits to return to Crete, or you wouldn't be here."

He paused with a grin. "All right, Zully. Name a reasonable profit that *you* expect for each senet piece and scarab. I'll find a merchant to give you that amount; then I'll negotiate for *my* profits above your desired earnings. I'll send rebuilding funds for Crete out of my portion, and we'll save separately for return passage." He lifted his brows. "Fair?"

I hesitated, knowing I could never enforce—nor trust—whatever agreement we made. "Will you truly take me back to Crete, Gaios?"

His anger drained like wine from an overturned goblet. "Yes, Princess Zuleika. I vow that someday I *will* return you to Zakros Palace." His dark eyes begged entry to my soul. I longed to depend on him as I once did. "Please let me hold you," he said, opening his arms.

I stepped back, memories strengthening my resolve. "No, Gaios. We'll do business but nothing more. I'll create. You'll deliver product, return my profits, and keep your portion."

A slight smile curved his lips as his hands fell to his sides. "We'll do as you say for now. I'll take care of everything, and I'll protect you from Potiphar. He won't harm you again, Zully. I promise." The street rat scurried over my wall, and his footsteps faded in the alley.

Oh, how wished I could believe him. Would he supply me with

clay, gold, and gemstones to make something truly valuable and then send the funds to help our homeland? Seeing a dolphin in the Nile seemed as likely. But even as I barred the door of my heart, I longed for at least a part of Gaios's promises to be true. *Someday I will return you to Zakros Palace.* Could I then return to the life I longed for, the life I was born to live? Might I even find a man who compared to the husband I'd lost?

PART III

When his master heard the story his wife told him, saying, "This is how your slave treated me," he burned with anger. Joseph's master took him and put him in prison.

GENESIS 39:19–20

THIRTY-THREE

*Though she spoke to Joseph day after day, he refused
to go to bed with her.*

GENESIS 39:10

Joseph

"It's Potiphar's third mysterious journey in as many months." Pushpa slammed brown dough onto the table, and a puff of flour shot into her hair. "He doesn't take a contingent of Medjays or tell Hami where he goes. He won't tell me either. I thought surely he'd tell you, Joseph." She pressed both fists into the dough. "He tells you everything."

"The master confides in you more than anyone, Pushpa." A basket of food for Ahira hung on Joseph's arm. He was trying to be patient.

"So, where does he go?" She turned the mound of dough, folded it, and shoved her fists into it again. "Some say he goes hunting in the Fayum. Why do men think it brave and daring to hunt lions near the pyramids of Giza? My son is not as good with a bow as he is with a sword."

Joseph stilled her furious kneading. "Your son is Pharaoh's best warrior and the king's most loyal friend. Maybe he simply needs to escape Avaris's relentless scrutiny."

"I feel like I'm losing him," she said, returning to her task. "I won't let him go." No tears today. Just the ferocious determination of a loving ima.

Joseph sighed. He'd felt a shift in his master, too, but couldn't define it. "We won't lose him, Pushpa. Elohim's favor has been extended to my master and this household. We'll all get through this." He walked away before she could argue. He didn't have any more platitudes to offer after using most of them to bolster his courage for another visit with Ahira.

As he descended into the underbelly of Potiphar's villa, Joseph's hope eroded like a river rock worn smooth over time. His first stop was always Ubaid's chamber to rouse the old man from his reed mat. He seemed to grow grouchier each morning.

"I don't know why you can't unlock the cell yourself." Ubaid coughed as he rolled off his mat.

"I've explained it a dozen times. We want no grounds for accusation."

The old goat coughed again, groaned, and grabbed the iron ring of wooden keys from the wall peg, then plodded through the main room to pluck a torch from its harness. In the narrow hallway at Ahira's door, Joseph placed his own lamp and the food basket on the floor, waiting with both dread and anticipation. The other prisoners didn't heckle them as Ubaid opened her door.

The warden stepped away and Joseph leaned against the doorframe. The odor from inside attacked him. "Ubaid! You promised to clean her cell yesterday!"

The old man walked away with a dismissive wave.

"Today!" Joseph shouted after him. "You'll clean it today!"

"Joseph, don't." Ahira's weak voice stole his attention. "Ubaid's cough is worse. He needs Pushpa's herbs."

He was jarred by her compassion and terrified by her breathy tone. "Why care about his suffering when you live in filth?"

No answer.

She'd asked him not to shine any light into her cell, but he needed to *see* her. Scooting over the threshold, he held the lamp aloft. "Ahira . . ." Words left him. The woman he loved was a shrunken vessel, poured out and withered.

Her eyes, sunken into a skeletal face, squinted at the dim glow. She smoothed matted hair from her face, and a small clump fell to the floor. "Go, Joseph." She extended an arm to block his view. It bore weeping sores.

"Your wounds need treatment."

"No, please." She lowered her arm. "If you wrap the wounds, cloth will stick. If you apply honey, the rats will feast. Let me go, Joseph," she whispered, curling onto her side.

He lowered the lamp and clenched his teeth to fight a sob. *Elohim, don't take her from me!* He skittered backward and breathed deep and slow. He couldn't lose control. *Elohim, I'm frightened. Please, don't let her die!*

A weak hum rose from the darkness. Fragmented and sparse. Though the shepherd's tune was barely recognizable, it was the sweetest sound he'd heard since Ahira hummed it months ago.

Joseph joined her, carrying the melody. He crawled into the darkness, feeling the rattle of fear's shackles. He lifted Ahira into his arms and pressed his back against the cell wall. Panting, heart racing, he focused on the open door and sang louder. They sang the tune again and again. Eventually other prisoners learned it and joined them. Joseph's heart rate slowed. His muscles relaxed. Their shepherd's song grew softer, and Ahira settled against his chest. Her singing faded.

"Ahira?"

No response.

Oh, Elohim! No! He lifted his hand to check for breath and discerned the warmth of life still in her. *Thank You, Elohim.* He sang again, rocking, alternately praying and weeping.

"Joseph?" Her voice from the utter darkness. "You're in my cell. Aren't you afraid?"

"No." His legs stretched into the doorway, his shoulders flat against her wall. She was draped over him like a blanket. They would never have been so familiar in another place or circumstance. Suddenly his body awakened—burning for a future with this woman. "You'll be my wife someday, Ahira."

"I'm dying, Joseph. If there's a resurrection, why not beg the master to end my suffering?"

"No." He pulled her closer, cradling her like a child. "Elohim is the God of life, Ahira. Only He determines our last breath. Remember the ancient records, my love, and tell me a story."

"Joseph, please." She buried her face against him. "I can't."

"You must," he said. "Think of a story when Elohim *saved* someone's life." Stubborn silence answered. If she weren't so weak, he would have argued with her.

"Hagar." It was barely a whisper.

"Yes." He laid his cheek atop her head. "Tell me the story."

"You know it."

"Tell me again."

Her little chuckle was like a fresh breath in the fetid air. "You're being a bossy prince."

She needed to eat if she were to have strength for a story, but Joseph refused to lay her in the filthy straw. Keeping her safe in his arms, he stood and felt his way to the door, then lowered her to the bare stones in the hallway. "I'll be back with fresh straw and a new oil lamp. Prepare your story while I'm gone." He nudged Pushpa's basket with his foot. "See if you can find something in the basket to eat." He heard no movement. She was too weak.

He hurried toward the torches in the main room, thrashing himself for not returning after yesterday's morning meal to check on Ahira's condition and Ubaid's cough. How could they have worsened so quickly?

"Ubaid!" He reached the main chamber and heard the old man still coughing. He entered his chamber and knelt beside his reed mat. "You stubborn old goat! Why didn't you tell me how sick you were?"

"I'm not drinking any more of that rancid tea."

"Don't be childish. I'll get your tea after Ahira has eaten and I clean the cells."

"Wait!" Ubaid sat up. "Cleaning the cells is my job, Lord Chamberlain." His rheumy eyes didn't meet Joseph's. "I've failed you and I'm sorry." A coughing fit overtook him.

"Rest, Ubaid!" Joseph snagged the iron ring of keys and a fresh oil lamp from a wall niche and returned down the narrow, dark hall.

Ahira lay on her side, the basket of food within reach but untouched. Joseph sat beside her, then retrieved a piece of bread and cradled her in his arms. "All right. You must eat while you tell me of Hagar."

She took her time, eating bites of bread and cheese and a few raisins while telling the familiar tale about the Egyptian slave woman who cried out to Elohim in the desert and named Him El Roi, the God Who Sees. Her cheeks seemed to have more color when she patted her belly. "I can't eat any more, Joseph."

"All right. Rest while I prepare your cell."

He began the arduous process of shoveling the soiled straw from her cell, piling it onto a rough-spun tarp and then tying the corners into a bundle he could haul up the prison stairs. After retrieving fresh straw from the storage space adjoining the main room, he sprinkled a layer of protection between Ahira and the cold stone.

"Clean mine!" a man shouted.

"Mine too!" another said.

"I will!" Joseph wiped perspiration from his forehead.

A faint whisper rattled in the chamber across from Ahira's but ended with a weak cough.

Joseph caught Ahira's glance in the dim lamplight. "He stopped speaking two days ago. A prisoner stops talking about three days before Ubaid removes the body from the cell."

Eerie silence fell. This morning, a simple oil lamp had illuminated more than Ahira's small frame. Pharaoh's prison was sorely neglected by a warden who was too ill to tend it—because the villa's chamberlain had let hopelessness and fear affect his judgment.

With renewed determination, Joseph carried Ahira into her clean cell. "I'll come back later today with something to clean your wounds." He kissed her forehead and left her cell door open while he used Ubaid's ring of keys to unlock the chamber next to hers. He mucked out each prisoner's dark world and found every man at least as weak as Ahira. Some were worse. The man in the cell across from her died in Joseph's arms. By the time he climbed the prison stairs with Pushpa's empty basket, his arms and legs hung like iron weights, and his heart was just as heavy.

He entered the kitchen just past midday.

"Aahh, get out! You're revolting!" Pushpa waved a towel at him but stopped abruptly when she saw his face. "Joseph—" She scurried toward the doorway where he waited.

He held out her empty basket. "Ahira ate more than usual today. We sang together, and she told me a story." She didn't need to know the other details. "She's dying, Pushpa. Ubaid is desperately ill too. It's my fault. I didn't realize any of it."

"Oh, no, you don't, Lord Chamberlain." She fisted her hands at her hips. "You may be a skilled administrator and good with words, but you'll not take credit *or blame* for things beyond your sway. You're no god." She raised a single brow. "Though in my younger days I might have noticed you look like one."

"Pushpa!" The unexpected jest brought the levity Joseph needed.

She patted his cheek and sobered. "I'll prepare the fenugreek tea for Ubaid. What can we do for our Ahira?"

"She has open wounds, but we can't wrap them or apply honey." He omitted the explanation of rats.

"Hmm." The old woman pressed her finger against pursed lips before waving him away. "Wash and change your robe; then serve Zully's midday meal. I'll prepare everything you need for your return to the prison this afternoon."

Joseph groaned inwardly at all the work that remained undone in his office as he left the kitchen and entered Potiphar's chamber. He washed in the fresh water he'd gathered earlier and slipped on his last clean robe. The laundress had been slow of late. Was the whole estate slacking? He ticked through a list of overdue tasks, and the critic inside said *he* was the problem.

You'll not take credit or blame *for things beyond your sway.*

If only his internal voices would bow to Pushpa's logic.

The sun had already passed its midday peak when Joseph raced into the kitchen and grabbed the tray Pushpa had prepared for Mistress Zully. The busy household hub was deserted. Its saucy commander often visited Wereni's wife—her childhood friend—or another gossiping noblewoman to gain information. The Minoan slaves usually rested in their chambers since their workday began well before dawn.

Joseph picked up the tray, his mind revisiting the woman he adored while he walked toward a woman he'd come to respect. Ahira was locked in a tiny cell, surrounded by suffering. Mistress Zully—what she'd insisted he call her—was a captive in her own home in an empty chamber with an equally empty life ahead. Both women had little hope of change in their circumstances. Joseph knew of only one instance in which Master Potiphar had made a decision and then changed it. He'd vowed never to marry. And Pharaoh changed that decision for him—with dire consequences for all. Life and joy in the villa had crumbled to ruin on the night of the lotus festival.

Joseph greeted the mistress's daytime guards as he approached. They were civil, though not friendly, and had fallen into the same dispirited service as the rest of Potiphar's estate.

"Is Pushpa ill?" the shorter guard asked. "She didn't send our meal trays yet."

Proof that even their cook was merely surviving. "Pushpa is fine," Joseph said. "I returned later than usual from the cellblock, which likely skewed her schedule. Unlock the mistress's door, and then go fill a tray for each of you. You can eat with Mistress Zuleika and me when you return."

"Thank you, Chamberlain." The guard slipped his key into the wooden lock, slid the bar aside, and opened the door. He and his partner strode away.

Zully peeked around the doorway. "Shall we run?" Her impish grin was a welcome relief from the morning's heaviness. He hoped she wasn't serious.

"You're probably starving." The words tasted bitter on his tongue. *Starving.* No one living above Pharaoh's prison was starving.

He startled when her hand touched his forearm. "What's wrong, Joseph? I can see you're upset."

Lowering the tray to her threshold was the most subtle way to avoid her touch. He lingered on one knee. "Ahira isn't well, Mistress. She's—" Joseph's voice broke as he kept his head bowed.

"But she'll be all right?"

"Yes." Would she be all right? He looked up. "I don't know."

"What do you mean?" Color drained from her cheeks. "You've seen her every day. How could you not—"

"I agreed not to shine any light into her cell, so I didn't realize how weak she'd gotten—or the heinous conditions of the other prisoners." He shook his head, the weight of the master's estate crushing him. "Hami hasn't spoken to me in weeks. Pushpa is worried about Master Potiphar. And the shepherds' reports are down from this time last year." Joseph raised his eyes to meet the mistress's and realized his mistake. "Forgive me, Mistress. I need not burden you with these sorrows."

She looked at her tray, picking at the dates but not eating. "I suspect you're nearly as lonely as I am, Joseph, with Potiphar away and Ahira locked in that awful place."

Lonely. He'd never connected what he felt with that emotion, but yes. That was it. Master Potiphar had been traveling more than he'd been at home. Hami seemed aloof and angry. Pushpa was either busy in her kitchen or gathering information from her noble friends. Because he'd been given permission to visit Ahira only once a day, all the time he was away from her, he yearned for that other half of his soul locked in the dungeon below. "I miss the woman I truly believe Elohim has chosen to be my wife."

Zully reached across the divide and rested her hand on his. "Do you know what I miss most about my best friend?"

He cradled her hand in his. "What?" He missed everything. Ahira's scent. The way she tossed her hair when she was nervous.

"I miss the way she hummed when she was working."

Joseph chuckled. "She hummed this morning—and sang. Even when she could barely whisper—she still sang." His heart warmed that the mistress remembered such a small detail about the woman he adored. He began the tune he'd shared with Ahira and watched the light of recognition brighten the mistress's features.

"Yes, that's it!" She clapped her hands and hummed along. After a short while, she fell silent. Her playful smile faded, and her eyes searched his. "You know I'd trade my life for Ahira's if I could, Joseph. She won't ever leave that cell." Her chin quivered. "We must face that truth, you and me. I've known only one man with your integrity, Joseph. The same kindness, intelligence, goodness—"

"Mistress—" He started to stand, but she captured his wrist and pulled him back to one knee.

"My husband, Minas, was a great man. You're very much like him." She tilted her head, eyebrows lifted. "Come inside, Joseph. Let me show you the scarabs I've created in my courtyard."

"Scarabs? How . . ." He stood and glanced inside the chamber. At the sight of her sleeping mat, his heart raced with warning. "Mistress, I can't."

"A desperate soul must fill the void, Joseph." Her eyes held him like shackles. "Please, come inside. We can leave the door open. We'll go quickly to my courtyard for a peek." She gently grasped his hands and lowered her voice. "You love Ahira, and I still love Minas. I'm not asking for your *love*, Joseph. Just come inside and fill the void."

He felt light-headed. "I should leave."

She tugged at him. "Before the guards return. Come to bed with me, Joseph."

The brazen words shocked him, and he stumbled back. "No, Mistress! How could I do such a wicked thing and sin against God?" Joseph turned and ran, ignoring the strangled whispers calling him back.

Her guards exited the kitchen as he slipped into Potiphar's chamber. "If you were a Medjay, Chamberlain," one of them called, "you'd be disciplined for leaving your post."

Joseph closed the door, then slid down it and landed hard on the floor. "Elohim," he whispered, "give me strength to love Ahira, to resist these stirrings, and to serve a master who seems to have abandoned us all."

THIRTY-FOUR

Let love and faithfulness never leave you;
  bind them around your neck,
  write them on the tablet of your heart.
Then you will win favor and a good name
  in the sight of God and man.

PROVERBS 3:3–4

EIGHT MONTHS LATER
Ahira

A chilling wail skirted the edges of Ahira's consciousness, drawing her from darkness to darkness. Opening her eyes to inky blackness was like waking to find herself still trapped in a nightmare. She uncurled her body, sat up, and pressed her back against one wall and her legs against another to stretch cramped muscles. Healthier now since her straw was kept fresh and she'd enjoyed two meals a day for nearly a year, she'd also become more alert.

Sounds of activity wafted down the cellblock hall from the prison's main room. Was it Joseph and Ubaid, come to share Pushpa's morning food offering?

Another wail sent a shiver down her spine. She covered her ears, unable to bear the sounds of suffering. Nearly every night, a prisoner was hauled from his cell to be tortured—some never to return. New prisoners appeared at all hours of the day and night. Some were tortured before being dragged to their new quarters. Others went straight to a tiny cell. Though Ahira's dark hole had become more bearable since two new slaves started helping Ubaid clean, increased tortures and executions made Pharaoh's cellblock far less hospitable than when she'd arrived. Whenever she closed her eyes, she wondered when her turn would come.

"Of course, Master Potiphar." Ubaid's familiar voice drew closer, quaking. "She's been no trouble at all, you know. I could clean her up and then bring her upstairs if you wish."

She? Ahira was the only woman on the cellblock.

"Hurry up, old man." Master Potiphar spoke in a low growl. Keys rattled outside Ahira's door, the sound mingling with moans emanating from the main chamber.

Would tonight be her execution? Worse, would she be tortured first? She held her breath as the wooden lock clicked and her door swung open. Master Potiphar's imposing silhouette appeared amid blinding torchlight.

"What have I done, Master?"

He reached into the small cell and lifted her off the floor.

"What have I—"

"Quiet!"

She tried to look at him, but the torchlight was too bright. "Forgive me, Master. The light—it's . . ." She lifted her hands to lessen the glare and caught a glimpse of his surprise.

"Where did she get a clean robe, Ubaid?"

"Lord Chamberlain distributes clean robes each month to cellblock prisoners."

Was he angry about her robe? "I don't need a clean robe. I can wear this for the rest of my life." A whimper escaped at the thought. "That is, if I'm to have a life."

Potiphar scoffed. "I'm not going to kill you, little Hebrew." He started down the hall, his hand a vise on her arm.

"Ahira?" A gravelly voice called out from the darkness, vaguely familiar.

Master Potiphar paused. She searched near the torture tables and found three figures cowering, groaning in pain. After blinking away tears from the bright light, she studied them more closely. "Gaios? Abasi?" Bloodied and barely recognizable from torture, Zully's wicked slave and the master's old steward had been those wailing in pain. She didn't recognize the third man, dressed in the flowing white robe of Egyptian priesthood, but his body was just as mangled, his priestly robe equally torn and bloodied.

"Ahira," Gaios said weakly. "Maybe you can get the master to let us go."

"Let you go?" The master stood over the battered prisoners. "You gave me nothing that helps me protect Pharaoh at today's festival."

"I told you King Rehor arrived last night from Cush. He connects Wereni to Pharaoh Sobekhotep *and* your Medjays."

"Mercy . . . mercy." Abasi, barely conscious, slurred the words.

The master leaned over him and rested his hand on the old man's cheek. "It will be over soon, old friend. If you want a swift and merciful death, you should tell me more—"

"We don't know more, Potiphar!" the priest cried.

Potiphar. Ahira recognized familiarity between them. Did he share a past with the master as Abasi did?

"We know of no violence planned for today's akhet festival," the priest whined. "Only riots are planned in Bubastis and On."

A Medjay jabbed him with the dull end of his spear. "Liar!" The priest cried out.

Gaios lifted his head, the most alert of the three, and met the captain's eyes. "You vowed to spare her life if we told you everything. We did. You gave your word."

The master's grin chilled Ahira. "Must an honorable man's promise to a liar be honored?"

"Please." Gaios's eyes slid shut. "Zully knows nothing of King Rehor's trade agreement with the Medjay chieftains and Pharaoh Sobekhotep."

"Why would I believe anything you say, cockroach?"

"Because I've loved your wife for as long as I can remember."

Ahira held her breath, waiting for a death blow to the cheeky Minoan. The two Medjays who flanked the prisoners exchanged a quick glance—a rare display of surprise—while the master slowly lowered himself to one knee.

"If you love her, then you should know . . . Zully had a miscarriage a few months after I returned from the Tehenu rebellion." He smiled. "The child was yours, cockroach."

Gaios's eyes widened, and his nostrils flared. "You're lying!"

"I don't lie." The master turned toward Ahira. "Let's go."

"Don't think you can trust your precious Medjays, Captain Potiphar," Gaios called after him.

Potiphar's steps faltered, but he clasped Ahira's arm and continued toward the stairs.

"Gaios doesn't know," the priest shouted after them. "He can neither be sure your wife is innocent, nor does he know which Medjays are involved. Pharaoh Sobekhotep alone knows every name and detail of our efforts to set him on Egypt's united throne. We've been successful because no one knows everything about anything."

Master Potiphar halted at the first step and turned to face the priest. "Repeat that."

"Pharaoh Sobekhotep alone—"

"No!" he shouted. "The part 'no one knows . . . '"

"No one knows everything about anything?"

Potiphar's attention shifted to the Medjays. "Where have you heard *that* phrase?"

They maintained empty stares. The one nearest Gaios saluted with fist to chest. "We are your loyal soldiers, Captain." The other guard saluted with equal passion. Tension crackled in the air. Ahira had heard Hami say the phrase several times in jest while he shared evening tea with her, Joseph, and Pushpa. The two Medjays guarding these three prisoners had been the master's chamber guards since she arrived at the villa less than three years ago. They were loyal. Faithful. Could they betray him? Had the world above her cellblock changed so drastically that even the most honorable Medjays couldn't be trusted?

"Upstairs," the master growled.

Fear, sudden and paralyzing, attacked her. "Master, where are you taking me?" Her legs collapsed.

He scooped her up and continued up the stairs like a man being chased. His arms felt like iron bars beneath her, but she dared not ask again. He seemed furious that the prisoners had offered so little information when, at least to Ahira, their testimonies seemed to condemn King Rehor and Vizier Wereni and alert the master to some of his own Medjays' possible connection to a conspiracy threatening Pharaoh Khyan's throne. Ahira's mind spun with all the details, and the ache in her eyes intensified as they approached the daylight spilling through the villa's open hallway door.

When they reached the landing, the master set her feet on the floor and steadied her. "Have you enough strength to walk to your old chamber?"

Mouth dry, Ahira nodded. "I might need to lean on something."

He offered his arm. Her eyes met his, questioning the kind gesture. Was it pity? Was someone waiting in the chamber to prepare her for execution?

"Seth's toenails, woman! I won't bite." He supported her waist, fairly carrying her through the doorway and down the hall. "Today is the akhet festival and Khyan's birth celebration. He allowed me to choose this year's freedom prisoner."

His meaning slowly dawned. "Me?" Shading her eyes from the hallway torches, she peered at the man who had imprisoned her for helping his wife deceive him. "Why choose me?"

"Because, after the festivities, you'll return as my wife's maid—and report her treachery to me."

"Of course, Master Potiphar, but how could Mistress Zully do anything worthy of report? Joseph said she hasn't left the guest chamber—"

He halted twenty paces from the chambers at the end of the hall. "You'll report to me any attempts Princess Zuleika makes to contact King Rehor, anyone in Cush, or others who might be conspiring with Pharaoh Sobekhotep."

"Conspiring?" Ahira squeezed her eyes closed and shook her head.

Surely this was another nightmare. When she glanced around, the hallway murals were as she remembered them. She looked again at her master. "Why would your wife care about Cush or *any* pharaoh when her single passion has always been to rebuild Crete and return?"

His features hardened. "You will remain free only as long as you are useful. Make no mistake, girl—I'll kill you now if your loyalty to Zully is greater than your will to live."

Loyalty. His need for it screamed in the silence, and she saw her master more plainly than ever. "That's why you can never forgive her." The words slipped out in a whisper, the truth proved by his widened eyes. "I knew you loved her, Master Potiphar, by the way you served her after the miscarriage even when she could give nothing in return. But Mistress Zully has never had anything to give a husband in Egypt. She left her heart in Crete. Which is the same reason she's incapable of supporting any pharaoh fully—Khyan or the other man you mentioned—or loving you, because she can only imagine herself returning to Crete."

He scoffed. "She can't love me because she's a princess who came to marry Egypt's king."

"No, my lord. It's because she's a princess who should have been a queen—in Crete. Instead, her husband and ima died, a few weeks later she married you, both you and her abba left her the next day, and she's experienced nothing but loss since."

His face paled, and his bearing became somehow less formidable. "You're much too generous toward the woman whose deceit put you in prison."

"I chose to obey Mistress Zully and help her sell her pottery in the market, Master Potiphar—as I make the choice now to never betray you again. Knowing how highly you value loyalty, it will be the way I show my high regard for you, Master." Ahira bowed.

When she straightened, the master's arm was waiting to escort her. "I hope you're right about my wife, little Hebrew. I would find no pleasure in killing her."

Ahira swallowed the lump in her throat and inhaled deeply the sweet smells of freedom. She was convinced Zully would never conspire in an Egyptian uprising, but Gaios's insistence on her innocence hinted at renewed familiarity and set off a warning shofar in Ahira's heart. But how had he contacted her in a locked, guarded chamber in the villa? As they neared the two rooms at the end of the hall, Ahira didn't recognize the Medjays at either the guest chamber or the mistress's old chamber. Both sets of guards saluted their captain with fists to chest. One opened the chamber where Ahira had spent nearly two years of her life with the woman now locked behind the door across the hall.

Pushpa's delighted squeal stole her attention. "My Ahira!" She showered her with a flurry of kisses and then clutched Ahira's hands. "You're here! My girl, you're back where you belong! I knew my Potiphar would find a way!" Pushpa wrapped her in a hug, warm and protective. Ahira buried her face against the woman's shoulder, her stinging eyes needing respite from the courtyard's sunny glare.

"Ahira?" The voice was familiar, its tentative tone not so.

Her head shot up, and she nudged Pushpa away, searching through squinted eyes for Joseph. He stood beside the master, stiff as a measuring rod, but the wonder on his handsome features was as bright as the sun. "Elohim heard our prayers."

Could he mean marriage? "*All* our prayers, Joseph?"

"No, not—" He grinned, glancing at the master, who lifted a single brow. Joseph sobered, returning his focus to Ahira. "Let's not test the master's patience by asking about our wedding on the day you've been set free."

The master's face reddened. "I've already said—"

"We'll discuss it later." Pushpa waved away his bluster. "Today we prepare the freedom prisoner. Ahira must glow with redemption and radiate gratitude." The dear woman guided her to a bright crimson couch and sat on a stool beside it.

Tears poured down Ahira's cheeks, partly because she still fought the brightness but also because the chamber, stripped to bare walls, felt lifeless. Zully's vibrant Minoan creations were gone, as was the circle of Minoan treasures so precious to her.

"Lie back, dear. Today you'll wear cosmetics, and I'll apply them."

Pushpa searched through her basket, distracted and frowning. "Oh, Seth's toenails! I forgot my pot of kohl. Rest a moment while I go back to my chamber to get it." She hurried from the room while Ahira melted into the lotus-scented pillows.

"Go with Ommi, Joseph." The master's gruff command stiffened Ahira's spine.

She exchanged a fearful glance with Joseph.

"Master," Joseph said, "what would I do to help—"

"Delay her return for a few moments."

"Yes, my lord." Joseph bowed and left.

Ahira closed her eyes, heart racing. *Elohim, have You followed me out of my prison cell? I need You now!*

When the door clicked shut, she heard the master's sandals shuffling nearer and opened her eyes to find him sitting on the stool beside her. "Because you'll carry more responsibility, I'm going to give you more information than I've shared with Joseph or Pushpa. Serve me well, and I'll allow you and Joseph to marry."

Relief shattered her angst. "Master—"

"Listen! We haven't much time."

She nodded, angst returning.

"Zully began selling art again six or seven—maybe eight—months ago. My informants saw an accomplice climb Zully's courtyard wall with an empty bag and leave shortly after with a shoulder bag full of the mud scarabs and senet games that have swept Avaris with their popularity. They followed the man to Wereni's villa after he'd sold the items to merchants in both the royal and the lower markets. Khyan himself has started collecting the scarabs. Thus far Zully has been protected from my wrath by her talent. I've known her accomplice was Gaios, but I waited to arrest him until—"

"You've known all these months, and you didn't stop him?" Ahira regretted the hint of accusation, but he needed to understand the danger. "Master, you saw what Gaios did to her while you were gone to Temehu. His deceit and manipulation made her an empty shell. He held her captive when there was no lock on her chamber."

"She deceived *me!*" He bolted to his feet, knocking over the stool.

"Yes, she did." Ahira slowly stood to face his fury. "A desperate woman, alone in a strange land with no friends, resorted to the only thing that gave her a sense of belonging—and Gaios used that weakness for his own gain. Whatever has happened with this coup or conspiracy, you can be sure Gaios has involved your wife without her knowledge."

He leaned close. "I'll never be sure of anything again."

The chamber door swung open, and Pushpa appeared with a tray of food and a basket over each arm. She halted abruptly, and her son quickly retreated from his threatening stance. Raising her brows, she gave a soft *humph* and continued into the room. "I thought we might break our fast together, but it seems likely you have other plans, Potiphar." She set the tray down on the empty couch and put the baskets beside it, then turned to her son with an outstretched hand. "I assume you stole my pot of kohl to force Joseph and me out of the room?"

The master sighed and produced the pilfered pot from his waist pouch. "There are some things you and Joseph can't know today, Ommi." He kissed her forehead and started toward the door. He paused when he reached Joseph, whispered something Ahira couldn't hear, and continued to the door. "I'll see you at the akhet ceremony, Ommi. I've arranged a Medjay escort for you—and don't argue. I *will* ensure your safety today."

THIRTY-FIVE

Hopes placed in mortals die with them;
all the promise of their power comes to nothing.
PROVERBS 11:7

Potiphar

In a crowd as large as the one gathered for the akhet measurement, Potiphar wished his friend were a normal-sized pharaoh—a smaller target for enemy arrows and spears. Pharaoh's army kept order in the streets, while Potiphar and his Medjays kept Pharaoh alive inside the palace complex. Potiphar scanned the gathered nobility, every face, every hand, every twitch. He'd placed a line of trusted Medjays between the king and his royal council members since Khyan insisted King Rehor stand among his most honored nobility. Ommi stood beside Wereni's wife. Not exactly where Potiphar would have placed her, but with his six best Medjays as her shield, even the wily vizier wouldn't dare attempt to harm her.

A hush fell, drawing Potiphar's attention back to Pharaoh Khyan as he bent low to read the water gauge affixed to the palace quay. "Sixteen cubits!" His shout drew a great cheer from those inside and outside the palace complex. Rather than reveling in the celebration, however, Khyan wrestled the gauge from its post and thrust it overhead. As more nobility glimpsed the king's unusual stance, merriment faded. "See the watermark for yourselves," he said, extending the marker like a sword. Issued like a challenge, his booming voice even quieted akhet festivities outside the walls.

Khyan donned his war face. Nostrils flaring and eyes wide with fury, he swung the marker in a wide swath. "You can see the measurement for yourselves. Your god and king never deceives you, and I demand equal transparency in *everyone!*" His final roar drove the whole audience back a step. "Shackle them!"

Khyan stared at Potiphar as he said the words. Potiphar glimpsed a contingent of Medjays descending on Wereni and shouted at Khyan, "How could you do this without—"

"No one should know everything about anything," Hami said as he approached him from behind with another contingent.

Potiphar whirled and reached for his sword.

"Potiphar, no!" Ommi screeched.

His glance gave his well-trained guards the advantage. With a great roar, Potiphar fell. His cheek slammed to the tiled pavement with the force of two men riding his back. One held his face against the tiles, three more locked his arms behind him, and at least twelve swords pointed at his neck.

Hami bent on one knee. "Mistress Pushpa will not be harmed, Captain—as long as you come willingly." His tone was utter calm, as Potiphar had trained him. Hami stood and stepped away. "If you show no resistance, we will release Pushpa when your trial begins in the king's throne room. Do you agree to these terms, Captain?"

Potiphar wiped the blood from his cheek and locked eyes with his commander. "Can I kill the Medjays involved in the coup after Pushpa is safe?"

Hami's eyes widened, but he recovered quickly from the surprise. "I'll help you, Captain," he whispered after a moment's hesitation. Nodding at his men, Hami stepped away, as did those who had restrained Potiphar. As he bolted to his feet, his hand went straight to his dagger.

"Potiphar, don't." The sight of Ommi in wrist shackles, weeping, drained his fight.

He glanced again at Hami, but he'd donned the unreadable mask of a warrior. Would Potiphar have to kill his commander someday?

"Captain!" That big voice had been the one he trusted most.

He looked at Khyan and pointed to the woman who had raised them both. "Nothing justifies *that*. Do whatever you wish to me, but don't make Ommi a casualty of your war with Wereni."

Pharaoh lifted one brow. "I thought it was *our* war with Wereni, Potiphar. Perhaps some of the accusations against you have merit after all." The king motioned to Hami. "Shackle the captain's wrists *and* ankles before you remove Pushpa's wrist irons. And be sure to take *all* his weapons. He hides a second dagger, sheathed on his right thigh beneath his schenti." Khyan marched toward the palace while Potiphar submitted to his Medjay commander.

King Rehor strolled toward the palace among the king's council members, occasionally casting a reproving glance at Potiphar. Why would Khyan allow a traitor to walk freely among his highest-ranking nobility after everything Potiphar had told him this morning about the prisoners' testimony? Well, Potiphar hadn't mentioned *everything*. He left out the truth that Zully had miscarried the Minoan cockroach's child, not his. Khyan still didn't know about Zully's adultery. Though he'd placed Potiphar in chains, their vow to protect and prosper each other might still include his wife's death if Pharaoh discovered she'd been unfaithful.

"Your clandestine journeys to On placed your own neck against Pharaoh's sword," Wereni hissed from behind him.

Potiphar refused to be baited.

"It proves your involvement in our cause."

His venomous statement answered many questions. Wereni now believed Potiphar to be a fellow traitor. His desire for the captain's demise was purely a personal vendetta. But Khyan knew of Potiphar's covert trips to On and his feigned sympathies to capture the priest he'd known since childhood. Khyan was the only one to whom Potiphar had confided every detail of his investigation, including the destination and purpose of his seven secret journeys, which led to the three prisoners' arrest and their unimpeachable testimony. When Potiphar left Khyan's private chamber this morning, the plan was to arrest Wereni *after* gaining more evidence on King Rehor.

So, why arrest me and honor Rehor? Potiphar's neck and face burned with shame as he climbed the palace stairs in shackles and was marched into the throne room like a common criminal.

The first face he saw was Ommi's. As she stood near the dais with Joseph and the maid, her despair was worse than a spear to his heart. Joseph, too, looked as if he'd been skewered. Beside him stood the freedom prisoner, Ahira, a woman whose courage continued to amaze him. She'd endured a prison cell longer than any other captive. If Khyan convicted Potiphar of treason today, there would be no prison sentence—only death.

Hami halted Potiphar in front of Pharaoh's throne and left him in the custody of four Medjays while he unlocked Ommi's wrist irons and then assumed the position of protector at the king's right side. If Potiphar's eyes could have thrust javelins, his Medjay commander would have dropped where he stood.

Pharaoh Khyan ascended the dais and faced his council members, who had gathered on his right, King Rehor still among them. Potiphar glanced around the quickly filling throne room and noted double the usual guards—both Medjay and regular army. Khyan expected a large gathering.

"A messenger arrived this morning," the king began, "with news of rioting in cities across the southern delta. Priests of Ra incited the unrest by promising blessing to those who pledged loyalty to Pharaoh Sobekhotep and curses on anyone who remained loyal to me, the *Hyksos* interloper."

What messenger? Potiphar hadn't left Pharaoh's side after giving him the information from the prisoners. When could a messenger have come without Potiphar's knowledge?

The king signaled to his soldiers at the rear entrance. Every eye focused on the opening cedar doors. Potiphar's two faithful Medjays escorted the bloodied prisoners toward the dais among ripples of whispers.

Wereni's face showed appropriate fear. "It appears, my king, that someone has beaten my personal steward. Is Captain Potiphar responsible?"

"Vizier Wereni, you stand accused of treason." Pharaoh turned to meet Potiphar's gaze. "As are you, Captain Potiphar. Which of you will speak first in your own defense?"

"I assure you, my king," Wereni said with a nervous chuckle, "any accusations Potiphar has made are fabricated and likely based on confessions forced through brutality." He motioned toward the three beaten prisoners. "However, the captain's crimes are all too real and most egregious. Perhaps Pharaoh would like to summon Princess Zuleika, who Potiphar has held captive in a scant chamber for nearly a year. I see that by divine wisdom our great pharaoh has already given Princess Zuleika's maid liberty as today's freedom prisoner—though she, too, was imprisoned by Captain Potiphar in Pharaoh's cellblock to ensure her silence about the crimes in his villa."

"Will you allow—" Potiphar's protest was cut short by the same threatening glare that Khyan had used to silence countless guilty men.

Whispers again rolled through the onlookers. "Captain Potiphar's worst offenses, however, were against you, my king," Wereni said above the rising clamor, "and against me, your humble vizier, when he tried to shift the shadow of blame for his stealthy dealings with the Cretan, King Rehor." He pointed at the suddenly pale Minoan king. "It was Captain Potiphar who worked with King Rehor and his daughter to establish secret and exclusive trade agreements with the Nehesu chieftains. Potiphar has secured the loyalty of key Medjays within your own royal bodyguard, Pharaoh Khyan, placing your life in dire peril."

Whispers turned to indignant shouts. Some accusing. Others defending.

"Silence!" Pharaoh stilled the chaos. "I'll clear the courtroom if ma'at is threatened." While Wereni quieted his supporters with confident whispers of assurance, the king caught Potiphar's eye with a barely perceptible bounce of his brows.

They'd often used the signal while interrogating a witness. Khyan was baiting the vizier. Potiphar set his features like stone, but at least now he understood. Pharaoh had arrested him to give the vizier false hope of escape. Khyan would ask questions until Wereni's own arrogance condemned him publicly. Another glance at the vizier, basking in his friends' support, and Potiphar believed it wouldn't be long.

"Mighty Pharaoh." Rehor stood among the officials, hands clasped humbly before him. "May I address the charges made against me?"

"I strongly suggest it, King Rehor." Khyan leaned an elbow on his armrest.

"I've known one of those witnesses since he was a child." Rehor nodded toward Gaios. "I've always referred to him as my street rat because he's good at finding unsavory pieces of trash from the darkest corners. I saw Gaios last night when I docked in Avaris. He confided that he'd been hired by Vizier Wereni some time ago to spy on Potiphar's household. It is your vizier who is elbow deep in treason, not Captain Potiph—"

"That's a lie!" Wereni shouted. "My king, look at those prisoners. Your captain obviously beat them into giving a testimony against me. One is my personal steward, a gift from Potiphar to spy on my household. The second is a Cretan slave who secured information for Rehor by the king's own admission. The third, as evidenced by his robes, is a priest of Ra from On's temple. Whatever they have to say will obviously be tainted by the rigorous beating they've endured." He paused as if hoping the king would suddenly dismiss all charges and get on with the festival.

"Is that all you have to say in your defense, Vizier?" Khyan's challenge stilled the courtroom.

"I haven't even begun, my king." Wereni straightened, his shoulders squared. "The captain knowingly shared his wife with the Cretan messenger—the *street rat* in King Rehor's employ—who then sent Princess Zuleika's art profits to King Rehor. Rehor used those profits with the funds brokered from his trade agreement with the Nehesu chieftains to rebuild his dilapidated island and strengthen Pharaoh

Sobekhotep's claim to a united throne—unseating you, Great Khyan, as Lower Egypt's king."

Potiphar's heart leapt into his throat when Wereni said he'd knowingly shared Zully with Gaios. Is that what he'd done by allowing the cockroach to visit her chamber for all those months?

Khyan glared at him now, frowning. "Tell me more, Wereni, about Princess Zuleika's adulterous relationship with Rehor's street rat."

"She's innocent." King Rehor left the council members' dais. "Zully would never sleep with a servant, and she thought Gaios sent all the profits for rebuilding." His regal calm shattered, and red splotches crept up his neck. A line of Medjays stood between him and the pharaoh he'd betrayed. "Please, Great Khyan, my daughter never knew where Gaios sent the profits."

"But you knew. Tell me about your agreement with the Medjay chieftains." Pharaoh motioned toward his second wife. "I gained a beloved wife through my dealings with them. Tell me what you gained, Rehor."

Uneasy laughter framed Rehor's pained tone. "Crete couldn't survive on Egypt's generosity alone, Mighty Pharaoh. Our trade died when word of the shaking and our destruction traveled ahead of us to the Canaanite shorelines. They refused to trade or even let our ships dock for fear of judgment from the same gods who destroyed our island." His eyes locked on Khyan's. "I couldn't ask you for more, and I couldn't let my island die."

"Now *you* will die, King Rehor."

"I know," he said, resignation seeming to have calmed him. "But please, believe me. My daughter knew nothing. I haven't written her a single message in all the time she's been in Egypt. I've left all her pleas for contact unanswered because I didn't want any suspicion to fall on her."

That's why he never wrote. Potiphar had been a fool. He should have known something was amiss when Rehor refused to write his only daughter. When Potiphar returned his attention to Pharaoh, the king was studying the prisoners. Abasi lay on a litter, too weakened by the loss of blood to walk. Potiphar's childhood friend—the priest of On—stood but was stooped, holding his likely broken ribs. The cockroach sat in a heap, head bowed. Had he heard the accusations against him? Against Zully—the woman he professed to love?

"Speak, street rat," Khyan said.

Gaios slowly lifted his head. Then, with no little effort, he reached for the hand of the Medjay beside him and struggled to his knees so he could bow his forehead to the floor. "Great king of the world, mighty of birth and giver of life in the Black Land and beyond, I will speak truth and only truth from this moment until I draw my last breath."

Potiphar gritted his teeth, wishing he could tear out the man's tongue for all his deceit. He could never be trusted.

Gaios raised his head slightly to speak. "Princess Zuleika and I share profits from her art sales, but I do not share her bed. She has no idea my portion of the profits are split between King Rehor and Pharaoh Sobekhotep. Zully saves her silver to escape Egypt and return to Crete, the home she longs for and adores." He returned his forehead to the floor, signaling the end of his testimony.

"You said nothing of Wereni's or Potiphar's involvement." Khyan leaned forward on his throne. "Whom do you serve?"

Gaios turned his head, leaving his forehead on the marble but peering at Potiphar sideways. "I'm a courier for a man who despises anyone not of pure Egyptian blood—Vizier Wereni."

The courtroom fell silent. Potiphar offered Gaios a single nod. He would die mercifully for his honesty.

Khyan whispered something to Hami, who immediately left the dais and strode toward the side exit—toward the villa.

Potiphar's blood ran cold. "Mighty Khyan, we've heard two witnesses declare my wife's innocence."

His eyes bored into Potiphar's. "Yet I'm not satisfied." Pharaoh motioned to the guards nearest King Rehor. "Shackle the Minoan traitor while we focus on something more pleasant." He turned his focus on the freedom prisoner, and the girl's legs buckled.

Joseph and Ommi caught her and supported her waist, whispering something as Khyan stood. The girl nodded and inhaled deeply before tilting her head back to greet the pharaoh who towered over her.

"I'm radiant with redemption and glowing with gratitude, great Pharaoh Khyan."

A compassionate *aww* swept over the crowd. Potiphar had to smile. Though her words had been stilted and rehearsed, the courageous Hebrew was facing a king after almost a year in total darkness. Joseph had chosen a remarkable woman.

Khyan's lips curved into an equally approving smile. "In previous celebrations, other freed prisoners—men twice your size and imprisoned half so long—have not presented themselves so well. You're a brave woman. Now you must continue to be brave and answer my questions truthfully." The girl nodded. "Who does Princess Zuleika trust most?" Khyan asked.

Without pause she said, "Joseph—and me."

"Then you two will escort your mistress to my throne. Assure her I seek only the truth and have no intention of harming her." He smiled and lifted his eyebrows as if soothing a child. "Can you do that?"

"Yes, my lord. I mean, my king."

"Good." Khyan shifted his attention from the rattled girl to Joseph, pleasantness fading. "Hami is waiting at the villa. If your mistress won't come willingly, the Medjays will bring her forcibly. Do you understand why you and the maid are to accompany the Medjays?"

"Yes, my—"

"Pharaoh Khyan." Ommi spoke for the first time. "Will you not hear my son's defense before forming an opinion?"

"Mistress Pushpa." Khyan was kind but firm. "Thus far your son hasn't lied to me. However, I believe his judgment has been sorely impaired by the woman I gave him as a wife. Keeping Potiphar silent is the only way to spare his life."

He looked at Potiphar, who nodded in defeat. Khyan was right. Potiphar would have said anything to save Zully.

But how could he save her from herself?

THIRTY-SIX

Be sure of this: The wicked will not go unpunished,
but those who are righteous will go free.

PROVERBS 11:21

Zuleika

Pharaoh Khyan's booming voice woke me, "Sixteen cubits!" The Nile's official measurement brought Avaris to life. All around me, festival celebrants cheered. Many had traveled from all the nomes of Lower Egypt to enjoy Pharaoh's free beer and free bread and to witness a captive freed from his prison. I wondered who they'd chosen. *Why couldn't it have been Ahira?*

I stretched like a lazy cat and ambled to my door. "Where's my food tray?"

No answer.

I made a poor effort at pounding on the thick cedar. Still not a word. Had my guards attended the ceremony? Was I alone? I chuckled at the irony. *You've been alone since you left Crete, Zully girl.* When I'd agreed to come to Egypt, I had no idea that Pateras would abandon me so completely—not even a scribbled message in nearly three years—or that Gaios was a leviathan beneath a caring facade.

Meandering into the courtyard, I glimpsed the bag of scarabs and senet pieces that Gaios was supposed to have picked up last night.

He'd probably started his akhet celebration early and was too drunk to keep his promise. Tonight perhaps. It wasn't like him to delay sales.

I tilted my face to the morning sun. How I longed for the sea. With a resigned sigh, I moved the three-legged stool into the shade of my palm tree. Deep ruts marred the ground where I'd stolen mud. I gained a little wicked pleasure from knowing Egyptians paid handsomely for scarabs made from the same mud they scraped off their sandals.

I grabbed a rock and made another mark on the east wall, adding one more day since Gaios had returned to my world—again. This time we were business partners if not friends. Though he occasionally pushed for more, he never forced his desires on me. I kept a carving tool hidden in my belt just in case, but my continued refusal seemed to stoke his respect. We weren't princess and street rat anymore. Gaios prowled through alleys and dealt with merchants, leaving me content to save my earnings for two passages to Crete—mine and a guardian's.

I peeked into last night's water pitcher and found it dry. Resting my head against the wall behind me, I closed my eyes, loathing idleness. When my hands stilled, my mind reeled, thoughts spinning faster than I could process them.

Did I anger Joseph yesterday? I shouldn't have pressed him so hard to come into my chamber. I can't even recall the fine details of Minas's face anymore. Now it's Joseph's face I see in my dreams. Will Ahira ever be released? I miss her company, and I don't want her to die in that awful place, but must both Joseph and I be alone forever simply because those we love have been taken from us? And why did Pateras abandon me so completely? Has he been killed too? It's the only explanation for his silence. He would never ignore my repeated pleas, refusing to send even a simple answer.

"Enough, Zully!" I pulled out one of my senet sets and drew a rectangle with the handle of my spoon in a flat area of my courtyard. After adding two long lines and nine short ones to make thirty even squares, I placed the five special pieces on my dust game board. Alternating cones and spindles on the first ten squares, I began the journey of the ka as if I were two opposing players. And wasn't I? Hadn't I fought reason and passion for months? Why was I so drawn to a Hebrew chamberlain who loved my closest friend? And worst of all absurdities, I wanted him even more for his integrity.

I used four mud scarabs as throwing sticks to determine my cone's first move—one space forward for every face-up scarab, five spaces forward if all landed facedown.

How had my life been reduced to a silly Egyptian game with Minoan mud baubles? *Oh, Minas, if you could see me now.* The thought of my husband's afterlife sent a chill through me. *Could* he see me?

El Roi. The God Who Sees. I remembered Ahira's story of the Egyptian slave woman Elohim visited with his angel. Did all the gods have angels? Ahira said her god had no form, so perhaps that's why he used these angels. Elohim seemed far more complicated than the Mother Goddess. She had a snake in each hand, a cat on her head, and breasts that would bring a sailor home. Simple. *And completely useless.*

I rolled the scarabs again and moved the spindles. The morning passed slowly, and I realized the akhet crowd had grown unusually quiet. They must have moved inside the palace for Pharaoh's birth celebration.

With only two cones and one spindle left on my makeshift board, I heard the bar slide against my door.

"Finally!" I hurried into the chamber to meet whoever carried my long-overdue morning meal. I stopped when the door swung open. It couldn't be. "Ahira?" The reed-thin woman wore fine blue linen and heavy cosmetics, but her smile belonged to my friend.

"I was chosen, Zully. I'm free."

I lunged at her with inexpressible joy, laughing and squeezing her. Only then did I realize how truly frail she was. I released her when I glimpsed Joseph and Pushpa standing in the hallway. "Come in. Everyone. There's not much room, but I think we can fit." I reached for Ahira's hand and led her inside. Was it her hand trembling or mine?

"Mistress," Joseph said, "we must—"

"Joseph, please." Ahira's fierce tone gave me pause. "I must speak with Zully alone."

Joseph bowed to her. Pushpa wouldn't look at me. "What's happening?" Cold fingers of dread crept over me when they remained without argument in the hallway with Hami.

Ahira began wringing her bony hands. "I was freed to *spy* on you," she whispered. "I must report anything you say or do that might prove you've sent aid to King Rehor or connect you with Pharaoh Sobekhotep's plot."

"Pharaoh who?" I choked out a laugh. "I've been locked in this chamber for almost a year. How could—"

"The master knows you and Gaios have been selling your art for many months." She pulled me into her arms. "King Rehor, Vizier Wereni, and Master Potiphar are in Pharaoh's courtroom right now—charged with treason. Gaios is one of three witnesses already sentenced to death. He testified against Wereni."

"No!" I pushed her away. "This is a trick! Did Potiphar send you to torment me?"

Joseph rushed in. "It's no trick, Mistress. King Rehor admitted to making a secret trade agreement with Cush and using profits sent by Gaios to aid in a coup to overthrow Khyan's throne. Both King Rehor and Gaios assured Pharaoh Khyan you knew nothing of their conspiracy, but Wereni insists both you and Master Potiphar are also involved. The vizier also accused the master of . . . of willingly sharing you with Gaios."

I cradled my belly, the words like a fist. Paralyzed by the irony, I almost laughed. I'd done so many wrong things since coming to Egypt. Would I now die for crimes I *hadn't* committed?

I gathered my wits but couldn't stop trembling. "I knew of no conspiracy, but I did share profits with Gaios—nothing else."

Joseph's kindness hardened into tight, deep lines between his brows. "You must testify to the *truth* before the king."

"You don't believe me." I saw the judgment in his narrowed eyes. "You should protect me. I did nothing wrong, Joseph."

"I can't testify to things I know nothing about."

Another man abandoning me. I spit in his face. "Testify to that."

I stormed past him, but Hami blocked my exit. "You must prepare to meet Pharaoh." He stepped back, extending his hand toward my original chamber across the hall. Pushpa waited beside a lonely couch with a new robe and several pots of cosmetics. "This will happen, Mistress, with or without your cooperation." Hami's low voice vibrated in my chest. "You will tell Pharaoh the truth today."

Everyone's eyes felt like daggers, a thousand stabs destroying the brave Zully from my courtyard.

"Come, Mistress. I'll prepare you." Ahira offered her hand.

"But you're not here to serve me, are you?"

"Can we pretend it's only Zully and Ahira—friends?" This woman had suffered intensely for *my* guilt and voluntarily confided she was a spy.

Yes. The one sent to betray me was the only one I could trust. "Friends." I linked arms with her and let her lean on me as we crossed the hall together.

Ahira took the robe from Pushpa, and the guards closed the door behind us. I stared at the empty chamber where I'd cried so many tears. The circle of Minoan treasures was gone. Nothing of *Zully* remained. "My life was a sandcastle built too close to the tide. The gods' plaything, Ahira, and now I'm to be washed away."

"Tell Pharaoh the truth, Zully." She slipped off my rough-spun robe. "I believe he respects honesty and courage."

She washed me with lotus-scented water and anointed me with oils. I drank in the memories of luxury and ease, almost as welcome as a swim in Crete's sea. When she slipped the soft linen robe over my head, I moaned with appreciation.

"Wait until you lie down on the pillows," she said with a knowing grin.

I melted into the pleasure. Insisting on light cosmetics, I also wiped the ridiculous red ochre from her lips and cheeks. "Who painted you like a street harlot?"

"Shh." Ahira glanced over her shoulder. "Pushpa might hear you."

I fell silent, the illusion of "only Zully and Ahira" shattered like the rest of my world. Pateras and Potiphar charged with treason and Gaios sentenced to death. Would the three men who claimed to love me be executed today?

"Finished." Ahira raised her voice, "We're ready!" The announcement summoned Joseph, his pinched brow convincingly concerned.

I looked beyond him to the stark chamber of my yearlong imprisonment. It held nothing I valued.

"Hurry," Hami urged from the threshold. "Pharaoh is waiting."

Joseph reached for my arm, but I pulled away, issuing a glare that could have melted iron. I stood and walked alone, recalling Joseph's accusing expression when he recounted Wereni's charges. Of course, he believed I'd taken Gaios to my bed because I'd pressed him to come inside my room. But I wasn't a harlot. I simply wanted what every woman wanted—a *good* man who loved her more than life itself. Was I asking too much?

The silent march only added to my despair. Ahira and Pushpa flanked me with Hami ahead and Joseph behind. Trapped, I couldn't retreat when the sounds of a nervous crowd grew louder. When we passed through the court's side entrance, my steps faltered. People stood shoulder to shoulder, packed into the room like barnacles on a hull. Only the giant pharaoh with Queen Tani and Ziwat seated on their dais behind him was visible above the rest.

I stayed close behind Hami, head lowered to avoid inquisitive stares. The big Medjay parted the crowd like a warm knife through butter, and an eerie silence fell. I halted at the edge of the crimson carpet, and Hami stepped aside, revealing a reality more horrible than I'd imagined. Gaios lay in a heap at my right, bloodied and beaten, with two other men who had been similarly abused. On my left stood three regal figures, two visibly shaking, one as solid as the crystal mountains of Crete. Pateras and Wereni quaked. Pateras avoided my eyes, while Wereni seethed with palpable hate. Potiphar looked at me with convincing regret, yet his squared shoulders hinted that his honor remained intact.

"Have you betrayed me, Princess Zuleika?" Pharaoh's deep voice demanded my attention.

Startled, I shouted, "No!"

Pharaoh's brows rose. "I'll be more specific. Did you correspond with King Rehor while living in Potiphar's villa?"

I glanced at Pateras, my heart breaking when he met my eyes for the first time. *I love you,* he mouthed. I shook my head, both furious and relieved. "No, Pharaoh Khyan. I received no answers from Pateras though I wrote to him several times." *He respects honesty and courage,* Ahira had said. After inhaling deeply, I exhaled more truth. "I was told Pateras tried to contact me many times, but I never received those messages."

Pharaoh rubbed his chin, letting the veiled accusation hang in the air for too long.

Potiphar stepped toward the throne, and three Medjays drew their swords. He lifted his shackled hands. "I merely wish to remind Pharaoh my wife has not been well since she lost her child. No one intercepted any messages. King Rehor himself testified that he never attempted to contact Zully."

"Never?" I shot a tortured glance at Pateras. "Even when I begged you?"

He blinked tears down his cheeks. "No, my girl. I couldn't risk involving you in any of this."

"In any of—" I looked at Joseph, trying hard to remember the exact charges he'd explained. *Making a secret trade agreement with Cush and using profits sent by Gaios to aid in a coup to overthrow Khyan's throne.* Gaios had accused Joseph of keeping Pateras's messages from me— more lies. I turned to confront him but saw his punishment already begun. "Gaios?" He couldn't raise his head.

"You've been deceived, Princess Zuleika, as have I." Pharaoh Khyan's declaration drew my attention and stiffened my resolve.

"I don't suppose it's a first for either of us."

His lips curved slightly, softening his expression. "While awaiting your arrival, I pondered the fate of the three men charged with treason—two of whom are likely the most important men in your life, Princess. Therefore, I'll ask you a question before rendering judgment. Let me warn you, however: I demand absolute transparency, which is different than honesty." He pinned Potiphar with a stare. "Honesty is telling the truth. Transparency is telling the *whole* truth. Some are honest but become deceitful in the things they choose to hide. So, Princess Zuleika," he said, returning his focus to me, "tell me exactly what you do with your profits from your art sales."

"I save it," I said without pause.

Pharaoh's quick glance showed his surprise. "What woman saves her silver?"

"A woman who wishes to return to Crete and must also pay for an escort to keep her safe on the journey."

"Zully, you can't." Pateras's plea was like an arrow to my heart, but he didn't even wait for my response before shifting his attention to Pharaoh. "She doesn't know what she's saying, Great Khyan. There's nothing for her in Crete. The Knossos king, Kostas, rules the meager existence of two districts, and Zully would be miserable there. She'll stay in Egypt. I vow it. Everything I promised earlier remains. Nothing has changed."

"Everything changed!" I shouted. The inane whispering of Egypt's nobility was like ants crawling on my skin. "My world died in Crete's quaking, Pateras, and I can't be whole again until my life there is rebuilt." I faced Pharaoh Khyan again. "You wanted transparency, so I'll be utterly candid. Your wives sold me to the underworld on the day I arrived in Avaris. The nobility treated me like a leper. My husband left the day after we wed, so I had no one to trust but a Minoan slave I'd trusted all my life. He used my pain and fear to force his will, and the gods made me pay with the life of our child." Control slipping, I had only one more truth to announce before begging for death. I glanced at Potiphar but bowed my head, not brave enough to face him. "I've tried so hard to hate you, Potiphar, but I can't. I could have loved you if my heart wasn't married to Crete."

"I know, Zully." The rattling of shackles drew my attention. Medjays shoved him back into line with Wereni and Pateras. "Get off me!" he shouted. His eyes found mine, approving and reassuring. How could he extend mercy yet again?

"Vizier Wereni, I find you guilty of treason." Pharaoh Khyan's thunderous declaration incited women's shrieks and men's shouts for mercy. Two distinct thuds quickly followed: a body and its head landing on marble—separately.

Vizier Wereni's punishment had been swift and severe. Now the great Khyan focused on my pateras. I raced around the Medjays that separated us. After squeezing through the crush of people, I clung to Pateras's waist.

The king's guards started toward me, but I held him tighter. "I love you, Pateras!"

"Leave her!" Khyan's command removed the Medjay threat—for now.

Had Khyan already decided Pateras was a traitor when the secret agreement with Cush was uncovered? Or had my honesty about leaving Egypt sealed Pateras's fate?

"King Rehor, you have built ties with my enemies." Pharaoh descended the dais and stood over us, imposing and grave. "Though you've broken trust, you can still be useful. You will convene a trade meeting between me, Pharaoh Sobekhotep, and the Medjay chieftains in which you'll use your negotiating skills for *my* benefit. If you survive the meeting and arrange uninterrupted trade routes connecting Lower and Upper Egypt to the mineral-rich lands of Cush, you will live."

"It would be an honor, Pharaoh Khyan." I released Pateras, giving him the freedom to bow to the merciful king who had every right and reason to kill him.

"Show King Rehor to a palace guest chamber, and place him under constant guard—immediately."

Panic replaced gratitude as two Medjays separated Pateras from me. "What about my daughter?" he asked as they led him onto the royal dais and toward the door behind the tapestries. "She knew nothing, Pharaoh Khyan. Please. Zully is innocent."

"Zully," Potiphar whispered, opening his shackled hands. "Come."

He'd heard my deepest truth and was still willing to hold me? My legs trembled violently. Was it a trick? Avoiding the growing pool of Wereni's blood, I balanced on wobbly legs for the few steps between us. Potiphar lifted his shackled hands. I tentatively tucked myself against his side, and he lowered his arms around me. I felt as if I'd donned my own special armor, protective and secure.

"I'm sorry for all you've endured," he whispered.

I choked on a sob and hid my face against his leather breast piece. What had changed so drastically since the last time he saw me—when hate radiated from him like heat from Egypt's sun? But his inexplicable kindness calmed me. I held his waist like a lifeline and lifted my head to face Pharaoh, ready to die if I must.

Khyan, however, glared at my husband. "Captain Potiphar, your arrest was never about treason. But you know that."

"Yes, my king. I'm on trial for being honest rather than transparent."

Pharaoh affirmed with a single nod.

Potiphar paused barely a heartbeat before looking down at me. "I love you, Princess Zuleika of Zakros Palace." He nodded to the Medjays and lifted his arms, releasing me to them.

"No!" I screamed, realizing he'd just said goodbye. "He's not a traitor! Please, Pharaoh Khyan! Listen!"

The Medjays had dragged me only paces when the king motioned them to stop and stared at me. "He's my best friend, Princess. I know he's not a traitor."

"Khyan." Potiphar's break in protocol stole the king's attention. "My life for your life, my king. If I failed to protect or prosper you, then take my life." He knelt and lowered his head to accept Wereni's fate.

"On the contrary, Captain. It is I who failed to protect and prosper—"

Pharaoh's dagger blurred and struck my face with searing pain, sending me to my knees. Deafening shrieks rent the air. I realized they were mine when I clapped my hand over the pain and felt blood. The room spun. Voices faded into a single roar.

One face hovered over me. "Joseph?"

"Ahira, give me your belt." He leaned over me. "Mistress, we have to stop the bleeding."

Fire shot through my face. "What's happening?" I writhed and whimpered on the floor, panic starting to rise.

"Shh," Ahira whispered, appearing beside Joseph. "Try to lie still."

"I request your permission to divorce Princess Zuleika." Potiphar's voice cut as deep as Pharaoh's blade. "I wish to remove her from my villa."

"Denied," Pharaoh roared. "Your wife's maiming was the debt she owed to Egypt for adultery. Your debt is owed to me—for the omission of truth—and will be paid by tending your wife's wound. I saw Princess Zuleika respond to your kindness in this court, and I believe you can mend this marriage, Potiphar. Hami will replace you as captain of my guard for six months. Then I'll determine if you're fit to serve me again—as the brother I once knew."

"Yes, my king!" Potiphar scooped me into his arms.

I cried out at the jostling.

"Take care with which Medjays you trust, Great Khyan." Potiphar's arms trembled with rage. "No one should know everything about anything."

Pharaoh leaned close and whispered to my husband, "I know everything about everything."

"I hope so." Potiphar pulled me closer to his chest and retreated. My head was beginning to clear as we entered the hallway leading to the villa. "I asked for a divorce so you could be free of me, Zully," he whispered. "I wanted you to recover somewhere safe from prying eyes and wagging tongues." He sighed. "Perhaps the ma'at you lost in Crete could find you in Egypt if you had a home of your own."

"Can't pay—" I groaned. Talking stretched the wound.

"I promised to provide for you as I provide for Ommi, and I will. I'll make my villa safe for you both. I vow it."

I forced my eyes open and glimpsed the determined set of his jaw. "Medjays?"

"Yes. There are traitors among them. Neither Khyan's palace nor this villa is safe until they're exposed."

I closed my eyes again. I wanted to scoff, but it would be too painful. My new reality was merely a disfigured rendering of the old. Ahira would tend me but never agree to help me die. Potiphar would be obsessed until he found the traitorous Medjays. At the end of six months, he'd win back his position as captain of Pharaoh's guard, and he'd always love his work and work at love.

Joseph had Ahira now. He'd dance on the edges of my life, having proved himself to be another accuser—no matter how silent—when I needed his support. Ahira was trustworthy, but how long would she continue as my maid? She and Joseph would likely marry soon. Would I have any influence over her future when I had no control over my own?

"No, in here." Potiphar's quick turn startled me, and I opened my eyes as we entered my original chamber. "Joseph, retrieve all Zully's furnishings from the storage closet. Have Ahira help position everything as it was before—including the art."

"Yes, Master." Joseph's voice sounded far away.

"Lay her on the couch," Pushpa instructed. When had she arrived? *Maybe I'm not as alert as I thought.* The old woman held a cup to my lips. "Drink this, dear. It's poppy tea. You'll sleep while I sew your wound."

Ahira sat beside me, humming her Hebrew tune while Pushpa wept against Potiphar's bloody chest. My blood. Thoughts chased themselves around my mind as the room started to spin. Pushpa hated me. Shouldn't Ahira sew my wound? A protest formed on my lips as darkness claimed me.

THIRTY-SEVEN

*Do not lust in your heart after her beauty
  or let her captivate you with her eyes.*
PROVERBS 6:25

Joseph

A puff of dust met Joseph when he opened the door to the first of four closets where he and the Minoan slaves had stored Mistress Zully's belongings. No one had breached the blockaded memories of the lotus festival for nearly a year.

Joseph started sorting through smaller items stacked on top of the furniture. When they'd emptied the mistress's chamber after that awful night, Joseph had felt like a thief pawing through the things she held dear. But he'd clung to hope since the master had placed her world in storage rather than discarding it.

He dusted off each piece of her art and pottery and placed it in the hallway so the larger furniture could be returned to her chamber first. After leaning nearly all the paintings against the wall, he paused and realized it formed a sort of time line, a journey through Mistress Zully's pain in Egypt. She'd kept her early floral paintings in a corner of her chamber where no one could see. Yet she'd prominently displayed the paintings and pottery, done after Gaios's arrival, that boasted Egyptian symbols rendered in Crete's vivid colors. She'd given one of the infamous little vases to Ahira and kept one for herself. Those vases had turned out to be her single most devastating work—and possibly her finest.

Joseph retrieved the most intriguing piece of her collection from the last storage room. After laying the rock-crystal vase on its side, he returned to the closet for its wire stand and placed the vase upright. As the center of her Minoan shrine, the vase had glimmered in the lamplight reflecting off its crystal surface. Now the torchlight gave it the same ethereal quality. *There must be a story behind that.* He surveyed the hallway filled with her talent and realized there was likely a story behind everything she'd done.

Joseph's chest ached. He could never admit that he'd been tempted to follow her inside her chamber when she pressed him yesterday. She'd promised she only wanted to show him the art project in her courtyard. He knew she wanted more—yet he almost went. Such recklessness would have marked him with catastrophic shame. Worse, to take his master's wife would forfeit the sacred favor of Elohim. He loved Ahira and respected his master. How could he have even considered it? Leaning against the doorframe, he bowed his head. *Elohim, I'm weak. Forgive me. Make me a man worthy of Your favor.*

"You look awful." Potiphar appeared at his side. "I'm the one who was accused of treason and watched my best friend maim my wife."

Joseph straightened. "You couldn't have stopped him, my lord. He's . . . your king." He would no longer refer to Pharaoh as his master's friend.

Potiphar sighed wearily and started toward the first closet. "Let's get the furniture moved. Ahira can arrange the rest as she remembers it."

"Should I get the kitchen slaves to help?" Joseph asked.

"No. Pushpa needs quiet while she's sewing Zully's wound. Her eyelid is barely scraped, so she'll keep her eye, but the scar on her cheek will run hairline to jaw." He cleared his throat and swiped at his eyes. He motioned Joseph toward the other end of a red couch. "Lift. Khyan was always better with his blade than I." They carried the first piece of furniture toward the mistress's chamber in silence and thereafter spoke only when necessary.

Ahira remained with Pushpa and the mistress but offered instruction on placement of both large items and small. "The crystal vase goes—"

"In my chamber," the master said, snatching it from Joseph's hands. He cradled it like an infant. "She gave it to me on the night I returned from Temehu."

"I can see it's precious to you," Ahira said, "but this vase will be even more meaningful to Mistress Zully now. The beauty of its imperfection will give her hope when she wakes forever marred."

Potiphar paled and returned the vase to its metal stand, then strode toward the door empty handed. "Report to my chamber, Hebrew, when you've returned everything to Zuleika's chamber. Let her maid arrange the room however she wants."

The door slammed, Ahira flinched, but Pushpa remained steady at her task. "Every time he lets himself feel, his heart is broken." The woman nodded toward the second cup of poppy tea. "Ahira, give her a little more. She's starting to wake, and I have more sewing to do."

Joseph continued moving furniture, and Ahira helped reconstruct the mistress's chamber as she remembered it. Finally Pushpa finished her harrowing task and rose from the stool to stretch her tired back and shoulders. Joseph reached out to pull Ahira into his arms.

She backed away. "No, Joseph." Glancing furtively at Pushpa, she kept her voice low. "After all that's happened today, I don't think we dare show any affection or mention our desire to wed. We must give everyone time to heal."

Elohim, more waiting? Frustrated, Joseph sighed and dragged his fingers through his hair. She was right, but he didn't like it. "Fine."

She hurried back to Zully's side and helped Pushpa tidy up. Was Ahira anxious to postpone their lives together? A spark of anger drove him out the door, down the hall, and into the master's chamber. Potiphar sat on a couch, his elbows on his knees, his hands steepled at his mouth. The master never sat quietly.

"Are you well, my lord?"

He slapped his knees and stood. "I don't think Hami is a traitor."

"Of course not." But Joseph's simple response seemed to incite a rush of fury.

"No one should know everything about anything, Hebrew. Hami said that."

"Yes, and?"

"The traitor priest from On repeated the same phrase during his interrogation."

The news drove Joseph back a step. "Hami would never . . ."

"We're all capable of betrayal, Hebrew."

Joseph's stomach turned. He knew the truth of that statement more than he would ever admit.

The master had started pacing, rubbing his bald head. "Hami is a skilled soldier with many high-level Nehesu contacts. He became well acquainted with Rehor during the two weeks he stayed in the villa before my wedding. Hami could have facilitated Rehor's negotiations with the Nehesu." He halted abruptly and looked at Joseph. "But I still don't believe Hami is a traitor."

Joseph was both relieved and curious. "How can you be sure?"

"I'm not sure, but when I used the traitor's phrase with Khyan, hinting at Hami's involvement, the king answered, 'I know everything about everything.' I believe he was trying to assure me that Hami was innocent."

"But you're not sure."

His countenance darkened again. "I'm not sure." He returned to his pacing, pounding the tiles with heavy strides. "I don't need a personal steward if I don't stand at Pharaoh's side each day, so you'll sleep upstairs with the Medjays, Hebrew. I'll give you a small blade to holster on your thigh. You do know how to wield a blade, don't you?"

"No idea, my lord." This was no time for false bravado.

"I'll teach you today." He waved Joseph away like a fly from his dinner plate. "Move your sleeping mat to the Medjays' bunk room, and report to me daily anything you see or hear that's different than when you lived among them before."

"I can't remember everything, my lord. How will I know what's important to report?" Joseph felt woefully ill equipped for what the master was asking of him.

He placed a hand on Joseph's shoulder. "You need remember only the inconsistencies and who's causing them, Hebrew. It's the *changes* that will reveal the bad grape in the cluster."

Before Joseph could ask another question, the master's dagger was poised at his belly. "And though Khyan is better than I, you'll be as skilled as any Medjay after today's training."

"In one day?" Joseph didn't want to sound cowardly, but the master seemed overly optimistic.

"Not in one day." Potiphar sheathed his blade. "We'll train in this chamber *every* day while I trust my instincts that Hami will protect Khyan." He lifted his brows. "And if your god still favors you and my household, we'll root out this conspiracy and regain Khyan's favor. Perhaps then I can reason with him and gain a measure of justice for my wife I never expected to love."

THIRTY-EIGHT

Who can say, "I have kept my heart pure;
I am clean and without sin"?

PROVERBS 20:9

Ahira

Zully moved her cone to the House of Life on the gilded marble senet board, and Ahira tossed the throwing sticks. "I saw Master Potiphar in the kitchen while preparing this morning's tray. Did he visit before he left for the palace?"

"He comes once a week, Ahira." She turned her face to display the angry red scar. "He can't even look at me."

Ahira's heart ached at the sight of the maiming that labeled her mistress as an adulterous woman. The throwing sticks had landed, but she paused before moving her spiral game piece. "You know he still cares for you."

"I wish he didn't," Zully said as Ahira moved forward three spaces. "The most courageous man in Egypt gave me his unguarded heart, and I crushed it. I'd feel better if he hated me." Zully threw the sticks and moved her cone out of the House of Life onto an open square. "But why would I expect a man to love me more than his work? Potiphar is no different than Pateras, and Minas was dedicated to me for only the first year of our marriage. Then he happily left me to rejoin our sailors for the next eight-month trading season." She met Ahira's gaze. "Joseph seems to be cast from the same mold. He's always with Potiphar or the Medjays. I think he spent more time with you when you were in prison."

Ahira was also frustrated by Joseph's seeming indifference, but hadn't she been the one to suggest they show no affection and delay their marriage? Her mistress needed encouragement, not fuel for rising resentment. "Didn't you receive a letter from King Rehor last month?" Zully had taken the letter to the rooftop and returned to the chamber empty handed—never mentioning its contents or what she'd done with the scroll.

She slid the throwing sticks toward Ahira. "It's your turn." Ahira tossed the sticks as Zully blurted, "Pateras wrote only to beg me for more funds to rebuild Crete—as if I had access to silver." She folded her arms. "I burned the scroll and left Crete on the rooftop. If I can't sell my art, then I can't earn my passage back. And if I can't return home . . ."

She left the ominous conclusion unsaid, so Ahira pressed her. "If you can't return, then what?" Zully had refused to reassemble her circle of Minoan treasures. The rock-crystal vase sat in a corner, shunned and gathering dust. "If you can't return to Crete, why not at least try to make a home here with Master Potiphar?"

"I don't belong here, Ahira, and I can't force my heart to love." Her eyes moistened as she bit her lip. "I don't belong anywhere anymore."

Ahira scooted the senet board aside and pulled her into a hug. "I know your life feels impossible, but you *can* belong to Someone, Zully. He can make this your home."

"I told you. I can't love Potiphar."

Ahira released her. "I'm talking about *Elohim*. You can belong to Him, and He can make anywhere your home. He was the one who sustained me in prison."

She scoffed. "Your handsome chamberlain sustained you in prison."

There it was. The diversion. Since she'd returned from the cellblock,

Ahira's attempts to speak of Elohim had been met with jesting or blatant ridicule.

"Has Potiphar given his permission for you and Joseph to marry yet?" Zully repositioned the senet board between them and picked up the sticks.

"Not yet. Joseph wants me to talk with Pushpa to see if she'll convince the master for us."

Zully's countenance brightened when all four throwing sticks landed with the uncolored sides up. "Look, Ahira! It's a good omen. You should go to the harvest festival today with Pushpa! Talk with her about Joseph. *Today.*"

"I don't believe in omens, Zully, but I do believe Elohim can use even silly little sticks to encourage us. And Pushpa did invite me to go with her." Ahira paused, looking into her mistress's hopeful expression. In the kitchen this morning, Joseph had overheard Pushpa's invitation and volunteered to serve Zully's midday meal to give Ahira some time away. She hadn't left Zully's side for more than a trip to the kitchen since returning as her maid. "I wouldn't feel right leaving you—"

"Go, Ahira." Zully swept all the pieces off the board. "I'm forfeiting the game—and you know I never let you win. I've got plenty of papyrus and paints to keep me busy." Her eyes sparkled with a mischievous glint. "I haven't left this chamber, and I won't start today. Perhaps I'll challenge Joseph to a game of senet."

"Oh, Zully, I don't know."

"Is Joseph a man worth fighting for or not, Ahira?" Her question seemed demanding, the tone almost resentful.

"Joseph delayed asking Master Potiphar to prepare our marriage contract because of our household's upheaval."

Zully's countenance darkened further.

"I meant the Medjay scandal and subsequent transition. Our household is finally starting to settle after Joseph helped Master Potiphar root out the traitorous Medjays. But the master still spends a lot of time with Hami—I mean, *Vizier* Hami—helping him adjust to life as Egypt's second-highest nobleman. I feel guilty asking your husband to consider a slave wedding when he's restructuring Lower Egypt."

"There's never a good time to interrupt a busy man, Ahira. And I've been thinking . . ." Her eyes grew misty in the silence.

"What is it?"

"There will never be a good time . . . to see my scar."

Ahira had dreaded this day. "I can't, Zully." Master Potiphar had ordered all the mirrors removed from the mistress's chamber.

"I know you have a mirror in your chamber."

"How—"

"You leave your door open when you think I'm napping."

Ahira squeezed her eyes shut, chastising herself. Why hadn't she stored her small bronze mirror with the others? *Vanity.* Abba Enoch had warned her of the sly tendrils that could bind a heart unnoticed.

When she opened her eyes, the mistress stood over her, hands on her hips. "I'll walk into your chamber and get it myself. Pharaoh didn't cut off my legs."

"I'll get it for you, and we'll look together." Ahira ducked into her small room to retrieve the mirror. Before offering it to her mistress, she said three words: "You're still you."

Zully took the mirror and paused for a fortifying sigh before facing the sight others had adjusted to. In that first moment of shock, her eyes widened. Then came horrified curiosity. She lifted her hair off her forehead to see the disfiguring genesis. With one finger, she traced the still-angry red scar down from her hairline. The fleshy marring skipped from her eyebrow to the peak of her lovely high cheekbone, then continued all the way to her jaw. Tiny dots marked both sides from Pushpa's skilled sewing. Though removing the horse's mane used as thread had been agonizing, Pushpa assured them the natural single fiber was less likely to fester than carded and spun woolen thread.

"Princess Zuleika is gone, and Zully remains." She offered the mirror back to Ahira. "Now I know what you look at all day long." Her smile seemed forced.

"Like I said, you're still you."

"Yes, yes." She waved away Ahira's encouragement. "Now, go to the festival." She gathered a piece of papyrus and her paints before settling on a cushion beside the low table. "You don't want to miss the great Khyan's first swath with his giant scythe."

Was that a tremor in her voice? Ahira started toward the cushion across from her mistress. "I don't really want to go."

"Leave!" Zully slammed her fist on the table.

Ahira froze. "I should never have shown you."

Zully closed her eyes and shook her head. "I need you to go, Ahira. Please. Give me some time alone." She looked up and offered what seemed a genuine smile this time. "Go, and convince Pushpa to talk with Potiphar. There's never a bad time for a wedding."

This was the Zully she'd known for the past two months. Her strength—body and mind—had returned soon after the master was reinstated as Pharaoh's captain. She'd been angry at first that the master had declined the king's offer to become vizier, but with that decision, Potiphar had proved himself the loyal brother Pharaoh remembered. Their villa had felt more settled ever since.

"All right. I'll go." Ahira bowed quickly and rushed toward the door. "Wait!" She turned with a giggle. "Is there anything you need before I go?"

"No, my friend." Zully waved her away. "Enjoy your day."

Ahira hurried out the door and down the hall toward the kitchen. Could she catch Pushpa before she left? She burst into the kitchen and ran headlong into Joseph, who grabbed her waist to keep her from tumbling.

His hands lingered on her hips. "This is the best surprise I've had for months." He gazed too long into her eyes and kissed her before she could object.

And then she couldn't object. Her arms circled his neck, and she responded to his longing. Yes, he would be hers. Not today. Likely not even tomorrow. But soon.

"Finally!" Pushpa's huff ended their passion. "Your god allows kissing now?"

"He does." Joseph chuckled, his arm still around her waist as they moved to Pushpa's chopping table. He glanced at Ahira. "Did you ask Mistress Zully?"

She nodded. "Pushpa, Zully gave me permission to attend the festival with you if you're still willing to have me."

After scooting the last batch of leeks into a pot with her knife, Pushpa wiped her hands. "Let me slip on a fresh robe, and we'll go."

Ahira nearly squealed. She turned to Joseph. "Zully will need her midday meal, and she might need a game of senet." She placed both hands on his chest before sharing her concern. "She demanded to see my mirror."

"Ahira, the master—"

"I know he said she mustn't see herself, but she needed to see the scar, Joseph. The wondering would have been worse than seeing it."

"Was it?"

"What do you mean?"

"When she saw it. Did her reaction prove the wondering had been worse?"

Ahira considered the question and Zully's matter-of-fact response. "Yes, I think it did. She was surprised at first, but I think she faced it with courage."

"And did you speak with her about *why* you were accompanying Pushpa to the festival?"

"Why is she accompanying me to the festival?" Pushpa asked, fists at her hips. "Can't we simply eat too much at the market, watch Khyan initiate the harvest, and enjoy some peace?"

Joseph sheltered Ahira under his arm. "We thought you might help us convince the master to draft our wedding contract soon as well."

"Oohh!" Pushpa clapped and squealed, then gathered them into a circle hug of three. "Of course! Of course! I'll talk to him tonight!"

THIRTY-NINE

*One day he went into the house to attend to his
duties, and none of the household servants was
inside. She caught him by his cloak and said,
"Come to bed with me!" But he left his cloak in her
hand and ran out of the house.*

GENESIS 39:11–12

Zuleika

I'd wondered whether guilt or pity had bowed Potiphar's head while in my presence. After one glance in Ahira's bronze mirror, I knew it was neither.

I was simply hideous.

Maiming. Even the word was ugly. I'd never considered the term until it defined me. Until it confined me to this room. To a solitary life. Ahira and Joseph would marry. They'd have children. Perhaps the king would allow Potiphar to take a mistress—since their brotherhood vow was to protect and prosper each other for life. Since my husband couldn't stand to look at me, perhaps he could enjoy the fruit of another woman's womb.

I'll never feel a man's touch again.

My whole body ached at the loss. My hair would turn gray, and my form would become as unsightly as my face.

I pushed away from my table, leaving the papyrus and paints untouched to tour my chamber. I'd filled it with paintings and pottery as full of life and color as I once was. Standing at the doorway separating my chamber and courtyard, I listened to the joyous harvest celebration outside my wall and stared at the grandeur around me.

How could I live amid the splendor and stare at Ahira's perfect face after seeing my gruesome reflection in that mirror? I glanced at my door, contemplating escape. The villa guards were on duty at the festival. Maybe I should simply flee to the guest chamber. Return to the simplicity of solitude. Removed from the tedium of life's demands and people's pity. The guest chamber was as empty as I and its courtyard as furrowed as the scar on my face.

I lifted a finger to my hairline and began the ragged downward trek, loathing the lumpy firmness. *Look again.* Curiosity warred with revulsion. It couldn't be as bad as that first glimpse.

Slow and reluctant, I entered Ahira's dark space to retrieve my forbidden accuser. I pressed it to my side, returning to my chamber, but refusing its punishing verdict. Why must I look again? Why not simply rely on others' reactions to tell me how repugnant I was? Potiphar hadn't touched or kissed me since the maiming, offering only a bow when he greeted me or said goodbye. The Medjays averted their eyes. Pushpa flitted about my chamber during her infrequent visits, chattering nervously and hardly glancing my way.

Look at the woman they scorn.

The mirror's call was strong, but I pressed it against my middle, refusing still. I meandered to the courtyard and lay on my favorite couch. Warmed by the midmorning sun, the pillows chased the chill from my bones. I glanced at what used to be my lovely pond. The lotus blossoms were gone. Potiphar had ordered the water drained so I couldn't see my repulsive reflection. He'd thought of everything . . . except Ahira's one rebellion.

Take another look. Zully needs to know.

Ahira said I was still me, but how could I know *me* until I saw what my unfaithfulness had done? Weren't the consequences of my past part of who I would become? I slowly lifted the mirror—and stared at my tormenter. The woman was a stranger. She had no voice. No words.

My finger traced the scar's familiar line, but seeing its hideous path felt different. The shiny skin felt hard, like Potiphar's armor. *Yes, a shield to keep love away.*

I slammed the mirror onto my lap and lifted my face to the sky. "Did *you* do this to me, God Who Sees? Was I so evil that I deserved to wear your punishment forever?"

I bashed the mirror against the couch's wooden frame. When I lifted it, the polished surface was dented, making everything appear as disfigured as my face. "A perfect picture of Egypt." I cast it under the couch, laid my head back, and closed my eyes. Why couldn't Khyan have punished me with death? *Because there is no mercy in Egypt.* No mercy in Egypt. No mercy . . .

* * *

"Mistress!" Joseph called to me from Crete's blue sea. "Mistress, where are you?" The dream faded into the blazing reality of Egypt's sun overhead.

I sat up on my couch. "I'm here." Hearing his footsteps approach, I turned toward the courtyard wall. How could Joseph's perfection bear my hideous appearance?

"Mistress?" he said in a whisper.

"Leave the food and go." I lay on my side and curled into a ball. *I can break one of my pottery vases and cut myself.* Surely Ahira would return from the festival too late to save me.

"You're upset." Joseph's nearness startled me.

I bolted upright and found him kneeling beside me. I covered my repugnance. "Leave me, Joseph."

Shuffling sounds too close proved he stayed.

"Ahira told me she let you look in her mirror." The tray he'd carried clanked on the table beside me.

"Please, Joseph, I . . ." Tangled emotions tied my tongue.

"Mistress, the courage you've shown amid your suffering has made you even more lovely." He gently pulled away my hands, the only shield from his pity.

But when I met his gaze, I saw none. Just kind, strong, faithful Joseph.

"Please, Mistress. You must eat something."

"How could you and Ahira look at me all these weeks and months?" Suddenly lost in his golden-green eyes, I confided in him what I'd never spoken aloud. "No one will ever love me again, Joseph."

His eyes widened. "The master loves you, Mistress. His guilt won't allow him to show it yet, but—"

"Joseph, I need to *feel* loved. I need to know I'm still desirable."

He started to rise, but I clutched his sleeve, near panic.

"Shh," he said, resettling on one knee. He gently lifted my legs onto the couch and guided my shoulders to relax against the armrest. "You're upset, Mistress Zuleika. It must have been a shock to see your scar for the first time."

Mistress Zuleika. His formality cut me to the core. "Say *Zully,* Joseph."

I knew with sudden clarity. Joseph was my only hope of a man's touch again. Could a good man's mercy override his conscience? "Please, Joseph." I leaned closer and slipped my hand beneath his schenti. "Come to my bed."

"No!" He bolted to his feet, a moment of shock, then horror—and then he ran.

Paralyzed with shame, I stared at my balled fist as if it belonged to another. In it I clutched Joseph's loincloth, still warm with his presence. The magnitude of my offense rained down. At first in a drizzle. Then in torrents of panicked gulps. I cradled his linen wrap like I'd held Minas's crushed body. Like I'd cradled my child's underdeveloped form.

Joseph was dead to me now. He'd never return. But where would he go?

Ahira! He'd find her. Tell her. *I'll lose them both!* My dearest friends.

My lifeline. I groaned, writhing in the destruction of this moment. Not a shaking of the earth but a shaking of my world.

Ahira would tell Pushpa, and the cook would tell her son. I screamed into a cushion, certain of my demise. Potiphar's mercy could extend no further. He could never forgive my advances toward his precious Joseph.

The loincloth was now cold in my grasp. A simple piece of linen that would determine life or death. But whose? If I truly wished to die, I could confess to Potiphar. But would he kill me? No. My husband, like Pharaoh, would think death too merciful for me. Ahira's recounting of her cramped, filthy cell came rushing back like a specter from the underworld.

I crushed the piece of cloth to my chest. I had only one path. It was dark and fraught with serpents and snares, but it was the only way I'd survive. I turned my face heavenward again. "How will you punish me for this, Elohim?" I whispered. Surely the Hebrew god's continued favor would protect Joseph from the accusation I must make.

Potiphar's trusted Medjays patrolled the palace complex on the other side of my wall. I inhaled a breath as deep as my hatred for Egypt and released a screech that set birds to flight. I bolted from my couch and ran the full length of the courtyard, shrieking until my voice failed. The guards would hear me. Spread the word. Send help.

Weary from the ploy, I went into my chamber and flopped on the bed, then coiled Joseph's loincloth on the floor. I squeezed my eyes shut. Regret seeped in like a noxious odor. But what was done was done.

After I'd waited for what seemed longer than a sowing season, Potiphar raced into my chamber with six of his guards. "Zully, what happened? The perimeter guards said—" He halted the moment he saw Joseph's loincloth on the tiles beside me.

Drawing on the injustices I'd suffered since the quake stole my life, I let anger erupt in irreversible destruction. "Everyone abandoned me here to go celebrate the harvest, so your prized Hebrew tried to force more than sympathy on his maimed mistress. He ran when I screamed for help." I leaned over to be sure the Medjays behind him heard me. "The Hebrew, Joseph, tried to rape me"—in case any of them misunderstood.

Potiphar roared and tossed the loincloth at my waste pot, trembling with fury when his focus returned to me. "You've told a convincing story—and in front of witnesses—Princess Zuleika."

"What story?" Ahira rushed in with Pushpa and glanced at me, then at Potiphar. "Zully, are you all right? We saw villa guards urgently retrieve the master." I'd prepared to face Potiphar but not my innocent friend's questions.

Potiphar sneered and folded his arms. "Yes, Zully. Repeat your story for Ahira and Pushpa so I can hear the details again."

I knew better. He'd find a way to twist my words. "I won't repeat what Joseph did until I testify before Pharaoh."

"Joseph?" Ahira's face paled.

Pushpa gathered Ahira into her arms while her glare pierced me like daggers.

Potiphar trapped me, his fists planted on both sides of my hips. "I will chew off my own tongue before displaying your hysteria again publicly. You will not cost me *two* friends this day." He stepped back and nodded toward Pushpa and Ahira. "You *will* tell them the accusation you've made against Joseph."

I stared at the loincloth hanging from the waste pot, because I couldn't look at my friend. "Joseph came with my midday meal and tried to rape me while everyone was at the festival."

The silence that followed was more painful than Pharaoh's maiming. "Why, Zully?" came Ahira's whisper.

I glanced up as Pushpa lunged at me. "You ungrateful—"

"No, Ommi." Potiphar caught her. "You need not trouble yourself any longer with Zuleika's continual commotion." He aimed his calm at me, which was more frightening than the fury I'd expected. "You'll not spend another night under my roof, Zully. The Hebrew maid will pack as much as you can carry. I'll provide a house for you in the lower city, because I keep my vows. You'll be free of me, and this villa will be rid of your hysteria and deceit."

"No! I don't know anyone in the lower city. How will I survive? How will I—"

Potiphar raised his hand as if to strike. I flinched, silenced by the threat, and looked at him when no blow came. "Your response should be 'Thank you, Potiphar,'" he said, "because the alternative is a cell next to Joseph's."

FORTY

Do not say, "I'll pay you back for this wrong!"
Wait for the LORD, and he will avenge you.

PROVERBS 20:22

Zuleika

"Come!" Potiphar commanded Pushpa and Ahira, extending his arm to shepherd them out of my chamber. Pushpa sneered at me before hurrying to escape my presence.

"May I stay and speak with Zully alone, Master?" Ahira's voice quaked.

Both he and Pushpa paused at the threshold, seeming as startled by her request as I.

"Should I remove all weapons from the chamber, little Hebrew?" He lifted an eyebrow. "The punishment for murder is death."

"I won't harm her, Master."

He scoffed. "Then you've proven again to be most courageous." He nudged Pushpa from the chamber and left me alone with Ahira.

She kept her eyes down, her whole body trembling as she drew near to my bed. "When Pushpa and I were running toward your chamber," she said, "your guards stopped us in the hall and asked if we'd seen Joseph." She looked up, eyes sparking like flint. "It's to your benefit we hadn't seen him, for if I'd helped them arrest the man I love, even the master's threats wouldn't save you."

The violence in her eyes drove me backward on the bed. She was capable, having killed predators to protect her flocks. "Ahira, I . . ." I turned away to gather my wits and weighed what the truth would cost me against what my lie had already cost her. Why confess the deceit and bring more pain on us both? When I faced her, she stood barely an arm's length away. "Ahira, it's not Joseph's fault. He's a man with needs like any other. When he saw I was alone—"

"No!" She held my face between her hands. "You can lie to others, Zully, but not to me. Tell me what *really* happened when I entrusted my betrothed with tending my best friend."

I heard a waver of doubt in her plea. If I painted partial truth with hues of loneliness, would she look at me through the eyes of compassion? "It began when you were in prison, Ahira. Joseph and I became friends, and his desire for me grew to more than friendship." It was true. I'd seen longing in his eyes though he'd never passed my threshold. I need not mention he looked like a snared rabbit whenever I begged him to bed me.

Ahira's cheeks paled.

"When I refused his flirting today, there was no one in the villa to help me. I screamed, so he ran, leaving his loincloth as evidence of his vile intentions." I nodded toward the condemning proof.

Ahira stood over me, shaking violently, rage evident in red splotches on her neck and face. "Hagar gave Elohim a special name in the wilderness, Zully. Do you remem—"

"El Roi," I answered. "Hagar called him El Roi, the God who sees me." Perhaps my eagerness would calm her.

"That's right. My God sees *you*." She leaned forward, menacing. "Though no one else can attest to Joseph's innocence, the God Who Sees knows exactly what you did to ruin my life—and Joseph's. He's watching us now, and He'll watch *you* until the day you die."

Fear crashed through me as she turned on her heel and marched toward the door. "Stop!" I bolted from the bed and reached for her. "Please, Ahira. Listen!"

She pulled away, glaring at me, but listening.

"I did it to survive," I said. "Everything I've done has been to ensure Crete's survival and mine."

"No, Zully. Everything you've done has been to regain a life you can't replace. You betrayed those who loved you, and Elohim will judge you—as He did Gaios."

"I'm nothing like Gaios." How dare she make the comparison!

"Didn't Gaios claim that his actions, too, were necessary to survive?" She rushed over to the waste pot, snared the loincloth, and lifted it like a banner. "Joseph ran because he refused *your* advances, but without witnesses, his accusation would bring certain death."

"Get out." I seethed, unable to deceive a woman who knew me too well. "Get out now!"

She held her ground. "Admit it."

I knew exactly what she wanted to hear. "I'll admit Joseph's innocence when you admit the God Who Sees is just a legend like all the rest."

Her nod and spiteful grin were chilling. "That's right, Zully. Keep denying Elohim exists with one breath and blaming Him with the next. At the end of time, after you've refused His every attempt to break into your life, you'll have only yourself to blame when He says, 'Away from Me forever, Zully.' "

I swallowed hard. "Is that really what happens?" She'd never lied to me before. Would she invent a horrible story about the afterlife to frighten me more? "Ahira?" Her hate throbbed in the silence. Without her or Joseph, there was no one to answer my questions about the God who saw *all* of me.

"Goodbye, Zully." She started toward the door again, and panic rose.

"All right, Ahira. I lied about Joseph." I stepped toward her, but she backed away as if I had leprosy. "Answer one more question, and I'll tell you everything."

"I promise nothing." She spat on the tiles at my feet. "You destroyed my life and Joseph's. You deserve—"

"Does Elohim know *why* I did it?" I swallowed hard, ignoring her hate. "Does the God Who Sees know my passion for Crete. For my people?" Ahira turned without answering, but I grasped her arm and fell to my knees. "Doesn't Elohim care about all I've lost? Does he know that I feel guilty because I'm relieved, not saddened, by Gaios's death? Does he know I'm drawn to Joseph because of his goodness—wishing to feel the touch of an honorable man one more time before I die?"

Ahira hovered over me. "Tell me, Princess Zuleika"—she ground out the reply—"do you think your vow to protect and prosper your people, or even yourself, justifies the horrendous things you've done?"

Protect and prosper. Potiphar and Pharaoh's lifelong vow. I involuntarily touched the scar on my left cheek. Ahira studied me as the phrase rolled over and over in my mind like a shell caught in a wave. *Protect and prosper.* I'd been taught my whole life to protect and prosper the people of Crete. Those words had even been part of the vows I'd pledged as a little girl when Pateras named me his official successor to Zakros's throne. How many lives was I willing to ruin—to take—in order to protect and prosper Crete? How many lives would I sacrifice to protect and prosper *myself*?

I stood to meet Ahira's fury, but her expression had changed. Tears clung to her bottom lashes. She wore the same sorrow as the day she'd told of shepherding a particular sheep that repeatedly wandered away from the flock. She'd eventually found it tangled in a thicket—torn and killed by a lion.

"I hope you get back to Crete," she said, sounding sincere, "because no one in Egypt is safe until you do, Zully."

I felt her words like a blow. "You're not much of a shepherdess if you leave me to be mauled by lions!" I shouted.

"*You're* the lion, Zully!" She glared at me as if I were Gaios.

Our eyes locked in silent battle. The truth of her accusation rolled like a boulder onto my chest, stealing my breath, crushing my heart. *I'm the lion?*

"Elohim is the only true shepherd," she said, opening the door to go. "His sheep believe and never need fear the lions."

"Help me believe!" I lunged at the door and closed it before she could escape. "Please, Ahira. I can't . . ." We stood like opposing warriors, shaking, Ahira with justified rage and me with increasing dread. "How could a lion believe itself a lamb?" Had I only imagined myself the prey, which turned my defense into stalking?

For the span of several heartbeats, she said nothing—only glared at me with tears coursing down her cheeks. Finally Ahira swiped at her tears. "I hate you with every bone and sinew. I want to walk out this door and never see your face again. But I know Elohim's heart for the broken—because I was broken like you are now. You are a lion, but your willingness to see it proves you may yet be a lamb." She groaned, pressing the heels of her palms against her eyes. "I don't want Elohim to help you. To forgive you. I wish He'd turn His back on you. But His heart is *for* you, Zully. Even for you."

I was astonished. "How could he . . ."

"I said Elohim saw you." Ahira's hands fell to her sides as she shuddered. "Though He never condones evil, neither will He turn away a sincere heart."

"I want to believe, but I don't know how."

She wrapped her arms around her middle as if holding herself together. "I'll ask the master if I can live with you in the lower city and help you adjust to your new life."

"Oh, Ahira, I . . . How can I thank—"

"Don't." She lifted her hand to silence me. "You say you want to believe in Elohim? Prove it by living differently in the lower city. Care for others. Show kindness. Serve. If I don't see changes in you, Zully, I'll leave, and then you'll truly be alone in Egypt."

"I'll change, Ahira. I—"

"You'll start by packing whatever belongings you think necessary for a secret life in the lower city." Her eyes swept over the chamber behind me. "Remember, Master Potiphar said you may take only what you can carry, and you must be sure no one recognizes you." She turned abruptly and left me alone to make my husband's commands reality.

Where had she gone? When would she return? I scanned my chamber and the courtyard and even peeked inside Ahira's small room to assess the contents and project our needs. I quickly realized I had no idea what I needed for life in Avaris's lower city.

You're the lion! Ahira's accusation hunted me. I'd seen only one lion—Pharaoh's catch—during my first two weeks in Avaris. Displayed in a deep pit near the king's harem, the beast had remained ferocious and wild since its capture a month before. Roaring at curious noble gawkers, it leapt and slapped at them with its powerful claws until it fell, exhausted, to the dirt. Day after day, I visited, watching its futile attacks. After drawing more attention and expending more energy, the poor creature died the day before my wedding—a shrunken shadow of its once-glorious self.

I found myself stroking the smooth, gleaming surface of my rock-crystal vase. Weeping. "I *am* a lion," I whispered. Having broken the silence, I scanned the empty chamber and for the first time marveled that I might *not* be alone. "Elohim, are you here even when Ahira isn't? Can you forgive a stupid beast such as me?" Though I heard no reply—as had always been the case when I cried out to Elohim—I no longer felt the need to swat at him with my claws.

Rejection and anger gave way to a curious peace. I lifted the vase from its metal stand and held it close to my heart, sliding my fingers around the slender opening to find the chip. I missed it the first time, so I tipped the vase upward and inspected the rim thoroughly. I blinked. Looked again. Rubbed my fingers over the cool, smooth stone. "It's gone!" The words escaped on a panicked breath. *It's perfect.* "How . . ." The vase Pateras had rescued from the Zakros Palace ruins had been chipped. But now? The rock crystal was filled in completely. Reborn. Not even a seam remained where the break had been.

Prickly flesh appeared on my arms, and I swallowed my rising fear. *Should I be afraid of You, Elohim?* What kind of God would destroy my life—and let me destroy others'—to reveal Himself to a Minoan princess?

But as quickly as the disquiet had arrived, so came a light breeze into my chamber with the scent of the sea.

I fell to my knees, bowing my head, my heart quieted in reverence. "You, Elohim, *are* the God Who Sees, and I finally see You. Forgive me, though I don't deserve Your mercy. Help me, though I deserve none of Your attention. Guide me, though I deserve none of Your wisdom. Show me how to mend all the damage I've done."

FORTY-ONE

*Joseph had a dream, and when he told it to his
brothers, they hated him all the more. . . .
When he told his father as well as his brothers,
his father rebuked him. . . . "Will your mother and
I and your brothers actually come and bow down
to the ground before you?"*

GENESIS 37:5, 10

Joseph

Joseph raced through the streets of the lower city, bumping shoulders
and jumping baskets. How could he have let the mistress get so close?
He dodged a bread cart, and the baker shouted curses. His short kilt
flared with every hop, revealing his shame, leaving a wake of lewd
shouts. Humiliated, he ran faster toward the slave village.

Hopefully, Maahir, his favorite old shepherd, would be away from
his home celebrating harvest's onset in the fields. Would Potiphar
remember that Joseph had chosen Maahir to replace him as overseer of
livestock and come searching? Maybe not. Joseph had mentioned the
old man's name only a few times. Come nightfall, Joseph would slip
into the wilderness, hoping to escape Potiphar's wrath and avoid
endangering Maahir.

He steadied his pace once he entered the master's pastures, waving and smiling at the shepherds. He must appear casual, as if gathering the monthly reports, loping from one field to the next. When he finally reached the edge of the slave village, he slowed to a walk and pressed against the cramp in his side. His duties as chamberlain had made him soft. He stood at the corner of the first mudbrick bunkhouse and scanned the deserted streets. Even the guards, normally posted beside each structure, were gone. *Thank You, Elohim.*

He marched straight to Maahir's one-room home. A fire ring, its embers now ash, lay in the alley beside the building, reminiscent of the late-night fellowship Joseph had known in Abba's camp. After pushing aside Maahir's tattered curtain, he entered the room barely large enough for two adults to lie side by side.

"Welcome, Lord Chamberlain." Maahir sat up on his mat as if he'd been waiting for Joseph's arrival.

"I didn't think you'd be here." Joseph wished the old man hadn't seen him.

"I live here." His smile disappeared. "Something's troubling you."

Joseph turned to go. "I don't wish to involve you."

"Sit, Joseph. I've seen you. I'm involved."

Joseph sighed and pulled both hands through his hair. He had nowhere else to go. "I went into Mistress Zuleika's chamber alone, and she invited me to her bed . . . and this wasn't the first time."

His bristly brows shot up. "Well. It sounds like quite a story. Sit down. Sit down." The old man waved him over.

Joseph lowered himself to the reed mat.

"Did you take her?" the old man asked, his eyes boring into Joseph's soul.

"Of course not," Joseph said, indignant. Maahir's unyielding stare stripped away the false piety. "But I wanted to."

"Wanting her isn't a crime, my friend. But you refused her. Noblewomen are seldom denied. She'll make it a crime."

Joseph had already considered the possibility. "Master Potiphar knows I would never—"

"Were there any witnesses that could testify—"

"She stripped off my loincloth and still has it."

The old man's rheumy eyes widened. "You're in a heap of sheep dung, Son."

Joseph snorted. "A profound insight, Maahir."

"You must leave at nightfall." The old man reached for a small jar beside his mat and removed two silver rings. "Take these. They won't get you very far, but it will be enough to buy bread for your journey back to Canaan."

"I can't return to Canaan, Maahir," Joseph said as he refused the old man's generosity. "My brothers shepherd flocks all around Abba's camp. They'd kill me before I could reveal their treachery."

Maahir wagged his head. "Trouble seems to follow you, boy. Where's this god of yours?"

Joseph fell silent. He'd thanked Elohim for the empty slave village, but he hadn't yet asked Him to intervene. Joseph leaned against the wall, closing his eyes to speak to the One who knew all things. *Search my wicked heart, O God. I confess my unholy thoughts and ask You to forgive my transgressions. Save me from the evil schemes against me, and fulfill the promises You revealed to me in dreams. Let it be so, Elohim.*

When he opened his eyes, Maahir was staring at him. "What did your god say?"

"He didn't speak to me yet."

"What good is a god that doesn't speak?"

Joseph had explained it to the old man before, but maybe today he'd listen. "My invisible God isn't bound by time or space. He seldom reveals Himself to our five senses but rather communicates to a deeper place than mortal flesh. There's a *knowing* I experience when Elohim speaks. The understanding nestles inside a part of me that will be resurrected after I die, when my body returns to dust and that inner me lives forever with Him."

Maahir's mouth hung open. "That sounds better than Anubis cutting out my heart to weigh it on his underworld scales."

Joseph laughed. "And the best part, Maahir? Elohim is *real.* He isn't simply a legend used by kings to control their people. Though you've never seen Elohim, you've seen how He favored me and, through that favor, blessed Potiphar's house."

Maahir's brow furrowed. "And yet here you are in a pile of sheep dung." Shaking his head, he waved away Joseph's words. "You can stay here as long as you like, Joseph. I would die before the master could torture me, so—"

As if summoned by the mention, pounding footsteps approached. A march at sprinter's speed. *Medjays.* Joseph bolted to his feet and started out the door—and met a Medjay face to face.

"Don't make me shackle you, Chamberlain. The captain wants no one to know what happened today." Only one guard waited beside him.

Relief surged through Joseph, and he pulled the curtain aside to tell Maahir. "Did you hear? Master Potiphar—"

"Take the old man," the first Medjay ordered his partner.

Joseph tried to block the doorway but was easily thrust aside. "No, wait! He's done nothing. He won't tell anyone."

"Captain Potiphar will decide."

"Let me carry him, then." Joseph moved past the other Medjay and bent over the frail shepherd.

"Maybe you should let me walk," Maahir whispered. "I might die on the way and avoid the master's wrath altogether."

"Quiet, old man." Joseph was in no mood for humor now. "If you're asked, I told you nothing about today's events."

"When did you start lying, Chamberlain? The truth suits me better. I'm too old to remember falsehoods."

Joseph grunted as he lifted the man and began the trek back to the villa.

The Medjays flanked him rather than marching with one soldier in front and the other behind, the way they usually did when escorting a prisoner. Carrying Maahir added to the illusion that the chamberlain, escorted by Potiphar's guards, was taking his favorite shepherd to the villa for medical care. All very plausible. Normal. On a day when *normal* would be stripped from Joseph's life no matter how plausible his explanation.

When they arrived at the villa, Maahir's eyes darted about as they passed through the banquet room, between the dividing tapestries, and into the hallway leading to Potiphar's chamber. "It's all so grand," he whispered. "So, this is why you've gotten soft and flabby?"

Joseph shushed him. "Don't you understand what's about to happen? We're going to die, Maahir."

A sad smile replaced his folly. "Only if your god wills it. Right, Joseph?"

Infuriating old man. But he was right. *Elohim, were my dreams just—dreams? Will my brothers never kneel before me?*

The master's chamber guards opened the door as they approached, and Joseph carried Maahir past them. The Medjay escort remained in the hall.

Master Potiphar halted his pacing when Joseph entered the chamber.

Potiphar nodded at the shepherd in Joseph's arms. "Who's that?"

"This is Maahir, your overseer of livestock."

"Why is he here?"

"Your Medjays thought it necessary to bring him." Joseph paused. Would he begin with a lie to protect his friend or tell the whole truth, which might mean they'd both die? "Because I told Maahir what happened in your wife's chamber at midday." Maahir was right. The truth suited Elohim better, and it was His favor—not Potiphar's—with which Joseph was most concerned.

"Lay him on the couch."

Joseph obeyed, then stood beside the old man, not because he could protect him if the master decided to kill them but because perhaps there was comfort in dying together.

"Have you betrayed me, Hebrew?" The master still called him Hebrew. A good sign.

"You know I'm innocent."

He advanced on Joseph, his smile dangerous. "You're not innocent. You delivered a food tray to my wife's chamber *alone*—and your loincloth remains as evidence of your nearness." He stopped close enough to draw his dagger and gut Joseph. "Have you told anyone except this shepherd?"

Joseph tried to swallow, but his mouth was too dry. "No, and Maahir won't tell—"

"He looks unwell." A glance at the shepherd, and Potiphar's intensity returned to Joseph. "Ommi needs someone new to tend since my wife will leave the villa today."

"She's leaving?"

The master's raised brows were like a warning shofar. "Perhaps I misjudged today's events. You seem overly interested in my wife's future."

"As your chamberlain, Master Potiphar, I'm interested in every detail of your estate—including *your* future. I've never lied to you, Master, but I haven't told you everything that's happened between Mistress Zuleika and me. When she arrived, she resented me but over time learned to tolerate me—even after I sold Gaios. We became friends when I served her midday meals during Ahira's imprisonment." *Elohim, protect me.* "Your wife hinted at . . . longings . . . and . . . asked me to put my arms around her. I didn't."

Potiphar's nostrils flared, so Joseph spilled the rest before losing heart. "The day before Ahira was freed, the mistress asked me to lie with her. But I never went farther than the threshold of her chamber." Joseph swallowed. "That is . . . until today. I was foolish to do so, I realize, but Ahira said the mistress had seen her reflection this morning for the first time. When I didn't see Mistress Zully in her chamber, I called out and delivered the tray to her courtyard. She was despondent." Joseph's face burned with shame. "She was so distraught, I lauded her courage and inner beauty, settling her shoulders against the couch. Then I realized she'd taken hold of—"

"Your loincloth."

"Yes, my lord."

"You're a fool!" He returned to his pacing.

"Yes, my lord." Joseph looked at his hands. He'd thought they would hold Ahira soon. Pushpa's attempt to help them wed would have to wait now.

"You confessed your wrong, Hebrew. I'll confess mine." The master halted. "I served a king with blind devotion, destroying any hope of building a life that really mattered. Ommi is my focus now. I'll make

Maahir my new steward so she can use her herbs to make him a new man. She comes alive when she has someone to care for."

"She does indeed, my lord. Maahir will make a fine steward." Joseph took a fortifying breath. "Will I take Maahir's place and resume my position as—"

"Guards!"

Joseph flinched.

Potiphar turned to face him. "You're going to a cell, Joseph." His face remained placid, unaffected by the explosion he'd set off in Joseph's belly.

"No!" Joseph darted toward the door as four Medjays entered.

"Must I shackle you, Hebrew?" Potiphar's tone held all the regret his features lacked.

Joseph glanced at the Medjays and at his shepherd friend.

"At least you'll live, boy." Maahir's rheumy eyes leaked tears into the wrinkles around them.

"I'd rather die." Joseph lunged at the guards. A sudden blow. Sparkling light. Darkness.

* * *

"Joseph," Ima Leah called from behind him. She was sitting beside Abba Jacob under their favorite acacia tree. "Come back to us." She was crying, but Abba looked away, indifferent to Joseph's return.

He ran toward them, rehearsing the dreams he'd been so certain were from Elohim. The eleven sheaves of grain, all bowing to a single golden sheaf.

Joseph's brothers had hated him even more after he told them.

Anger rose at the memory. "My brothers *will* bow to me, Ima," he said, arriving at the acacia. Still Abba ignored him. "Even you and Ima bow in the second dream, Abba, the sun and moon joining the stars at my feet."

Ima Leah pressed her finger against her lips. "Not yet. You must wake now, Joseph. Please, wake."

Joseph blinked but saw only darkness. Was he still dreaming? He pushed himself up, and his hands sank into something prickly. He tried to straighten his legs, but a wall kept his knees bent. "No," he whispered.

Reality dawned, and panic with it.

"No!" Joseph thrust his feet against the wall in front and pressed his back against the wall behind. Pushing with all his strength, he screamed into the darkness. "Aahh-Uuubaid! Let me out!" He drew a quick breath to push again.

"Joseph . . ." The gentle call chilled him.

"Leave, Ahira."

"The God Who Sees, my love."

"No!" He pushed against the walls again. Straining. Grinding his teeth. Trembling. Sagging. Falling. Hopelessness seeped into the damp emptiness. Weeping. Sobbing. "The cistern." He groaned. "I'll die, Ahira."

"You won't."

"I *want* to die!" he shouted.

"I know."

"Leave!" Her calm infuriated him.

"I'm staying."

Silence.

He held his hands in front of himself, unable to see anything. "The darkness feels like an iron blanket, crushing me."

"That will pass."

Pounding startled him.

"Follow my knocking, Joseph. You'll see my lamp's glow at the bottom of the door. Do you see?"

Such dim hope. "I see where Ubaid shoves the prisoner's rations into the cell." Barely a glimmer lit a square the size of his hand.

"Come toward the light, my love." Something moved into that space. He was drawn to it like a moth to flame.

The moment their fingers touched, he pulled away. "No, Ahira. Leave." He pressed his face against the cold, damp wall. "I'm Potiphar's secret. He'll never release me because Pharaoh can't know I'm here. You must never tell—"

"I'm leaving the villa, Joseph."

The news both distressed and relieved him. "Good. You'll be safer. Where?"

Silence.

What could be so horrible that she wouldn't say? "Not Canaan. It isn't safe. Simeon would kill you this time."

"I'll live with Zully in the lower city."

"You would . . ." Fury boiled up at the thought. "Did the master exile you with her?"

"No, Joseph." Her voice quaked. "Master Potiphar offered to let me serve as Pushpa's kitchen maid."

"Then why?" He pounded the cell door.

"Elohim has a purpose for Zully in Egypt—just as He does for you and me."

Joseph huffed. "Yes, God brought the Minoan princess here to ruin our lives. That's what she's done, Ahira."

More silence. "How did she get your loincloth, Joseph?"

The question shattered him. "Isn't a dark cell torture enough?"

"I'll leave if you no longer love me, Joseph. If you can honestly say your heart belongs to Zully, I won't trouble you again."

Perhaps now was the right time to lie. If he told the truth, Ahira would visit him until he died in this hole. Denying his love for her would be the most merciful thing he could do.

"Don't you dare lie to me, Joseph ben Jacob."

"If I were a better man, I'd say I don't ever want to see you again." He paused. "Would you believe me?"

"No."

"Then why ask about my loincloth?"

"Because you knew she wanted you yet you got close enough for her to strip your undergarment? I need to know if she possesses even the smallest corner of your heart, Joseph."

"Aahh!" He pressed his thumbs against his eyes, hating the shame and fear and humiliation roiling within him. "I wanted *you,* Ahira. After our kiss in the kitchen, my passion was stirred, and I wanted—"

"You wanted the *passion,* Joseph, not me."

He shook his head, though she couldn't see his denial. "I wanted passion *with* you, but when the mistress offered the heat of passion, I moved too close to her flame." Squeezing his eyes closed, he flayed his heart. "I feared she might harm herself over the distress about her scar. When I didn't see her in the chamber, I took her meal tray into the courtyard."

"I found my mirror under the couch," Ahira said. "It was bent. She'd been more upset than I realized."

"She seemed desperate. When I tried to calm her, I got too close and didn't realize she'd grabbed my loincloth until I ran."

Ahira's quiet sniffing proved he'd heaped more pain on the woman he adored.

"Leave me. Please. I love you too much to let you waste your life in that hallway."

"And I love you too much to let you doubt Elohim's promises."

He set his jaw, bitterness surging through him. "Will my brothers travel all the way from Canaan to bow at my prison door?"

At the sound of shuffling in the hall, he sighed. He'd offended her enough that she'd finally left. Pushpa would surely find an honorable man for Ahira. The thought of it rolled into a ball of hate inside his belly. Mistress Zuleika deserved the fires of Sheol.

"I'll see you tomorrow morning with a food basket from Pushpa."

"Wait! Ahira, no!" He leapt to his feet. "Don't come back!"

The sound of retreating sandals was her only answer. Joseph pounded the rock walls until his fists could pound no more.

FORTY-TWO

*The warden put Joseph in charge of all those held
in the prison, and he was made responsible for all
that was done there.*

GENESIS 39:22

SIX MONTHS LATER

Ahira

The soft melody of a shepherd's tune nestled into her consciousness, pulling Ahira from a restful sleep. She'd enjoyed many peaceful nights during the last few months, something she'd never imagined possible after the turmoil of her first few years in Egypt. She turned onto her side but made no sound, watching Zully stir the embers of their cook fire as she continued humming the shepherd's song. They often sang it together now. One of the many parts of Ahira's Hebrew legacy she'd offered as encouragement while Elohim transformed Zully's heart.

"He'll forgive you." Ahira's whisper startled Zully.

Zully turned, her face aglow in the predawn firelight. "Joseph may never leave that prison because of me. How could he forgive *that?*"

"He'll forgive because he'll see Elohim shining through your eyes—as I do. Just as Elohim replaced Simeon's betrayal with Joseph's love, the God Who Sees is redeeming all the tragedies—Crete's quaking, the miscarriage, your maiming—with the joy of a new life: selling art in your own booth at the market."

"It's more than joy, Ahira. It's peace and fullness and hope and—" She pressed a trembling hand against her lips. "But at Joseph's expense. *Your* expense. You two will never have a life together because of me."

Ahira rolled off her mat and closed the distance between them. Today it was Zully's turn to need reassurance. Yesterday Ahira had struggled with doubt and fear. "When you see Joseph this morning," Ahira said, "you'll understand our hope. Elohim isn't finished with Joseph's story or mine. That's why I'm sure Joseph will forgive you when we visit him. I haven't told him you are coming, because I wanted you to see his true reaction. It will prove the absolute healing of his heart, Zully."

She squeezed her eyes shut. "If Potiphar catches me in the villa . . ."

"That's why we're going through the kitchen. You can apologize to Pushpa first." After seeing her friend's shocked expression, Ahira added, "I *have* told her you're coming, and her heart is softened toward you." She emptied their water pitcher into a basin for them to share. "We need to hurry, though. It's best if we greet Pushpa and get our morning meal to share with Joseph before the Medjays take all the best food."

They splashed their faces and shared a hand towel, then slipped on fresh robes before lighting a torch for the trek from the lower city to the villa. Shabby mudbrick buildings with palm-frond roofs loomed silently over them while they crossed dawn's vague shadows on deserted streets. Ahira kicked a grimy ball made of thatch, a toy abandoned when darkness chased a child inside. This was the lower city because these good people dwelled at the base of the knolls and peaks where Avaris's wealthy nobility perched—and sewage rolled downhill.

"I didn't know."

Zully's whisper drew Ahira's attention. The Minoan princess had pulled her crimson scarf tighter, covering the lovely right side of her face so only the ugly scar showed. It was how the common people of Avaris knew her: Leika, the artist. Accepted and genuinely loved.

"What didn't you know?" Ahira asked.

"Before we came to live among these wonderful people, I'd only visited the lower market a few times and only during the hustle of business. Never the back streets or neighborhoods." She smiled through her tears. "There's so much more to love than the goods they sell."

Ahira pulled her into a sideways hug. "And they'll miss you, my friend—as will I—when you leave us someday."

After clearing the lump in her throat as they approached the palace complex, she greeted a familiar guard. He nodded toward her friend. "Who's this?" When Zully lifted her head, the Medjay's training failed in a moment of recognition before he returned his attention to Ahira. "I can't allow—"

"Pushpa asked me to bring her." Ahira's urgent plea wasn't exactly a lie. Pushpa's constant questions about Zully's welfare were certainly a form of invitation.

The Medjay gave her a sidelong glance.

"We'll enter through the palace kitchen and go directly to the prison." Ahira waited silently, knowing begging would only harm her chances.

"Please," Zully whispered. "I must apologize to Joseph."

His eyes widened. After a heartbeat of indecision, he stepped out of their path. "Go, but don't linger in the kitchen. The captain often retrieves his own morning meal."

"Thank you," the two women offered in unison. They clasped hands and hurried past the gate and through the busy palace kitchen. Ahira led her through a small side door into Pushpa's calmer kingdom. Zully's grip tightened.

Potiphar's ima stood near the cook fire, staring into the pot of gruel and stirring as if intently searching for something.

Ahira lifted Zully's hand to her lips. "Go ahead," she whispered. "I'm right here."

With a deep sigh, Zully bravely squared her shoulders and stepped closer. "Pushpa?"

The older woman's hand jumped on the spoon, clanking it on the side of the pot. She turned to face her son's wife. "Good morning,

Zully." A tremulous smile pushed her rosy cheeks into soft, wrinkled mounds. "I'm glad you came."

Zully ran to her without invitation and gripped her waist in a fierce embrace. "Oh, Pushpa, I'm so sorry."

Pushpa's arms enfolded her, spoon and all, her cheek pressed against Zully's. Their whispered words were private treasures for their ears only while Ahira packed the basket of food she and Zully would share with Joseph and Ubaid.

Two months previously, Ubaid's compassion had outweighed his fear, and he begged Master Potiphar to make Joseph his assistant warden. The master agreed, and the softhearted warden gave Joseph a fresh reed mat, where he now slept in Ubaid's chamber. The old man received the benefit of sharing Joseph's morning feast, and he'd put the prisoners' well-being in Joseph's capable hands. Ubaid had never been happier, and the prisoners had never been healthier than under Joseph's watchful care.

"Zully." The master's coarse whisper stole Ahira's attention. She whirled and found him halted at the kitchen door, mouth agape.

"She's here to speak with me, Son." Pushpa nudged Zully behind her. "And she's determined to apologize to Joseph."

Emotions tumbled across the master's features, changing so rapidly Ahira couldn't guess how he might react. "Apologize." Not a question. "Which means Joseph will know that you've confessed your deceit and that his continued imprisonment is solely my decision. You're still scheming, Zuleika. Trying to turn Joseph, Ahira, and Pushpa against me."

"I'm not scheming or trying to turn anyone against you." Zully stepped around Pushpa. "Your reasons for keeping Joseph imprisoned are between you and Elohim. I came here to apologize to Joseph. To Pushpa. And to *you*. Nothing else. Your gracious provision saved my life during the transition to the lower city. The debt I owe you is too great to repay, Potiphar, but my art sales are going so well, I'd feel better if I could pay the rent for the house now. Can you ever forgive me for the suffering I caused you?" She bowed, waiting for his reply.

The master's eyes darted toward Ahira. "Is this another of my wife's tricks?" He didn't seem angry but almost . . . fearful.

"No, Master. Zully is sincere." At the burgeoning hope in his eyes, Ahira added, "Though she remains determined to return to Crete."

"I see." He bowed his head, hiding his reaction. When he looked up, he eyed Zully with suspicion. "Why would Joseph forgive you?"

"I'm not sure he will, but I must face him because Elohim asked it of me."

He scoffed. "I won't release Joseph unless the god on Egypt's throne asks it of me."

"Potiphar, please. Joseph has done nothing—"

He silenced Pushpa's plea with an uplifted hand. "I'll continue to pay rent on your house, Zuleika, so you can save more quickly for passage to Crete. You'll be an unmarried woman by then. You mustn't travel alone." Zully stared in awe, but no one dared interrupt for details. "When you've saved enough for travel, send word through your maid. I'll provide a Medjay to escort you." As he strode from the room, the three women exchanged astonished glances.

"Did he just release me to return home?" Zully asked Pushpa.

With misty eyes, the old woman embraced her. "He did."

It was a miracle only Elohim could have provided. But how would the master persuade Pharaoh to grant the divorce? Or would he somehow convince the king Zully was dead? Perhaps the latter would be easier since *Princess Zuleika* hadn't been seen in public since the maiming. Those in the lower city knew her only as the eccentric artist, Leika. Her paintings and pottery boasted shades of crimson, each piece bearing a purposeful imperfection—resembling the red-scarfed artist herself.

"Are you ready to go downstairs?" Ahira asked softly.

Pushpa released Zully and traced the exposed scar on her left cheek. "You are more beautiful than the princess who left this villa."

Zully took her hand and planted a kiss on her palm. "Take care of him, Pushpa."

She left the kitchen, Ahira close behind. The master's chamber guards already waited for them with the prison door open. Zully covered her nose and mouth as they descended. Ahira had warned her about what she'd see, hear, and smell, but experiencing the horrors of Pharaoh's prison was a very different thing.

Ahira carried the food basket on her arm and reached the bottom step first. "Joseph?"

Ubaid's chamber door opened right away, and he appeared. "My water clock stopped a while ago. You're late—" His smile drained like water from an overturned jug. "Mistress Zuleika?"

Zully stepped to Ahira's side. "I'm simply Leika now, Joseph."

Ubaid emerged from his room. "Goodness. That's some scar."

"Ubaid!" Ahira scolded.

"Meet Leika," Joseph said, and then lingered in a bow. "She's someone who has endured much, Ubaid, and deserves our respect." When he finally straightened, his features had softened, and his eyes met Zully's. "Thank you for coming, Leika. Ahira tells me you're quite successful with your own booth in the market."

"Joseph, I need to say something."

Ahira offered the basket to Ubaid. "Take the food into your chamber. We'll join you in a moment."

"Of course." He grabbed it like a thief and closed his door. Zully stared at her feet, and uneasy silence filled the cavernous main room.

Joseph pulled Ahira to his side. "I'm glad you brought her. Thank you."

Zully's eyes darted toward the man she'd wronged so deeply. "How can you be glad to see me, Joseph? I ruined your life. Even now, Potiphar knows you're innocent, but—"

"I've accepted my imprisonment," he said, "but I know my life won't end in this prison."

"But how . . ." Zully's chin quivered. "How can you forgive me?" The words, strangled by emotion, came out as barely a whisper.

"Perhaps I can forgive because Ahira's love gives me hope and Ubaid's mercy proves Elohim's favor. My God will deliver me from these dark halls just as He delivered me from the cistern."

"Just as I know Elohim has delivered me from the dark streets of

Lower Egypt." Zully removed her crimson scarf. "Potiphar has been an instrument of Elohim's mercy and promised to free me from our marriage. By next month, I'll have saved enough silver to pay for passage to Crete."

Ahira's heart skipped a beat. "So soon?"

Zully offered her hand and a tender smile. "I asked Pushpa to make a place for you here in the villa. She plans to move into my original chamber and hopes you'll take the guest chamber across the hall— fully furnished and no longer bolted from the outside." The three of them chuckled, hard memories crushed in the hand mill of time and forgiveness. "I'll leave you two alone to enjoy your morning meal with Ubaid," Zully said. "I've got art to sell and travel plans to make." She leaned forward and kissed both Ahira and Joseph on their cheeks before hurrying up the stairs.

Joseph turned to Ahira, his lips curved into a knowing smile. "You could have warned me."

"You wouldn't have let me bring her."

Sobering, he stepped back. "How did you know I'd forgive her? I've been so angry anytime you speak her name."

"Ubaid set you free from your cell, Joseph, but your bitterness toward Zully was eating you alive." He reached for her waist, the desire in his eyes as strong as her own. "No, Joseph." She intercepted his hands and pulled them to her lips instead. After a gentle kiss, she released them and stepped away. "We're free now in this place to enjoy our meal together each morning, talk about our separate lives, and wait for Elohim to complete the work He's doing. But until then we must take care not to abuse our freedom."

He groaned. "I don't want you to be sensible and wise right now." He traced the length of her jaw with one finger, weakening her knees and her resolve, then lightly brushed her lips before stepping back two paces. "But you're right, my love. We must guard our freedom as slaves in Egypt while Elohim writes the rest of our story."

EPILOGUE

Those who find me find life
and receive favor from the LORD.
PROVERBS 8:35

FOUR YEARS LATER
Zuleika

Seated at my writing desk in our modest palace, I watched angry autumn waves crash onto Zakros's shore. A cool breeze ruffled the papyrus trapped under the chunk of unchiseled crystal Kostas had given me on our wedding night.

A warm breath on my neck stirred my desire. "You're home early from the council meeting, Husband."

Kostas offered his strong arm to help me rise. I struggled to my feet as gracefully as possible for a woman eight months heavy with child. "You're most beautiful when you're pregnant," he said with a grin.

"You've always enjoyed whale watching."

A deep rumble of laughter drew me into his arms.

"I've finished the ledgers," I said, "for both Zakros and Knossos Districts. Now I get a nap."

"Mitta! Patta! Wook at dis!" Our two-year-old, Minas, ran toward us—his nurse two steps behind as usual. "It a goat!" He carried a sculpted mud ball that was more like an oblong glob with a bulge for the head and four lumps as legs.

"Minas, it's stunning!" My husband—both king and sculptor—applauded as if the glob were made of gold. "Don't you agree, Mitera?"

"It's a most unforgettable goat."

"For my brubber, Mitta." Minas hugged my legs with mud-caked hands.

I chuckled. "What if Elohim gives you a sister instead?"

He looked up, his dark brown eyes identical to my first husband, Kostas's older brother. "I get brubber."

Kostas laughed. "Perhaps Minas and Elohim have an agreement we know nothing about."

A servant raced across the garden with a scroll. Assuming it was for the king, I reached for Minas's hand, thinking I'd forego my nap and take him for a swim. "Queen Zully, wait! A message arrived for you on the merchant ship from Egypt."

My heart did a little flip, as it always did when Egypt was mentioned. I'd received six messages from Ahira since returning to Crete. She and Joseph had written them together, never using their names but giving me updates on Avaris and encouraging me to remain faithful to Elohim.

I thanked the servant and broke the seal.

Kostas peered over my shoulder. "Read it aloud," he said. "Your Akkadian is still better than mine."

I had nothing to hide. I'd shared every detail of my life in Egypt with him.

Your friends and humble servants in the Place of Confinement send warm greetings to the gracious king and queen of Zakros and Knossos Districts. We pray you and your family are well and hope with great anticipation for Elohim's imminent miracle.

The one who writes these words may soon be released from Pharaoh's prison. A few days ago, I interpreted dreams for two

*of the king's servants who had been imprisoned for treason.
One of the servants was chosen as freedom prisoner for Pharaoh's birth celebration, and the other was executed—exactly
as the dreams foretold.*

*I wait now for the freed prisoner to reveal my name—as he
vowed to do—at which time my innocence will be revealed
and I'll be free to marry the woman Elohim has chosen for me!
Join with us in praising the God of all creation—and remember the One who sees you.*

I clutched the papyrus to my chest, laughing through tears. "Can
you believe it, Kostas? Elohim gave Joseph the interpretation of those
men's dreams. Pharaoh will finally discover his unjust imprisonment.
Oh, but—" Joy twisted into fear at the thought of Potiphar's fate.
"What will Pharaoh Khyan do to Potiphar when he discovers his captain has been engaged in deception, Kostas? What if Khyan discovers
I escaped Egypt?"

"He won't." Kostas pulled me into a tight embrace. "Potiphar buried his *wife's* mummy in his family's tomb, and Elohim brought you
home to me. He gave us a life here and prospered Crete's trade. As
long as your pateras appeases both Egypt and Cush—and leaves Crete
to us—Egypt will never send more than merchant ships to our shores."

"Mitta, I hungee." Our son's voice returned my focus to the new life
Elohim had given me.

"Come, my sweet boy. Let's talk more about Elohim." I pulled
Minas close and then looked up at Kostas. "He's the only God who
sees and protects us and can satisfy our hunger completely."

AUTHOR'S NOTE

Who doesn't love the biblical hero Joseph? I certainly do and began researching his life with zeal . . . but quickly discovered I'd kicked an academic hornet's nest. On my first day of research, I read the following statement (paraphrased) and saw a version of it repeated in almost every resource: *No one can definitively determine the dates for Joseph's sojourn in Egypt or the pharaoh he served.*

For a fiction author who relishes biblical truth and historical fact, such hopelessness could have been discouraging. Nevertheless, I reminded myself—and remind you now—that *Potiphar's Wife* is a work of *fiction*.

In every novel I write, biblical truth forms the foundation on which historical facts become the building blocks. Creative fiction is then used as mortar to construct a story that invites a place of exploring. I hope the following details give some insight into the adventure we've shared in *Potiphar's Wife*.

Date and Location
In an effort to determine the patriarchal time period described in Genesis 37 and 39, I consulted well over one hundred resources (print, digital, and online) to examine the relationship between ancient Egypt, Crete, and the Levant. Though I make no assertion of proof or fact, I placed Joseph's *fictional account* in Egypt's Second Intermediate Period (c. 1800–1550 BC) and the Hyksos dynasty.

The Hyksos—literally *foreign rulers*—reigned at a time unlike any other in Egypt's history. Ancestors of the Hyksos kings were driven out of Canaan and into Egypt by an influx of wealthy Bedouins.

The Bible records Abraham and Isaac as having large livestock holdings that caused serious land issues with the Philistine king, Abimelek (Genesis 21, 26); and Jacob, on his deathbed, bequeathed to Joseph a ridge of land he'd taken from Amorites (Genesis 48:21–22).

Most historical resources agree that six non-Egyptian kings ruled Lower Egypt's fertile delta in the capital city of Avaris (called Tell El-Dab'a today). It was a prime agricultural and grazing area of the Nile delta, matching the area the Bible calls Goshen.

History affirmed Scripture in recent findings at a site very near Avaris. Archaeologists discovered a stele (inscribed pillar) from the reign of Rameses II (c. 1279–1213) in which he mentions a Hyksos king that ruled four hundred years before him.

Why is that information so important? While researching and writing *The Pharaoh's Daughter,* I determined 1250 BC to be the date of the Exodus and Rameses II to be the pharaoh of the Exodus (see *The Pharaoh's Daughter* author's note for more details). If Joseph brought his family to Egypt during the Hyksos Dynasty (Genesis 46ff), then God's promise to Abram (Genesis 15:13–16) was affirmed by the Ramses Stele:

> The LORD said to [Abram], "Know for certain that for *four hundred years* your descendants will be strangers *in a country not their own* and that they will be enslaved and mistreated there." (Genesis 15:13, emphasis added)

Nations and Tribes

Ancient Egyptians divided the human race into four classes, placing themselves at the pinnacle of humanity (see www.temehu.com /temehu.htm). The second class was the *Nehesu* people who lived on their southern border in the nation of Cush (sometimes called Nubia, modern-day Sudan). Special respect was granted to a single tribe of warriors among the Nehesu, called Medjay, who were first mentioned serving with Egypt's military as early as 2400 BC (see https://oi.uchicago.edu/museum-exhibits/nubia/pan-grave-culture-medjay for more information).

To Egypt's east and northeast was the land they called *Retjenu*, which included biblical Canaan and beyond. Its inhabitants were deemed *Amu*, regardless of tribe or national borders. All were Semites—descendants of Noah's son Shem. Their origins can be found in Genesis 10:21–31 along with Ham's son, Canaan, in Genesis 10:15–19. The fourth recognized nation, Temehu, spread south along Egypt's western border. Its Tehenu tribe shared the fertile soil of Lower Egypt's delta.

Archaeological findings confirm generations of drought, including that foretold in Genesis 41–47, that changed the Tehenu's landscape from lush pasturelands to what we know today as the Sahara. Egypt and surrounding lands were brought to their knees, which provided necessary historical data for the novel's military and conspiracy threads.

Tensions continued to rise, and cooperative trade became a necessity for all four people groups to survive. In the sequel to *Potiphar's Wife* coming in 2023, discover what role Joseph's wife, Asenath (a named biblical character), might have played in this crucial period of Egypt's history!

Names

Who's real and who's imagined? We know Potiphar's and Joseph's names from Scripture (Genesis 37:36; 39:1–20). Though the Bible refers only to "Potiphar's wife," rabbinic literature and the Koran give her the name *Zuleikha*. Scripture depicts her as a foil character to emphasize Joseph's commitment to Elohim. Historical texts paint her as a troubled woman who cared too deeply about what others thought but who eventually repented.

Very few names have survived on the Turin King-list (the Egyptian resource I rely on heavily) to definitively identify the names and dates of the reigns of the Hyksos. Most scholars agree that Khyan and Apophis were the two most stable kings of the dynasty, Apophis following Khyan but with no family correlation. Yanassi has been proven to be

Khyan's son, but there's no record of Yanassi ever ascending Lower Egypt's throne.

Some would suggest the omission of Joseph's name (or his Egyptian name, Zaphenath-Paneah) from Egypt's history as reason to doubt the Bible's validity. However, it seems to me another affirmation that Joseph—a foreigner—was given the second most powerful position in Egypt during this period of "foreign rulers." Perhaps Joseph's name will someday be found—along with the lost Hyksos pharaohs!

For more historical information from the sources I relied on heavily, see the academic works of these four leading experts: K. S. B. Ryholt, Manfred Bietak, Anna-Latifa Mourad, and John Van Setters. Most online research was done through academia.edu and jstor.org, which I highly recommend.

Afterlife

Hebrew beliefs about the afterlife during the patriarchal period are underdeveloped compared with those of most other religions during the same period. My depiction of Joseph's belief in resurrection comes from the book of Job since he was living at the time. (See my debut, *Love Amid the Ashes,* for the story of Job and Jacob's daughter Dinah.)

Truth

I hope you've enjoyed exploring Joseph's story, but most of all I hope it has stirred your curiosity enough to send you to God's Word for more of *His* truth. Many blessings, dear reader!

ACKNOWLEDGMENTS

This book wins the award for the most difficult I've written to date and was finished only by the grace of God shown through many faithful people.

Thanks to His creative gifts through my dear OBX friends who in the fall of 2019 helped brainstorm with me the biblical bad girl of Potiphar's wife.

Beta readers—Tracy Jones, Meg Wilson, and Carol Ashby—helped avert early mistakes in characterization. My team at Waterbrook handled every obstacle with a tenderness beyond the call of duty; each of you is amazing in a unique and beautiful way.

Thank you, Sherril Odom, for helping with various projects along the way (even during an extended illness!).

My newsies (newsletter subscribers) and BFFs (launch team) prayed faithfully with every panicked SOS I sent.

Special thanks, as mentioned in the dedication, to the Woodalls for allowing me to deem their basement apartment my writing cave for nearly five weeks.

And, last but most of all, thank you with all my love to my precious family, who supported me through a year of compulsive work habits with relentless prayer and unflinching encouragement.

ABOUT THE AUTHOR

MESU ANDREWS is the Christy Award–winning author of *Isaiah's Daughter,* whose deep understanding of and love for God's Word brings the biblical world alive for readers. Andrews lives in North Carolina with her husband, Roy. She stays connected with readers through newsie emails, fun blog posts, and frequent short stories. For more information, visit mesuandrews.com.

The Old Testament book of Daniel comes to life!

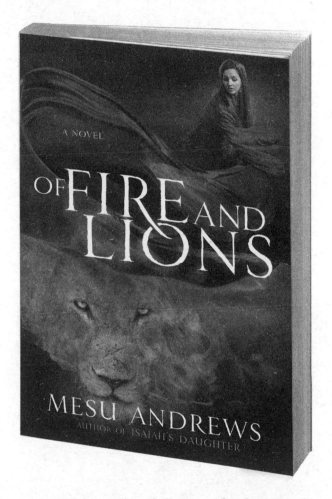

A young Hebrew girl and the son of Judean royalty are forced into Babylonian exile, where they bear witness to the limitless power of a sovereign God.

WATERBROOK

waterbrookmultnomah.com

Step Back into Bible Times!

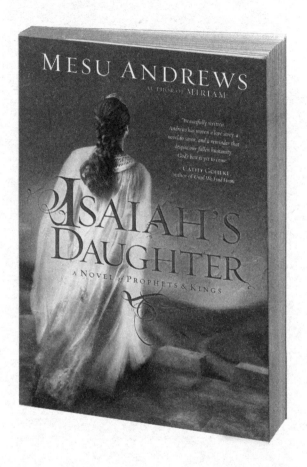

In this epic biblical narrative, a young woman taken into the prophet Isaiah's household rises to capture the heart of the future king.